The Story of a Girl: Back to the Game Board

The Story of a Girl: Back to the Game Board

"And when your fears subside
And shadows still remain, oh yeah
I know that you can love me
When there's no one left to blame
So never mind the darkness
We still can find a way
'Cause nothin' lasts forever
Even cold November rain"

- *Guns N' Roses*

Prologue ~ 48 Hours

September 22nd, 2012

And so here I was, trekking along an exceptionally long and winding road in this adventurous, sometimes unpredictable game of so-called life, although right now I was hardly feeling adventurous. You see, I've always been more of a planner, the kind who writes lists so I know what to expect. My method had seemed to work perfectly for most things but when it came to certain 'aspects' of my life, it repeatedly came up short because the one 'to do' I never listed was love. I guess it just hadn't been as important to me as other things, like achieving my goals or being successful. But that all changed the minute I had opened my eyes.

I'd thought I'd been doing pretty well up until recent months, when things had precipitously shifted in the wrong direction. I felt alone, disappointed in the powers that be for having left me stuck in the middle of a pond of quicksand. It was like I'd drawn the card from the deck that puts you back 10 spaces into the land of gumdrops or jail or in my case, all the way back to the damned starting line- empty-handed, without an ounce of candy, a single property or one dollar to my fucking name. I never intended on anything like this happening and now everything I had worked so hard for, including the one thing I hadn't planned on and never thought I'd actually *find*, was hanging in the balance and it had all been my fault.

Just how in the hell had I ended up here? And why had I been so deaf, dim-witted, and blind? Why couldn't I have listened to or seen what was right in front of me this entire time? My cousin was right- for someone with years of schooling and a medical degree I could be so dense sometimes and *this* was definitely one of those times.

I thought back to where it'd all begun. It was 2008 and after four years of practicing veterinary medicine and way too many years of being lonely, I'd lost my way *and* my focus on what it was I truly wanted and began questioning life's (and fate's) big plans for me (or if they'd actually had any). I remember it vividly: it was yet another absurdly busy day at the office, otherwise referred to as a 'day from hell'- a shitshow of never-ending fun involving animals, their all-too often difficult owners and the onslaught of emergencies that should've been brought in way earlier.

I'd been off daydreaming about a different life and in popped this crazy idea for a change of scenery- out on the west coast, ya know for a short break, intent on coming back recharged, refreshed and ready to move forward with my same old eternally single, lame-ass merry-go-round-of-a life in hopes that somehow, some way it might improve. But as we all know, it hadn't *exactly* turned out like that; I hadn't returned home as planned and my life had become *anything* but lame. It had also taken a few unexpected turns along the way...

That summer on a random San Diego day, my life changed forever when I'd met the man of my dreams. Yes, that *actually* happened and *yes*, he'd been real. At the time Patrick Wade Thomas had been a household name to every teenage girl and young woman in America. I admit I was a little *older* than many of his fans, but I had the same rights as they did to drool being that I, too, had been a longtime fan. Anyway, I digress from my point which is that not only did I *meet* him, I began *dating* him. And, for those of you wondering (and who obviously *didn't* read the first installment which you clearly need to do...), *YES*, that also actually happened.

Fast forward to this very moment, nearly 4 ½ years later where, because of my actions (or lack thereof), I stood to lose any and all ground I'd gained in both the career and personal departments. I'd fucked up badly and I wasn't sure if it could be fixed. And instead of landing in the happy ending I had anticipated and so desperately wanted, I had landed here- lost, afraid, unsure of which direction to take. Should I leave the pieces where they lay or face my deep-rooted fears, go for the gold and take a chance on what I believed in my heart to be true?

Surely, no one would think I was serious. I mean if they really *knew* me, they knew this kind of thing wasn't like me at all. Normally I was meticulous and thought things through, that annoying list person, like I said. I almost never did anything without some kind of forethought. But *time* was exactly my problem- and I didn't have much left.

And then it hit me- This was the calm before the storm. I had just *two* days to come up with a feasible plan: that's only 48 hours. *Hours.* The mathematical equivalent of 2,880 minutes or 172,800 seconds. Maybe there *was* enough time to fix things; maybe not, but I had to find out. One thing's for damn sure- I had little of it to spare, even less to waste and absolutely *nothing* to lose. Actually, scratch that- I had *everything* to lose, including my sanity if this didn't work. If only I could just go through with it...

It was time...time to put myself back in the game well, onto the gameboard.

Part One:
Perfection

"No shit, honey. What do you think this is, *real* life?"

-Andrew Dice Clay

The Adventures of Ford Fairlane

Chapter 1 ~ Big

April 2011

"And when I grow up, I wanna be an *Army* vet."

"Well, Owen, that's kind of a special way we describe some of our soldiers who have fought in the military," answered the teacher.

"No, I mean I wanna be an Army *veterinarian*," he said.

"Oh. Oh, well okay. But honey I'm not so sure veterinarians can *be* in the Army."

"Um, yeah, *yeah* then can," I heard a few soft giggles in the room, including my own.

I stood at the back of the classroom watching him proudly with teary eyes and a huge smile. He had gotten so big so fast. Where had that little 8 ½ pound chubby-faced, olive-toned baby, the one who used to fit in my arms, gone? He stood nearly four feet at age 6, his head down slightly with doubt. I caught his attention with a loud psst sound and he looked up. I nodded my head assuredly and when he saw that he looked back at his teacher, his confidence restored. I sighed and smiled again. Because I knew him. Once Owen was adamant about something there was no stopping him.

"My aunt's right there," he pointed at me. "She told me they can and that I can be whatever I want when I grow up."

The teacher immediately spotted me and then, with a notable embarrassment to her tone and a newly forced smile she said, "*oh*, well, then of *course* you can."

He sauntered back to his seat, a minor clumsiness in his walk, his dog tags jingling against the stethoscope around his neck. God I loved that kid. I had waited what felt like forever for my nephews to get older, wondered what it'd be like to take them to The Museum of Natural History, the U.S.S. Intrepid or the Statue of Liberty, things we had done as kids. What had felt like forever had gone by in the blink of an eye. It seemed like just yesterday that I had taken my oldest nephew Luca to his first baseball game. He was now 9 and playing baseball himself.

Erin stood next to me, tissue in hand. "I'm so glad you were able to come to career day- it means so much to him," she smiled. "I know how busy you've been lately."

"Who, *me*? You make it sound like you're not," I laughed. "And he's my *Godson*. Plus, ever since we hired another doctor, we've had more flexible schedules so it's really no big deal.

Owen came running over. "Lea!!" He leaped at me, throwing his arms around me. I prepared myself constantly for the day he'd be a linebacker.

"Hey, awesome job up there, kiddo I mean, Dr. Camioni!" I hugged him tightly back. I understood the feeling now that moms got holding their children- I never wanted to let him go.

"It's Sergeant Dr. Owen Camioni, Aunt Lea," he stated.

"Oh, yeah, right. Sergeant," I smiled. He grabbed my hand and hurried me down the hall.

"I guess we'll see you at the reception," I stated, my voice trailing off as I was pulled away. Erin waved back at us.

How is it that the hallways of an elementary school feel like a labyrinth when you're a kid and when you're older, you feel like Alice trying to fit through that tiny door into Wonderland? I wondered where all the time had gone for myself, too. They'd set up the cafeteria- rows of tables were decorated with crafts and refreshments. He steered me towards a place setting with his name on it.

"Aunt Lea, I made this. Look." On the scrapbook's cover was a photo of Anthony, Erin, Luca and Owen. I perused through it, laughing and sighing at the work this kid had put into it. The last picture was of me and him at the hospital, dressed for surgery. If I needed a future partner someday, I might not need to look very far. And then, as if I were six years old again myself, I jumped at the sound of the school bell ringing, that familiar tone signifying the end of yet another school day.

"So? How'd it go?"

"The handsomest little man in uniform I've ever laid eyes on." *Well, almost.* "You should've seen him- camouflage pants with a scrub top, wearing a stethoscope *and* dog tags. I was beside myself," I giggled.

"Sounds like you guys had fun."

"Totally," I answered.

"Any future actors in the mix?"

I laughed. "*Seriously*? You forget this *is* the East Coast- nothing but firemen, police officers, maybe the occasional doctor thrown in."

"*Really*? Come on. It's a very prestigious profession, ya know. We serve the community just like everyone else..."

"Ah hem," I interrupted. "Aren't *veterinarians* real doctors? I mean, I like to think that's what I sacrificed all those years, money and my free time for eternity for. I'm not just some PhD who's, of course, *always* referred to as one…"

"I wasn't leaving you out," he laughed. "Whatever, you're like the most trusted profession. I mean *I* trust you." If it's one thing that hadn't gotten old with us, it was the constant sarcasm and friendly bantering. No matter how far apart we were, we'd found a way to make it work, and to keep the foreplay interesting.

It'd been almost three years since we'd met (well, the *second* time, not the time when I nearly bowled him over with coffee) and a year and a half since our first date (well, our *official* first date he'd asked me on at my brother Donnie's wedding, not the blind date we'd been set up on months before), and I can honestly say that I was impressed with how well it was going. I'd always wondered if this kind of thing was possible- and it *was*. I never thought I'd be lucky enough to find someone like him, but it turned out not to be luck at all; it had been fate- and God, was fate doing me good right now…

"Hey, is that Patrick?" Luca and Owen yelled from the other room.

"Yeah. Why, you wanna say hi?" I paused, turning around.

"Yeah! Yeah!" They both answered excitedly. They absolutely loved him.

"Hang on a sec. The boys wanna say hi. They're sleeping over."

"Okay. Put 'em on."

"Hi Patrick!" They said in sync.

"Hey guys!" he answered. "What are ya doing- driving your aunt crazy?"

"Yeah," said Luca.

"*No*," stated Owen. I rolled my eyes. "We're making pizza."

"Pizza? Wow I could sure use some good pizza right now," Patrick said.

"Where are you?" Luca asked.

"Toronto."

"Where's that? California?" Luca persisted.

"No, buddy. It's in Canada." Patrick continued to appease them.

I took the phone back. "Alright, go rewash your hands cuz I *know* you guys were playing with dirt. I don't want dirty dough." They hurried off.

"They love sleeping over don't they?"

"Yeah, well, I'm the best aunt. They were hoping to see you but we have the whole summer," I added.

"Definitely, babe; just gotta check my schedule."

Chapter 2~ How to Marry a Millionaire

May 7

Unlike many Italians, my parents hadn't owned a bakery or a pizzeria. I guess that wasn't a bad thing, since I might've been guilted into working in one instead of going off to college. Sometimes I wished we would've owned a winery, but of course then I probably would've ended up awaiting a liver transplant by now.

It smelled so damn good in this place I wished I could put it in a jar. As much fun as I'd been having working here the past year there was so much more taking shape in my life that I was beginning to feel like I had less and less room for it, which made me sad because I loved baking and, more than anything, I loved working with my oldest and best friend.

Our mothers often told Rachel and I growing up that we were two peas in a pod. As we got older, it was apparent that as much as we'd always made fun of them, we couldn't argue that we weren't too different from them at all. Not that that was a *bad* thing. We'd not only inherited some damn good genes in the 'aging gracefully' department, we'd learned more than a few important words of advice over the years: Nothing beats a classic Beatles' record; a great bartender is only as good as his best martini; always look your absolute best when you're around a gentleman because he could unsuspectingly be a millionaire, and never *ever* serve dinner without dessert. Overall, I think Rachel and I had made our moms proud, especially when it came to our careers- the marrying the millionaire part? Not so much. If I had a dollar for every time Rachel's mom had said, 'Rachel, *please* don't tell me you're leaving the house looking like that- you'll *never* marry rich', I would've had a million dollars a long fucking time ago.

But disheartened and irritating mothers aside, we were a force to be reckoned with when in the kitchen. But we hadn't gotten *all* our sweet teeth from our moms. Although Italians are well-known for their savory cuisine, we pride ourselves on dessert. We were lucky enough to each have scrapbooks (aka disorganized pieces of paper with scribbles of broken Italian and English) of old family recipes, and this is where Rachel and I got some of our greatest ideas from.

Rachel and I were thrilled with how the bakery had been doing. Cupcakeries may have been a dime a dozen in places like California, but they were few and far between in the New York area and we knew we wouldn't fail. Rachel's husband Tom had disagreed with us in the beginning, that there wasn't a market for cupcakes, but he'd been wrong. And she didn't let a day go by without reminding him of that.

We were in the middle of testing one of our new recipes- a raspberry and Campari (a bitter Italian aperitif) infused yellow cake with a Prosecco Italian meringue buttercream. Oddly enough, Campari made me think of Carriacou, the tiny sister island to Grenada, where I'd attended veterinary school. Speaking of vet school, I had completely forgotten to register for the upcoming conference.

"Damn," I stated, nearly spilling the raspberry syrup.

"What?" Rachel was standing next to me fidgeting with the mixer.

"I just realized I forgot to register for the conference."

"What conference?" she asked.

"The AVMA." I continued filling the cupcakes with the raspberry-Campari infusion. "This year it's in San Diego, which works out great for me, 'cause I'll already be out there."

"*Nice.* I wish I could go," she said, adding the egg whites to the bowl. "When is it?"

"July.."

"Is it at the convention center?"

"Yep."

"That must be the popular place these days," she smiled, amusing herself.

"Maybe," I paused.

"You ended up with a superhero that time. so it didn't turn out *too* badly for you." We smiled at each other. "Speaking of which, when are you gonna see each other again? Is he coming here anytime soon?"

"He was supposed to the end of this month but he's been so busy between wrapping up the show, trying to move back to L.A. and starting this new project, I'm not sure I'm gonna see him before I head back out there. And then he starts filming like immediately, so…"

"When's the last time you saw him?" she inquired, adding Prosecco to the meringue.

"March," I sighed, a little sad. I perked up quickly, continuing on. "I headed up to Vancouver for the finale weekend celebration with everyone. But still I'd hoped I'd see him before he had to start filming. Thank God for Skype."

"Totally," she said. "Hey, taste this." She handed me a dollop of buttercream.

"Wow. That's really good. Tell me why we don't use booze more often?"

"I don't know. What should we call this anyway? I was thinking *The Godfather*- the red reminded of blood, which of course reminds me of that movie."

"Oh, I *love* that idea!" I laughed beside myself. "There's also *Under the Tuscan Sun*." I started lining up the cupcakes for icing.

"Right, how could I forget? I mean, after all *that* she doesn't even get a hot guy? What kind of shit is that? Like having a wedding for a couple of teenagers you just met a month ago is going to make you forget that you just got dumped by your husband. *Bullshit*."

"It's no wonder we're best friends. At least in *Must Love Dogs* she gets the fucking guy." We both laughed, as she filled the pastry bag with buttercream and began icing.

"Speaking of movies, don't forget to grab Emilio Estevez for our Brat Pack girls' night. Tom's going out so we have the place to ourselves."

"Got it. Be there at 7."

As kids Rachel and I had gotten accustomed to *Gilligan's Island*, *Wonder Woman* and *The Munsters*, but we were too young to have crushes on Buck Rogers or Captain Kirk. By the mid-eighties, however, we'd started to pay more attention to the boys of television, like Michael J. Fox, Ricky Schroeder and Jason Bateman. But who could ever forget that decade of absolutely awesome movies?

I arrived at Rachel's with piping hot pizza from Mario's and wine, ready for an evening of boy toy fun. I was glad that after all these years we had not only remained the closest of friends, but still lived near each other. I had remained close with many of my vet school classmates, but sometimes nothing beat hanging with an old friend who understood you like no one else could, rehashing memories of growing up, laughing at the things you said and did and wore back in the day.

Rachel and Tom lived 'up in the sticks' as she still referred to it but as bad as she made it seem at times, they weren't really that far from anything. It was still a short ride to catch a train to the city. It had grocery stores, restaurants and a gym. Your neighbors weren't on top of you like when we were growing up. But she had some valid points. If you wanted to go to a more upscale place than The Blazer Pub or needed something after 9 pm other than beer or cigarettes, you were shit out of luck.

Looking at their house now, it was hard to remember the way it used to be. Tom had transformed a small cape into a two-story piece of heaven that I would have been happy to live in. Of course, I myself would have had to trade something in order to live there but look what I'd traded for being with the guy I was with right now. I walked in to find Rachel in the kitchen, kneeling on the floor, her head stuck in the cupboard.

"Damnit. Where the hell are those martini glasses? I know I put them in here." She was rifling through boxes of various glassware and gadgets.

"What do you need those for?" I asked, confused.

"What do you *mean* what do I need them for? *Martinis*," she huffed.

"*Martinis*? I thought we were having wine? What'd ya do, change it to *James Bond* night?"

"*No*. I've been dying to try out a recipe from that book I got for my birthday. There's an amazing recipe for a blood orange martini. Here, got 'em." She pulled out one. "Aren't these fuckin' cool?"

"Dude. If those don't scream Vegas, I don't know what does."

"I know, right? And check out the name- 'Sinatra Martini Set'. It even says it right here on the box- 'the colorful contrast of retro swirls will set the mood for your intimate gathering'. I love this shit." She studied one in her hand, its thick stem bursting with swirls of blue and gold. "They're made of hand-blown recycled glass."

"Let me guess- they're from your mom."

"Of *course*. You know you always have to drink and eat ice cream in style. Otherwise, what's the point?" she laughed, setting two glasses on the counter."

"Right. Okay, so what's in this martini?" I asked, as I put the bottle of wine in the fridge.

"Um, let's see," she said, turning through the book. "Cointreau, blood orange juice, fresh lime juice, and… vodka- of course."

"Of *course*."

We whipped up a batch and headed for the living room with our pizza. "Wait. And, to make us feel like we're eating a healthier meal…*here*," Rachel added, placing a slice of blood orange garnish onto each rim.

"Perfect. And to cancel *that* move out, I'll grab the grated cheese."

"Perfect," she laughed. "So, what are we watching first?"

"I figured we'd start with *The Breakfast Club* then move on to *16 Candles* or *Weird Science* followed by, last but not least, the underrated favorite, *About Last Night*."

"Sounds great. I've already figured out the next couple of girls' nights- I'm thinking…a little *Anchorman* and *Old School*, followed by an evening of Eddie Murphy…*Beverly Hills Cop* I and II…or maybe just his standup."

"Oh, *hells* yeah. '*Look*, man, I ain't *fallin'* for no banana in my tailpipe'," I quoted. We were already hysterical and the first movie hadn't even started. Hell, we hadn't even finished our first drink.

Chapter 3~ A Bronx Tale

Sunday, May 8

My family rarely celebrated any holiday at a restaurant, but Mother's Day was a unique tradition on my mom's side, one that held a very special place in my heart. We'd pack into the station wagon and head down to Little Italy for the day. Of course, I'm talking about New York's *real* Little Italy- Arthur Avenue. At least, that's the way *some* of us feel.

The Belmont section of the Bronx is certainly not for everyone- you either get its distinctive sentimentality and welcoming charm or you don't. You might feel a strange puzzlement when you first see it, but that's the magic of a New York state of mind- it lures you in and grows on you.

The streets of Belmont looked different than they had back in the day. Handsome guys no longer hung out on corners and sung Doo-Wop; old men weren't selling fruit or shaved ice from street carts and Italian immigrants weren't the only friendly people in the neighborhood. The area surrounding 184th and 187th Streets had changed drastically. Even in 2011, it wasn't hard to see that much had stayed the same. The bakeries and the delis, the butcheries and the cheese shops, the religion and the pride- the tradition lived on and anyone who came here could see that Italy was very much alive in the heart of the Bronx. It's sad to think that one day it could all disappear, a memory in the minds of those who had once been here to live it or like myself, been fortunate to have experienced first-hand just a small part of a much bigger piece of history.

Much of my mom's family was from the area and like most Italians who grew up nearby, they visited Arthur Ave often. I'd spent a lot of time in New York as a kid- it felt like a second home growing up. I was often jealous of my cousins learning Italian and hanging out with the crew at the rec (aka the recreation center), talking New York slang and arguing over whose dad made the gravy.

The great thing about my mom's family being smaller was that we *knew* everyone and unlike my dad's side where I was only close with a few cousins, I was close to most on my mom's so close, that my first and second cousins were like brothers and sisters. Not that her side was *that* small. They just made a point to stay close, even if they lived hours away from each other.

I parked in the same spot I always had, two blocks away on East 187th, in front of one of my favorite pastry shops, Artuso's. There were so many to choose from it was nearly impossible to pick a bad one, although my Uncle Tony still claims Sal and Dom's in Pelham is the best around. 'Fuck Arthur Ave. You want pastries? I'll tell ya where to go fa good fuckin' *pastries*, the best schfoyadel and bishgot around.' For those of you who *don't* happen to speak New York dialect, that translates to sfogliatelle (flaky pastries with filling) and biscotti (cookies).

I knew I should have come down more often over the years- it felt like an obligation to my ancestors to check in at the local home base every once in a while- but like most people, that never happened. I loved Arthur Avenue, from the people to the food to its authentic sense of 'home'. It was a feeling difficult to relate to for non-Italians. Part of me wished I'd grown up here, my parents owning a bakery or cheese shop; that I had married a local and lived the simple life, speaking fluent Italian and passing old traditions down to my children; that nearly all my relatives lived on the same block, or even in the same building. Wait-*what?* I would never argue that I was lucky to have most of my extended family living within an hour of me. But would I want all my cousins in my face 24/7? *Hell* no.

My cousins and I stepped out of the car. We walked past a store that held great memories, a tiny hole-in-the-wall religious store. Years ago my grandmother had taken me there to buy my first deck of Italian playing cards. My cousins and I still played Briscola and Scopa at family gatherings. "Oh my God. Is that where grandma used to take us?" Adriana asked. "Shit, these people don't take Jesus too seriously or anything. Look at all the crucifixes and baby Jesus's in the window!" she commented, stopping to peek inside.

"Yeah, those rosary beads in the corner- I think they've been there for 20 years." All four of us laughed as we moved on. "And not only are we smack dab in front of a mini church, it's Sunday- you better watch it; Jesus is looking down." I poked her in the side.

Adriana, Maria and Tara were first cousins and besides Rachel, the closest things I had to sisters. They still lived around the corner from each other not far from where our moms had grown up, which made it easy to see them often.

We had been here countless times, but it didn't matter-with each first step onto the notorious street it was like stepping back into another time. Storefronts housed in centuries-old brick buildings, their windows packed with items for sale. Now I know people may like to 'window shop' on classier streets like Fifth Avenue or Rodeo Drive, but I will stand by the fact that you can't beat the kind of window shopping that exists here. There isn't a place in the world with this spread of pastries, breads, meats and cheeses, toys, household items and such a vast collection of religious shit you'd think you were at The Vatican.

But I wouldn't be doing Arthur Ave. justice if I left out the *best* part- the assorted heads and carcasses strung upside down, dangling up for all to see, including children, who are usually scarred for life; pig, lamb, goat, rabbit, pigeon...if they could've fit a horse in a window, they would have. You name it- they *had* it.

"So, Adirana, you cookin' up some rabbit cacciatore this week for dinner?" I chuckled, as we walked past Vinny's Meat Market.

"*No*. I don't get how people eat that shit," she answered, speeding up her pace.

"Grandma used to eat it all. I even saw her eat squirrel once. And remember how she used to suck on those pigs' feet? I gag just thinking about it." I motioned with my hands.

"Ugh. I'll pass," I continued, nearly tripping over a manhole. I stopped; my eyes suddenly fixated on the tall, husky figure standing at the curb. I quickly caught up with the girls ahead.

"Trip much, Lea?" They all laughed.

"Did you *see* that guy? I mean, and I'm sorry it's Sunday God but, Holy *shit* was he hot!" All three of them paused, turning to see the striking man in uniform standing behind me with his buddies. There's a reason New York firefighters dominate annual calendars- many could be models.

"I would've been perfectly happy with one of them, too." I continued to stare at him, his big strong arms clutching his hat at his waist, his jacket half-open, exposing the tight muscles beneath his shirt. "Ouch!"

"You already *have* 'one of them', remember? His name's Patrick, aka hottie slash previous model slash soon-to-be starring in the new Tom Clancy movie?" Tara had smacked my arm.

"Yeah, I *know*. But *look* at him. There's just something about firefighters," I smiled. "I'm sorry- I've just been a little lonely lately." I sighed heavily. "I think I'm in withdrawal."

"*Relax*, Lea, you'll see your man soon enough. We better hurry through the market before we're late for brunch." Adriana led us inside.

The Arthur Avenue Retail Market was built in 1940, to replace the hundreds of push-cart vendors that so often roamed the streets of New York. It was considered a landmark, one of the few remaining markets of its kind in the United States, and inside was like a moment from the past frozen in time.

"Ah, looks and smells just like home," I said, scanning the multitude of merchants. "Well, not really, seeing as how I haven't *been* to Italy yet, nor do I own pots so big you guys could fit into 'em. I mean, how much fuckin' sauce do you need- enough for a village?" I wasn't kidding- my cousins could literally fit into some of the pots they sold here. We meandered through a plethora of fresh produce and imported goods.

"They don't waste a square inch in this place," Maria said, referring to how they jam-packed so much under one roof: you could buy everything from espresso to dish towels in here. After picking up some cheese and soprassata at Mike's Deli, we grabbed a quick espresso then dropped our goodies back at the car before meeting up with the rest of the family.

When I was a kid, very few people knew about Dominick's. It was like you had to know somebody who knew somebody to know about it. And that's how my mom's family started going there- they *knew* people. Dominick's was an institution. There were no tables for two or even four. Shit, there wasn't even a menu. You had the choice of eating whatever they were making that day. If they had veal scaloppini and chicken cacciatore, you ate veal scaloppini or chicken cacciatore. If they had mussels oreganate or zuppa de pesce, you ate mussels or zuppa de pesce. You didn't even *think* about asking for meatballs. And...there were no *prices*. When you were done eating, they walked over to your table and told you how much it was gonna be. And every time you went back it would likely be a different price.

When we arrived everyone was already there. My brothers and their wives were seated at the far end of one big table next to my mom. My aunts and uncles were next to them. I noticed my cousin Toni and ran over to greet her.

"Hey, girl!" Toni and her family lived two hours north which meant we only saw each other on special occasions. Still we remained close. She jumped out of her seat to hug me.

"Yo, Lea! You made it," Anthony shouted.

"Yeah, what the hell were you guys doing?" Donnie had to chime in. They'd clearly already gassed a carafe of wine.

"Yo, what's going on?" I asked Anthony.

I stood behind Moira and Donnie and poured myself some red wine with a splash of Pellegrino, as I observed everyone conversing at the long table. There were easily 20 of us. I smiled. Family was something you just couldn't reproduce. They could be overwhelming, overbearing even frustrating at times, but that's what families were for- to be there, even when you think you don't need them to be, to love you...*and* to get on your fucking nerves.

"Hey, Lea, how's the vet business?" I hadn't even sat down yet and already my Uncle Joey was at it. And I knew exactly what was coming next. "And where's that guy a yours? I heard he was an actor or somethin'. I acted when I was young, too. I did one of them school plays. I could a done more wit it but ah, ya know, I had to get a *real* job." He laughed, spooning some bruschetta onto his bread. I nodded in response. He didn't mean it. After all, he didn't know any better and it really didn't bother me all that much.

"Good. It's going okay," I paused, "and he's not here- he's out of the country-*working*."

"Workin'!?" His voice echoed throughout the restaurant. The entire table turned, all eyes on me. "*Where*? It's Mutha's Day for Christ's sake. He should be with his mutha." Like he even knew the guy.

"Uncle Joey, it's 2011. People actually *do* work on Sundays and holidays now," I rolled my eyes. "I'm sure he'd be with his mother if he could. Geesh." I took a sip of wine.

"How long you been wit this chump anyways? Isn't it about time you two tied the knot? I mean, what the hell's this guy waitin' for?" I couldn't even get a word in; he kept rambling. "Well, when ya get tired of waitin' around, lemme know- I know someone wit a real job- my buddy Jimmy's kid, Lorenzo. Good kid, comes from a good family, works as a contracta."

I tried not to lose my cool, seeing as how it was Mother's Day. The last thing I wanted to do was upset my mother, of all people. "Patrick *has* a real job. In case you hadn't noticed, actors actually make a decent living." Italians came from a long line of hardworking, honest (well, *mostly*) people and most people in my family didn't believe in acting as a profession. None of them would argue, however, that Robert Deniro and Joe Pesci weren't talented.

"Sure- paycheck ta *paycheck*." Before I had realized it, I'd finished my glass and was shaking for a refill. "*Patrick*? What is that anyway, *Irish*?"

"You mean, he's not even *Italian*?" my Aunt Lena chimed in. And you think those stereotypes in movies *aren't* real, huh? Although many Italians and Irish immigrated to the United States around the same time and had things in common, they didn't get along very well.

"What does it matter anyway? This isn't 1950, not that it shoulda mattered then. You may wanna watch somethin' besides *Boardwalk Empire* or *The Sopranos* every once in a while. You know your TV won't blow up if you change the channel," I chuckled.

"Lea, don't worry," Erin interrupted, "If you ever get tired of waiting, I'll have him- You won't mind, will ya honey?" She patted Anthony on the hand.

As usual, the spread had been nothing short of a feast and, in keeping with tradition, the bunch of us headed to my cousin Tara's to play cards.

"So," Tara said as we walked back to the car, "who's dealing first?"

Chapter 4 ~ Song of the South

Memorial Day Weekend

I'd been a little restless lately. Not only was I missing Patrick, I needed a break from work. It'd been way too long since Mac and I had revisited our southern roots. You might wonder why two New Englanders would willingly submerge themselves in such a dramatically different culture for their last year and a half of veterinary school. Having already lived in a faraway place that lacked most comforts of home, Mac and I had returned to the states yearning for more exploration. Plus, who *wouldn't* choose booze and beignets over I don't know, *anything*? And it had paid off- we'd not only left Baton Rouge with new friends, but a new 'appreciation' of the south.

It was 2003. Neither of us had been that far south of the Mason-Dixie line before (except Florida) and when we'd first arrived, it was a culture shock, and a far cry from the island life we had experienced. We were both eager and nervous to get through the last grueling months of veterinary school. The curriculum would be challenging, not to mention having to pass boards. To make things more trying, we'd entered the senior year of *another* school's class, one far larger than ours and one who'd already known each other. Our class of 35 had been tight, almost like family. To head off to different schools after three years had been hard. But like all chapters, that one had to eventually end if we were to embark on our journeys as doctors.

Mac and I had stood out overwhelmingly amongst the locals *and* LSU's students, about 90% of whom *were* locals, and it'd been no surprise that we'd butted heads with more than a few. To them, the Civil War was far from over and they even considered people from northern *Louisiana* to be Yankees. It'd been an...adjustment. Grenada had been an adjustment, too and it hadn't been easy being away from everyone we knew, but it'd come with advantages- a year-round warm climate with one of the world's best beaches, unbeatable sunsets, an endless supply of rum...

Louisiana was *very* different in its own ways and, although I appreciated the drive-thru liquor stores and the term 'y'all', there were things I just couldn't wrap my head around- the overwhelming number of terrible fast food chains like Whataburger and Krystal, the crappy 'pizzerias' and the fact that no one gave a shit about *anything* else in life except LSU football. The bombardment of purple and yellow was consuming year-round. It was a world we hadn't been used to.

If that hadn't been enough, Louisiana State University itself was intimidating. It sat on 2000 acres along the banks of the Mississippi, with 25,000 undergraduate and over 500 veterinary students. But however impressed Mac and I had been with the veterinary school, it was kind of hard not to notice the massive structure we had to drive past every day to get to the vet school.

Tiger Stadium towered over the entire campus. It was the eighth largest on-campus NCAA stadium in the country and the eighteenth largest stadium in the *world*, its one-of-a-kind, renaissance-inspired architectural design, earning it the title of "Death Valley". And then there was Mike, who wasn't just *any* mascot, but a live Bengal tiger and the heart of the university's spirit. This cat had it *good*- and I don't mean he ate Fancy Feast.

On home game weekends, RVs were camped out all over the city *and* on campus leaving hardly any parking spots. Fans from opposing teams rolled into Baton Rouge days before a game, outlandish paraphernalia proudly displayed, ready for a fight. It was a scene out of *Braveheart*, warriors storming in revolt, their faces painted for battle. And to these diehard fans, they wouldn't hesitate to slaughter the enemy over some piece of pigskin.

We exited the small Baton Rouge airport. After being greeted by a ginormous Mike the Tiger statue at the baggage claim, we grabbed our stuff and headed outside, spotting Leann's Toyota pickup immediately, its windows decorated with purple and yellow 'Geaux Tigers' decals.

"Hey y'all!" She ran around the truck, her arms wide open with excitement. I compared her size to her vehicle, wondering how the hell she managed to get in and out of the damn thing without a step stool. She and Mac were about the same height, all of 4' 10", and they had about the same amount of gumption, too. Her family still lived off the same 100 acres of land, which had been in their family for generations.

With that smile you wouldn't expect her to have had a mean bone in her body, but she hadn't earned the nickname 'fireball' for nothing. Leann may have spoken with a friendly Mississippi drawl but trust me- you didn't wanna cross a girl who could shoot a mean target and butcher a cow blindfolded. It was friends like her we never would've met had we not taken that chance 10 years ago and landed on some remote Caribbean island. We set our bags in back before taking turns hugging our dear old friend.

"So good to see y'all! 'Bout time y'all made it down! Wait till y'all see the house," she shouted.

"Right, how's it coming?" Mac said, sliding into the truck.

"Would y'all just get in and stop yappin'? I'll tell you while we're drivin' home. I gotta stop by my friend Billy's- he's got some moonshine for me."

"*Moonshine*? Aren't you startin' us a *little* early?" I asked.

"We're not drinkin' it *now*," she added. "Besides, it's too early for moonshine."

"Ok, good. You were beginning to worry me for a sec." Mac stared out the window as we drove past a Chick-Fil-A and straight into Daiquiri Café. "Ok," she paused, "you're officially worrying me now."

"*What*? Come on, did y'all forget where y'are? This is *Louisiana*. It's never too early for huntin', drinkin' or tailgatin'. I said it was too early for *moonshine*. Everything else is fair game," she enforced her best smile. "First off, it's *practically* the weekend. Second, y'all are on *vacation*. Were y'all gonna be doin' surgery?" She gave us her 'what's wrong with you, you're a chicken shit' look.

"To *hell* with that. I don't see any doctors around here do you, Camioni?" Mac was now all in.

"No," Leann and I both answered adamantly.

"Then I say we get this vacation started off right," Mac insisted. "There's only one problem- do I get Peach Bellini or Hurricane?"

Leann's home sat on a cozy, fenced-in two-acre lot. An early 1900s, Acadian style farmhouse, it was different from the farmhouses I'd been used to. Her family automatically thought it was haunted, her mother insisting on placing odd family heirlooms around the place to protect it from evil spirits.

Where Mac and I were from 'haunted' usually involved witches, poltergeists, or ghosts from horrific murders like *Amityville*. Up North we didn't have slaves who'd been tortured and heinously murdered running around haunting plantations. Voodoo was a much *different* kind of magic than witchcraft and for some reason it scared the hell out of me more.

I was impressed and jealous with both Leann's property and her barn. It housed horse stalls, an expansive loft and two outdoor, chicken coops. Equipped with a pool table, darts and a flat screen TV for none other than football season, this place not only trumped any man cave, it could've literally passed as a bar.

Maybe having a rooster could come in handy on works days, but *not* on vacation. No thanks to Chester, the next morning all three of us were up much earlier than we'd wanted.

"So y'all ready to visit one of your favorite places? It'll get you geared up for tomorrow."

"Absolutely." I was more than enthusiastic to revisit an old favorite.

The Myrtles Plantation may have appeared tranquil and inviting, but its dark and harrowing past dubbed it one of, if not *the* most, haunted homes in America. Its history was steeped in mystery, romance and tragedy, not that you'd guess it from the outside. Centuries-old oak and myrtle trees lined its curvy driveway, which led up to the beautiful Greek Antebellum home. It had a grand entrance front and rear, with lacy intricate ironwork framing its veranda, its tall windows and columns holding up an expansive covered porch. The carriage house sat by the beautifully manicured courtyard.

We walked through the double-entry doors past the infamous 'magic' mirror, said to harbor the spirits of two little girls who'd been poisoned. As the tour guide continued his story of The War of 1864 against The Yankees I tried not to stare into the mirror, fearing I'd actually see something or *someone* looking back at me.

At the end of the tour, we stood attentively at the bottom of the grand staircase gathered around the guide, listening to the details of William Stirling's heart-rending death on the seventeenth step. We cautiously gazed up picturing the tragic scene as if it were the first time we'd heard the tale, listening for the heavy sounds of footsteps of the wounded soldier said to be heard at night. There was no other way to say it- shit was just creepy in these old plantations. Jealous murder and bloodied soldiers were one thing- slaves hung in courtyards and voodoo raising the dead was another. I was thankful this had been a morning tour.

Speaking of history, I couldn't *wait* to see New Orleans tomorrow. We spent the rest of the day relaxing and after dinner and drinks, headed to bed early. Besides, we needed to conserve at least *some* of our liver function for a weekend in The City of Sin...

Chapter 5 ~ King Creole

In 2004, a year and a half after we'd left Grenada, Hurricane Ivan blew in and devastated it. The tiny island we'd called home for more than three years, known as "The Spice Island of the World", had had most of its crops destroyed and would not recover for some time due to the severe damage to its economy. But few lives were lost and with help they'd been slowly and steadily inching upward.

Fast forward to 2005 and bad juju had been hot on our tails. After Mac and I'd finished rotation, Hurricane Katrina unleashed a wrath upon the Gulf Coast more powerful and devastating than it had ever seen. Louisiana was no stranger to hurricanes; it'd been an unfortunate part of New Orleans' past. At six feet below sea level, it was poorly designed to ward off natural disasters, and repeated trauma had broken down its only means of protection over the years. The lack of improvements had remained a mystery. Either way there was no going back to the way things were. No matter *what* they showed on T.V.; No matter *how* many trips celebrities like Oprah made down to better their names- things would just never be the same.

We were headed East on The Bonnet Carre Spillway, on the Southern border of Lake Pontchartrain. Crossing the causeway into Orleans Parish for the first time since Katrina had almost reminded me of returning to New York from Grenada after 9/11. New Orleans was a sad sight after Katrina hit, but the parts hit the worst were hardly ever seen by outsiders. As we neared downtown, I felt that familiar stomach drop, because I knew hidden behind what we *could* see was a city constantly struggling to return to a new 'normal'.

I imagined what it might've been like to lose my family, my pets, my home- my *life*. Visions flashed in my mind...people yelling and screaming, pleading for help, for anyone to come save them. A widespread panic among those trying to get to any high point to safety. But once the levees broke residents of the Lower Ninth Ward, had five seconds before they were flooded to nearly 12 feet. I remember the chaos, everyone in complete upheaval, in fear of their loved ones. I remember the videos, the aftermath *and* the statistics:

80% of New Orleans flooded, 90,000 square miles of land severely marred, $800 billion in damage, thousands of people died.

Animal deaths could not be counted. It was complete and total devastation and fear and that had only been the beginning. The anarchy that ensued turned into far worse. Thousands of people had stayed behind instead of evacuating, but it hadn't been because of pride- they were disproportionately poor and had had nowhere to go, couldn't afford hotels and didn't have a means to leave. The nonexistent mass transit system, limited buses and streetcars had proven to be a matter of life and death.

We exited at the Superdome onto Poydras Street. As we crossed Canal Street, I watched two streetcars pass each other, full of locals and tourist, a warming welcome. Four years ago, on our last trip down for a conference, it'd been pitiful to see a lone, half empty car pass by every 90 minutes. You could still get a sense of how much these people had lost, but somehow they'd kept it all going; they never gave up. It's not the bars, the vampires or even JazzFest-You can just feel their overwhelming passion for life streaming from their souls. You can hear it in their music, see it in the art and taste it in the food and coffee...

We turned left at South Peters Street past Harrah's Casino, heading into the Quarter. I watched all the people walking, laughing and enjoying themselves. Down a side street I caught a glimpse of storefronts: 5-foot water stains and cracked foundations, broken windows still held together by tape, others simply abandoned with or without an 'out of business' sign...So many residents had fled to start a new life; Six years later most hadn't returned, and it showed. But what *had* survived? A plentiful supply of love- for a place in desperate need of healing and a heartbeat that hadn't stopped after tragedy had struck. And the combination of these two things fed the fuel for regrowth, a rebirth. And you could see that now, a city that had finally started sprouting its limbs.

Dozens of establishments were busy with tourists and the seductive sound of jazz floated through the air. We'd decided to stay in Marigny, just outside The French Quarter. Frenchman Street was another world compared to Bourbon Street, the place tourists flocked here to see. It attracted a more low-key audience- true fans of classic jazz and blues admixed with a younger, hipper artsy crowd. People traded in their Mardi Gras beads and Hurricanes for costume jewelry and gin fizzes. Known for its old school clubs and classy fare, it was somewhat less rowdy and more relaxed atmosphere.

"Now *this* is what I'm talkin' about," I said as we pulled in front. The Frenchman Hotel was just a short walk from The French Market. The valet appeared to greet us.

"Mornin' ma'am. How all y'all doin' this fine mornin'?" He said, smile beaming.

Mac stepped aside. "Mornin'," she greeted him back. "Fine, thank you, and yourself?"

"Not too bad, ma'am. How long all y'all stayin'?"

"Till Sunday." Mac turned to me, now smiling, "God I love this city- it's good to be back."

"Sure is," I answered. "Have a good day, sir." He nodded shyly and went about his way.

"Me, too, but I'll still take my bayou and moonshine over a Hurricane. And y'all can keep that voodoo here, too." Leann's comment sent us all into a fit of laughter. "The bayou's got enough haunts and mysteries of our own- we don't need anymore...So," she paused, "where to first?"

Chapter 6 ~ Interview with the Vampire

After our Café du Monde fix we checked out the art galleries along Royal Street before visiting the tomb of Marie Laveau, New Orleans' most famous voodoo priestess. The whole time Leann could hardly stop shaking her head, calling Mac and I out on our obsession with the dead.

As one of the most historically beautiful cities in existence, New Orleans is best experienced on foot. But as beautiful a city as it has been for nearly 300 years, its beauty isn't *exactly* what keeps people coming back. Countless tales of voodoo, spirits and mythical creatures set it apart from almost any other place in the world. Some believe it literally wreaks of the dead (not just sex and booze).

But walking around knowing that among us had been *true* evil, evil that still lingers at every turn, now that just creeped me the fuck out. Being anywhere near that kind of darkness sent chills down even my spine. We made our way back through the Quarter and as we neared the corner of Royal and Governor Nicholls Streets, the eerily familiar three-story residence made me cringe, in a way even The Myrtles Plantation couldn't.

I remember the time Mac and I had driven to New Orleans and gone on a haunted walking tour. LaLaurie Mansion was the most popular and feared house in New Orleans- Popular because of its elegant architecture; feared because of the little shop of horrors that had been uncovered in 1834. Once owned by Dr. Louis LaLaurie and his wife Delphine its rather plain-looking exterior hardly reflected the grandness and lavishness behind its front doors. But the couple themselves hid behind their own façade. On the outside Madame LaLaurie carried herself with great style. There was a cruel, cold-blooded insane side to her, though, one of pure evil. Because the things she had done could only have been done by someone with evil coursing through their veins.

I recall the tour guide urging us to take pictures, in case we'd catch an orb or apparition peering out a window, namely the attic, where more than a dozen slaves had been found mutilated and tortured; bound by chains, shoved in small cages, mouths sewn shut, body parts cut out and/or off. To this day no one has lived in the house for any substantial amount of time, making it New Orleans' very own Amityville Horror- a cursed entity many are obsessed with, but few are brave enough to take up residence in, me included- you wouldn't catch me dead inside 1140 Royal Street- no pun intended. But you better believe I still have those pictures, the ones with green orbs...

"Hey, I meant to ask, what was that pyramid-like tomb we saw near Marie Laveau?" I asked, as we neared Jackson Square.

"Oh, yeah, that's Nicolas Cage's. He bought it a few years back- wants to be buried here. Weird right?"

"What the fuck. I don't get it."

Mac chimed in, "*no* one gets Nick Cage. I mean he named his son Kal-El. *Who* does that? Didn't he own LaLaurie Mansion for like a minute?"

"Well I guess when you're a Coppola you can do whatever you want..."

Overlooking the Mississippi River, Jackson Square's 2.5-acre lot was one of New Orleans' most recognizable landmarks. Inside was a beautifully gated park, where a towering statue of Andrew Jackson watched over the city, representing the Louisiana Purchase in 1813. At its north end was St. Louis Cathedral and across from its entrance along the river sat the world-famous Café du Monde, known for its beignets and café au laits. Surrounding the park were various shops and restaurants, making it a bustling place during the day. But it was during the late-night hours that things got interesting.

Local craftsmen and performers were replaced by darkly dressed tables covered with crystal balls, tarot cards and voodoo dolls, and musicians and sketch artists swapped out for fortune tellers. But innocent-looking gypsies sitting at tables reading fortunes weren't the *only* odd things in Jackson Square; people believing they were pirates or even vampires roamed about, taking bizarre and creepy to a whole new level. The unexplained was not unique to New Orleans. Salem, Massachusetts had its own haunts, but New Orleans held a very different paranormal atmosphere, one with a long history of the occult and haunted happenings. They may not have had witches, but everyone knows witches aren't the only ones who do magic...

We walked around scoping out prospects until finally, we decided on a woman set up in a dimly lit spot away from the action. She had dark eyes and long, black hair that wrapped down around her neck like a scarf. With her inviting smile she motioned us over.

"Welcome, welcome. My name is Willow. So, which one of y'all is first?" she asked curiously. I felt her gaze go through me. I looked down at her table- a lone candle, a feather and a few rocks had been placed almost strategically. "What about you, honey?" I stood there momentarily, questioning my decision. I shook my head 'no'.

"*She* does." I gently shoved Mac in front of me.

"Ahhh, I see your friend has volunteered you..." the woman said smiling, waiting."

"Uh, I'm Mac."

"...Mac, interesting. Come, now sit," she continued, shoeing us away. "I hope you don't mind if I ask y'all to wait 'round the corner. I can feel the spirits better." *Yeah, right.* Leann and I backed away.

Almost 20 minutes later I got a text from Mac saying she was all done. Before I could speak, Willow cut me off, "come on and have a seat, will you?"

Mac quickly moved aside, "You're up," she said, touching my arm, "psss... she's *good.*" I rolled my eyes at her. *Good- yeah right. She's gonna tell me I have a long lifeline, I'm gonna be wealthy and live happily ever after with my twin flame...*But something inside told me to trust her. After all, Mac had an even stronger intuition than I did.

"She'll be fine, don't y'all worry. My customers area always in good hands with the spirits, isn't that *right*, Mac?" Her coy wink albeit comforting to Mac hardly relieved me. Maybe they had some Wicca connection. I shook it off and watched as my friends disappeared around the corner.

How we'd ended up over here I had no idea. But it was too late to back out now. I turned to face her, a small knot in my throat. "So, anyway...um, how does this work? Do you need me to pick a significator card or something?"

She just watched me, smiling still. "Honey child, have you ever been here before?"

"Um.... Yea, a few times."

"Ever had a reading?"

"Yes, why?"

"I just wanna let you know what *not* to expect."

"I'm sorry did you say, *not*?"

"I mean, whatever you've experienced before, with cards or crystals, don't expect to see any of that here. I do my readings strictly through spirit guides," she said. Then lowering her voice to a whisper, she added, "and a little old-fashioned voodoo, but we won't tell anyone that." *Another wink- just great.*

"Oh, okay," I laughed. This was sounding eerily like *The Skelton Key*... "and I've been told I'm hard to read so sorry in advance."

"That's cuz you're a Scorpio, child." *What?* "And you ain't hard to read, now give me your hands. Come on, now. Don't be afraid." *I am not afraid- just hoping that voodoo thing was a joke.* I laid my arms on the black cloth, feeling a subtle jolt as if I'd crossed into some other space. *Shit- Maybe she wasn't kidding.*

"Uh, huh. Let me see," she continued studying me. "Wow, you have beautiful skin- what's your secret?"

"No secrets- just a bunch of fading scars and lots of olive oil," I joked.

"Scorpios *always* have secrets, child." Her demeanor turned serious. "You have an old, ageless soul, like an angel." *Weird, but...* "Your destiny is far greater and your journey far from over. You have a lot yet to do." She paused as if she could read my hands. "You work hard in this life, almost too hard, like in all your past lives. I see the greatness that you are, what you have done for others. But what is to come well...well let's just back up a minute."

"Okay."

"I see a great presence around you, masculine, strong, *very* strong, someone here among the living; he cares greatly for you. I feel a tight bond between you two, but..." She paused again in thought, lifting her head, "somethin' holds you back- fear. Fear of solitude, sadness but also of another. I see a separation, maybe not physical, but it is there and still you hold back."

"I'm already..."

"Shh, shh. Let him in, they say, trust in what you know to be true."

"How?"

"You'll have to figure out that one yourself, but it'll all be fine. Children... I see lots of children, all around you, many little lights."

"I don't have children. To be honest it's getting a little late for that..."

"Figuratively, and the love you have for them is unconditional. These lights, they are what drive you. You have a way of bringing hope to those who are not able to help themselves. It is a special gift. And it is never too late, remember that. But be careful not to let the darkness take over. It can be tempting, especially for a Scorpio." She looked away then back, making sure no one was around. "Hmm, you have a powerful shield. They were right about you." *Wait till Mac hears that one.*

"You'd give it all to a stranger, but not to those closest to you, hmm?" I didn't move. "Been that way your whole life, haven't you? Scorpions..." she murmured to herself. "Yet...you're different from most." *I'll say.* "You're special, for many reasons. You...have many abilities and...you don't seem to have that curse they typically get."

I looked at her, confused, "curse?" *Great- that's all I fuckin' need.*

"That deep-seeded urge for revenge. That's the downfall for most a y'all." She smiled surely, clinging to my right hand and placing her right hand on my chest, catching me off guard. "This," she said turning serious again, "this right here, is one of the most powerful weapons there is and yours well it's...I don't quite know. Sorry- haven't ever been told to do that before," she apologized, catching herself, replacing her hand to the table. "They said to tell you that is your biggest strength and to hold on to it because you will need it and they will need you."

"Who?" she didn't answer. *"Who?"*

"All those who depend on you..." Suddenly her cards flew violently of the table onto the ground. She jumped back, releasing me abruptly. Everything around us appeared unaffected and no one seemed to have noticed. The trees were still. There wasn't a hint of a breeze. *What the shit...*

"Are you okay? Willow?" Why I was asking a voodoo queen if she was okay, I had no idea. Moments later she was back, as if having been temporarily transported out of body. She had a look of sheer terror on her face, barely making eye contact with me. "Whelp, I guess that's it. We can end here; I'm good," I bent down to pick up a rock. "You sure you don't want any water or...ow!" She grabbed my arm firmly.

"No! I am not finished. Sit *down*." Her voice had changed to a deeper, more scary tone and her eyes seemed a blackish blue. *'There is no Dana, only Zuul'...* I followed her back up to the table. "I'll get those. Just go ahead and sit back down." Then in an instant her voice had changed back.

"Do you know what that was?" I asked, afraid of the answer.

"Oh, nevermind that. Give me your hands again." I did as she said. Up until now everything she had said was pretty accurate, all but the part I *didn't* understand. She started to speak. "I need you to listen to me. A darkness is coming."

"Excuse me?" *Gulp.* "A *darkness*?"

"Shhhhhhh!" She leaned in closely, lowering her voice. "Shhh. Yes, child, darkness, despair and...danger. You must heed warning. Now listen." *What the hell?* "Right now, you're happy... but there are challenges ahead." I nodded. *Original.* "There is always hope; your guardian angels are watching over you but...you will be tested- you *must* be tested. And you must *listen*- listen to your intuition and pay attention to the signs, they will lead you."

"Lead me where? Tested? What danger? I don't understand. And how will I know what to do? Please, there must be something else you can tell me."

"When the time is right, you will know. But remember this, honey. Things are not what they seem. They have one final message for you- Listen to your heart, it will guide you toward all that you need. That's all I can tell you, child. That's all I can see." I stared back at her, confused.

Out of the corner of my eye I saw Leann and Mac. I waved, my arm still shaking, and as they walked over I put on my best smile, careful not to let my uneasiness show.

"All finished?" I nodded 'yes'. *Hell yes. Let's get the fuck out of here.*

"So, how was it? You gonna be rich or..." Leann asked. When I didn't answer Mac immediately sensed something was off.

"Uh...yep, yep." Willow appeared unphased, like she had hit the reset button, ready for her next customer. *Victim is more like it. Why the hell was Mac so happy after her reading and I got the message of destruction?* I threw a twenty-dollar bill on the table, "okay, that does it, let's go. Uh, thanks again," I said to Willow. *For what I'm not sure...*

"Everything okay?" Leann asked.

"Yeah, totally, all good," I pressed. "It's getting late. Isn't it getting late? What time is it?"

"For N'awlins? *Shit* no. We got at least one more stop before we call it a night and I know just the place..."

Chapter 7 ~ Must Love Dogs

June

It was much cooler than where I'd just been. The temps began to soar well into the 90s come May in Louisiana and between the sticky, stagnant air and all the bugs, 75 degrees was a nice welcome. I wish I could've said the same about work. You know how you never feel like getting back to your day-to-day life after a much-needed break?

In addition to all the work I had waiting, my brain was bogged down with something else- that crazy fortune teller, or spirit guide, whatever the fuck you want to call her. That so-called 'reading' I'd gotten from a seemingly sweet, yet all-too suspecting, blue-turned-black-eyed gypsy, which had left me with more questions than answers about my future. I guess she could've just been high on incense or vampire dust, but what she'd said had stuck with me. Why? Because what may have appeared harmless, even mysterious fun between the covers of a novel could be scary as hell if it actually came true...

"So," Maureen said, "how's it being back in real life?"

"Not bad," I said, reading a chart. "Did I miss anything exciting?"

"No, not really, but you know I hate it when you leave."

"You should've come," I joked.

"True, I could've had my own Jewish version of Patrick by now, I know, I know..."

"I *meant* to New Orleans...but I did hear Larry David is single now..."

"Oh shut up. I am *not* that desperate," she argued.

"But you could be *rich*. Think about it. Anyway, did you happen to see Baxter's record? She was supposed to see the dermatologist..."

"It's in referrals."

"You mean, she *actually* made the appointment? I'm shocked."

"Uh huh. I swear these fucking people get on my nerves more and more every day. I'm a *doctor*, not your therapist, your only friend or your personal assistant," we laughed.

Maureen had a point; the same one *all* veterinarians would agree with. Everyone assumed people loved their pets, brought them in when they were sick and actually *listened* to medical advice. Unfortunately, that *wasn't* always the case. Yes, it was true we had some of the most loyal clients, but we also had some of the craziest, neediest, most annoying, confrontational, noncompliant ones so many, that it drove us absolutely out of our fucking minds at times. No, scratch that- *all* the time. There's nothing like spending minutes, hours, even days of your valuable time on one patient, giving it your all, making the proper diagnosis and treatment plan, only to find out that an asshole owner was never going to either spend the money or listen to you anyway.

"Yeah, no *shit*. Next thing you know they'll expect concierge service," I joked.

"I already know someone who does that- in *The Hamptons*, of course- *if* you want that kind of life. This sucks out enough of my soul. I'm sure living in The Hamptons is nice, but you couldn't pay me enough to be called out in the middle of the night to check Fluffy's fucking watery eyes."

"Unless it was Ina Garten. She'd probably pay in Beef Bourguignon or chocolate mousse; I'd take that."

"Okay, *maybe* her. Speaking of Patrick, when is he coming?" she asked.

"Next week."

"Doing anything fun, ya know, besides tons of hot sex?" she teased.

"Oh shut *up*," I blushed. "Well, we're supposed to go to a show, we're having dinner with my mom and we're going shooting with my dad and my brothers."

"Of *course* you are," she chuckled to herself. "Does he even know *how* to shoot?" she asked.

"He's gonna *learn*. When it comes to my dad, you don't have a lot of choices, you know that. It'll be fun though. I mean, I'm excited."

"Of *course* you are."

"He'll be fine. I'm sure they won't beat up on him *too* much. Besides my dad likes him, I *think*, plus he's looking forward to teaching him some skills for his upcoming movie."

"I bet he is. Anything good?"

"*I* think so- another leading role with some bigwig director. He's excited."

"Wow, so he's really beginning to take off then, huh?"

"Yea. Pretty soon people will recognize him as more than just some guy who once played a superhero on TV."

Chapter 8 ~ Lethal Weapon

A week later...

Patrick and I were at my mom's by 6 pm. She'd made her signature dish- penne a la vodka, a secret family recipe that had been passed down through generations. My mom was about the kindest person you'd ever meet. She rarely had anything bad to say about anyone, especially Patrick. She absolutely loved him, almost too much it seemed at times, but I'm pretty sure it's because she was so excited for me to have found someone so good-hearted (it also might've helped that she, too had been a fan...). God knows the last one hadn't exactly been up to par, but I digress...The first time they'd met I thought he was gonna suffocate from her hug. A year and a half later, things hadn't changed one bit.

"Oh, honey, so glad you guys made it!" she exclaimed, grabbing hold of Patrick as she welcomed us inside.

"Hi, mom. Yeah, of course we made it; you're only 10 minutes away," I said, shaking my head at the ridiculousness of her statement.

"How are you Mrs. Camioni?" Patrick asked.

"Patrick, how many times do I have to tell you to call me Lorraine? Now, come in and relax. What you want to drink?"

"If I remember correctly, you make a killer martini," he winked. What a player, I thought, smiling to myself.

"Damn right I do," she laughed. In a moment she was back with his drink. "So," she said, "how's work? Anything new I need to set my VHS for?"

"That's DVR, mom."

"Whatever- DVR, VCR, Betamax," she answered. "I am *not* getting rid of my VCR- how else am I supposed to watch *The Creature from the Back Lagoon*?"

"*Some* people buy the version on DVD or Blue Ray, ma. Come on, get with times, will ya?"

"Don't feel bad, Mrs. Camioni, uh, I mean, Lorraine. My mom does the same thing. Actually," he said as we went into the dining room, "I've got a couple of cool projects coming up, but they won't be out until next year."

"Any new James Bond?" She was just relentless sometimes.

"No, ma. I think Daniel Craig's got that one covered," I laughed.

I waited for my mom to leave the room. "Sorry about that- she can't help it. You know how much she loves you."

"It's fine, don't worry about it. I *love* your mom. She's so sweet."

"Yeah, until you piss her off. You see that wooden spoon over there? In an instant that thing can become a deadly weapon in the hand of a pissed-off Italian woman," I joked.

He looked at me quizzically, "a wooden spoon, *seriously*?"

"Yeah, seriously, right ma?!" I turned around, yelling towards the kitchen.

"Oh, she's joking, Patrick," my mom answered.

"No, I'm *not*. Let me check my arm. I think I still have a scar somewhere..."

"Okay, who's ready for dessert?" she asked excitedly.

"Oh, I'm sorry but I'm kind of fu..." Patrick began to say.

"Shhhhh!" I said, hushing him, "don't *ever* say those words around here."

"What words?" he asked dumbfounded.

"F-U-L-L."

"Honestly, I am..."

"You *can't* be. Two key rules whenever you're invited for a meal at an Italian household- never show up emptyhanded and *always* show up hungry."

"But what if you really can't eat anymore?"

"Then you make *room*. We are?"

"Great! I've got cannolis and tiramisu from Artuso's. I would've made the tiramisu myself, but I ran out of time," she admitted. "So, what are your plans for the rest of the week?" she asked.

"Donnie and Anthony are taking me, us, shooting tomorrow," Patrick answered.

"Oh, well, have fun and tell your father I said hi. Any other big plans?"

"Maybe a show in the city, but other than that, just hangin' out."

"Oh, nice."

The next day...

It was just after 11 am when we arrived at the hunt club. The positives about bringing your famous boyfriend to places out in the middle of the quiet New England countryside? The odds of any paparazzi finding you were slim and the odds of someone recognizing him were even less, which made for a more relaxing time all around- *unless* you were in certain company. My dad had always preferred hunt clubs over smaller ranges due to their more rural locations and lack of hot-headed guys who were typically dumbasses with guns, the kinds of guys people like him would more than likely want to beat the shit out of.

My dad was one of the most hilarious, bad-mouthed, non-politically correct people around but when it came to certain things, he was 150% serious, especially when it involved two of his passions- scuba diving and weapons. And anytime we were at the range the one thing he never joked about was gun safety, to the point where anyone who was around would always have this look of awe combined with sheer terror on their faces. Of course, if you'd ever seen what he *brought* to the range, you'd look the same way.

"Yo!" My brother Anthony shouted as we walked over.

"Patrick, good to see ya, buddy!" Donnie chimed in.

"Hey, what's up guys?" Patrick said as the three of them shook hands.

"Hey, *Hollywood*, ready for gun skills 101?" And there came the ultimate wise ass from around the corner. *Please be nice, please be nice...*

"Hey, dad," I said, giving him a hug and a kiss.

"Hey, sweetheart," he said.

"Hi, Mr. Camioni. Good to see you, sir." Now unlike my mom, my dad *never* corrected guys when they addressed him by that. Probably because it made him more intimidating. Not that my dad needed any help with that one. At over 6' himself and with the 'experience' he made known to those around him, he had that one pretty much in the bag.

"How's them palm trees treatin' ya?" my dad asked.

"Not too bad, sir. Not too bad. I was actually gonna ask you for some pointers..."

"Oh *shit*," I heard my brothers both say. I watched Patrick's clueless face. He'd met my dad before; he knew the story; he'd even seen my dad with a weapon. But this was going to be a whole different experience, one he'd likely wish he'd never signed up for, let alone forget.

"What?" he asked me.

"Oh, you'll see." I smiled as we continued hauling the bags of weapons out of the trunks of their cars. "Here, hold this," I said handing him a rifle bag.

"What's all this?"

"Well, we *are* at a gun range..."

"Why are these bags so big?" he asked, suddenly unsure.

"Where the fuck did you think you were going to today, the *golf* course?" my dad joked.

"I mean, my AR-15 wasn't gonna fit in inside my pants, dude," Donnie said, walking away.

Patrick leaned in, lowering his voice, "did he just say *AR-15*?"

I just smiled and tapped him, "ah...yep. Good luck." Minutes later we were ready for action.

"So," Donnie asked as he set up his gear, "is this new movie you're doin' any good?"

"Ah, yeah, actually. Christopher Nolan's directing one of Tom Clancy's novels, *Rainbow Six*."

"Wow, that's pretty fuckin' cool, I gotta say."

"Thanks," Patrick answered.

"I don't know if it'll be as good as *Patriot Games*. Anyway, back to business. I don't give a shit *what* they tell you out there in 'la la land', listen to me and you'll get it right every time. You'll be so good they'll be asking *you* for pointers." And that was just the beginning of my dad's rant. "First things first: Always make sure you're familiar with basic firearm safety. Consider all guns *always* loaded..."

An hour later, my dad was still talking and miraculously, Patrick hadn't run for the hills. "Now, listen up. New shooters tend to pull the fuckin' trigger too abruptly. What that can do is move the gun quickly out of alignment and cause the shot to miss. Obviously in the fuckin' field you don't want that shit to happen..."

"Got it, sir," Patrick agreed. I don't know how the guy was so patient with him and then it hit me- he hadn't spent enough *time* with the man. Because anyone who had, recognized the beginning signs of a very long story and began to back away.

"Now," my dad continued as we reloaded, "if you want something with more of a kick but still easy to use, there's the Colt 1911. Comfortable to hold, not as nice as a Smith & Wesson .45 ACP, but decent. One of my favorites is the Glock G29. It's compact, about the size of a 9mm, but the 10mm cartridge delivers power almost equal to a .41 Magnum..."

My brothers and I watched as Patrick maintained an attentive look, even though we knew he had no idea what the hell my dad was talking about. Most people who knew something about guns could recognize a 9mm or a .45 but those who didn't, like Patrick, couldn't tell a BB gun from a water pistol. We kept our distance so he wouldn't see the comical looks on our faces.

"Now I love a Mag just like the next guy, but nothin' beats a fuckin' Sig."

"A *Sig*?"

"Jesus fuckin' *Christ*. Did they fuckin' teach you *anything*?" my dad asked. "A fuckin' *Sig*, as in Sig *Sauer*? This one I had engraved special. Here, hold it. 9mm, fully loaded with a second sight, undetectable by your enemy. Check it out- I feel sorry for the unsuspecting bastard on the other end of that shit..."

A few hours and a couple of beers later, we'd unwound at a local restaurant. Of course, *some* of us needed more than beer to 'unwind' from the weaponry lessons and war stories, two things that went hand in hand in the company of my dad, whether you were at a gun range or not.

"So, you made it past phase *I*," Anthony's commented to Patrick as we left the restaurant.

"What's phase I?" Patrick asked.

"That's where my dad doesn't *kill* you for sleeping with his only fuckin' daughter," Anthony joked.

"Oh. We were shooting guns- I assumed that was at *least* phase II," Patrick said jokingly as if trying to fit in.

"*Fuck* no," Donnie added, "phase II's where you go shooting with him *alone*." I could swear I heard Patrick gulp from where I was standing.

"Do I even wanna *know* what phase III is?"

"Uh, no, no you don't."

Patrick nodded silently as we all continued towards the parking lot, my dad staying behind to settle the bill. "Why not?" he asked, curious.

"'Cause no one's ever *made* it to phase III..." Anthony said.

Patrick leaned in towards me, "what's *that* supposed to mean?" I tried to hide my smile.

"That *means* that even if they've lived to tell about it, they've never been seen again, at least not around here," Donnie stated.

If people thought *I* was hard to read, my brothers could be even harder- especially Donnie. They were, of course, completely fucking with Patrick and I felt kind of sorry for him, but it came with the territory. After all, I *was* their only sister and my father's only daughter.

"You okay? Sorry about them- they like to try to act tough," I said in the car ride home.

"You mean they were *acting*?"

"You thought they were *serious*?"

"Weren't they?" he asked.

"I mean, maybe a *little*," I smiled, "but they just like screwing with any guy I bring around."

"Oh, so...there's no such thing as phases I through III then," he sounded relieved.

"Oh, well, I'm afraid *those* are real," I answered. "I mean, when I think about it, the last guy I brought around my dad kind of *disappeared*. I haven't even heard of his last whereabouts." I laughed as we drove. "At least he got some pointers to take with him- wherever he went, anyway..."

"Funny, Lea. *Real* funny."

Part Two:
Scrabble

"Life is what happens when you're busy making other plans."

- John Lennon

Chapter 9 ~ Gross Anatomy

Attending lectures was like being in school all over again, and not in the best way. No matter how many degrees anyone had accumulated, some things just never changed. It was an all-too familiar scene: the ass kissers who fought for front row seats as if it'd somehow get them a better grade; the overachievers who never looked up from their notes or my favorite, the ones who felt the need to ask obscure and unrelated questions, desperate to appear smarter than everyone else.

I remember my second year of veterinary school. Neurology had been difficult enough without the constant interruptions of one of my classmates, Ivan, who'd managed to piss us all off to the point where we'd wanted to strangle him.

"Question," he'd begin, obnoxiously raising his hand, "so you're saying that a unilateral lesion in the left C6-T2 region of the spinal cord would cause lower motor neuron signs to the left thoracic limb and upper motor neuron signs to the left pelvic limb..." I'd cringe every time he spoke, biting my lip, half-crazed. Ivan had thought he was so clever, when all he'd done was repeat what the professor had just said making it clear that he hadn't had a fucking clue. He'd apparently had enough of a clue, however, to have made himself one of Los Angeles' most well-known veterinarians and was currently running a very successful spay-neuter clinic, nearly earning him a key to the city. I still didn't have a key to my *boyfriend's* place and although some knew who that 'boyfriend' was, I was far from well-known.

Neurology was a popular topic at conferences. Most anything could affect the nervous system, leaving many general practitioners intimidated and many specialists confounded. Seizure disorders were only the tip of the iceberg and there were not only multiple underlying and intricate etiologies but also variable clinical signs, which often made a definitive diagnosis next to impossible. Anything from trauma to infections to cancer, not to mention the innumerable amount that fell into the "idiopathic" category, which I like to call the "no one knows what the fuck caused it so let's give it a mysterious title" etiology. So, not surprisingly neurology was typically jam-packed, often to the point where they ran out seats, forcing people to have to sit on the floor. It was a good thing we'd arrived early and hadn't been one of the unfortunate. Colleagues asking obscure and unrelated questions? Now *that* was unavoidable.

So far, this lecture hadn't' been bad and I'd been able to stay decently focused but honestly, if one more asshole disrupted the talk with another stupid question, I was gonna kill someone. "*Ouch.*" I felt my arm being pinched.

"Sorry," Jeanine had unintentionally pushed her chair against mine. "Hey," she lowered her voice, "what do you think so far?" A woman three seats down gave us a dirty look.

"Other than the constant interruptions? Good." I gave Jeanine a thumbs-up as I flipped through my notes, eyeing her back with a smile.

It was a new age with all the technology, something I admit I was still having trouble acclimating to. In a matter of only a few years things had advanced so quickly it was hard to keep up. People used to *look* at the lecturer and actually *pay* attention. Now they hardly looked away from their laptops or tablets, a bunch of zombies not doctors. On the other side of Jeanine was a woman, the lecturer's notes pulled up on her screen. She hadn't looked up once in 20 minutes. I mean, why travel all the way here and take up a clearly valuable seat when you could just stay home and *read* the fucking notes? If this asocial twit had bothered to look, she would've noticed all the great slides which were not included in the conference proceedings.

At the end of the lecture the three of us exited the room and went out on the terrace, coffees refreshed. It was only 10:00 AM and I needed a boost. "So, what'd ya think? I thought there were a few good points in there," Alex mentioned, walking to the terrace's balcony.

"And you haven't even seen the ocean yet." Jeanine approached from behind, pastry in hand. "Only been here once and I couldn't wait to come back. That was a fun trip, remember, Lea?" She smiled. I nodded 'yes'. Two years ago, Mac, Jeanine and Maureen had come to visit and we'd gone down to San Diego. The San Diego Convention Center *hadn't* exactly been my favorite place at the time and I certainly hadn't given a shit about its views...

"Is it true it's sunny here 300 days a year?" I nodded.

"Well, even if it weren't, all the men around are like rays of sunshine," Jeanine pestered.

"Yea, yea," I rolled my eyes in response. "Capelli, didn't you know they call it *Sun* Diego?"

"No shit. Nice." She paused, looking out ahead. "So you get down here often, Lea?"

"Not as much as I should. When I finally got over my Comic-Con PTSD I really came to like this place-it's just got such a different vibe than L.A. Just don't make the time, I guess."

"Yea, cuz you're too busy running around with Mr. Hollywood, right?" Jeanine was not known for her subtleties.

"Whatever." I looked across to The Coronado Marriott. Further to the right Navy ships stood guard and the constant flyovers of Navy jets made their distinctive sound.

Alex followed my gaze across the water. "Hey, is that Coronado?" I nodded. "What's over there?" She probed.

"Besides one of the U.S.'s top beaches? Mostly residential and military. There's a Naval Air Station to the right where you see all those vessels? And down past the hotels is another base."

"Cool. Can't wait to see it," she said.

"And maybe we'll get to see some *other* sights, right Lea?" I shook my head at Jeanine.

Alex studied our faces, "what does that mean?"

"It *means* hot guys at the beach." Jeanine could hardly contain the drool forming at the corner of her mouth.

"Get a hold of yourself, J-Lo." I turned back to Alex, "I doubt we'll see them."

"*Who*? I'm good with shirtless pilots playing volleyball."

"Those *aren't* the guys we're talking about. If we get lucky, maybe you'll see. Anyway, back to why we're *really* here? I'm gonna stay for the next lecture with this lady. I'm interested in that new medication class she was talking about."

"I'll join you," Alex added.

"I'm gonna hit rehabilitation, so I'll see you at lunch. Anyone know where the girls are at?"

"Not sure. I'll text them. We can meet down at the exhibit hall for that shitty lunch we have to stand in line for," I threw my coffee cup in the trash as we walked back through the double doors.

12:15 pm

"Camioni, in front of the Roadrunner Pharmacy booth." I looked over quickly spotting Dana.

"Hey." Alex and I looked for Mac. "Where's Mac?"

"Chatting with the Zoetis rep," Dana shook her head. We watched her speed over, avoiding eye contact with the other hungry company reps. "Anyone seen Jeanine?"

There were over 100 booths with everything from pharmaceutical products and surgical lasers to the latest laboratory and computer software, each claiming to outdo their competitors. It was kind of fun sometimes to play them against each other. Mostly we just walked around looking for free pens, candy and dog toys.

"There she is...and she's not alone." The look on Mac's face was priceless.

"Hey!" Jeanine shouted from nearly 50 feet away, "look who I found?"

"I don't believe it," Alex stated, as in shock as we were. Jordan, Tyler and Evan were with her- even at this distance they hadn't changed one bit.

"Wassup ladies!?" Evan was of small stature but in great shape. We used to work out at the gym together at school and I could still hear Godsmack blaring in the background like it was yesterday. He blamed his height on his Mexican roots, but you couldn't downplay his golden skin, good looks and a smile that brightened any day.

"Sanchez! What are you doin' here? I didn't know you were coming! How long has it been? Haven't seen you since what, Sedona?" I smiled back, giving him a brief hug.

"Yea, I think so," he thought. "That already four years ago? Damn time flies. How you doin'?"

"Good. You?"

"Not too bad."

"You guys get here today?" Jordan continued, "I landed few hours ago."

"Last night," Dana answered, the rest of the girls in agreement. He still looked good. Jordan's dark, lightly bronzed tone and buff body made him the spitting image of an Egyptian God, which had not only earned him first dibs at many girls but the title of 'Best Looking' in our entire university two years in a row.

"Cool. So where are you guys staying? You all at the same place?" she continued.

Feeling left out, Tyler interrupted, "I'm at The Omni."

"Nice," Alex and Evan stood back.

"My uncle works for the company." Tyler shrugged his shoulders.

"We're at The Hyatt," Jordan said pointing at himself and Evan.

"Yea, figured it'd be fun sharing a room, just like the old days, right bro?" Evan winked at them both smiling wryly.

A sardonic look crossed Tyler's face, "which is why I had my own room with a separate entrance- thank *God*." Tyler hadn't exactly shared the same 'ideals' with the other vet boys, but he'd moved into the multi-level house they all shared off campus and had actually ended up enjoying it more than he'd wanted to admit. He was right, though; their parties *could* get a little crazy.

"Whatever dude, *your* loss. Just kidding, bro." Evan may have been spoken fluent Spanish, but his accent was 100% Texan. He was damn lucky for it, too, otherwise he would've been slapped by a lot more women a *lot* more often- he had this funny knack of pissing them off.

"You going to the alumni reception tonight?"

"Yeah, probably. What time?" The guys looked at each other.

"6:00 pm. Supposed to be a decent turnout and I heard the rooftop bar is pretty kickass. Know anyone else who's here? I hardly ever run into anyone," I added.

"Ok, cool. Then catch y'all later" Evan turned to Jordan. "What are you doing?"

"Practice management. My dad'll kill me if I don't come back with some useful information."

"He retiring anytime soon?" Evan asked.

"No, not yet. Anyway, you gonna talk to some reps, too?"

"Yeah, especially that red head with the inappropriate top," Evan winked.

"Hey, Evan," Jeanine played, "better grab her before she takes a break." We eyed his prey skeptically as we exchanged numbers.

"She has no idea what she's in for," Mac whispered.

6:00pm

Atop the Hyatt, The Sky Lounge held up to its reputation, offering an unparalleled panorama of San Diego's harbor. Its small, upscale lounge feel and generous floor to ceiling windows attracted guests' eyes to its perimeter, making most stop dead in their tracks at its entrance, just as Jeanine had done.

"Shit, J-Lo, what the fuck?!" Dana blurted out. "I almost tripped over you."

"Sorry." Immediately I realized why she'd been so distracted.

I smiled as we exited behind her and walked over towards the hostess stand. To the left a sign welcoming the alumni of The St. George's University School of Veterinary Medicine stood. A young man led us to a reserved area where people were already gathered around the bar.

Alex motioned for a drink. "What does everyone want?"

"Dirty vodka martini." Jeanine had clearly already thought about this.

"Jack and Coke right here," Mac smiled proudly.

"Nice call on the martini, J-Lo. I think I'll have one, too, no olives though."

"Okay. So two dirty vodka martinis, a Jack n' Diet and two light beers. Dana come, on."

"So I see more than *one* of us has improved our palates since the island days."

"Yeah, a few steps up from Grenadian rum and warm beer," Jeanine added.

"I wonder where the Tufts alumni are tonight..." Mac nudged me jokingly.

"Probably somewhere with club sodas and sushi. And here I thought we'd be banished to some supply closet." There was no doubt in my mind she'd had something to do with this evening's scene.

We'd gone to a then new school in somewhat unchartered territory. It didn't matter how well-established or reputable a school was the AVMA, The American Veterinary Medical Association, saw 'foreign' education on an island as substandard. Although the education was equivalent if not better, it would be years before we were accredited *or* accepted.

I remember deciding to attend veterinary school so far away from home. My parents had not only approved my dad had been thrilled (and then had proceeded to fill me in on his 1983 'visit' involving a rescue mission as a result of a Cuban invasion and a botched military plan...). Some saw it as odd, but I'd seen it as a chance of a lifetime. I mean, studying on an island with an average year-round temperature of 85, palm trees and pristine beaches? And it had more than paid off. Not only had I received a top-notch education I had made lifelong friends and countless connections.

But not everybody saw it that way. The veterinary community had jumped at the chance to judge and condemn, labelling us nothing short of outcasts and second-rate. But when our charter class graduated in 2003 earning higher than the average national board scores, higher even than Tufts, UC Davis or UPenn, they had little to say. And when an SGU veterinary graduate had been the first to discover a new tick-borne illness they were silenced. Finally, it became known that luck had had nothing to do with it and our once-deemed inferior school had made it known the kind of doctors it was capable of producing.

"Here, Tyler, gotcha a Bulleit Rye," Alex handed out drinks after her and Dana had returned from the bar. He quickly thanked her and called the boys over.

"Cheers to that," Dana and Alex toasted, lifting their glasses.

"Hey! You gonna wait for me or what?" I didn't have to see him to recognize that voice. A tall guy with a husky build and buzz cut strolled over, interrupting.

"*Dude*! What the hell are you doing here?" Evan offered his best bro hug. Ya know, the one where guys go in for a real 'I missed you' hug but don't follow through for fear they might be labelled homosexual?

"I *live* here." Ivan smiled. "Well, L.A. Hey- you didn't *tell* me you were coming," he said to me, "we could've carpooled."

"I was able to sneak away for some CE. Sorry, it was last minute, "I answered.

"Sweet. So," Jordan asked, "you here for the weekend?"

"Whoah." The gang suddenly had eyes on Ivan and I. "Are you guys..."

"*No*," we both answered. Ivan held up his left hand. "Happily married well, I think anyway." Ivan wasn't my type of guy and I have to admit when I'd first met him, I didn't really like him. His arrogance could be off-putting, but after getting to know him that had all been a front. He was a good guy- and one *hell* of a doctor.

"So, you guys working together?" Tyler hinted.

"I was at a pitbull rescue fundraiser and we ran into each other about what, Lea, six months ago, and it kind of spiraled down from there." His smirk was killing me. "In all seriousness we've been helping each other out. She's even worked for me a few times."

"Wait a minute. You never told me you had a license to practice in California," Dana cut in.

Jeanine immediately started with the 20 questions. "So, does this mean you and Patrick..."

"No, I was just getting too limited in what I could do."

"Oh, that's cool. So," Alex continued, "Has he met Patrick yet?"

"Actually...yeah, once," he answered. "Cool guy." He turned his attention to Mac, who'd been scanning the room. "So, Mac, on another note, Lea told me you're doing pretty well at SGU? When the hell are you inviting us all down for a *real* reunion?"

"That could probably be arranged. Remember that run down resort at the end of L'Anse aux Epines Road? The school turned it into professor housing. It was kind of *my* idea." He looked at her confounded. "Well, I *was* President of the entire student body. I got to know the Dean pretty well."

"*Pretty well*?! You were just at his house in Miami." Mac's humbleness amazed me. She rarely put herself above anyone else and she would never admit it but despite all her achievements, she saw room to improve.

When we were in Grenada the medical school had been well established and, if having been frowned upon by the veterinary community *hadn't* been enough, we'd also been mocked by hundreds of medical students who hadn't taken us seriously, either. But Mac had bigger plans, forging her way through politics. So, when she had been elected as first female *and* veterinary President of the Student Government Association (SGA) tables had been turned, faces shocked and history had been made. In all seriousness that will probably never happen again and why? Because there will never be another Maria DiMacchio.

"No shit, and I thought *I* was doing well. What are you like Assistant Dean or something?"

Dana cut in again, "Before you know it she'll be running the fuckin' place."

"Wow, DiMacchio. Which brings me back to my original point- when are you having us down? We're just missing one person." I looked up from my drink. "Has anyone been in touch with Nate? What's that bastard doing these days?" *Shit. And just how did I know he was gonna be brought up?*

"Last I heard he was studying for medicine boards," Jordan said.

"*Boards?!*" Shocked, Ivan blurted out.

"What!? I didn't' see *that* coming. I thought he'd be on some ranch working for his dad."

"Nope," Tyler interjected. "He's still on the east coast, I think." We all listened in. "I ran into him at a conference in Atlantic City a couple years ago." Dana and Alex looked at each other then stared at me. I stared back at them with equal shock.

"I hit him up a while ago to see what he was up to and if he was coming, but I never heard back," Tyler said annoyed.

"Typical Nate." Mac shook her head as the group all muttered in agreement. "I think we can all agree we're definitely not surprised." She was right- Nate hadn't been one to keep in constant touch with anyone after Grenada.

"So what's your guys' plans this weekends? Doing any excursions? I saw there's a pub crawl.."

Chapter 10~ Blast from the Past

Educational 'vacations' were great, but long days were never fun and anyone who willingly participated in 'Early Bird' 7:00 am sessions was just fucking nuts. Spending eight hours a day for five days in any classroom was far from mine or anyone else's idea of a vacation and so...I didn't. I'd spent too many years in lecture halls- do you really blame me for having an aversion? I chose lectures I knew I'd get the most out of and skipped the rest. It's not like anyone took attendance or graded us and we sure as hell deserved to have a little fun *once* in a while.

But don't judge me if I, along with some of my classmates, had ditched classes to go on a Carnivale 'field trip' to Trinidad with one of our then veterinary professors. It may have involved excessive amounts of rum, all night Jouvet parties and street dancing, but it'd been a once in a lifetime opportunity and things like 'Da Wee Wee Truck' and travelling rum carts we'd likely never see again.

"Yo, Camioni, make sure that shit's on straight. Don't wanna get yelled at by Mr. rent-a-cop." Dana's hallmark New Jersey attitude was a ray of sunshine even at 8:00 am.

"Yea, no shit, right?" I looked down the bottom of the escalator at the older gentleman in uniform. "Like someone really wants to sneak into a fucking *veterinary* conference and listen to people talk about vomiting and diarrhea." We all laughed.

"What are you headed to first, Lea?" Mac searched her bag for a pen as we walked off the escalator to the breakfast 'buffet'- if you could call it that. For $800 you'd expect a little more than stale bagels, muffins that belonged in an elementary school cafeteria and days-old apples. Not to mention the coffee that was so watered down it made 7-11's look like espresso.

"Probably internal medicine. I've seen an increased amount of IMHA lately, so it piqued my interest. You?"

"There are a couple of exotic lectures I wanna hit." Jeanine, Dana and Alex stood in line behind us eyeing the lame food choices.

"They call these *bagels*?" I saw heads turn. Leave it up to my friends to make a scene. "I may not be a New York Jew but I still know my bagels."

"I'll probably join you, Mac." Dana wrapped her bagel and put a container of cream cheese in her bag. Dana and Mac were the exotic vets in the group. Most of us only worked with dogs and cats except Alex, who worked for the USDA.

"I may split the morning between agriculture and infectious disease," Alex remarked.

Alex had started in mixed animal practice, but it hadn't taken long for her to wear out. It may have sounded fun, but the days were long and grueling. Farm calls in any weather at all hours, being paged too often with barely any time to eat or even breathe- all for less pay than a dental hygienist. So, after being overworked and underpaid for too long, she'd been fed up *and* exhausted- to the point where she'd questioned her choice of profession.

That life would've done the same thing to anyone. In fact, it *had* happened- to nearly every veterinarian I knew. We were seven years out of school, just three years until what's called the '10-year burnout', yet we'd already felt burnt to a crisp. This job could get to you in a way that most others couldn't and believe me it took its toll, but our love and passion for what we did kept most of us in check. For others, though, they ended up leaving the profession altogether for their own sanity. As years passed, we were finding our individual niches in the field.

"It's 8:20. Let's go get seats, J-Lo." Jeanine topped off her coffee and we headed left.

Mac looked at her phone then began walking. "Which way you heading Dana? I'm at 24C."

"Think I'm in 21C, so I'll walk with you."

"I'm that way," Alex turned away.

"Text you guys after." Jeanine and I continued down the hall until we reached our room.

It was double the size of yesterday's. Sometimes they actually matched the right lecture with the appropriately sized room. I was excited for this morning. Immune-mediated hemolytic anemia was a complicated disease. Yet another often labelled as 'idiopathic', IMHA had only an average survival rate of 50% in dogs and cats and with all the tick-borne illnesses on the rise throughout The United States (and the World) cases had also been on the rise.

We got seats closer to the front and sat down. "I can take some good pics," I said to Jeanine. "I get all the pics of the stats, graphs and case examples that aren't in the notes." I sipped my latte.

"Good idea. So," Jeanine asked, pulling out the notes, "who's the speaker?"

"What do you mean? I thought it was Susan Little."

"It *was*. See?" She pointed at the screen. "It says TBA. I hope whoever it is, is good." We both scanned the room looking to see if any of the guys had popped in, but they hadn't. Then the announcer walked to the podium.

"Good morning, everyone. If I could have your attention. Thank you." The room settled, people still trickling in. "Before we get started, I'd just like to make a few quick announcements." "First, welcome. The exhibit hall will be open today at 11:30. There will a two-hour lunch break so you can roam around. Second, unfortunately, Dr. Little is unable to make it due to a family emergency." The room oohed and aahed. I smirked, flipping through notes.

The woman continued, smiling. "I'm glad to say that we've got a fantastic stand-in who was able to come on such short notice." The audience hemmed and hawed with both disappointment and curiosity. I listened in, my head still down. "He received his Doctor of Veterinary Medicine degree from St. George's University and completed his internship and residency in internal medicine at The Animal Medical Center in New York. He has done extensive research on autoimmune disease and we're lucky to have him. Please welcome Dr. Nathan Peterson."

I froze, momentarily unable to look up. *What the fuck?* I nearly stopped breathing. I felt Jeanine hit me. "Ow!" I jumped. "What?" My eyes told her all she needed to know. They were filled with horror and shock. Thankfully, the clapping snapped me out of it.

"What do you mean, *what*? You *know* what," she stressed. "Don't you wanna at least look up?" she nudged me. "You should; he looks hot."

"Oh shut up." Even without having looked I knew I was only fooling myself.

"Well, you're gonna *have* to at some point- He's the speaker."

I took a deep breath as my eyes slowly moved upward. He was different somehow, a new and improved version of the guy I had known what seemed like so long ago. Different, yet familiar, and handsome. I'd never thought of him like that. Probably because we were all running around in scrubs, shorts and flip flops. Nate was never the dress-up type (not that we had much to dress up for on an island)- the laid-back Midwest guy from Iowa. He still had the most beautiful brown hair...

"Right," I blurted. Jeanine looked at me.

"Right- *what*? What are you talking about?" she asked.

"Oh, nothing, nothing. I don't know, nothing."

"Whatever you say." I rolled my eyes and pretended to pay attention.

"Good morning," Nate began. "I'll put up my email address in a minute- I promise to get you my notes. They're a little different than Susan's but still on topic." *Susan's? Since when are they on a first name basis? She was our professor for shit's sake...*

I couldn't take his smile- and I wasn't sure I could stare at it for three full hours. *I hope he doesn't see me. Who am I fucking kidding?*

"Okay," he continued, "let's get right into it. IMHA- those dreadful letters, almost as scary as 'DIC'..." *How about N-A-T-E?*

Forty-five minutes later, the first of three lectures in this series was over. I was hoping for no break so I could sneak out some side door when he was done. But there was no way that was going to happen, for two reasons: (1) I needed to use the bathroom and (2) there was only one exit. So, I had no choice but to face him, especially since Jeanine was already in line with a question. It dawned on me that if he'd shown up that meant that I wasn't gonna be able to avoid him the *entire* weekend.

"Nate?" Jeanine hadn't wasted any time- she'd dove right in while I'd started to feel the water quickly rising around me. He paused for a moment then realized who she was. I gulped, knowing that he'd notice me, too.

"Jeanine? Hey! What are you doing here?" *Yup. Just saw me.* He looked right at me, smiling even more. I just stood there unable to speak, as he hugged her.

"Um, duh we're here for the conference," she said, shoving me forward, "Lea actually had the question, not me, about the... the spherocytes..." *Bitch.* I nearly fell into him, embarrassed beyond all belief. "Anyway..." She quickly moved aside, leaving me alone with the angry she-wolves awaiting their turn behind us.

Trying to keep my composure I finally spoke, "um, yes, about those spherocytes...you said at 100X magnification they can be..." I lowered my voice. "Hi. Sorry about Jeanine..."

"It's fine," he said. *Reign it in, Lea.* Out of nowhere he pulled me in for a tight squeeze. Suddenly my brain began to fill up way too much with days past. I quickly turned to see the two women behind me and their dirty looks. "Well yeah, there's this trick I like to use- works really well. You just do all four quadrants of the slide, careful to identify the normal RBCs and platelets, then compare their sizes and central pallor..." he winked, whispering in my ear, "meet me outside in a few," then kissed me on one cheek, sending chills down my spine.

"Okay," I played on, "well thanks for the tip, Dr. Peterson." I stepped back but he held my hand briefly before releasing me. I blushed, returning the smile, then turned for the door. Jeanine was right outside waiting, eagerness seeping through her pores.

"*What*?" I tried to ignore where she was going.

"Oh, come *on*. You haven't seen the guy in what six years and you're not in the *least* bit curious?" she pressed.

"Seven, and *no*."

"Whatever. So, what did he say?"

"Nothing. Okay, nothing *important*," I said crossing my arms. "Spherocytes."

"*Spherocytes?* You talked about *spherocytes*?" She was getting impatient.

"What the hell did you *expect* him to talk about? You *did* ask about that, didn't you?" She wasn't satisfied. "Plus, you pushed me into the line, and into *him*, thank you very much."

"You're welcome."

"There were two hyenas behind me waiting to attack- they nearly bit my head off for stealing his time. And," I added, "it's not the time or place for this anyway and you know it. This, this... whatever this is, which is...not, is nothing."

"For what? You said it was nothing," she argued. *Shit.*

"Hey, there you are." Nate was outside the lecture room closing in fast.

"Hey," I said. He smelled so good. I needed the next lecture to start already.

"I got five minutes," he said looking at his watch. "You staying for the next two?" How could I say no?

"Of *course* we are," Jeanine answered. "Are you here for the whole conference?" she asked.

"I'm leaving Sunday. What about you?" He asked, looking over to me.

"Yes." I caught myself, "I mean, Sunday. Me, too. Actually I think most of us are." *Whew.* "Lucky for me my drive isn't long."

"She lives in *L.A.*," Jeanine answered before I could speak.

"Well, not *all* the time." I noticed Nate's quizzical look. "I still live back home but I have an apartment in Marina del Rey. I kind of split my time between Connecticut and..."

"Patrick's." God I wanted to smack her. I shot her a pissed look.

"Patrick?" Suddenly I felt guilty, not that I should have.

"Yea, my uh, my..."

"Boyfriend?" he asked. I nodded.

"Uh, yup." That word was always difficult to say aloud.

Jeanine interrupted again. "Ah, *hot* boyfriend, hot *actor* boyfriend. Go ahead, *tell* him."

"Excuse me, Dr. Peterson?" he turned towards her. "We're about to start back up."

I watched him make his way back into the lecture room. He looked like a celebrity himself the way women were hawking him. Patrick certainly wasn't the only one with a magnetic personality, killer smile and a knack for aging well. I heard trouble knocking at my door and I suddenly wished it would go the fuck away.

"Hey, guys, how was the morning?" Dana asked.

"Not bad."

"What do you mean, 'not bad', Lea? Nate was *great*," Jeanine insisted. They stared at us in disbelief. "They asked him to lecture last minute. In place of, get this, Susan Little." Mac's eyes widened in shock. "You almost wouldn't recognize him, all prim and proper, speaking in front of a crowd."

"I'm just still trying to picture it," she laughed.

"Well we better see him at the pub crawl tonight," Alex said. "Haven't seen him since graduation."

After lunch Mac and I paired up to roam the exhibit hall.

"Let's stop here. I promised Paul I'd scope therapeutic lasers out for his new practice."

"The one who left that horrific corporate conglomerate in Boston?"

"*That's* the one- he took a bunch of clients, too."

It was true- those fuckers had it coming: turning bright young minds into heartless machines who, all because of dangling incentives and worthless promises, began to care more about material things than their patients' well-being. They claimed to practice 'high quality', 'cutting-edge' veterinary medicine, while simultaneously contradicting the very essence of what veterinary medicine was: compassion, dedication and improving the lives of others. The only thing 'cutting-edge' was their ability to drain peoples' bank accounts without a conscience.

First on the scene was Banfield, opening pet hospitals (if you wanna call them that) inside PetSmart. It wasn't long before other greedy assholes followed suit- buying up smaller hospitals and molding them into what they deemed an appropriate veterinary medicine care model, their intentions filled with false promises and illusions. The practitioners who sold out ultimately lost all control, along with the heart and soul of the very practices they'd sadly poured their blood, sweat and tears into.

Slowly the veterinary world was beginning to change, mimicking the human world, the layers of personalized and compassionate medicine being stripped away by greedy corporate monsters and insurance companies. Mac's friend Paul was one of countless doctors who'd loved his job until a company called VCA (Veterinary Centers of America) took it over little by little, changing every decent aspect of it into a hellhole that no one wanted to work in. And it didn't matter *what* position you held- no one was safe and everyone was a disposable commodity. Even if you could squirm your way out of an iron clad contract, they'd screw you. They'd not only *screw* you, they'd have people lined up to take your place and by the time they figured out it was a losing game and were ready to leave, they'd have their replacements waiting.

It was a revolving door of poorly trained employees and shitty management, which translated into inconsistent and sometimes shitty medicine, which was *not* was veterinary medicine was all about. It pissed all of us off. The number of privately owned facilities was decreasing, and it was a detriment to our field. It made me sick. There's a reason I called them Veterinary Cannibal Centers- they were literally eating their own alive.

5:00 pm
"So..." Alex said as she got on the treadmill, "...Nate..." Jeanine and I snagged machines on either side of her. "Weird he just showed up, right?" I remained silent, hoping she'd shut up. No such luck.

"He's a *speaker*." I scrolled through the machine's settings. *Where the hell's the 'memory burn' mode on this thing?*

"I know. It's just...doesn't it worry you that things with Patrick might change now that he's becoming 'bigger'..." Jeanine asked, "And what about the whole long-distance thing, especially how things turned out the *last* time?"

"That was *different*. "Plus, I was stupid- I didn't see it coming. I know better now. Not really, no. And I'd never ask him to give that up. Just like he wouldn't ask me to give up on my dreams." I scowled, continuing at a quicker pace.

"All I'm sayin' is that maybe that lifestyle is okay for *now*, but do you *really* see yourself with him in ten years?"
Did they still think of Patrick and I as some farce, that we couldn't last? I admitted the thought of being with someone for a long time still freaked me out and these days there was no guarantee that a relationship with a *normal* person would last, never mind one with someone in the entertainment business. My ex-boyfriend had been a stand-up guy (or so I'd thought), my brother's good friend *and* a Marine. Being honest and trustworthy should've been a given; but I guess people of *all* kinds eventually show their true colors and I'd been shown way more than I'd ever deserved or wanted to see.

"Look, I trust him and he trusts me." For once in my life I was focusing on here and now, so I *wouldn't* freak out too badly, run or scare him away and things had been going well, but now suddenly a few little comments and doubts were beginning to surface. I didn't wanna think about what might happen down the line but...

"Patrick's a great guy, but don't ya think you might want someone more 'normal', to have a more realistic future with, who shares similar interests, maybe lives in the same hemisphere..." I knew exactly where she was going and I didn't like it. "What if he's here for a reason?"

"And what if he's *not*?" I didn't understand why the sudden change in opinion.

"Admit it, Lea. You're on the east coast more than you are here. Your family is *there*, not here. It's just a thought."

"A *thought*? To consider throwing away everything I have with Patrick? Nate's been here for like what, five minutes? He's been MIA for over five *years*. You don't just pick up where you left off. We have *different* lives now." What had she just done? I actually had to think about that for a second. "Anyway, everything is just fine." *Isn't it?* "Did everyone suddenly forget I'm with an amazing guy who I happen to...to...really, *really* like and he feels the same way about me? Why can't you just be happy?"

"We *are*, but it doesn't bother you that you spend more time Skyping than actually, *physically* seeing each other?"

"Of *course* it *bothers* me, but it's just the way it is. He does his thing, I do mine. We don't have to live together." They remained silent. "We're all adults. Who says Nate and I can't hang out as friends?"

"Well, you've got the whole weekend to find out, I guess," Jeanine teased.

"Ha, ha, funny." I unplugged my headphones, stepping off the machine. "I wouldn't worry- I think I can *more* than handle Nathan Peterson."

8:15 pm

There were about 30 of us on the pub crawl in the heart of The Gaslight Quarter, a historic 16-block neighborhood downtown and an easy walk from the convention center. Everyone was having a good time, but by the time we'd hit the third stop, I was ready for a break. Tyler, Ivan and Evan were with some vets they'd met earlier. Meanwhile, Jordan and Nate had stolen the attention of nearly every girl. It wasn't a surprise. Together they were like a super magnet- few women could resist.

Although quite amusing, watching Nate and Jordan talk to girls was not the kind of fun I'd had in mind for this weekend and I felt my anxiety creeping back. *I wish Patrick would call. Where is he?* I had no reason to be so bothered or uneasy. *I'm dating Patrick Thomas for Christ's sake!* But it *did* bother me- seeing Nate with other girls. Could I *really* still have feelings for him?

I left my unfinished drink at a table and walked outside. I stood against a lamppost, looking across the street at some partygoers at a sidewalk bar. I checked my phone again. *Nothing.*

"What are you doing out here all alone?" A graze of something behind me made me jump.

"Oh, shit. You scared me."

"Sorry," he grinned dotingly. *Gulp.* "You seem surprised." I just stood there, looking at him in his t-shirt and faded jeans. It brought back memories I hadn't thought about in a long time. Damnit, Jeanine had been right- Nate was looking pretty damn good right now. "Lea?" I felt his stare, his head cocked to one side lackadaisically. *Yup- definitely the alcohol.*

"No. Okay, well, maybe a little. I thought you were inside with Jordan. How did you even know besI was out here?"

"I *was*. I saw you leave. I hope you don't mind I'd rather talk to you."

"Of *course* not. We haven't really had a chance to catch up."

"Yeah, right. Just kidding. I know your *boyfriend* probably wouldn't be too happy if..." He stepped closer. Our faces were now in striking distance. "...if he saw another guy so close to you..." He leaned forward, taking in a breath, his cologne mixed with the warm San Diego air intoxicating me. I pulled back.

"Right," I answered, almost disappointed. Almost seven years had passed since I'd seen him, five since I'd even heard from him. He could do whatever and whoever he wanted, couldn't he? Still, it *had* always been kind of easy with us...

Grenada had been a time of endings and new beginnings. We'd crossed paths in the middle of a storm. He was exactly the opposite of the guy I'd been dating at the time and getting to know him had been a much-needed light in a time of darkness. He'd been a good friend and more...but I'd screwed up.

"I'm glad we ran into each other. We should have lunch when you're back east..." Just then two obnoxious punks came storming out of the bar.

"Yo, Pete, where the hell have you been?" "Jordan was lookin' for..." Evan stopped abruptly, noticing me. "Oh. *Oh*, sorry to interrupt. Ready for the next stop?" he asked, "Cuz we're ready to roll."

Evan was a little over enthused, but it was only because he loved a good time, sometimes *too* good. Part of it was from his innate competitiveness, the other his myriad of 'workout supplements'. We all knew from way back that Evan dabbled in a little more than 'protein supplements' and 'fat burners', but there was little we could do and when it came to Evan's workout regimen, he did what he wanted, which sometimes made him a little out of whack.

"So, where were we?" I suddenly hoped the others would appear. Dimly lit streets, a hot guy talking to me away from the crowd...this was somewhere I'd been before, somewhere I didn't belong...

God, he had me there for a minute. "We were talking about food...lunch."

"Oh, right," he said. "I was serious. When you're not too busy leading your double life and...how exactly does that all work- the job, or *jobs* and stuff?"

"I'm in Connecticut mostly but...I think I'm actually starting to get the hang of this cross-country thing."

He looked at me attentively. "Hmm. And what's his name- Patrick? He lives here?"

"Yup, well, mostly."

"Look at you," he continued, "livin' the life, landing the rich and famous, I'm kinda jealous."

"*Really*? Look at *you*. How many letters are after your name now? *I'm* the one who should be jealous, but you can have an autograph from Patrick anytime..." I smiled, snickering.

"That's not what I meant, but he does have it pretty good right now- he's got *you*."

I blushed uncontrollably, trying to shake off his comment. "Oh- oh well, I don't know about *that*. I think I'm running on a little luck. Still hard to believe, really."

"Don't be so fuckin' modest, Lea. You don't think *you* played any part? You can't tell me your award-winning smile and sarcastic charm didn't help win him over? Not even a *little*? Anyway," he cleared his throat, "I'm sure he's a good guy, otherwise your dad would've had him killed by now."

"Nah, he would've done it himself," we laughed. "So, Dr. Peterson, you *really* liking the big city life and what's the story with...what's her name?"

"Actually, yeah. Oh, you mean Tina." *Sounds like a New Jersey housewife in the making.* "No story, it was a blind date. She's not bad, I guess." *Why do guys always refer to girls as seasonal beer?*

"Not *bad*? What is she a slice of pizza? I thought you were gonna say something else, like she's pretty cool or she can recite the alphabet."

"Well, she's no Camioni." His all-too familiar sincere smile threw me for a loop. "She *is* pretty good in bed though," he winked facetiously.

"Oh my God. I *so* didn't need to know that," I said.

"Yea, but I figured I'd tell you anyway. Plus, you're the only girl I know who can handle it," he laughed to himself. "Looks like I'm gonna be around for a while, in New Jersey, I mean."

"You are- oh, that's great. I'm so happy for you. I mean, you're *happy*, right, with the job and the...the...and stuff?" Inside I silently wished he'd say 'no'.

"Yeah." *Oh well.* "And how about you? You seem happy." I nodded quietly. "Tell ya what, let's not talk about dating and just enjoy the rest of the weekend, deal?"

"Deal," I smiled.

Chapter 11 ~ Top Gun

Seeing Nate so unexpectedly had not only dredged up old feelings but was now making me question myself. There were just certain things about certain people that stayed with you and no matter how much time had passed, even one brief meeting could instantly bring you back in time. Memories and regret had this unavoidable way of sneaking up on you and seeing him yesterday had thrown me for a loop bigger than I could've imagined. Was there really some deeper meaning for his sudden return, or was it all just a weird coincidence?

Mac, Jeanine and I had gone for an early walk along the harbor. "Just try not to overthink it," Mac continued. Early bird or not it was way too early for *this* conversation.

"I'm *not*," I answered curtly, wishing I'd ventured out solo.

"Right-says the girl who overthinks *everything*. I know you more than *you* know you."

I looked at the peaceful harbor trying to breathe deeply. 'Smile, it helps', I could hear my yoga instructor Julian saying. *God I could really use some yoga right now.*

They both looked at me in disbelief. "You *sure* about that?" I shot Mac an angry look. *Definitely too early for this bullshit.*

"Yeah," I sighed with a shrug of my shoulder, "Maybe I'm just...it's just Patrick was supposed to call last night and he didn't so...so it's probably that. I don't know what's wrong with me..."

"That's what happens when your past shows up. It throws you off," Jeanine added. "There's nothing wrong with you well, *mostly* anyway," she said trying to lighten things up.

"I feel a little more than *off*," I mumbled, walking full speed ahead, leaving them behind.

"What's with her?" Jeanine uttered to Mac, "I mean Alex and I may have brought it up yesterday but..."

"It's not you. We went to New Orleans a couple months ago."

"*So?*"

"So, we had our fortunes read and...I don't know what the medium said to her, but it spooked the hell out of her."

"I thought you guys were into that spooky shit. Did she ever tell you?"

"No, but now...it's like she's flipped a switch."

"Do you *really* believe in all that stuff?" Jeanine was somewhat of a skeptic in all things mystical.

Mac looked at her strangely, "Then I guess I shouldn't tell you that I actually studied Wicca." Jeanine's face turned sour. "I don't think you understand. Getting your cards read in New Orleans or Salem isn't the same as some medieval fair. They're almost *never* wrong; they don't just tell you the unicorns and rainbow bullshit, either."

"So, what do you really think they said?"

"I'm not sure, but I have a strong suspicion that whatever it was is beginning to unfold. She's just acting too weird."

I finally slowed down my footing. "You *do* know I can still hear you guys. If you're still talking about Nate, you can drop it, 'cause nothing's happening there. In fact, the *only* thing happening is me, walking away well, after tomorrow, I guess." We all stopped in our tracks and looked up.

At the northern edge of Tuna Harbor Park was "Embracing Peace", a 25-foot tall statue that towered over anything around it. Behind it was the USS Midway, an historic aircraft carrier. It struck a chord with me each time I saw it. Maybe it was how perfectly it'd been erected amongst the trees and Bob Hope Memorial or the image itself, the romance and whimsicalness of the moment, that made a girl wish that it would happen to her. That some handsome sailor would take her into his big, strong arms for an enchanting kiss in front of a crowd if strangers. I'd had a quasi-hero once, although he was no sailor. I couldn't wait for him to come home from overseas; that feeling of being swept up into arms that would love you and keep you safe. But that had all gone away the moment he'd betrayed me and any happily ever after had been flushed down the fucking toilet along with my heart. All these years later, I wasn't sure how much I had recovered.

"Lea, come on," Mac said. I hadn't even realized I'd stopped walking. "Are you okay?"

"Yeah." I was still lost in the moment. "Oh, about that," I resumed my quick pace. Sorry to get so unnerved. I don't do well with surprises. Meeting Patrick was dumb luck. I'm surprised *he* hasn't run away yet. I don't have the best track record with relationships."

"You can't count the ones that weren't your *fault.*" I didn't speak. Mac was pissed. Anyone who knew the whole story had shared her opinion and if 'he' hadn't been one of my brother's friends he'd be at *least* six feet under by now. Too bad…

"Okay, *fine*. Maybe *that* one wasn't completely my fault but…"

"Don't be ridiculous. The dude cheated on you for months and didn't tell you. After all the times you sat home worried *and* faithful while he was off in some other country, he pulls that shit. I still can't believe your brother didn't fuckin' kill him. What a *dick.*"

"Which is why I no longer trust Marines- lesson learned," I answered.

"And why I don't trust guys period, *especially* from a distance." Jeanine caught herself just a little too late. "Sorry, Lea, I didn't mean…"

"It's okay." She had a point. After adamantly promising myself I wouldn't go through the stress and feared heartache that could happen in a long-distance relationship I'd done it again. Only this time I swore it'd be different, and it *had* been, so far. Still, doubts and uncertainties circled my head, and I began to wonder deep down if we'd last. That happens to everyone, *right*?

"That statue is beautiful. Wish that'd happen to me," Jeanine stared at its largeness adoringly.

"Yeah," I added. "Too bad it's *bullshit*." But it was true.

"What?!"

"You're ruining her Hallmark moment," Mac responded to Jeanine's angry look.

"You don't know the story." I paused. "That's from an old photo from 1944. When World War II ended the sailors returned home to New York and this guy grabbed some random lady and laid one on her, right in the middle of Times Square. Someone snapped a picture and it became famous."

"Oh, well that's a bummer," she answered. "Hey, what time is it?"

"7:48." Mac stopped to look at her watch. "we should back."

1:30pm, Coronado Island Ferry Landing

"Do you see them?" Alex asked, leaning on a railing overlooking the harbor.

"We're wasting valuable sun time." Mac didn't fuck around when it came to the beach, one of the many reasons we got along.

We'd head to Grand Anse Beach with our notes for a change of scenery from the lab or the school's only library. We got tired of the medical students taking up all the spaces- leaving their shit on tables, disappearing for hours. But I guess when most of their learning came from memorizing old exams, they could do that. It's not like they were treating sick animals or performing surgery, like us.

"I think that's them." Just then a small group of guys was approaching in a Marriott water taxi.

"Yup, that's them alright. This *really* is starting to feel like old times. Remember those catamaran sails?" We watched the guys make their way off the boat. One rafter the other they filed up the dock. "Well, well, well. Look who finally showed up," I said. "Bring anything good?"

"Some beer and shit." Evan opened the cooler. "And water for the losers."

In no time, we'd made it to our destination. With its backdrop of homes along Ocean Boulevard and killer views, Central Beach was an iconic spot. Dana, Jeanine and Alex were quickly fixated on the hunky men at the volleyball nets who were no doubt, military. It was a scene right out of *Top Gun*, where Goose and Maverick team up against Iceman and his cohorts Cougar and Slider, vying for the title. With the sounds and sights of naval jets above and Kansas City Barbeque back on the mainland, it may as well have been Miramar. I had to pull my *own* eyes away. I could sit and watch men in shorts all day, especially military men, but there were two problems: these weren't exactly my *type* of Navy men and the afternoon sun was calling.

The stretch of beachfront just passed The Del tended to be less crowded than the main beach. We kept going until we neared the last set of condos and claimed a large area for ourselves. The girls continued to scope. Meanwhile Jordan had already removed his shirt and was drinking a beer. He was pretty damn good to look at himself. I watched as Evan, Tyler and Ivan followed suit. Then Nate's shirt hit the sand. *Stop it, Lea.*

It certainly did feel like old times. Students spread out across the white sand sunbathing and drinking while stray dogs ran by and locals sold loofa and spice necklaces. We'd camp out until dusk, enjoying every moment. We never tired of the sun, the waves or each other and to most of us, our three-year stint down there had been incredible. Evan and Jordan paired up against Nate and Ivan for some football while Tyler sat out the first game. I was so lost in my memories of Caribbean days past that I hadn't noticed Dana, Alex and Jeanine had gone MIA.

"Look at those bitches making themselves cozy," Mac said, referring to the group of girls who'd seamlessly made their way over to the guys- and into *our* space. They couldn't have been more than 27, I thought.

"Twenty-*five*," Mac said aloud.

"What does it matter? They're hot," Tyler smiled as he stood up, his hormones standing attention along with the rest of him.

"Yeah, if you call fake tits and Botox hot," she argued. "Jesus, are they *trying* to look 50? I mean you'd think someone would tell them that shit doesn't even look good."

I remember some of my brother's friends and their takes on women. Getting laid was all a matter of perspective and sometimes you just had to pick from what was on the menu, even if there were slim pickings. You made the most of it so whether chunky or boney, imperfect or butt-ugly, you learned to improvise, adapt and overcome- just like the military had taught you to. One of the guys had said, 'ya just put a fuckin' bag over their head and pretend its Carmen Electra'.

That crew of my brother's buddies was a bit out-of-whack, to say the least.

"I turned to Mac, curious as to the girls' whereabouts. "I don't see them."

"You're looking the wrong way." She spun us both to the left. Jeanine, now at a fast pace headed in our direction with Dana and Alex behind her, was looking way too enthusiastic for having returned from a casual stroll.

"Whoah, what are you all hyped-up about?"

"Oh, nothing." Her sly look said otherwise.

"Yea, nothing," Dana interjected, "nothin' but asses and *abs*."

"What? Where?" Mac and I were confused. "I don't see any." Besides the boys, we didn't see anything.

"Where did you guys go? Oh *shit,*" she answered, finally realizing what Dana had meant.

"That way. We wanted to walk further but there's a blockade on the beach." She pointed out the sign stuck in the sand. "Guy stopped Jeanine, almost pulled out his rifle. He didn't even smile."

"Well, they *are* pretty serious around here," I said, catching on. More memories from days past flooded back. Several small groups of men jogged onto the beach in a line, each carrying a boat over their shoulders, as they chanted aloud. It was a sight few were lucky to witness and you couldn't help but stare at not only their bodies but their determination, strength and stamina, a unified team.

"Oh my God," Mac caught herself, grabbing her beer for a toast.

"*I'll* say," Jeanine said, barely taking her eyes off the parade of hotness. My eyes were glued, too. They stopped at the water's edge on their side of the enormous "NOTICE- US NAVY PROPERTY- NO TRESPASSING" sign and took a brief reprieve. A group of instructors began yelling.

"I think I'm in love," Alex growled. "Lea, how did you never land one of those?" I eyed her, cautious of my words. The answer wasn't that simple. There were things she didn't understand, like the fact that guys like that seemed fun, cool and sexy on the outside, but being with them was a completely different story. It wasn't like dating or marrying *other* types of guys, civilians *or* military, and this was definitely one case where movies strayed greatly from real life...

"She has brains, *that's* why," Mac defended as the girls stared at me confused.

"True, but honestly? You don't *really* want one well, maybe for a *little* while. Beyond that it gets...complicated."

"But your dad..."

"Warned me to stay away." Of course I hadn't. "You forget he was never around. Hence, my parent's divorce. Don't get me wrong, they're great guys- trustworthy, dependable, nice to look at, good in bed- but at the end of the day you don't want one- you don't wanna wonder where they are or what they're doing or if they may not come back. They..." I had stopped mid-sentence. The men had moved closer towards us. I swore for a second one of their voices sounded familiar. - *Nah...*

"Ladies, we're not here to put on a fuckin' show so move your God Damn asses, *now*! Smith, your fuckin' grandma can do a better job- she's even got a tighter ass... you ladies want Smith carryin' you out of a fight or his grandmother?" Even from where we were standing you could see the poor kid's trepidation and embarrassment, something unwelcome and frowned upon. He was sure to get it later from his teammates. And for damn good reason- if you didn't have your buddy's back you didn't belong here. "Pussies aren't welcome here, Smith, are they?"

"No, *Sir*!"

"What'd you say boy?"

"No, Sir!!" He was running out of breath, struggling to maintain his hold his end of the boat.

"I can't hear you ShitSmith!! And you're sinkin'. You sink, you *die* and you take your brothers with you. Look who's the weakest link in this crew- ShitSmith pussy boy! I bet your grandmother likes pussy..."

"Sir, no sir!" The instructors sounded too harsh, insulting, or racist to some, but they were that way for a reason- these guys needed to able to withstand *anything* that came their way and if they couldn't handle some simple name-calling they may as well ring that bell and cry all the way home. But the technique worked, not only to toughen up recruits but also to weed out the weakest links, the ones that'd likely fail due to their lack of heart. Because heart's exactly what it took to get through SEAL training. People thought it was muscles or size or brains even. Sure, you needed those things but without heart, you'd never make it past day one, which is why 95% failed.

"Quittin' is for the enemy so I want 200% or we start at the beginning." *Definitely familiar...*

"They...*what*?" Alex asked, still awaiting my answer.

"Of *course*," I said to myself. "How could I be so *stupid*?"

"About what? What the *hell* are you doing Camioni?"

"I just remembered something." I stood there, trying to locate the familiar voice. I stopped when I found it. He'd apparently noticed me, too. *I was right. Holy shit.*

"What is that guy doing? Is he coming *over* here?" Alex asked.

"Are we in trouble?" I shrugged. "Are we not allowed to watch?" Jeanine asked, legitimately concerned.
"Of *course* we're allowed. It's a public beach. Otherwise they wouldn't be out here in plain sight. Trust me," I added, annoyed at their unfamiliarity on such things, "the *real* shit is behind closed doors."

"Hey! Camioni, is that *you*?!" the guy shouted, now only 20 feet away. I smiled craftily, shaking my head.

Cal was an attractive guy. He and my brother had trained together and been stationed on the east coast, where I'd met him years earlier. I broke out in laughter as he approached, thinking back to when I'd met first met him. He was still quite the character, attractive no doubt, but I'd had my sights set elsewhere at the time...

By now the guys had stopped their game and had joined us on the sidelines. Ivan and Jordan were shell-shocked. "What the fuck?! She *knows* him?" I heard the comments behind us.

Mac interjected, "Well yeah, *sort* of..."

I answered awkwardly, "yea, it's kind of a long story." What else was I supposed to say? It really was. Then Cal spoke again.

"Christ, Camioni. What the *hell* are you doing here? You *live* here or somethin'?" He swooped in, his small super strength lifting me up off the sand.

"Or something," I paused. "So...Donnie said you were an instructor. I didn't put two and two together until I heard that voice. How you been?"

"You saw my moves, don't lie." His cockiness was typical and oddly bordered on charming.

That still didn't stop me from playing a little hardball back. "Fuck you."

Alex and Dana stood there, stunned. "Did she just yell at a Navy SEAL?"

"Ha, ha. Yea, I'll retire one of these days but right now I'm havin' way *too* much fun." He turned around, motioning to someone, "and you'll never guess who else is." It didn't take me long to single out the very tall, attractive tatted-up blonde he'd been referring to. *What. The. Fuck.* Who was now walking our way...

"Yo, Mad Dog! Look- it's Camioni!" Cal shouted.

The tall blonde shouted back, "where? I don't see him!"

"Not *that* one!" he yelled, pointing me out.

I watched the look on his face when he suddenly recognized me and grinned widely, jogging over casually like some lifeguard straight out of *Baywatch*. *Oh shit...*

Nate had snuck up behind me, making me jump, "wait- you know *him*, too?" he whispered.

I turned, looking him dead in the eye, "*Well*? Kind of, um...*yeah*."

"I'm afraid to ask," he answered impartially.

"Better not," I sighed, "that's an even *longer* story." And with that, I barely had time to react before Mark scooped me up away from Nate, my feet floating in the air. "Whoah!" I exclaimed.

A guy like Mark had never been my 'type' but he hadn't been easy to ignore. Standing 6' 3" and covered in tribal art his natural dirty blonde locks completed the quintessential 'surfer' look so predictable of Californians. His effortless style and personality attracted women of all ages and I had been no exception. As much as I'd tried to resist, I'd been sucked in with no chance of escape.

"You look *great*, Lea."

"Yeah, so do you," I smiled back. Like many of his teammates Mark's looks were unintentionally deceiving. If you saw him running down the beach, you'd never suspect what his day job was or the shit he could do. He was 100% California surfer- rough hair, dazzling blue eyes, a body worth exploring every inch...His shyness made it hard to imagine him flipping a switch and getting to work.

"I hate to interrupt this little reunion but we gotta get back," he hit Mark comically. "If you guys wanna join us later, a bunch of us will be at O'Neill's. Usually we avoid the place like the fuckin' plague on weekends but it's my buddy's birthday. Just warn your friends." His smile was purely sinful.

"Lea?" Mac asked, suspiciously. I stood there still admiring the view, all proud of myself.

I blinked, shaking my head at what had just happened. I turned to her and the rest of the gang. "Um yeah?"

"What the *hell* did you just sign us up for?" I continued to smile, knowing that the only person who *truly* knew the answer to that question was in New York right now and the minute she found out about my day she was gonna flip.

Chapter 12~ The Other Guys

O'Neill's was a legendary landmark on Coronado. Once a frequented spot by many team guys back in the day it was now mostly visited by tourists and 'frog hogs', women looking to score one for bragging rights (and if they were lucky, a husband). It was a typical, run-down Irish pub, its inside generously decorated with various military memorabilia. We were all outside on the patio. I'd quickly snuck away to call Rachel. I just couldn't keep this to myself any longer.

"You're never gonna be*lieve* who I ran into today."

"*What*? You're *kidding*. What the *fuck* is with that city anyway? Every time you're there, men come out of the woodwork. First Patrick, then Nate, now Cal…"

"There's one more…"

"Who else *is* there?"

"Funny you ask because…" I sensed her apprehensiveness from nearly 3000 miles away. Before I could sense *Cal*, he'd wiped the phone out of my hand.

"Who you talkin' to, Camioni? You're supposed to be hanging out with *us*."

"Wh…Who the hell is this?" Rachel asked.

"I'd say I recognize the voice, but I've just been with too many chicks, sorry."

"It's *Rachel*. You know New Yorkers aren't phased by you guys." And she was right. Unlike most women who squabbled and squawked and put on their best skimpy, tit-showing outfits for an ounce of attention, Rachel and I hadn't. We were no doubt bowled over by their sheer hotness and well-muscled physiques, but we'd remained immune to the infamous SEAL charm (until we'd both eventually given in…). When my brother's friends had met Rachel and I they'd instantly accepted us into their group. They'd even designated us their wingmen, helping them score (not that they really needed help).

"*Yo*, Rach, what do ya think about that one over there?" one of them would ask. She'd respond, "She looks like a fuckin' whore *and* she looks stupid. That one's better." Guys like Mark and Cal were used to women fighting over them and in places like Virginia Beach and San

Diego where their numbers were high, the women were constantly circling like vultures. They hadn't exactly known what to think about us when we hadn't sprouted wings.

"Oh, *yeah*, *Rachel*, I remember, but don't get how you'd forget me," Cal laughed.

"I *didn't*, but I don't think my husband would be too happy if he knew who I was talking to." I laughed loudly. SEALs never took well to defeat and I could sense the dent in Cal's pride.

"Is that *right*? Married...that's too bad."

"Yup, missed your chance- *sorry*." Of course *she* wasn't. We both knew the life that came with guys him and as reliable as they were out on the field, they didn't *exactly* have the best track record- plus, it wasn't a life any girl really wanted.

"Yeah, you're right. Sorry if I had to run over to Afghanistan a few times," he shrugged. "But we did have some good times, though." His wise-ass smirk was quick to return.

Those had been good times for Rachel and I. Seeing Cal and Mark today made me think back on all the fun we'd had, albeit too short-lived. It also made me miss my brother. If it hadn't been for Donnie I never would've met any of them and Rachel and I never would have gotten an inside look into their crazy world or had so much fun.

I saw Mark at the patio bar and my mind jumped back to that summer. I'd just been dumped, was absolutely miserable and Donnie had convinced me to visit him. I'd planned on staying a few days but Donnie had refused to let me sulk and forced me to join him and his friends on bar crawls (Rachel and I called them night missions because they were always on the hunt for chicks). Well, it'd been the first of many great times there and some of the best I can still remember. Mark had been an unexpected bonus and the main reason I'd not just extended my stay but had returned.

Cal wasn't giving up, "So, you comin' out anytime soon?"

"I just told you I was fuckin' married, asshole" she laughed, "and, no." Didn't I mention some other key SEAL traits, like 'never waiver'; 'never back down' and 'never leave a potential piece of ass behind'? He gave me my phone and waved to Mark. "So, let's talk about how the *fuck* you ran into those two. So ridiculous! I cannot *believe* I'm missing all this."

"I would've bet on them being married before becoming anything close to responsible adults."

"Fuckin' right. So," she added, "how does he look?"

"Who, Cal?" I asked.

"Well, yeah. But I meant Mark."

"*Yeah*, he looks good, I guess." *Damn right he does.* "Okay, fine, looks fuckin' *hot*."

"I wonder what would've happened if we'd both stayed the course, ya know, way back when..."

"We were wrapped up in the fantasy?"

"Yeah. But that would've been pretty *fuckin'* cool. Lea, I'm pretty sure you're the only one I know besides Paige who's livin' the fantasy-for *real*. That's more than I can say for myself. So," she quickly changed the subject, "what's up with Nate? How does *he* look?"

"I see you get right to the good stuff." I noticed Nate out the corner of my eye chattin' it up with a few of Mark and Cal's friends.

"Well? Spit it out. I can't wait all night. You got two exes there and *one* of mine, all to yourself." *I hate you*.

"O-kay, I guess."

"*Okay*? Bullshit. I know what that means."

"Okay, so he looks a little more than okay, alright?" I walked off to find a quieter spot. "Oh shit."

"What?"

"He's coming over here."

"Who?"

"*Guess.*"

"Oh shit. Alright, call me when you're back home, your *other* home." Click. *Just in time.*

"Following me again?" Nate had appeared with a drink in hand. He passed it to me, smiling.

"Not really." I sipped my refreshed vodka seltzer and nodded. Being this close to him two days in a row was beginning to unnerve me. "Somethin' bothering you?" *Am I that obvious?*

"No. Why?"

"You just seem so serious. In the middle of an important call?"

"Oh, uh, no. Just my friend Rachel. Um, nevermind, it's a..."

"Another long story, right." I agreed shyly. "Kind of like...*Mark*?" he looked over his shoulder at the group of guys. "So, how exactly do you know them again, your *brother*?"

"Yeah. Met them about 8 or 9 years ago." *You did a helluva lot more than meet them...*

"Cool guys. I have a lot of respect. I'm feelin' a little lame standing among such an elite group with just a medical degree."

"*Two* medical degrees," I corrected, clearing my throat. "Just pointing out the obvious. You're hardly lame," I nudged his arm teasingly.

Evan had found us. "That chick keeps asking for your number." A blonde in a fluorescent pink tank with slits in all the wrong places was visible near the bar. *Ugh.*

"Oh, *that* one," Nate recalled. "I don't know, I'm kind of 'taken' at the moment so..."

"*So?*" Evan wasn't budging.

"So, talkin' to someone is one thing, doin' shit is another."

"Well if you can't, *I* can." He scurried off.

"He hasn't changed a bit."

I looked at him, a small head shake showing Nate I agreed. "Neither have you well, mostly."

"Is that a *good* thing?" he asked, leaning in slightly. *Gulp.*

"I haven't decided yet." I paused, thinking of a quick recovery. "I better catch Jeanine before she leaves with that excuse for a guy over there." I felt my phone buzz. I pulled it out of my pocket. *Shit. Bad timing.* I immediately stopped in my tracks. "I kinda gotta take this, sorry." Nate didn't need telepathy to tell who it was.

"I'll take care of Jeanine." He winked before disappearing into the small but dense crowd.

'Thanks' I mouthed, putting the phone up to my face. "*Hi,* I was wondering where you've been. Did you get my texts?"

"Hey, babe. *When*? I'm so sorry I meant to call you earlier but every time I went to, something came up. I *miss* you."

"I miss you, too. So, how's it going? You're not doing all those stunts, right? Bet you're missing the beach right about now. How's the weather there?"

"Tell me about it. Toronto doesn't exactly have those. And it's cold. Everything okay? You seem distracted."

"Uh, yeah, yeah. Just making sure my friend doesn't make a big mistake with some loser. You know how guys in bars are." I laughed, referring back to when I'd unknowingly met Patrick for the first time at one. I heard him snicker on the other end. "My friends and I ran into a few of Donnie's buddies and ended up at some dive bar in Coronado. Don't ask."

"*Coronado?*"

"Yea- I'm in San Diego for that conference, remember? We wanted to go to the beach." I giggled, a little embarrassed.

"Oh, right. Skipping class again, are we?"

"You know me and lectures."

"Good, cool. Wish I was there with you. I love San Diego. Well I don't wanna keep you from your friends- I know you rarely seen them. Call me tomorrow? I'll just be enjoying my downtime, awaiting your call and beautiful face."

A year and a half and I still hadn't gotten used to calling Patrick Thomas my boyfriend or him calling *me* beautiful. Probably because somewhere deep down I still thought he was under some kind of love spell; particularly when he was constantly surrounded by what I, along with the rest of the world, considered to be drop-dead gorgeous women, especially on movie sets like he was on right now.

I smiled to myself, already looking forward to tomorrow's call. "Oh, stop. You're too much."

"You are, ya know. Well go save your friend and call me tomorrow."

"Okay, good night, and Patrick? I wish you were here, too."

Chapter 13 ~ Fast and Furious

The next day...

I had a lot of work awaiting me back in L.A., which I knew would be the perfect distraction; work was good for that sort of thing. Sensory overload couldn't begin to describe the past few days I'd had. The rest of Saturday night had been entertaining. After I'd gotten off the phone with Patrick, I'd caught up more with Mark and Cal, who updated me on their latest shenanigans which surprisingly in no way involved women, night raids or rescue missions, but a clothing line designed and launched by veterans and I was more than impressed.

But Patrick calling at the just the wrong moment had thrown me off even more than comingling with not one, but *two* exes, and now I had to call him and pretend that I was perfectly fine when I knew I wasn't. The drive back to Marina del Rey had been an easy one. I was home in less than three hours, unpacking aimlessly, collecting my thoughts, as I continued filling Rachel in on the weekend.

"Honestly? I don't know. Everything was *fine*. I mean it *is* fine."

"You don't sound fine."

"I don't?"

"Not really."

"It was just a slight overload of the uh, opposite sex. It's all good, seriously."

"Right," she laughed. "Patrick's away and leaving for Europe in a couple of months, you haven't seen Nate in a *very* long time, not to mention you also hung out with tall, blond, tattooed and gorgeous. Anyone's feelings would be stirred up."

"Yeah, you're right."

"Look- don't overthink it-I know how you get. I mean, it's not like you're gonna see either of them anytime soon, right?" *Maybe, Sigh.* "And keep me in the loop about Cal and Mark."

"Will do. Got their contact info. I'm just not so sure that was a good thing," I joked.

"*Their*, as in Mark, too?" Rachel was just looking out for me but she didn't have to worry. What had happened with Mark and I had been fun- that's *all*. Neither of us had been looking for much more, although seeing him this weekend had sort of made me wonder if a future had at all been possible. He was doing well- 'technically' out of harm's way. Plus, he was one of the most genuine guys I had ever met. "Anyway, speaking of Cal, he brought up a good point- I need to start planning my next visit."

"Shit, yeah. You're missing this view right now." I was looking out my bedroom window at the marina, the one that had drawn me out here, among other things...Nearly every morning I had my coffee out on the deck. And every night the well-lit moorings and streetlights in the foreground made the marina look almost magical so magical, it still seemed fake.

"*Don't* remind me," she said angrily. "I'm gonna check my schedule and let you know. When are you coming home?"

"After Labor Day, not sure yet. I gotta see when Patrick's..."

"So, when *are* you gonna see him? I feel like he's been shooting for almost the *entire* summer. He still in Toronto? When's he leaving for Europe?"

"Yeah, not sure yet. I'm trying desperately not to think about it. I know it's gonna come up fast. I'm actually gonna talk to him right after I meet my friend Jamie to work out. I need double the workout after this fuckin' weekend. But he should be back next week. He's got this golf tournament coming up so..."

"Don't tell me you're gonna take *that* shit up next."

"Hell, no. I like mini golf. I don't know- I guess I could be open to it- He looks pretty fuckin' hot in golf clothes." I picked up a picture of us from my nightstand.

"He looks good in *anything*, Lea."

"I guess you're right," I answered.

"Alright, go work out- you *do* probably need it. Oh, and say hi to Patrick for me."

"I will."

Chapter 14 ~ Caddyshack

August 5th
SAG Celebrity Golf Classic, Newport Beach, CA

"How did I let you talk me into this again?"

"I'm really good in bed?"

"Nice *try*," I mocked him, "but I don't think so."

"*Really?*"" My eyebrows raised at Patrick as he tried to keep the wheel steady. "*Foreplay?*" I was sure having fun with this. "*Kissing?* Everyone knows I'm a *great* kisser. It's even gotten me some good parts."

"*Oh?* Who's *everyone*?" I scowled.

"Uh, it's a well-known fact. Do I sense some *jealousy*?"

"At the parts you've gotten for your supposedly award-winning kissing or because you've kissed God knows how many girls?" I laughed again. "Okay," I admitted. "Maybe a little."

"Only a *little*, huh? Hmmm," he thought. "I don't know how to put this, but I'm kind of a big deal- people *know* me," he smirked, knowing instantly I had picked up on his movie quoting.

"Ha, ha, very funny, Ron Burgundy, but I don't think you're *that* big a deal. Your point?"

"My point is that I don't think you realize what a great catch you've got here," he said, referring to himself. "You know, lots of women, and *men* FYI, swoon over me." I rolled my eyes at him, not that he could see them with his eyes focused straight ahead. "I even had this girl once who was *so* into me, she snuck into Comic-Con just to *meet* me."

"I didn't sneak in- I had a *pass*." My cousin Mike had invited me to San Diego Comic-Con, where he'd been promoting his sci-fi comic. I'd made an ass of myself not once but twice. First, I'd spilled coffee on him and then, after having gotten completely lost in the convention center, I'd mistakenly barged in on the cast and directors of *American Justice*, along with a room full of nearly 1000 die-hard fans. It was a day I'd never forget and one I'd never live down.

"Personally, I thought the whole coffee-spilling, damsel in distress routine won out that day."

"I was *not* a damsel in distress," I stressed.

"Could've fooled me. You still didn't answer my question. About the kissing."

"Oh, right." I let him wait. "Hmm, I think you'll have to remind me. I have a *very* bad memory." Just then he leaned over to kiss me, our lips barely brushing. "Hey, keep your eyes on the road, loverboy."

"Are you trying to make me crash?" I grinned, my eyes wandering down his shirt. Whoever said women had the true power over men wasn't kidding. They were suckers, alright.

"So anyway, what am I supposed to do all day while you're out on the course?"

"Tee time's at noon but I gotta be there early. I don't know- you can hang at the pool or go to the spa or... It's a really nice resort."

"Or...mingle with *The Real Housewives of Orange County*? You know I won't fit in with those people."

"Oh, why not?"

"Well for one thing- we're not married, which makes me even further from a housewife than I already am. Two, there's nothing fake about me."

"True. Come on, what's the third thing? I know you and your lists."

"You're not rich enough."

"Yeah, you're right. So, I guess that makes your last option more appealing."

"There's a *fourth* option?"

"You- standing on the sidelines watching me play." I looked ahead at the 405 which as usual was backed up. We were in Long Beach, about halfway to Newport Beach.

"That depends," I loved this game.

"On what, wiseass?"

"On *who* else might be playing in this 'celebrity' thingy."

"Well, I heard Dermott Mulroney and Joe Pesci will be there. Sorry, Brad Pitt and John Cusack can't make it."

My face showed my disappointment. "Oh, then forget it."

"Oh. I'm not good enough to look at, huh?"

"The spa is looking pretty damn good right now," I teased.

"Ha, ha." I looked at him adoringly, the way I couldn't help look at him every time he poured on the charm. I mean he was just too irresistible.

"Well you're no Superman, but you *are* awfully available."

When we'd pulled up to the main building, I'd already lost my bearings. Although not far from the freeway the Pelican Hill Resort was an overwhelming piece of prime property, perched atop over 500 acres of beautiful coastline. Our bungalow was just a small part of the resort's expansive layout. Private villas, rooms and condos made up the housing while dozens of resort amenities, as well as a world-class golf club and spa, offered the ultimate relaxing vacation-or living community- *if* you could afford it. All it was missing were rides and it could have been Disneyland.

"Holy shit," I caught myself, attempting to be more ladylike. Not that he minded- he'd gotten somewhat used to my imperfections, my foul mouth being only one of many. "I thought you said it was a nice resort." I set my bag on the floor next to the wet bar, staring ahead.

"It is."

"How many golf resorts have you been to?" I asked him.

"Enough. But this one *is* nice, I guess."

"You have some definition of 'nice'" I said, pushing past him through the living area. "This place is fucking ridiculous." I unlocked the sliding glass doors and slid them open, exposing the view. The furnished terrace was surprisingly private. "I think I'm living in the wrong place."

I felt his warm hands slide around my waist from behind as he gently kissed the side of my neck. The tingling sensation was enough to make me jump. I'd lost my train of thought. How he could always do that to me I hadn't quite figured out. I tilted my neck further to the right for more.

"It is nice, but we better go check one thing before we go any further."

"Whoah, hey! What are you doing?" I shrieked as he whipped me around. He gazed down at me with his fiery eyes and I could feel them beginning to sear into me. "But what abou…"

He pulled me close and kissed me hard before rushing us inside. I didn't even see the bed. All I remember is falling onto a fluffy cloud. I mean, do people *really* come to these places to golf?

I hated to admit it, but Patrick had been right- watching him play hadn't been so bad. Golf was something I hardly ever paid attention to and I could never understand how the hell people watched it on TV because to me it was *so* boring. But I guess it was better than watching cars go around in a circle a million times. I was standing behind the ropes at the 9th hole, admiring the view and I don't mean Patrick Thomas.

Gazing out at the course's jaw-dropping scenery it was hard for me to keep my eyes on little else, no matter *what* A-List stars were playing. There were perfect panoramic ocean views from every hole and the breathtaking cliffs stole my attention so many times I'd lost concentration, which I know you must be wondering how I could've let that happen when someone like Mark-Paul Gosselear was on your boyfriend's team…I mean here I was dating Patrick Thomas and then one of my major crushes growing up suddenly appears. I guess I was *never* gonna be able to hold it together in front of certain celebrities.

I couldn't help it- I had to snap a shot and text it to Rachel. We'd seen every single episode of *Saved by the Bell* a hundred times, including the movie when Zack and Kelly get married, not to mention *Saved by the Bell: The College Years*, a poorly attempted sequel. Like every other teenage girl, we were in love with him and wished we could be his high school sweetheart. I mean, Zack Morris playing golf *who* knew? And he was even hotter now. He hadn't aged at all. Patrick hadn't told me who was on his team. He wouldn't have let me tag along if he'd known how in love I still was...

After the tournament had ended and they'd finished autographs I met Patrick at the club house, where he introduced me to a few of his teammates. It hadn't been long before I'd had to excuse myself to the ladies' room to regroup. It'd been an all-too familiar 'celebrity crush' feeling and I fought to hold myself together. Patrick kept asking if everything was okay- I could only answer him with silent nods, my legs shaking most of the time.

"So," he asked, changing into a new shirt and a more comfortable pair of khakis after we were back at our bungalow, "what did you think?"

"About...the...tournament?" An hour later and I was still trying to wrap my head around the fact that I had just touched *the* Zack Morris.

"Yeah, what did you *think* I meant?"

I tried to picture greenery and sand pits but all I kept envisioning was him. "Oh. Um, yeah, it was *beautiful*, just beautiful..."

"*Beautiful*, huh?" He combed his hair, eyeing me curiously in the bathroom's mirror.

"Yes. I guess I never really gave it a chance. It really *is* better up close." *Damn right he is.*

"Uh, huh- bullshit," he smiled. "You probably weren't even paying attention. Did you even notice our team got second place?"

"*Yes* I was." *To Mark-Paul Gosselear and Benjamin Bratt.* "And it's not *bullshit*- for your information I was trying to follow along." *Follow men like William Baldwin.* "I never knew how green the turf really was or just how deep those sand pits were."

"Uh huh. How about the celebrities?"

I cleared my throat and took a big gulp. "Okay, okay, I admit there were some pretty cool people there. What did you expect me to do, sit there and act normal?"

"Ha, ha. Like *that* would ever be possible," he joked.

"Okay, fine. So maybe I *don't* exactly have the best track record for first meetings with famous people. I can't help it- I get *nervous*." I finally got into the bathroom to touch up.

"*Nervous*? I don't think you were that nervous when you met me." *What are you nuts?*

"That's because I didn't know it was you."

"You weren't even *nice* to me. You were *way* nicer to them by the way. They thought you were as cool as a cucumber." *What?* He kissed my cheek.

"Sorry, but I... *really*? And I was *nice* to you. You just had on that stupid Red Sox hat."

"Gee, thanks. Mark asked me where I'd met you and said you were sweet. I told him he was only seeing the tip of the iceberg."

"Funny. Wait, *what*? What did you say? Oh my *God*- he's gonna think I'm a total ass. I can't believe you called me out in front of Zack Morris! And now I gotta sit at a *table* with him tonight?"
"Why do you keep referring to him as Zack Morris?"

"Because that's his nam... oh *forget* it. I am officially a loser in his eyes now."

"Jesus. Were you this crazy with me? Wait. *Don't* answer that."

I chuckled to myself, "that was different. I've known him longer. You don't understand."

"Well, maybe *he's* single," he joked. "Is this what goes through the minds of crazy female fans? Well," he continued still amused by my ranting, "just try to act semi-normal, okay? It's only a few hours. Think you can handle it?" His warm hands dug into my tense shoulders. I looked at his reflection in the mirror and smiled. "Should I be worried?"

I turned around to kiss him. "Ok, we gotta go, hot stuff." I let go of him, heading for the door. "I'm not making any promises," I winked.

"Right. I better keep a tight leash on him then." He kissed me again. "Now keep your shit together and don't embarrass me," he kidded.

"Don't worry, I'll be fine," I said. "As long as I..."

"You what?"

"As long as I get a picture. This is the closest I'll ever be to being Mrs. Zack Morris so I wanna take advantage."

He shook his head amusedly, "let's go, *Kelly*, before I change my mind and tell them you got the flu."

Chapter 15 ~ Who's That Girl?

The clubhouse was lavishly decorated, packed with celebrities and media, and just as intimidating as any Hollywood premiere. I'd been to a few events with Patrick, but I'd rarely mingled with any 'stars'. Patrick had mostly 'non-industry' friends. He may have been off to bigger and better things but still, he remained untainted and low-key.

I observed the variety and caliper of people scattered about, from wealthy moguls to 'once hot and now not' celebs, to some of the most well-known in all of Hollywood. I did my absolute best to focus on my immediate surroundings and stay calm, like I had been to a million of these things before. I was sipping my cranberry martini trying to maintain confidence and act nonchalantly whilst not staring at every single celebrity who walked by, which was nearly impossible- everywhere I looked was a recognizable face. Peyton Manning chatted it up with Andy Garcia across the room, while Alice Cooper strutted past in a rock-inspired suit.

"So, what do you think of Chris O'Donnell up close?" Patrick teased, trying to help. "You sure you're ok?"

"Not too bad, but I wish L.L. Cool J played golf- I'd love to meet him. Okay so far..."

"Good," he answered, "because don't look now but there goes Mark Walhberg." He pointed to our far right. He moved confidently through the crowd, smiling and greeting nearly everyone he passed.

"Whoah- I still remember those Calvin Klein ads," I mumbled. "Now why couldn't *he* have been on your team?"

"If he *was*, I wouldn't have invited you." I gave him a dirty look.

"Come on, you don't think I'd forget what a huge NKOTB fan you are, do you?"

"Donnie's not here, is he?"

"Don't know, but since Adrian's on our team, maybe you'll get lucky." Perplexed, I stood there.

"You still have never watched *Entourage*, have you?" I shook my head 'no'. "Well don't tell him that. Here we are- table 32." I noted the 'Patrick Thomas & Guest' place card, right next to one that read 'Mark-Paul Gosselear'. I almost fainted at the sight of it, never mind the *real* one, who hadn't arrived yet.

Across from us were two women, a taller light-skinned African American and a petit blonde. Both were drop-dead gorgeous and wore huge wedding rings. I assumed they were each married to whomever was in those seats. Before I could speak Patrick held out his hand to introduce us. It was no surprise that even married women couldn't resist him. I praised myself inside, knowing that this handsome and talented man was all mine. But still, being around any rich or famous I felt inferior.

I inspected my outfit. I had wanted to buy something new but hadn't had the time, so I'd worn one of my nicer casual skirts and a Vineyard Vines polo shirt. Together with a pair of simple sandals it was the best fit-to-wear-at-a-celebrity-golf-tournament outfit I could come up with.

"Hi, I'm Patrick. This is Eleana."

I smiled sheepishly. Normally if I wasn't nervous I'd say, 'hey, what's up?' or 'hi, how are you?', but somehow I always felt like I had to pull out some bullshit etiquette (not that I actually knew what that was).

"Nice to meet you Patrick…and Eleana," the taller one said. "I'm Chris and this is Michelle." I looked at them blankly. "I'm Alfonso's wife. Michelle's married to Scott."

"Oh, nice…pleasure," I quickly recovered my composure.

"Well, why don't you ladies get acquainted?" Patrick said, "I'll be back. There's a few people I wanna say hi to." And just like that he'd left me.

"Um, so," I said, turning my attention to them as Patrick wandered off, "you been to this before?" *Get aquainted? I don't have anything in common with these people.*

"Our husbands were on the same team a few years go so we've remained friends since. You?" It was like a pair of deer staring at me.

"Uh no, no. My first one."

"Do you golf?" Michelle asked. I was afraid to answer. I shook my head 'no' and waited.

"Me neither. Scott has tried but honestly I'd rather be at the spa." They giggled in unison as if rehearsed.

"Yeah, me too. I mean I've *tried*, so Alfonso can't say shit." *A swear? Well that makes me feel a little better.*

"I like mini golf, though." They listened in closer. "There's this place back home- they have glow-in-the-dark mini golf- it's pretty awesome."

"You don't live here?"

"Uh, not…" *Where is he?*

"Oh, there he is." Alfonso Ribeiro wasn't a tall guy but his presence was. It was almost theatrical; no wonder he won *Dancing with the Stars.* He got to the table at nearly the same time as his teammate,

Scott Wolf. Yes, Scott Wolf. It was then that my nerves began to steadily rise again.

"Honey," Chris said adoringly, "this is Eleana, Patrick's um...Patrick's..."

"Date," I interjected, a cunning grin across my face. I guess I could've said 'girlfriend' but for some reason my mind blanked.

"*Oh*. Oh, hey, I'm Alfonso. Nice to meet you." He gently shook my hand. "Nice place, huh? A little better than some crappy room and an average course."

"Yep, hi."

"So, *you're* Eleana, huh?" *Did Scott Wolf just talk to me?*

"Um, yep," I frowned, "Why? What did he say?" *Gulp. They were talking about me?*

"I'm Scott. It's a pleasure to meet you and I'm glad you're here- it's a fun night."

Alfonso looked around, "where are the guys? I just saw them a few minutes ago."

Just then a familiar voice registered. "Hey, there's our table." I looked left, my temporary level of comfort now diminishing. "Hey guys and *ladies*," he corrected himself. "Sorry, ran into some...photographers. Oh, hey there, *hi* again." Mark-Paul Gosselear was like a Zack Morris poster come to life. His beaming smile was so sincere I almost couldn't breathe. His hand, still held out for me to shake, was beautiful and strong. Suddenly I was back at Bayside High along with Slater, Screech, Lisa and Jessie, horrible 90s outfits and all.

I felt a breeze. Patrick was standing beside me, a jealous look on his face. "I bet, dude," he said.

I stood there embarrassed. Then finally I said, "oh, hi, hi, again."

"She's a *big* fan, *huge*." I glared at Patrick, squinting my eyes in true scorpion fashion.

"Of your swing, yeah your swing." He looked at me.

"Oh, thanks. So, you follow golf?" He was being serious.

"Not really."

"Not *ever*," Patrick corrected.

"Should be an interesting night. Oh hey, Adrian." He looked around me. Out of nowhere Adrian Grenier had appeared.

"Bro," Mark-Paul quickly said to Patrick, "come with me for a sec- there's someone I want to introduce to you. You don't mind if I steal him, do you?" he asked me.

"I think she'll manage," I heard Adrian say. I nodded 'okay' and they were off. I sat down to give my now shaky legs a rest.

"Ahem." Obviously trying to make conversation with the consolation prize he'd been stuck sitting next to, Adrian offered his hand. "We haven't formally met- Adrian."

"I know who you are," I answered smugly. "Eleana, Lea actually. It's nice to meet you."

"Same here." A moment of silence passed before he continued, "so, *you're* the one." God he had an alluring smile. No wonder he'd been cast by Mark Walhberg. Thousands of girls would kill to meet him, let alone touch him and here I was.

"*Excuse* me?"

"The one- his 'plus one'." His smile expanded to the edges of his face.

"What is that, like 'code' for something?"

"Chill, I just mean I've been to these before and I've never seen him bring anyone."

"Oh, well maybe he thought most girls would find this boring." *Which, aside from the stars, it pretty much fucking is.*

"Or maybe he just never found the right girl to bring." He was becoming more attractive by the minute. Before now, I'd never really thought of him as hot. Was everyone around here this hot?

"I doubt it," I answered, "but thanks. You don't have to say that to make me feel like I'm special or anything."

"I don't need to." *What?*

"So, where's your 'plus one'? You don't seem like the kind of guy to go emptyhanded."

"Most girls wouldn't handle this, like I said."

"Handle what? It's a golf tournament. All they gotta do is show up and look pretty. Most of 'em don't even eat or speak proper English. How hard can that be?"

"You'd be surprised and that's totally cool," he said, laughing. "You know, Patrick left out how fuckin' funny you were..." I was having so much fun I hadn't even noticed Mark-Paul and Patrick return. Everyone sat down and continued talking. New projects, old projects, down time...surprisingly it had been anything but the usual superficial shit I expected these people to talk about.

"So," Adrian asked me, "how long have you two been dating?" *Why does that still sound weird? And why does this guy care?*

"Um, about a year and a half," I replied in a low voice, although obviously not low enough for the others not to hear.

I heard someone speak. I looked across the table directly at Chris. "And what do you do Lea? In the business or..."

I tried not to snort, scoff or choke on my water. After all it was a fair question. "Uh...*no*, not so much. I'm more of a, uh, *science* kind of person."

"So then, what do you do?"

Before I realized Patrick had completely cut in. "Don't let her fool you," he said. "She's a doctor- a veterinarian, and a very *good* one. I don't know why she's always so modest," he smiled.

"Impressive. She really is smarter than you," I heard Mark-Paul say. *I think I'm gonna die.*

"Hardly," I responded shyly, now hating that I had suddenly become the center of attention. Which apparently wasn't ending any time soon.

"I hope you don't mind but how did you guys meet? I mean you two don't exactly seem like you'd cross paths easily," he added curiously.

"On a blind date. Well, actually we kind of met before..." They looked clueless. "Okay, the 'cliff notes' version is that his brother walked into the animal shelter I was at...and I kind of gave him a hard time."

"*Kind* of?" Patrick stared me down plainly.

"Okay, *fine*. So I told him that I didn't care *who* his brother was, he couldn't adopt a dog for someone else."

"What did you do when he told you his brother was Patrick Thomas?" Michelle asked.

"Well, he didn't- he left."

"He *left*? Ok, I'm confused. So how did you find out who his brother was?" Scott asked, obviously into the story.

"Oh *that* fun came later." I could tell that Patrick was thoroughly enjoying this. "I didn't see him again... until weeks later when..."

"...when he brought his very attractive brother back to adopt the dog?" Chris asked.

"Well, no, umm, uh..." Suddenly they were all silent, waiting for me to continue "Then I kind of ran into their family on a wine tasting and that's when I *officially* met him." *And made a complete ass of myself, just like I'm doing now.* I hung my head low, wishing I could disappear.

"She's not telling you the whole story." I kept my head down. "She left out the part where she crashed my sister's wedding." I could have killed him right then and there.

"Excuse me, I was invited by your sister," I defended. "Plus, it was a good thing I was there since your 'date' showed up halfway through the wedding," I blurted, my confidence returned.

"And this is the *'cliff notes'* version? I wonder how long the whole *story* is," Scott said.

"Nope, nope, that's it. Anyway, I would just like to say that I'm a huge fan of all your shows," I continued left to right. When I made eye contact with Adrian I had to stop myself, "well, except yours, sorry."

"You haven't *seen Entourage*?" He was shocked I shook my head 'no'. "*Everyone's* seen it."

"Sorry, it wasn't intentional, but I just haven't gotten around to watching it." *Oops.*

"You too busy watching *Save by the Bell, The Fresh Prince* and *Party of Five* reruns?" he joked.

"Ah *hem*." Patrick cleared his throat annoyingly. "What about *American Justice*?"

I turned to him, smiling, "I don't need to see your reruns- I know all ten seasons by heart."

"I *bet*," Adrian said.

"*Wait* a minute- I though you said you met at Comic-Con?" Scott asked. I was about to cross *Party of Five* off my favorite show list and replace it with *Dawson's Creek*. If a group of people could have been shocked twice, these people were.

"You *told* them?" *Gulp*. It was now clear to the entire table how much of an idiot I was. "*Great*. I get invited to a harmless golf tournament and I end up at my own *Comedy Central Roast*. You know what? I think I see an empty seat next to Joe Pesci."

"Relax, babe, it's no big deal," he winked and smiled so adoringly I could hardly be mad.

"So, the entire day instead of birdies and golf swings and you talked about me*?*" I asked.

"I never had a fan go that crazy for me," Mark-Paul said. "Don't worry about it," he said.

"Well I have, *obviously*," Adrian interrupted.

"Yea, right, they're probably all after Wahlberg," Patrick noted, "speaking of which, you know Lea is a huge Wahlberg fan..."

"Is that *right*?" he asked me.

"Okay, I think that concludes this evening's entertainment. Let's move onto something else."

"I'm sorry," Adrian apologized, "we got a little carried away in your story, which was great by the way. You should write that down." Those gorgeous dark blue eyes and black eyelashes would bowl over and win the forgiveness of any girl, including me, I hated to admit.

"I just hate being the center of attention, especially around people I don't know *and* people of your caliper. Thanks."

Most in Hollywood were the exact opposite of who'd been at our table; even Adrian had surprised me. The night had quickly come to an end and I'd been proud of how well I'd handled myself. I had met *the* Zack Morris and had remained mostly calm (at least, that's what I'd *hoped* he thought), even when he'd introduced me to a costar from his current TV series. But I was in for one last shocker of the evening. Just before leaving Adrian had led me over to a crowd of people. I hadn't had I time to react until it'd been too late. Without barely an introduction he'd had thrown me into Mark Wahlberg (yes, *the* Mark Wahlberg), who'd stared at me, a dumb look on his face. He had a unique charm of his own and was one of the few big names in Hollywood who hadn't lost his genuineness. It was a miracle I'd lasted almost a full minute talking to him without fainting.

"Yo, *who* was that girl again?" Mark Wahlberg asked in his unmistakable Boston accent.

"Patrick's *girlfriend*." Adrian answered.

"Oh- I like her. Pretty cool. Most girls can't say a fuckin' word around me- drives me nuts."

"Yea, I know what you mean."

I left feeling accomplished on a few levels, one of which was being minimally accepted into a club of elite. I'd met some celebrities, even enjoyed their company and made a decent impression on them (or so I'd hoped), except for the moment when I'd almost spilled my drink on Bill Murray.

"So?" Patrick asked me as we walked out.

"It was...*fun*. Not what I expected, in a good way. I'd come again." My elation was undeniable.

"*Fun*, huh? Because of *Mark*?" he kidded.

"Probably," I teased. "A chance to meet Marky Mark only comes along once in a lifetime."

"*What*?" He stopped, all confused.

"What?" I played it off as if I had no clue what he was referring to.

"I was talking about the *other* Mark."

"Oh yeah, him, too."

"Is there any type of party you're *not* successful at crashing?"

"Hey, I was *invited* to this one *and* Kelly's wedding, remember? Jealous of my skills?"

"Hardly," he bent down and kissed me. "Besides, I have *more* than a few skills of my *own*."

Chapter 16 ~ License to Drive

Friday August 12

Before living in Los Angeles, I hadn't realized how strange its layout was; to me, it was confusing. A scattered cluster of bunches of small neighborhoods, each with its own unique culture and population, made Los Angeles similar to many others like New York, however. It had no true central location unless you count Hollywood which, of course *was* the center of their universe.

People in entertainment usually lived in either Central L.A., The San Fernando Valley or the Westside. The Valley, the largest and 'most affordable', included Burbank, Glendale and North Hollywood, while the Westside boasted more expensive neighborhoods like Santa Monica and Beverly Hills. Aspiring actors and entertainers wanted to be close to the 'action' and if they wanted *any* privacy, they needed the means and know-how. California real estate was costly- Los Angeles and San Francisco surpassed New York in price, with far less available space. In addition, Los Angeles' public transport system was rudimentary, forcing most to drive- not that they *could*. So, no matter what time of day L.A. traffic was a fucking mess, and although there were buses and a Metrorail the areas serviced were severely lacking.

At times I wasn't that bothered, but right now while I was stuck on the I-10 behind some half-cocked pothead in an old, beat-up pickup, I was annoyed beyond belief. No matter where you were headed, the amount and variety of idiots on these roads was disturbing. I don't care what kind of bad rap New Yorkers get, at least they knew how to drive. Out here they handed out driver's licenses to any moron, maybe even pulled them out of a Crackerjack box, creating some of the dumbest, incompetent drivers on the planet.

I'm sure *some* of these people could drive but trust me, they were few and far between. They were unaware of their surroundings and no fucking common sense. Despite its five lanes, the I-10 was a constant shitshow of people coasting from lane to lane without signaling or even looking, which drove my blood pressure up every fucking time I had to get on it. I mostly rode my bike to the shelter which was only two miles away and drove only when I had to. It didn't take too long to get to Patrick's but I had no choice but to drive. There was no train and the buses doubled my driving time.Patrick's new place was less than 15 miles away, but it sometimes took an hour. For years he had been splitting his time between Burbank and Vancouver, Canada renting, but he'd finally decided to put down some roots. Burbank was home to the major studios. It was decently affordable and at one time private, but it was becoming more popular and more inundated with people making privacy (and space) harder to come by.

Los Feliz, on the other hand, lacked anything that had to do with the glitz and glamour of Hollywood. Its eclectic and historical architecture and cultural diversity set it apart from L.A.'s more well-known locales and its central location made it a prime spot. Just east of Hollywood, it was known for its cozy, chill and artsy vibe, its tight-knit neighborhood maintaining a balance between old school charm and refined creativity.

Everyone knew I wasn't the biggest fan of Los Angeles although yes, I was currently residing there, however. Los Feliz was *different*. And my favorite part of it besides Patrick? Griffith Park, one of the largest parks in the United States. It 'protected' the neighborhood with its rustic, evergreen-lined hillside, and its own version of Hollywood Hills known as Los Feliz Hills, one of the wealthiest areas of L.A. Sprawling 4000 acres, Griffith Park was unquestionably a unique presence in such a busy, reputedly one-dimensional city. Until I had actually seen it, I hadn't believed I'd ever love it, but I'd been wrong. Its harbored hiking trails, caves (including the famous Bat Cave!), museums and my personal favorite, The Griffith Observatory, made it more than unique. It was easy to forget you were in L.A. unless you ventured to the park's northern edge. The Hollywood sign remained one of the world's most evocative symbols and an ongoing (albeit fake in my book) representation of an industry (also fake), a lifestyle and an ambition to make peoples' dreams come true (can we say... *bullshit*?!).

Patrick's house may not have been grandiose or extravagant, but it was pretty sweet. Of course, he'd had the 2 million to buy it, scoring a piece of prime real estate at the foot of Los Feliz Hills, where digs seldomly sold for less than 5 million. It was up the road from Los Feliz village, yet its surprisingly quiet location offered privacy and beautiful city views, especially at night.

I turned left, crossing Los Feliz Boulevard and continued up windy Lowry Road, whose lush greenery hid away many of its homes. After a few bends I was at Patrick's. Spanish revival homes were popular out west. Despite its 'mere' 2500 ft2 size it felt bigger. Its main entry and garage doors were arched like those of a castle and its windows were almost medieval, yet somehow it delivered in a modernistic, classic kind of way. The light grey color and simplistic design fit Patrick to a "t"; I could see why it had caught his eye, but it was what awaited through its doors that really sold me- European Oak floors, white coffered ceilings admixed with a modern, open-floor plan... it gave it a grand yet beachy feel despite its façade. As I opened the front door, I could hear music coming from the back. I called out for Patrick- nothing. Nothing but Jack Johnson. *Where is he? And why is that so loud?*

I set my bag down and meandered through the sizable open living space, a trend I hadn't ever been a fan of. Call it yet another New Englander syndrome. Growing up I'd been accustomed to old houses and actual rooms. Now people wanted every wall down with a clear line of sight from their toilet to the back of the house. They also, it seemed, needed to coordinate every space together, which fit Angelinos perfectly since they only ever seemed to like the color white. I had become quite familiar with the L.A. sense of 'style', lame attempts at interior design which ended up being about as creative as an empty cardboard box. But I suppose it went well with their superficial personalities.

Most 'normal' people I knew had no problem maneuvering a plate of hors d'oeuvres through a doorway or two, but I guess that was just too much effort for some. The rich and famous thrived on one-upping each other and seeing who could throw the best A-list or B-list parties and what better than a wide-open, one-note space with floor to ceiling pocket glass doors that allowed for a perfect view of their fake little world?

I followed the music trail, chuckling to myself. Here I was again bashing the rich and famous while Patrick's own floor to ceiling pocket glass doors were wide open, offering killer views of not only his backyard and beyond it downtown L.A., but of Patrick himself doing laps in his pool. I stepped onto the patio and sat on one of the comfy couches. I thanked God daily for the gift he'd given me.

"Ah hem." I cleared my throat to gain his attention.
He wiped his eyes and waved at me, poking his head out of the water. If there's anything sexier than watching a man strut down the beach, it's watching one swim. You could see nearly every muscle in his arms and shoulders working, contracting with each movement. Handsome hardly fit the bill when it came to describing him; it almost hurt my eyes.

"About *time*. I was wondering when you were gonna get here. I thought I was gonna have to change our dinner reservations again," he laughed as he swam closer.

"Funny. Well I would've been here earlier if it wasn't for this fuckin' L.A. traffic."

"Uh huh," he said, approaching the pool's edge. "Knowing you, you probably left late. I guess L.A. *does* one-up New York on a thing or two..." His grin was purely sarcastic. "Anyway, why are we still talking about traffic and why are you still dressed?" He raised a brow, waiting impatiently.

"What do you mean? I just got here. Give me a minute to settle in, why don't you?"

"You've been here enough it should feel like your other home," he continued, "so stop whining, try to relax for once and change so you can get in here and join me."

I couldn't much argue with that and he was right about one thing- strangely this place *was* starting to feel more comfortable, even though it wasn't near the ocean *or* on the other side of the country. It had nothing to do with views. Somehow all the stupid minutia about L.A. seemed to fade into the background when he was around.

"Well," I remarked snidely, "I suppose since I've got a half-naked, *very* attractive man at my disposal I should take advantage...wait a minute," I paused, looking around, "speaking of L.A.'s most eligible bachelor, where's my favorite tallish, brindle and handsome guy Fenway?"

"Probably upstairs taking a nap. Guess he didn't hear you come in. Either that or he hates his doctor so he's hiding."

"Not possible- who could hate me?" I narrowed my eyes and cocked my head.

"I'm sure he'll realize you're here soon. Now shut up and change already."

"Don't push it, Thomas. Just because you're...you're in there with water dripping all over your half-naked body...don't think you can just order me around and seduce me with your slick moves." I stood there miffed.

"Why *not*?" My eyes didn't waiver. I put one hand on my hip. "So, I'm guessing that's a 'no', you *won't* grab me a drink on your way back out?" Cheesy grins were his specialty. Still I remained steadfast.

"Hmmm, I'll think about it. Don't go anywhere, I'll be right back."

"Oh, don't worry your pretty little face off- I'm not." I turned, smiling sassily, then walked inside. He may have been doing laps, but I was about to do a whole lot more to him. Besides, it wasn't everyday I got to seduce a man like Patrick Thomas in his own home.

Chapter 17 ~ House Party

Saturday August 13

I rolled over and noticed the time- 8:00 am. I couldn't believe I'd slept that late. I rarely slept past 6:30 and although I didn't need coffee to wake up it was the first thing I wanted in the morning. Well, among other things...

I went downstairs, careful not to wake Patrick *or* Fenway. He really was a good dog. To think, some asshole dropped him off at a shelter. I really hated people sometimes. Patrick had the dream kitchen but what I always found fascinating was that he stocked it with top-notch appliances and cookware that any chef would kill for, yet he never even used half of it. I filled the tea kettle with water, turned on the gas and waited patiently for it to boil, reaching up in the cabinet above for coffee.

"If you're looking for my stash it's in the safe." I heard Patrick's gruff morning voice behind me. Gruff and *sexy* that is. It was nearly impossible for him to ever *not* be sexy, especially in the morning. His voice alone could get my innards reeling.

I removed my head from the cabinet under the utensil drawer next to the stove, nearly hitting my head on the granite countertop as I stood up. He was at the bottom of the stairs. He walked around the island and greeted me with a morning kiss, one hand wrapped around my waist.

"What are you doing up?"

"What does it *look* like? I'm trying to make coffee."

"Coffee? It's *Saturday*. Can't you sleep in like *one* day?" His puppy dog eyes drew me in, as his arms pulled me closer.

"I'm an early bird," I smiled. "Where's Fenway?" I looked toward the staircase.

"He didn't wanna get up, either. He needs his beauty rest."

"Right," I said pushing him aside and opening another cabinet, "where's that French press I bought you? I swear it was up with the coffee."

"Maybe the cleaning lady moved it. Turn that off and come back to bed."

"Well, I don't know. Once I'm up, I'm up. You're gonna *really* have to get creative. My brain starts going and I can't slow it down."

"I figured *that* out the second I met you. But don't worry..." He swooped me up abruptly, carrying me upstairs to the bedroom. Yea, he was one of the few things that could shut my brain off, alright. The only problem was that sometimes my body paid for it later.

"Oh. My *God*." I stared at the wall, Patrick's arm tight around my waist as we lie still.

It was a feeling that had been unfamiliar to me most of life. Before him, I'd gotten good at jetting the scene of a crime or kicking someone out to avoid any emotional bullshit. But that was probably because most guys I'd been with had never *meant* anything to me and had hardly qualified as relationship material. I couldn't blame it all on them, though. It was *me* who'd had the problem- I never let guys get too close to me, and unlike most girls, cuddling and spooning had never been in my repertoire.

So, what better way to eliminate any possibility of actually 'feeling' anything than to avoid the entire situation altogether? Another stellar Camioni trait that had made my life a sad collection of very brief relationships well, except a few...

"That *good*, huh? Yea, you don't have to thank me."

I smiled, hiding my facetious expression, "that's not what I meant." I groaned. "The clock- we better get moving."

"I thought that's what we were doing."

"Funny, but it's almost 10:00. We have to shop, walk the dog and I have to get in *some* kind of decent workout today."

"Again, weren't we just *doing* that? Wait a minute- *decent*?"

I giggled to myself. "Ha, ha, ha, um yeah, but we..." I paused, rolling over to face him. "I'm sorry I..."

"Can't help it, yeah, I know. *Relax*. You're not going into surgery today, are you? It's dinner. About that," he added, "I've been meaning to ask you...if you could make that kick-ass vodka sauce?"

I guess it could've been worse. "Wait. What? You're just asking me this *now*?"

"I didn't think it was that big a deal."

"Says the guy who hardly cooks..." I argued.

"Hey, I cook."

"Uh huh- hot dogs. Besides, there isn't enough time. There's a precise recipe, a process..." he stared at me blankly.

"A *process*? Come on, how long could it possibly take? I thought you just threw a bunch of stuff in a pot and..."

"And...what? *Poof*- it's done? I can't work *magic*," I sighed, irritated. "Why didn't you ask me this yesterday? Or last night?"

"I guess I forgot. We *were* a little busy making our *own* magic," we both laughed.

"I could've at least *started*." He was clueless. "There are steps to follow." He waited for me to continue, silent. "You need to soak the vodka. Shit. Now what am I gonna do?"

"Improvise? You're pretty good at that," he said kissing my arm.

"Real slick," I eyed him, "You don't *improvise* vodka sauce," I said. "Besides which, do you even *have* any vodka?"

"Yea, it's hiding out with the percolator," he said noting my look. "Well, well, look who can't take a joke...I think so, in the bar, *doctor*. I'm sure you can find it."

"What about crushed red pepper?"

"What do I look like?"

"Right now? A guy who doesn't *cook*," I remarked.

A few hours later...

"Where were you?"

"Eating samples. Between this morning and the gym I worked up an appetite. You're not hungry?" Patrick asked as he came around the corner.

I looked at him strangely. "What kind of a question is that? I'm *always* hungry, unlike most people around here."

"Oh, they're hungry- they just don't eat," he joked.

"Anyway, back to business. Did you grab butter and cream? Salted, not unsalted."

"Yep, right here. Two of each, right?"

"Whoah, what are you *doing*?" I turned around, my arms overflowing with boxes of penne.

"Um, I'm *shopping*."

"For what, a football team? Exactly how many pounds of pasta is that?"

"Four. I thought you said 10 to 12 people were coming."

"That just looks like a lot."

"*Clearly* you're not Italian. Are you having a bunch of models over? In *that* case I'll just buy seaweed," I couldn't hold in my laugh.

"They're *guys*."

"Well are they manorexic? *Ugh*," I huffed as he shook his head, "then it's always better to have extra. God forbid there's not enough food, my grandma used to say. That's how Italians roll." I dumped the pasta into the cart and kept moving.
We made it out of the store without being harassed or even noticed, which was a relief, especially on a Saturday, and were back at the house. With bags barely unpacked I set myself on autopilot and got to work. At least I tried to.

"Can you stop messing with that?" Patrick's Bose system was nice I admit, but boys and their toys... He was now in love with his latest toy, satellite radio, and I could hardly pull him away from it.

"I thought you were just unpacking. Besides how the hell can you see what I'm doing from over there? There's a wall between us."

He couldn't see me roll my eyes in response to his dumb question. "*Wall*, huh?" I took out a small bamboo cutting board. "Of *course* I can see you. I can see all the way into your neighbor's fucking kitchen. You *do* realize your entire first floor is one room?" I grabbed a knife from the butcher's block. "Unpacking was supposed to be *your* job- I've got work to do."

"I'm making sure this satellite is hooked up for tonight." He stood up and moseyed over. "I can't wait to listen to Howard Stern whenever I want."

I remember when Howard Stern took that giant leap over to satellite from FM radio back in 2006, a movie critics swore would sink him. But his fans never doubted him, and he led a new revolution- *again*. Free 'streaming' radio online, Pandora, Rhapsody, iTunes...and *then* SiriusXM Satellite. In 2011 nearly everyone had it in their cars and could 'stream' it from home. Patrick had had the old iPod home stereo, which limited you to only the music you had collected by either saving CDs to your computer then putting songs into iTunes or downloading. With satellite, music and sports were both at your fingertips.

"Yeah, just no NESN- I ain't listening to the Red Sox," I said, finely chopping some basil. I watched as he took out the assorted cheeses and put them on the counter alongside the crackers.

"Fine, fine, no Sox."

"Hey, can you get out those two large pots, will ya? Thanks," I winked. "You sure you don't mind Mike coming? He's been going through a lot lately and could use the night out..."

"I told you it's fine, he's cool." He leaned on the counter watching me cut vegetables. "So, *Rambo*, what *else* can I do for you?"

"You could get me a glass of wine."

"Anything *else*?" he asked curiously. "The outdoor candles?"

"Here Martha Stewart," he said rolling his eyes, a glass in hand. "I'll grab those candles. Fenway," he called out over his shoulder, "let's go outside, buddy."

I heard the front door open and shut.

"Hey," a male voice said from around the corner. *That doesn't sound like Mike.* "Where's the party at?" In a flash Kevin was standing in the kitchen, awaiting acknowledgement.

"Oh. I thought you were *Mike*," I said, barely looking up.

"Gee- hello to you, too. Who's Mike?" I made eye contact saucily, tilting my head.

"My *cousin*." I smiled, holding in a laugh. "Did you come early to help?"

As if ignoring me, Kevin made his way towards me. His hug matched his headstrong, egotistical personality. It was forceful and aggressive and could border on inappropriate. There was no doubt Kevin was himself easy on the eyes and underneath his sometimes bullshit exterior was a nice guy.

"What's up, doc? Miss me?" I hesitated, as he pulled back. "That *much*, huh?" he played facetiously. I shook my head, smiling. "Come *on*, how can you resist this?" he pestered.

"You're right, I'm holding myself back."

"Sure you don't wanna trade up? I'm officially off the market. Plus, I won't be half-way across the globe next month like my brother," he winked facetiously.

"Hmm, tempting," I answered, "but I think I'm good."

"Your loss. So, where's the guy who stole you away from me?" I pointed behind him.

"*Stole*, huh?" Patrick had been standing there watching.

"Hey bro, wassup?" Kevin was a master at graceful recoveries.

"*Let* me? Is that how it went? I'm not even gone yet. What happened to what's her name?"

"I forgot."

"I'm guessing she found better fish out in these rough L.A. waters."

"*Hardly*. Got any IPA?"

"I *told* you to stick to brunettes," Patrick said, throwing one arm around me. "I got some out in the fridge," I watched as they made their way out to the patio. It was times like these that really made me miss my brothers. Despite their tendency to get on my nerves (like only brothers can do) I missed them. Suddenly, I heard the doorbell ring.

"Coming!" I shouted, running to the front door. "Ah, *finally-* reinforcements," Mike and I exchanged a solid hug and kiss. "So glad you could come." I had no issues with Patrick's inner circle, but it felt good having family around. Mike was my only family out here and since being in L.A., we'd gotten closer.

His shoulder length hair was pulled back in a ponytail, a few strands of grey poking out through black locks. He had on his trusty *Cujo* t-shirt, jeans and more than likely his actual Converse from the 80s, a style he'd no doubt be able to rock to his grave.

"Shit," I heard from behind, "you kiss *all* your family like that?" Kevin had approached like an unwanted zit. Mike and I both turned around.

"Usually we make out for like three minutes," Mike kidded. "Hey, I'm Mike, Lea's cousin." He stretched out his hand.

"Oh, hey, man, nice to finally meet you. I've heard great things."

"So do you act too or..."

"Not really. Patrick and I are doing a few projects together, got our own production company. Lea said you're on your like 20th comic or novel or something?"

"15th dark comic, 6th novel and, thanks man," he laughed. "I miss being behind the camera. I majored in TV production and music. Unfortunately, that never paid the bills if you know what I mean.

"I hear ya," Kevin added. "Yo, Patrick, Mike's here!" he yelled out back.

"Come out back!" Patrick called. "Help me get the pit going."

It was beautiful evening. The sun was slowly sinking and the deep colors were gorgeous. I had met Colin, Morgan and Steve a couple of times before. The other guys, Paul and Craig were from Patrick's hometown back in Minnesota. And then there was *James*. I mean what L.A. BBQ would be complete without an appearance by a money-hungry, shallow Hollywood agent? James wasn't the worst guy I'd come across, but his presence irked me. He sauntered over as if going in for the kill.

"Patrick was right about you, Eleana, you *are* good. I can't believe you did all this. You sure you didn't hire a party planner?"

I smiled politely. "Thank you. Well if you'll *excuse* me," I said, cutting our conversation short, "I need to check the pasta and I think I hear my phone..." I left and returned five minutes later in hopes James would be on the other side of the house. When I came back out, he was still right where I'd left him. *Damnit.* Lucky for me, the last guest had arrived- and just in time to save the day.

Mike grabbed my arm discreetly, "Psst- is that who I *think* it is?" I nodded. He looked at me, surprised. "Why don't you seem fazed?"

"Well," I explained, "I... we met sort of recently. He's pretty cool."

"Hey, Lea, right? How's it goin'?" He asked, walking over with Patrick. Yes, Adrian Grenier had arrived- and was about to eat my vodka sauce. *Holy Shit, no one would believe me if I told them.*

Mike may have been a horror fanatic, but he'd been a huge fan of *Entourage*. "Oh, sorry, this is my cousin Mike. Mike, Adrian. Adrian, Mike."

"Oh, hey man. So, you visiting or..."

"Nice to meet you. Love the show. I live here." Mike must've picked up a few acting pointers living out here, because right now he was playing it off like Adrian was just another guy.

"Nice, yea, good meeting you, too."

A little over an hour later dinner had finished, bellies were full. Colin and Morgan had left right after dinner while the rest of us kept the party going on the rooftop deck. Mike blended in seamlessly and I'm certain acquired a few new fans in the process. We stood side by side, admiring the killer lit-up view of downtown Los Angeles.

"So," I nudged him with my shoulder, "I'm really glad you came."

"Me, too." He turned back in Patrick's direction.

"What's on your mind?" I asked.

"I was just thinking."

"About what?"

"Patrick's a good guy, with his *shit* together," he hesitated, "ever think about moving here permanently?"

"Not really, right *now*. Not sure I could leave it *all* behind...I don't know how you did it."

"Well for one thing your family's always been closer than mine. Plus, I don't have that many ties back there anymore. This is home now, has been for a long time. I mean, home will always be *home* though. When I first came out here, I was scared shitless- of failing or letting people down, being thought of as a joke; that I might forget everyone and everything about home or be forgotten. You've been out here long enough to see it."

"See what?"

"The emptiness, the illusions and *delusions* of grandeur that embody Los Angeles, the ugly parts people *don't* necessarily see. But it's not so bad once you accept things for what they are- *then* you'll be okay. I think wherever you call home is somewhere you can see yourself being happy in the long run; not because of its palm trees or beaches, its bright city lights or its claim to fame or fortune, but because there's just something or *someone* that makes you whole. This place definitely has its quirks- maybe that's why it suits me; twenty years later the sun still sets on the wrong side; there are no tides or seasons; year after year the smog worsens, the draughts continue, and I *still* can't find a decent slice of pizza." We laughed. "But it's where I feel the most *whole* and at the end of the day."

"But I can't fit in here; I'm not like you," I laughed.

"Lea, you don't *have* to and you're *not* alone- you've got *Patrick-and* me," he added. "You're not so different than I was- you're scared you'll forget everything, or it'll forget you. But that will only happen if you let it. Lea, no matter *where* you are you're only gonna make it as far as you're willing to go, if you're willing to sacrifice things you may have never have thought you'd have to. It's up to you."

"Mike," I smiled, "you're right, on so many levels, but I just don't know..."

"I think one day soon you're gonna have a harder time than you think when it comes to choosing a side," he winked. "I know *I* did." I looked at him strangely. "A coast. No one can do it all, even you cuz." He kissed me gently on the cheek.

"I don't even know where Patrick and I will be a year from now. I keep waiting for the floor to fall out from under me and this all goes away."

"Don't sell yourself short, Lea. He's the lucky one."

"Oooh!" I exclaimed. "Oh my God- you *scared* me. Don't *do* that. Are you following me?"

"I came down to grab some water," Patrick said, sneaking up behind me. "Everything okay?" he asked, immediately concerned.

"Yea, *why*? I was just walking Mike out," I lied. I wondered, if I had to decide on a permanent home, *could* I? Obviously, Patrick had. I shook it off; I'd have to worry about that later...

"What were you talkin' about up there? You looked so serious," He moved a stray hair from my forehead.

"Nothing- family stuff and...you."

"Should I be flattered or scared? I know how your family can be," he murmured.

"How many times do I have to tell you my family is *not* in the mob." I rolled my eyes.

"Somehow I don't believe you," he said, laughing. "Come on, let's go back upstairs."

"You watch too many movies," I said reaching up to kiss him. "Why does everyone always assume all Italians are in the mob?"

"Because they probably are. I should *know*- I'm from New Jersey," Adrian said, he and Steve moseying downstairs. "We're gonna take off. Thanks for a great time. Lea, a pleasure."

"So, what did your cousin *really* have to say?"

"Why is it so important to you anyway?"

"Because it's your *family*. You don't get it." *Apparently not.* "You won half my family over when they first met you- that says something."

"Yea, that I don't know how to hold my liquor," I lowered my head.

"No, I mean you have this warmness about you, this light. I don't have to worry about you. For guys, it's not so easy. I thought your dad was gonna tie me up and question me when I met him."

"He was just fuckin' around. He's all talk- *trust me*." I hit him playfully on his chest., "Mike was just saying how lucky I am."

"Oh please- *I'm* the lucky one." He laid a deep kiss on me and we went back up to the roof.

Chapter 18 ~ Best in Show

Monday, August 22

I had a busy week ahead. I was scheduled to be at *two* shelters *and*, no thanks to Ivan Kolisnyk, I'd also been volunteered to help out with some apparently big fundraiser.

It was almost September and soon I'd be transitioning back to E.S.T. so I had lots to do. Plus, the surprise weekend for Patrick I *still* hadn't finished planning, which was days away. Before long he'd begin filming in Europe and this time, we'd be apart for much longer, which I was *so* not looking forward to. Seeing each other intermittently was trying, but we never went more than one or two months without meeting face to face.

Being apart from someone you cared about was difficult- I knew that all too well from my parents and my own past experience. I'd only seen my ex a handful of times in the four years we dated and it took its toll. Back then the only people who had cell phones were the very wealthy (like Zack Morris), the police and the military. When your boyfriend disappeared for months to another country you couldn't go on Facebook or use your smartphone- you *wrote* letters using *real* pen and paper. Why do I feel like talking about 100 years ago when it was only 1999?

I remember writing him about nearly anything and everything: the sunrise, the sunset, the falling leaves... The XO's, hearts scribbled on envelopes...ya know, all the stupid bullshit you do when you miss someone. 'I love you', 'I miss you', 'I can't wait to see you and hold you again'. 'But I love you *more*', bla, bla, bla. It was a scene right out that *Dear John* movie with Channing Tatum (which I can't believe I even watched but I was drinking...). But I was young and I loved him, and every nine or 10 months I'd see him and it'd all seemed so worth it. But then he'd have to leave again.

So, when all that had finally ended, I vowed never to put myself in that position again because in the end I wasn't so sure it'd been worth it. But almost a decade later, here I was doing the same exact thing. At least I'd stepped up my game- Patrick was honest, independent and successful and despite fame, had remained himself; he wasn't gone all the time and probably the biggest improvement? We were *friends*, something I hadn't exactly had with the last guy.

Past relationships aside, the one thing that I still couldn't bring myself to do, that annoyed me to no end, was being forced to name what Patrick and I were. As if two people couldn't just 'be' and enjoy each other's company. There always had to be some label. Like, are we 'dating', 'seeing each other', are we an 'item', are we 'friends with benefits'? I hated that everyone always wanted to label your relationship *for* you, instead of leaving you the fuck alone. It just made everything more stressful than it needed to be. Maybe it was the fear that labels made you more vulnerable to attack or to falling apart and not having one made it feel like there were less expectations. As opposed to the usual outside interference, urging you to take your relationship to the next level until eventually it seemed everyone was bugging you for a wedding date.

These days with such high divorce rates I was surprised at how much people still felt the need to pressure themselves into the act of marriage, to sign a piece of paper, and for *what*? To prove your loyalty or love? Ask Goldie Hawn and Kurt Russell about that one. I grew up with strong family values, attending church, believing that marriage was not only sacred, but something you just 'did'. At the age of 37 I had been to nearly 20 weddings and although they were beautiful, I always had a hard time connecting. Patrick and I had what we both thought was a decent relationship, but were we going to be together *forever*? Every time I remotely thought about it, I freaked out. He never brought anything up and neither did I.

All summer I had prepared myself mentally for Patrick's departure. A few minor distractions hadn't changed my feelings or my commitment to him. It was gonna be tough, but I was gonna have plenty to keep me occupied. Going home meant getting back into the swing of things at the animal hospital and the bakery, plus you can never escape your family and God knows I had enough of them to keep me busy for an eternity.

Ivan had made quite the name for himself in L.A.'s shelter scene, which had its own Hollywood vibe. Sometimes all it takes is for a few people to spread the good word and these days with social media the good word on Dr. Ivan Kolisnyk was all over L.A., which is how he'd met Tia Torres. Her and her boyfriend had an uncanny ability to rehabilitate and place abused and abandoned dogs, a unique talent that had landed them their own spot on Animal Planet.

Ivan and Tia had met at a rescue event and had instantly hit it off, and their combined efforts had now culminated into Los Angeles' largest ever animal fundraiser. I'd been dumbstruck over the amount of publicity the event had received and the names who'd signed on, including none other than Ellen Degeneres herself, a well-known animal activist herself, which explained how it'd been at all possible to secure such a grand venue as The MacArthur. It'd gotten so much press that it'd practically needed its own planning and zoning committee.

I was excited for the fundraiser (and to dress in true Mardi Gras style, since I'd never actually been to Mardi Gras) and the make-shift dog show that we'd planned, which was of course to only use dogs for adoption. I wondered how many celebrities I'd get to meet at *this* famed event and knowing Ivan, there'd be more than a few on that list.

In the meantime, however, the clock was ticking on my surprise for Patrick. I'd decided on Catalina Island, an obvious choice in my book due to its romantic and secluded setting. Patrick had to be on set on Labor Day which meant we wouldn't have much time to enjoy it but still, I was excited go out with a boom. Now if only I wasn't too late to book the reservation

Part Three:

Chutes and Ladders

"The only easy day was yesterday."

-unknown

Chapter 19 ~ 9 to 5

September 22

I'd been back in Connecticut almost two weeks. Things were beyond busy at the animal clinic and the bakery, which had left me with little time to relax. I'd hit the ground running while simultaneously readjusting to such a quick-paced east coast life. I loved the west coast for its scenery (among other things), but there was just something about coming home that was comforting. The familiar New England landscapes and smells of the tides were a warm welcome and a constant reminder of why I couldn't see myself leaving it behind anytime soon. No matter that most of my family still resided here or that it was where I had spent my whole life- it completed me in a way that no other place could. I could have cared less what part of the world I had yet to see because I knew that it wouldn't matter; nothing could ever compare to a place I'd come to love so much, no matter *what* Mike had tried to stress.

And that's the same way I had felt about Patrick. In many ways, he filled in the missing pieces to my life and so far, no one else had compared to him- or so I'd thought, until a certain person from the past had randomly reappeared. Up until that night my cousin Mike had brought it up, I hadn't really given much thought as to where I wanted to put down permanent roots. I cared a lot about Patrick, and maybe I did love him, but I was still uneasy about the word. I mean it's not like we'd said it aloud or anything. I had a lot to think about, but one thing remained constant- I was dead set on seeing this through; it wasn't going to be like before: all the worrying and wondering about what wouldn't work, where it would go wrong.

My brain had this tendency to go on a track to negativity and doubt, which had in some way always prevented me from moving forward with relationships. And my calling card, my signature move? Never let any guy get too close or see the real me, which would guarantee minimal casualties. I would over-analyzing shit to the point where I basically talked myself out of any decent relationship. And so here I was with Patrick well not now I suppose, since he was out of the country. I was really happy to be home, but Mike *had* been right about one thing- a part of me felt alone because Patrick wasn't here. We'd see each other soon but right now that 'soon' felt like forever.

"Hey."

I turned around. "Oh, hey, I didn't hear you come in."

"I brought you an iced green tea latte, *with* almond milk. They just started carrying that." Maureen's curious face stood in mine.

"Thanks. I needed that."

"Whatcha doin'?"

"Oh, just scrolling through emails." I took the plastic Starbucks cup from her, anxious for a sip. "You, know, when the hell are they gonna start using something *other* than plastic? Don't the landfills have enough?"

"Good point. So, when's your first appointment?"

"2:30. Tully O'Malley has yet another ear infection." Maureen and I had been practically adjoined at the hip since we were down a full-time doctor.

She paused, flipping through some papers. "So...how's life home treatin' you, or retreatin' you, should I say? Have you heard from Patrick? I wonder how London is. Oh, and you never finished telling me about San Diego."

"What else is there to tell? He called the other day. We have a Skype date this week," I smiled shyly.

"*Oohh* a *Skype* date. Sounds thrilling," she winked, "Wonder if he'll ask you to visit while he's there? I'm not sure how all that movie stuff goes," she uttered. "Anyway, about San Diego..."

"What *about* San Diego? There was a conference. Some of our classmates attended. It was a lot of fun." I could tell she was looking for something more. "*What?*"

"*Seriously?* You wanna try to weasel your way outta this one?" "Out of what? The conference?" I huffed at her supposition. "I can't believe..."

"*I* can't believe that he showed up and I had to hear about it from Mac." I froze in a mild panic.

"Hear about *what*? What are you two conspiring behind my back? Oh, now I get it. Patrick's in Europe; I'm here and so is Nate. And now you think...Just what exactly did you *hear* anyway? We *all* had a good time and that's the truth- nothing happened." I caught her eyes roll. "Wait a minute. I thought you *liked* Patrick."

"I do."

"You said he was the perfect guy."

"I did."

"So what's the problem all of a sudden?"

"I don't know it's just...aren't you the *least* bit curious?" She was killing me.

"About..."

She looked at me with doubt. "About what he's doing over there."

I sipped my tea again, huffing. "As long as he keeps in touch I don't see the major issue. Skype's better than you think," I sent her a wink of my own. *Point- me.*

"Not London- I meant over there, as in Jersey." *Of course you did.*

"I know how your mind works. I'm happy, Maureen, so stop prying."

"That's not what I heard."

"What is this middle school? Tattletales, note-passing and rumors?" I collected myself, trying not to seem upset. Maureen was, after all, a great friend and was trying to help- not that I needed it. "Let's hear it."

"It's nothing- just that it was kind of hard not to notice some of the old sparks flying."

I laughed uncontrollably. "*Sparks*? *Flying*? *Seriously*?" *Okay so maybe a few stray embers were still a little hot to the touch.* "Come on. You know what I think? I think everyone had a little too much to drink that weekend and they weren't seeing clearly."

"You know as well as I do Nate ain't hard to forget."
"Neither are a lot of people. We caught up, reminisced about the island days. That's what old friends do, in case you hadn't noticed."
"Oh, I *noticed* alright."
"Noticed what?"

"You." Now she was really annoying me.

"It was a weekend with *friends.* I don't see what the big issue is."

"Figures you wouldn't."

"What the hell is that supposed to mean?"

"It means that despite being so intelligent and wonderful, I can't believe how deaf, dumb and blind you can be."

"I don't what you're talking about and whatever anyone including Mac might've *thought* they were seeing, they were sorely mistaken. Two people catching up over a weekend hardly qualifies as broadcast news. And maybe Mac left out the fact that Nate's with someone."

"So?"

"Why don't you stop worrying about my social life and get one of your own?" *Take that.*

"Oh I *am*, don't worry. Sorry for prying it's just that you really do seem different since last time you were home and I have this weird feeling that it was more than just some strange coincidence."

"I don't see how- you weren't even *there*."

"*So,* does this mean you're attending the New York State Vet Conference with me then?"

My eyes toggled back and forth. "I was planning on it. Why?"

"Good, because Nate's gonna be there- I already checked." *Great. I wasn't ready for part II...*

"Look, it's not that I don't appreciate you lookin' out for me, but everything's fine. I finally feel like I'm right where I'm supposed to be and the last thing I wanna do is screw it up."

"Well if it feels right then you have nothing to worry about. But Mac did say he's lookin' pretty good these days; too bad I'm not in the market for a farm boy myself..."

My eyes squinted reflexively at her comment. How could I argue? As much I had been trying to deny it, Nate *did* look good. More than eight years had passed yet somehow all of us being together again had made it seem almost like no time had passed at all. The truth was those days were fun and we'd had some amazing times, but they were gone. And if it's one thing I've learned over the past decade, you can never get them back; There are no do-overs. I know that because every time I'd tried it never worked out, so why would I think that miraculously the universe would make an exception?

Chapter 20 ~ Ferris Bueller's Day Off

Saturday September 24

"Hello?"

"Miss me?" I joked.

"I *always* miss you," Mac replied matter-of-factly.

"I'm surprised you answered; I thought you'd be at the beach already."

"Oh, I'm getting there- *trust* me. I just have a few things to finish up at the office. Apparently even on an *island* I have work on Saturday. You off today?"

"Yup. I was gonna go apple picking but it's fuckin' 78 degrees." I peered out over my kitchen sink studying the squirrels outside. "I feel like I'm in California, not Connecticut."

"How's E.S.T.?"

"Not bad...except my family, whose already being a pain in my ass," I laughed.

"oh, right- *them*. You've been back what, two weeks? What now?" she asked.

"Oh, everything. You know Italians."

"Do I? They can't keep themselves outta anyone's fuckin' business. Well, if you need a quick getaway, the door's open."

"Thanks. I may take you up on that. Speaking of SGU, how's the term going so far?"

"So far so good. We've got a new large animal surgeon lined up- Dr. Hamburg isn't doing too well."

"Oh, that's too bad. I really miss his classes," I kidded.

"Bullshit. You used to build stacks of pens in the back of class- I even have pics to prove it."

She was right. Large Animal Medicine and Surgery was probably *the* most boring of all our classes, with the exception of that dumb ass ethics class they forced us to take first term. Dr. Hamburg used to read his notes line by line for nearly two hours and none of us ever paid attention. It was the biggest waste of time.

"Okay, you're right, but I still feel bad. Anyway hope he/she works out."

"I'll probably be able to sneak away unnoticed mid-term, so you and I can meet up somewhere. How's the clinic? I bet they missed you."

"Good. Trying to find my groove again. It's harder than I thought switching back from shelter to real-time medicine with needy, pain in the ass clients. Thanks, Ivan."

"I'll say. I didn't see that one coming, even more than Nate. Speaking of which..." *here we go- you, too?* "I heard Nate's lecturing at the New York Conference. You going?"

"I don't know, I *guess*. I had told Maureen I'd go a while back."

"You should go. Maybe it can be another mini reunion..."

"I thought we already did that."

"Since when do we ever get sick of each other?" she asked.

"Oh, *never*," I giggled. "And I thought I'd had enough fun that weekend to last me a while. We had some good times."

"We still do. Anyway, I just meant th..."

"Alright, stop, I know what you're doing," I said, now annoyed.

"What? What am I doing?"

"Sticking your nose where it doesn't belong, like a true Italian. Look, did you and Maureen suddenly forget that I'm dating someone?"

"No, it's..."

"Then stop acting like I need to be doing something I'm not and leave it alone."

"Okay, fine. I will. But just remember one thing."

"What's that?"

"The past is the key to your future."

"What?"

"Isn't that what that fortune teller said?"

"I *knew* I'd regret telling you even one ounce of what she said," I grumbled. "She was wrong. Remember that time the lady said you were gonna have twins in the next year?"

"I *did*. I adopted two cats from the same litter."

"That's not what she meant."

"How *do* you know? Can *you* read fortunes? My point is that you don't need to relive anything, but I'm sure there was a clue in there somewhere. You never know, maybe there's a hidden treasure out there."

"If there is, it's *not* in the past. I'm all about looking forward and for once, it's not so scary."

"Just keep telling yourself that and you'll be fine."

"I *am* fine."

"Alright, let me go, Miss negative. Call me later if you want, although I might be passed out from my sunburn."

"I hate you."

"Did I forget to mention I'm staring at a six pack of Ting right now, ya know, the stuff I'm gonna mix with my vodka later?"

"Now I hate you more."

Chapter 21 ~ Weird Science

"Here, taste this." I reluctantly accepted the spoonful of batter into my mouth."

"Hmmm...smooth, silky, a little tart but I *like* it."

"Okay, *good*. That's what I thought too, but I wanted your opinion. It's the new Limoncello Lava Cake recipe I've been working on." Despite what people may have thought, baking was more of science than anything else. As Italians Rachel and I had been accustomed to a pinch of this or a handful of that when cooking and all-too often recipes were taught from memory, but baking required exact measurements and any alterations had to be carefully thought out and tested. Sometimes I felt like I was working in a laboratory.

"That's different. What are we gonna frost it with, cream?"

"I was thinking maybe that or a meringue or a less sweet Italian meringue buttercream."

"Yum- I could eat an entire bowl of that." She walked into the office and was back in no time, a notepad in hand.

"Better write these ideas down before I forget. We're getting' old, ya know." She laughed, setting the pad on the counter next to the large mixing bowl.

"Don't remind me."

"And damnit, for once I should've listened to my mother and married a millionaire." Her cackle nearly made me over pipe the cupcakes. "I guess I fucked that one up," she added.

"It's never too late to trade up. Besides, I think Tom is worth at *least* a million, right?" I winked playfully. "But I guess you could always find some decrepit, old rich guy who can't walk or get it up."

"Totally. I mean at least I'd be able to afford plastic surgery and that dream beach house I've always wanted. I damn sure ain't got that now. Mahopac is no castle in the sky and if that husband of mine doesn't finish that deck soon I might just consider it," she laughed.

"Ha, ha, ha. True, but at least there's more than there used to be and more importantly, you have me to help keep you insane twice a week."

Rachel jotted down some notes then, clicking her pen continued on, "oh yeah. I'm just glad that your work schedule allows you to. Even with that other doctor out you still make the time." She was right. Luckily Maureen's friend had been able to fill in so we could each get a little leeway. God knows the other two owners of the clinic weren't willing to- yet more bullshit we had to deal with...

The bakery was in Mount Kisco, a small quaint village just south of where Rachael and Tom lived and a little north of where I worked. It wasn't much of a ride for me to get from one to the other and my commute from my apartment wasn't bad either. I continued piping cupcakes until I'd finished the entire tray. I refilled my pastry bag, reassuring Rachel of my commitment.

"Nah, don't even worry about it. I mean we're partners, aren't we? We've only known each other since we were in diapers. And you're not the only one who didn't marry a millionaire. My mother's still bothering me to settle down, vomit..."

"Yeah." She began pouring the liquid egg whites into the stand mixer.

I loved modern baking. Having grown up with hand-held mixers, wooden spoons and whisks, these latest appliances and gadgets could be a Godsend. Kitchen Aids, bread machines, mandolins and vegetable spiralers...the list went on. And now instead of having to separate a million eggs or scrape dozens of vanilla beans people had liquid egg whites and vanilla bean paste at their fingertips. I watched out of the corner of my eye as the mixer did its work, whipping at full speed with ease. That sure beat the hell out of well, hand beating.

"So," I continued, "speaking of that back deck, anything special in store? I know how Tom's creative carpentry mind works."

"Not sure but he did say a part of the design was a surprise. I hope it's a fuckin' hot tub, not that it makes where I live any more desirable." She joked.

"Me, too. Maybe he'll build us a tiki bar."

"Yes! While we're on the significant other subject, how's Patrick?"

"Good- Skyped him yesterday. I don't know, they just started filming so I guess."

Rachel continued adding sugar a little at a time to the egg whites. "Some Bourne movie or something?"

"Tom Clancy. Same author, different series. He's been pretty psyched about it. Apparently they chose him over Ben Affleck *and* Ryan Reynolds."

"Seriously? I guess he really is moving up in the world. I *love* Ryan Reynolds. He's fucking hilarious. So how long is he supposed to be there for?"

"Not sure. They're moving locations a few times, like to Amsterdam which I've been wanting to visit; tentatively another four months. I guess there's a lot of action shooting, etc."

"Wow, that is long. Then again, what the fuck do I know about making movies?"

"No shit. But I think he's able to come to New York over Thanksgiving and we are supposed to spend New Year's together. Of course, that's all tentative, too," I sulked inside.

"Thanksgiving? Where in New York?"

"Remember I told you he's from upstate? Rhinebeck."

"No shit," she commented, looking up momentarily in thought. "So like, you might meet some more of the family then? What's your family doing this year? I think we're going to my dad's."

"Yup. Don't remind me- I'm already nervous and it's not even *close* to Thanksgiving yet."

"Why are you so worried? It's not like you haven't met any of his family before *and* it's not like you haven't done the long-distance thing before."

"I know. I'll just try my best not to think about it too much and stay busy."

"Yup. Speaking of hotties...Oh shit. Damn I'm not even paying attention. Don't wanna overwhip these," she said, removing the stainless-steel bowl from the mixing stand and placing it to the side. "So, what were you saying?"

"Oh, nothing. I was just wondering if you ever heard from what's his name." Her look was more than obvious.

"What's his name, hmm. Now we're calling him 'what's his name'? Go on, you can say it," I pressed, curious to hear now *her* input on my love life.

"Okay, I will. *Nate.*" I stood silent. "So...have you heard from him?"

"*No,* why would I?"

"Oh I don't know, maybe because you said you exchanged numbers and now you're...home."

"So what if we did? That doesn't mean he's calling me and I'm not calling him- I got enough shit on my plate."

"There's always room for more. You're *Italian*- you know that."

"Whatever. I'm already stressed out as it is with the guy I'm *actually* dating."

"You're classmates- it wouldn't be that awkward." *Says who?* "Didn't he wanna do lunch or something when you got back here?" I was beginning to wish I hadn't had so many close friends- this shit was getting repetitive.

"That was just friendly chatter. People say that shit all the time, it doesn't mean it ever happens. But maybe at some point, yeah, I'll see him."

"What's the harm?" *Unless you're making it a bigger deal than it actually is...*"

"I'm not- everyone *else* is."

"Like who?"

"Oh the usual- Maureen, Mac and Jeanine. It's annoying it what it is."

"That's because Nate isn't just anyone else."

"Fine, but they need to get over it- *I* did, not that there was really anything to get over..."

Her stare pierced me with attitude only a New Yorker could deliver. "You *sure* about that?"

"*Yes*, I'm sure. Come on, Rach, what is this *13 Going on 30*? It's been *eight* years. I've moved on. Like I did with dickhead and Nate? I mean it was great to see him, but..."

"Yeah, but what if people *can* change? You certainly have, for the better of course."

"Right, I can make a better buttercream and do surgery more effectively," I countered.

"You know what I mean. Nate is nothing like dickhead- he never was and you said it yourself- he's a great guy."

"That was never the issue. It was...everything else, which is best left back on the island where it belongs. Seriously, it's all good."

"I guess so, but maybe they were just looking out for you ya know, in case maybe this thing with Patrick doesn't work out. Like maybe they were thinking what I kinda thought this summer."

"Spit it out."

"That maybe for the first time in your life, the timing with a guy you care about is spot on. You gotta admit it's a little weird."

"Honestly? Beats the shit out of me. Anyway, I don't need to call Nate because apparently he's gonna be at that conference next month." My cheesy grin appeared.

"What?" *Exactly.*

Chapter 22 ~ Ghostbusters

October

I looked out the window as the train passed Orchard Park in the Pelham section of the Bronx, where the scenery began its transformation to the familiar cityscape of New York City. Houses and condos morphed into narrow brick townhouses and tall apartment complexes. Front yards shrunk to a patch of grass before disappearing altogether, leaving only paved paths along busy city streets and subway signs. I was headed into the city for the New York Veterinary Conference. Maureen and I had taken separate trains into Grand Central Station and had planned to meet up with the others after.

Before I knew it, I had arrived. I walked quickly onto the platform along with the hundreds of other commuters and headed into Grand Central's main hub. A work of art and historical landmark of its own, Grand Central Station was a sight to see and I was in awe every time I set foot inside it. Looking around, it was obvious how some things never changed: thousands of curious tourists gazing up at its notoriously decorated fresca of constellations and stars; commuters coming and going; couples on a day out in The Big Apple.

Other things *had* changed, though. Metro-North Railroad cops had been replaced by stricter police patrol, along with the occasional bomb-sniffing canine. Men and women in military garb now carried rifles, a sure sign of the times. Less than a month ago had been the 10-year anniversary of the 9/11 attacks and not only had security measures tightened all over the United States, no one had forgotten, including the city that had endured the brunt of it all.

I remember it well- it was Tuesday, September 11th, 2001. I was in Grenada beginning my second year of veterinary school. We'd been out drinking the night before and I'd been so hungover I'd felt like I was gonna die. I had survived just fine, but nearly 3000 innocents had not, no thanks to the then newly emergent, evil group of brainwashed assholes known as Al-Qaeda.

They say tragedies bring you closer and make you stronger and I believe that, but this evil act of terrorism was to date the worst the world had ever seen and those affected were forever traumatized, their worlds torn apart, without the culprits being punished. Ever since that day the people of New York City had been different. It'd reminded me of *Ghostbusters*: the dead rising from their graves, buildings up in smoke, panic everywhere, complete mass hysteria. Only John Venkman and Egon couldn't fix it and shit certainly hadn't been as 'simple' as roasting a God from another dimension masquerading as a marshmallow the size of *Godzilla*.

My roommates and I hadn't had a TV, but we'd heard it on BBC Radio. Thankfully, I hadn't witnessed anything live. To this day I refused to watch any footage of that horrific day- the pain and gut-wrenching feeling, even from the Caribbean, was still too much to bear and I hadn't even known a single person directly who'd been affected. I wasn't sure I could bring myself to visit the site of where the Twin Towers used to be, aka 'Ground Zero', where they had begun construction of what was to be deemed 'The Freedom Tower', set to open in 2013.

Years had passed and the people of New York City and its surrounding counties in New York, New Jersey and Connecticut had learned to move on and 'Never Forget' those who had died or given their lives for others, a motto that would stick forever. The sadness would always remain and the anger would fuel everyone's passion to keep The United States of America the safest and best place in the world to be – The Freedom Tower was to be a symbol of that commitment for the entire country and the world to see.

I made my way to the information booth and waited for Maureen. I checked the subway schedule as I watched hundreds of people hustle around me. Then my phone rang.

"Hey. Where are you?"

"Standing at the info booth. I'm in a red shirt."

"Be there in a minute."

"Hurry up, I need more coffee." I spotted Maureen coming out of Track 21 and waved to get her attention.

After acquiring our much-needed caffeine fix we headed downstairs to the subway and were at our destination in less than 15 minutes. We exited the 34th street-Hudson Yards subway station and walked three blocks. The Javits Center was huge. I had only been there once for the New York City Car Show years ago with my dad and brothers. Once inside, we registered and put on our badges then looked to see where our first lecture was.

"What are you doing?" she asked me.

"First, I'm trying to figure this map out. I can do surgery, but I can't find a room. Second, I'm looking for Dana. She said she was coming."

"Oh, right. I don't see her yet. Did you text her?"

"Just did. No answer yet."

"Maybe she's in the subway- shotty service, ya know?"

"True. I just told her to meet us at the Purina booth. That's always easy to find."

"Oh, okay. Good idea. I'll be right back. If I see Dana I'll let you know," she said.

"Alright, I'll wait here. We've got some time to kill anyway." I watched as people lined up to register then wander to the exhibit hall. As I walked over to throw out my coffee cup I noticed a few men gathered by one of the two long breakfast buffet tables. I couldn't hear their conversation, but they looked like veterinarians and as I got closer, I recognized not one, but *two* of them.

"Dr, Matthews?" They all stopped and stared at me. "Sorry to interrupt but..."

"*Justin*, please. How many times do I have to tell you, Eleana?" Justin Matthews was one of the best internists around and he wasn't bad looking, either. Hardly taller than me, he had always reminded me of Noah Wylie on *E.R.* His demeanor was calm and professional, and he didn't have a mean bone in his body. I had had the pleasure of referring patients to him for the past five years. He had an excellent reputation in the New York Tri-State area and I was fortunate to know him.

"Okay, *Justin*." I smiled before hugging him briefly. The man standing immediately to his left seemed more surprised to see me than Justin had been.

"Wait," he interrupted, "you two *know* each other?" The look on Nate's face was almost priceless. He'd been standing there in awe, watching Justin and I exchange words, impatiently awaiting an acknowledgement. "And you, why didn't you tell me you were coming?"

I shrugged my shoulders. "Hi to you, too. And I didn't realize I had to. Besides I've been a little busy ya know, *working*."

"Okay, I guess that's fair," he winked. "When did you get back?"

"Last month. And I've known Justin what, five years?" I turned to Justin.

"Six, maybe," he answered. "How about you two?"

"Vet school," I said.

"Oh, didn't realize."

"What about *you* guys?" I asked, turning back to Nate. "I thought you worked in New Jersey?"

"Yea, but I interned with him." He turned to the other gentleman on his left, "I'm sorry- this is Paul. We work together."

I held out my hand, "Oh, hi, Paul. I'm Eleana. Nice to meet you." He returned the sentiment.

"So, are you here alone?" Nate asked.

"Ah, no, actually. Maureen should be...*Oh*, there she is." I waved her over. "Hey! Over here!" My phone buzzed. "And that would be Dana. She just got here." Maureen walked briskly to where we were standing.

"Hey, there you are. Nate- is that *you*? I was wondering if we were gonna see you." His face looked surprised again.

"How have you been? You guys work at the same place?"

"Yes, actually technically we're part owners, a small part, but still." I could see Maureen was showing off a bit, probably because she'd seen Justin. "Oh hey, Justin." *What a flirt. Wait- Justin?*

"Hopefully they'll offer more at some point before they retire or die, whichever comes first," she laughed it off as I shook my head.

"Hey, Maureen," Justin answered back. "Well I hate to cut this short, but I better go set up for my lecture. Staying the whole day?"

"Pretty much," she said anxiously. "Anyone up for drinks after?"

"Um, sure, sounds great."

"Yea, I'm in. Paul?" Paul nodded. "Cool. I'll text you later," Nate said to us.

"Sounds like a plan," Justin said just before slipping away. Just then I heard her.

"Fuckin' trains," Dana exclaimed, storming over.

"Hey Jersey, glad you could make it," I smiled.

"Yea, right. It's only 8:09 and I'm already fuckin' annoyed. Is there any Jameson for my coffee?" She pointed to her cup. They looked at her, perplexed.

Those of us who knew Dana well were amused, while those who didn't, including the group of innocent onlookers she'd nearly plowed over, were less than impressed. To me it was normal, and everyone knew the difficulty I had keeping my own mouth in check. Not that Dana couldn't control herself- she just hadn't thought before speaking.

"Yea, I made it," she continued ranting, "I swear sometimes I hate public transportation. I feel sorry for people who do this every day. Oh, hey, Peterson," she said, finally noticing Nate, "good to see you. How's it going?"

"Hey Dana," he smiled. "Not bad. Just about to check out Justin's lecture before my own."

"Cool. What are you talking about?"

"Oh, just some shit on respiratory disease."

"Nice. Well, we'll see you later maybe?"

"Definitely." We waved goodbye as Nate and Paul walked away.

"Hey, what happened to the *other* Jersey? I thought she was gonna try to come."

"*Try* being the operative word. Never heard back. Maybe she'll still make it- you know how she is- work, work, work. That shelter medicine can be a real *bitch*."

"Totally," I agreed, "well I hope she makes it later. I know she's not far and it's been too long. I really want to see her."

We were talking about another of our classmates, Sharon. Our class had been tight in vet school. When we'd started there'd been only

40 of us but with dropouts and transfers, we'd become an even smaller group and those who remained had gotten even closer. Few of us rarely ever saw each other at conferences. The last time a group of us had been in NYC was for graduation. It was sort of like *The Muppets* when they'd invaded Manhattan...a bunch of misfits who'd met on an island of misfit toys, roaming the streets of New York.

"Yea, me, too. I'll text her in a few hours and see what's up."

"Good," Maureen added. "Alright ladies, ready to learn or at least *act* like we wanna learn?"

Chapter 23 ~ Boomerang

"How the hell is it 4:00 already?"

"I don't know, Camioni, but I'm ready for happy hour. I don't remember the last time I was even *at* a happy hour." The bothered expression on Sharon's face was obvious.

"I don't think if I've *ever*," I said.

"How the fuck can we when we work all the time?" I was pumped Sharon had been able to make the afternoon sessions. We were headed to the exhibit hall to meet up with Dana and Maureen. The time seemed to pass quickly. After they showed up we walked the hall bullshitting while we waited to hear.

"Anything yet?" Dana asked. I checked my phone reluctantly.

"Nope." I wasn't gonna lie. I'd been half-hoping Nate would forget and blow us off. This whole thing had given me the willies, ever since San Diego. I didn't like being caught off guard or the fact that seeing him had disrupted my happy little life.

"It's after five," Sharon mentioned, gazing at her watch.

"Well, I say we text him or you, Lea, *you* text him that we're grabbing drinks and they can meet up with us. I'm too thirsty to wait." Dana had a point.

I found Nate's number and sent him a text, "So, anyone have any idea what's around here?"

"There's a bunch, a couple blocks from here."

In less than twenty minutes we were at Scallywag's, drinks in hand. It was after 6:00 and still nothing from Nate. I'd be fine, I told myself. I wasn't even sure what the hell I was making a big deal about. We were friends. Any other bullshit from the past had been said and done, there was nothing left to unravel.

"Man, this really makes me miss Grenada," Dana said, finishing her beer. "Who's ready for another round?"

"Not me," I answered, "I'm pacing myself."

"What are you slowin' down in your old age Camioni?" Dana asked. "I'm Irish- these go down like water." She looked around. "Anyone else?" I felt my phone buzz. *Of course, the one time I wish for a guy NOT to call me...*

"On second thought, I'll have a dirty vodka martini no olives," I said.

Just then in walked Nate, along with Justin, Paul and another guy I didn't recognize. They were checking out the scene, eyes on every lady in their path. Guys were so obvious. Taken or not, they couldn't help but stare. Without even noticing us they bee-lined it to the bar.

"Think they saw us?" Sharon asked, smiling. "Should we wave them over?

"Nah, they look like they're having *way* too much fun," Dana pointed out. Their attention was fixed on a small group of twenty-somethings who clearly weren't giving them the time of day.

"Yeah right," I snickered, "Oh wait, they just saw us. Dana, see if you can snag that high top next to us- they're leaving." Hands now full, the guys joined us.

"What's up, ladies?" Nate's smooth tone drowned out the noise around us. "You guys know Paul and Justin. And this is Ted- he works at the VCA in midtown." We exchanged hellos. "Ted just moved here, one of the new ophthalmologists."

"Cool, cool. So how you liking New York so far?" I asked politely.

"I mean it's *different* from Nashville," he answered in his twang, "but I like it." Ted was an attractive guy with a genuine aura about him. Of course, most guys from the south or Midwest were like that. I remember meeting the guys in our veterinary class: Kansas, Texas, Florida, Nevada...and thinking there was something wrong with them, that they had to be faking the smiles and the charm- but they weren't. I guess they were just bred like that.

I smiled at him. Ted's blonde, almost sandy strawberry curls accented his strong features. *Another farmer's son, I bet.*

"Well, nice to meet you ladies. So all y'all work around here?"

"New Jersey, Westchester and Connecticut."

"So, what did you guys think of the conference? Pretty good, huh?"

I noticed Maureen checking out Justin from across the table. "Me, too. Justin, your lecture on pyelonephritis was great," she flirted. *Since when the fuck is pyelonephritis great??*

He thanked her passively, sipping his beer. Justin had a reputation of not only being a phenomenal clinician but a ladies' man, *ladies* being the operative word. He was a great guy, but that was a game I just didn't play. I'd never be a fan of 'open' or 'noncommittal' relationships, at least not in this lifetime. I was a one-guy-at-a-time kind of gal and I wanted a guy who thought the same.

I tried to warn Maureen about Justin, but she didn't want to hear it; as nice a guy as he was his newly found, quasi-celebrity status in the veterinary community had gone just a little bit to his head.

"Yeah," Sharon interjected, attempting to break up the monotony of medical talk, "I got some good tips, thanks. Anyone coming tomorrow?"

"Probably not," I said, "I'll be at the bakery." I saw the guys' heads whip around.

"*Really*." I saw Nate lean closer from the corner of my eye as his colleague spoke, "aren't you a vet?"

"Among other things, yeah."

"You don't give yourself enough credit," Dana said, looking around the table before looking back at me.

"She's right." Maureen backed her up, "doctor, baker, writer, volunteer…"

"Don't forget therapist."

As much as none of us ever wanted to talk about work in a social setting, it was nice to be around people who understood the job. I mean you just couldn't go out with your regular friends and say, 'I had to stay late again because this dog relapsed from IMHA because the stupid owner decided to take her off her meds and suddenly it's an emergency, after the owner noticed she'd been nearly moribund for 72 hours'. First you gotta say what IMHA is (immune-mediated hemolytic anemia), like five times, *then* you have to explain *why* the dog is so pale she could be Casper the friendly ghost and why a simple PCV (packed red cell volume) *isn't* sufficient, and *then* you have to try not to sound so heartless when you complain about the owner not following your instructions- *again*. See what I mean?

Patrick was a great listener and easy to talk to, but I couldn't really ever talk to him about work stuff. As much as I had sworn off dating any medical doctor of *any* kind, I had to admit that not having to spell things out around colleagues was pretty awesome.

"Fuckin' right on with that shit," Sharon said, speaking for everyone.

"So," Nate asked, "baking?" Why Nate had suddenly shown interest in my work I had no idea. And where is this place anyway?"

Maureen nearly jumped out of her seat to answer for me, "Mount Kisco."

"No shit," he said. "What's the name of it?" Justin asked.
"Simply Irresistible."

Sharon intervened, setting her glass down, "I hate to change the subject but anyone ready to skip out after this round and grab some food? I'm starving."

"So, Justin," Maureen asked, "tell me more about this 'new' place? You didn't finish earlier." Doe-eyed and sexy, she was laying it on think, alright. Not that she had to right now- he was clearly interested.

"Oh well, I'd been thinking about doing my own thing for a while, breaking away from the corporate chains, so I could finally do things my way..."

"I hear that, brother." Nate held up his glass to toast.

"Where? Down here?" *More doe eyes...yak.*

"Westchester. Just a few logistics to work out so shouldn't be much longer."

"Whoah, *wait* a minute," I interjected. "You mean you already *have* a place? Why didn't we know about it?" He shrugged. Just then Justin and Nate exchanged looks.

"Don't worry, I will. It'll be public real soon. In fact, you guys are some of the first to know."

Justin Matthews was what I liked to call 'good people', a man out for animal kind rather than his own fortune. His talents lied far beyond internal medicine and it was because of that that he was so sought after *and* admired. People like him were way too good for corporations, abused just like any of us often were, so I was glad he was escaping their clutches. Plus, I wasn't the only one sick and tired of corporate referral hospitals and their declining quality of care, compassion or general lack of professional courtesy and so privately-owned facilities were a huge welcome.

"Okay, so..." Sharon continued, questioning Justin, "MRI, the works?"

"The whole nine yards," he said.

"That's cool. I'm glad we've got Oradell and Atlantic Coast Specialists- I fucking *hate* VCA."

"I'm sure it'll be *great*- can't wait to see it." Maureen then excused herself to the bathroom. I couldn't help myself- I just had to know what was going on here.

"So," I continued as he sat there unsuspectingly, "how's the dating scene lately?"

He cautiously answered, unaware of my probing, "you mean do I *know* anyone?" He laughed, lowering his voice, "because I may know of a few eligible bachelors, ah hem." It was hard to miss the utter look of annoyance on my face. *Seriously?*

"*Seriously*, Justin?" I lowered my own voice to a whisper. "What are you talking about? He's not single and neither am *I*."

Justin got closer, "yeah, but no one likes her. I'm not really sure how much *he* even likes her," he laughed again.

I smirked at him, "A-*who's* asking you and B- *why* do I care? I was asking about *you*."

"Oh, my bad, I guess I just like keeping my options open."
Clearly

"Well that's not for everyone, Justin. I was wondering about Maureen, or couldn't you tell how into you she is?"

"You *sure*? Okay, but I wasn't kidding. Who knows, maybe that hot shot boyfriend of yours will decide to run off with one of his costars and you'll change your mind..." My eyes seared through him like a laser. "Okay, kidding, kidding. Anyway, *really*?"

"Watch it, Matthews. It's one thing to have fun but burn my friend and I burn *you*," I poked him facetiously. "I may not be so dead set on settling down but girls like Maureen *are*."

"Yeah, I always liked that about you."

I answered playfully, "shut up."

"Like what?" *And she's back. Shit.* I kept my cool, pretending to talk shop.

"Her ability to work up a case so thoroughly. *Phew.*

"Oh," she said. *And the doe eyes are back, too apparently.*

"Whelp, this air's getting a little thick for me, what with the pheromones and all so I think I'm gonna step outside for a minute"- and throw up- "Be right back."

I excused myself and exited the bar. Just then I noticed two messages on my phone. The first was from Patrick saying hello in his sexy-as-hell voice and he'd try to call again tomorrow. I grinned to myself all smitten, sending him a quick text back filled with a smiley face. The second was from Mac. Her message instantly wiped the grin off my face. Halfway through it I froze, blocking out most of what she'd said. It felt as though something had come of out thin air and whacked me in the head senseless only *this* time, it had nothing to do with Nate.

Chapter 24 ~ The Truth about Cats and Dogs

Two Days Later

The news about Evan hit us all hard. Anything could spiral into a shit-show of hearsay these days, especially with social media; tales so tall it could be hard to discern fact from fiction- which movie star robbed a bank, had cancer or died in a car crash. But even normal people could have their lives nearly destroyed by 'home-brewed', tabloid bullshit, drama stirred up to create chaos or seek fame. Hollywood folks weren't the only ones vulnerable to the shortcomings and pitfalls of the real world and what had happened to Evan *had* been real, as much as we all wished and hoped for it not to.

I'd prayed what I'd heard had been wrong, that it'd been some kind of mistake, but it hadn't. Mac hadn't known details, just that he'd been found unconscious and couldn't be revived. It was like she was talking about someone I didn't even know, some stranger, like I'd been reading about yet another *'True Hollywood Story'*.

So far the 2000's had been one banner of a decade, beginning with the 9/11 attacks in 2001, of course. In the past five years we'd lost some major stars, all from drug overdoses (intentional or not) and all *way* before their time: Michael Jackson (2009), Heath Ledger, Anna Nicole Smith...the list went on...but one had been tough for me. Corey Haim was only 38 when he died, just two years older than me at the time. After all he'd been through (which wouldn't be publicly known until much later) he'd tried to make comebacks, even teaming up with his longtime costar and friend Corey Feldman, but he eventually lost his battle. In the years ahead, we would also lose Whitney Houston, Prince, Scott Weiland (Stone Temple Pilots) and Chris Cornell (Soundgarden, Audioslave), all to drug addiction. It just wasn't fair. Corey Haim was only one of many who unsuccessfully overcame their demons, breaking millions of hearts like mine because he could have and would have been able to accomplish so much more had he only been able to win.

In many ways Evan was no different in some ways- extremely talented, a dedicated veterinarian who loved his job. We had just seen him less than three months ago and he'd seemed great. His job was going well. He even talked about partnering with one of his buddies and a TV show. But maybe he'd had us all fooled. One thing was certain-depression and addiction were not only common in the veterinary field, but were on the rise, a fact few people knew.

Veterinarians kill themselves at four times the rate of the general population which is twice as much as all other medical professionals. We also have the second highest rate of alcoholism. Some think it's because the amount of debt we come out of school with (which now averages over $250,000), but that's not the real reason. Many of us choose this profession driven by an unrealistic, perfectionistic ideal that leads to compassion fatigue, hopelessness and depression. Remember when I mentioned future major deaths? Well, I left a key one out- Dr. Sophia Yin: renown veterinarian, animal lover, behaviorist and pioneer. Thought to be happy and fulfilled, she'd fooled everyone, too. I often wondered if physicians ever killed themselves over losing patients or not being able to fix someone. They definitely never have to kill anything or make decisions for people. Can you imagine if they did? Think all we do is vaccinate and play with fuzzy animals? Think *again*. This is the *real* truth about veterinary medicine.

But none of us really believed that Evan wanted to leave this planet, at least not without saving another 1000 animals or banging another hundred chicks. His mission was far from over and his life far from complete. I wished I could go back in time to San Diego, talk to him, see if I could have done anything to prevent what happened (There goes that guilt and unrealistic ideal again...), but I know no one could have. I hadn't known anyone who had committed suicide or overdosed, at least not up to this point in my life and I wondered if I had just been that lucky.

"So, have you talked to anyone else?"

"No, only Mac and Maureen," I hesitated. I could sense the sadness in Dana's voice.

"I just got off the phone with Alex. This fuckin' sucks, man."

"I know. I can't even believe it."

"And we still don't know what happened?"

"Not the whole story, no." Part of me didn't really wanna know. Mysterious deaths, I thought, sometimes put me at ease. Other times the not-knowing was worse.

"I personally think there's no way he'd..."

"I know, me, too. I just wish...well you know."

"Yeah, I know. If you wanna meet up for dinner let me know. I'll make the time, McSorley."

"Absolutely- he deserves a toast."

"Or seven," I answered.

"Man, I miss already."

"Me, too." I hung up, feeling sad. A little curve of a smile crept up the side of my mouth and I looked up. "Miss you, man."

Chapter 25 ~ Sleepy Hollow

The next week was tough. Normally work was a great distractor, but I had just lost one of my friends and it was hard for me to concentrate, so I tried another strategy. I didn't care what pain in the ass client or problem came my way, I jumped at any chance for a challenge, just to get my mind off of things. Fall was beginning to take over full force and with Halloween just around the corner it never failed- full moon or not, the crazies began to come out and for some reason they liked to gravitate towards veterinary hospitals.

I'd been talking (or in this case, listening to bullshit) to the same client for more than 15 minutes and at any moment my head was going to explode.

"*God.*" I hung up, irritated as all hell. My technician Pam was standing before me with several charts in her arms. She giggled, containing herself.

"What now? Let me guess- another satisfied customer."

"Nope- Pookie's owner just got through all the magical online shit she found to cure her Cushing's disease. "

"Seriously, if I had a dollar for every 'cure' these people find on the internet..." She shook her head in agreement, placing the charts on my desk.

"When are they ever gonna learn- *no* one can work magic, even us. If we could we'd be rich *and* famous. Are those for me?" I frowned.

Pam nodded, "Speaking of famous- I think someone called for you, a *guy*." She winked. I didn't exactly go around telling people who I was dating. Most who worked here knew to keep their mouth shut or they'd be answering to me.

Hmmm... *Patrick wouldn't call me here- weird.* "Oh, okay, I'll grab the message after. Thanks."

I focused my attention back on the charts. There were some things that needed long explanations, or 'special needs' clients who always had a million questions. Mrs. Johnson didn't understand her cat's high blood pressure. Mr. Kramer couldn't grasp that *both* eyes needed glaucoma drops *twice* daily, *forever*, or Precious would be permanently blind. Mr. Knight wanted to know *again*, why we were scheduling an abdominal ultrasound for his dog and last but not least, my brother had called me twice to remind me he needed more heartworm meds for his dogs.

What the fuck. It was a never-ending circle of what felt like at times (or most of the time, actually) the same conversations about the same shit. And I know it's part of the job, but sometimes I just didn't wanna deal- with *any* of it. I went to go check the message board. If there had been a message from Patrick, I didn't see one, so I popped by reception.

"Leaving Dr. Camioni?"

I smiled at our new receptionist, shaking my head 'no'. She was looking down at some paperwork. "I *wish*. I don't know why I save the worst call for last sometimes. I gotta stop doing that. Anyway, Pam said someone called for me, but I don't see any message."

She immediately searched through her papers. "I had it right here. Wasn't sure if it was a new drug rep or...oh, *here* it is," she said, handing me the note. "He insisted it wasn't urgent and not to bother you." *Probably Patrick.* "Sounded real *cute*, too," she winked. *Definitely Patrick.*

I took the piece of paper, "no worries." Looking down, my smile flattened. *Or not.*

After finishing my calls I dialed the number, anxiously tapping my fingers on the desk.

"Hey. Uh, what's up? Something wrong? Why didn't you call my cell?"

"Miss me already, huh Camioni?"

"Dream *on*," I remarked.

"Definitely missed me." God he irritated me sometimes. "I did try your cell- *twice*. You didn't answer. You gave me your business card, remember?"

"Oh." I looked at my phone. "Shit- I forgot to plug it in- it's dead." I heard him snickering. "I wonder who else's calls I missed," I said under my breath.

"You mean, Mr. Perfect?"

"Funny, Peterson. Why were you bothering me again?"

"Actually, it's part business, part personal."

"Meaning?"

"Well to be honest, I haven't exactly had the best week, ya know, after everything. I've been trying to keep busy but...I don't know. I just can't shake it...it just sucks. Anyway," he continued, "I was wondering if maybe you wanted to grab a drink."

"Feeling lonely Peterson? Where's your woman?"

"Around," he answered. *Why do guys always have to be evasive?*

"*Around*? What is she a tree? And what about your friends?"

"It means she wouldn't understand. And I've been living here almost two years- of *course* I have friends but it's just not the same. They're not...us. You're the only one from our class that I really know around here- well. You know me."

"Oh," I smiled, dipping my head, partly shaken. I was beginning to sound like a martini, the kind of martini I suddenly wished I *didn't* like.

"Well, sort of. So, you're not flattered? I mean I *do* have chicks lined up outside my door so..."

"Uh huh, sure."

"Sure, you'll come for a drink or..."

"That depends."

"On..."

"On when you wanna meet up. I've got a pretty packed schedule."

"How about this weekend?"

"I'm working."

"At the clinic?"

"No, the bakery."

"Can't someone else make cupcakes?"

"Hilarious. Let me see what I can do. We make more than fuckin' cupcakes."

"I'd love to see your bakery, since you brought it up." *I did?* "And while I was up there I thought I'd give you a tour of the new place." *What?*

"It's already built? Wait a minute," I paused. "Are you telling me...he asked you to *work* for him, didn't he?" I could feel his egotism through the phone. His silence answered my question. "How come you didn't say anything last week?"

"The final contracts aren't signed."

"Oh, that's um...that's...congratulations, that's great. So where is it anyway? And how do you know where my bakery is?"

"I got that card, too."

"From who?"

"Justin."

"Justin?"

"Maureen." *Of course.* Apparently, they *had* hit it off."

"Oh. I'll let you know."

"Sounds good to me." We ended our conversation and when I'd hung up I got an eerie feeling. Maybe it was because it was nearing Halloween. Or maybe it was something else entirely.

Later that evening...

"I don't know why you're feeling guilty- you haven't done anything."

"I *know* but for some reason it feels like I have." I sipped my drink. It was cool and refreshing and just what I needed after the week I'd been through.

The crowd at The Palm was a mix this cool October evening. Still winding down from happy hour, we'd snagged two seats at the bar. One of our friends worked here and so every now and then we liked to stop by. Plus they had amazing fried zucchini.

"So," she continued, "what time are we meeting tomorrow?"

"I don't know. Does three sound good? I told Rachel I'd work. Plus, Nate wanted to check out the bakery. I told him it was not on the way to the hospital, but he insisted."

"You didn't tell me that," she said, browsing over the drink list.

"You didn't tell me about *Justin*, either." *Ha.*

"What's there to tell? We're just hanging out," she answered nonchalantly.

"*Hanging* out, huh?"

"Yeah, I'm taking it slow for once."

"I didn't realize that word was in your vocabulary."

"Huh?! How dare you!" She burst out laughing, scaring the two older gentlemen to our left. "My Jewish mother raised me well."

"Yeah? If only she could see you now."

"Don't change the subject. So, Nate has a sudden interest in bakeries?"

"Oh, it's back to me. Who's changing the subject now?" I sneered at her, "I don't fucking know- maybe he likes dessert." Meanwhile she was the one who had something juicy going on. I'd have to find out more later. "It isn't a date; it's business. Plus, you know how close he was with Evan in school; he's just feeling a little lost this week, like the rest of us. You can't blame him for wanted to preoccupy himself."

"I guess I can't argue with that."

Two Days Later

"I didn't realize Sleepy Hollow was a real place."

"Seriously? What did you grow up in a cornfield?" I was enjoying hearing Maureen mock Nate.

"I *am* from Iowa," he answered in his usual midwestern drawl. She smiled at him from the back seat, a hint of incredulity in her voice. "I saw the movie."

"Actually," I continued, staring out the passenger seat window, "It used to be called North Tarrytown. They didn't change it to Sleepy Hollow until the 1990s."

Maureen jumped up from her seat. "I didn't know that."

I turned around and smiled, "that's because you're from Long Island." She deserved the poking. After all, she'd practically shoved me into the front seat. As if Nate and I needed any more bonding. Nate had come to the bakery as planned. From there we'd met up with Maureen and were now on our way to the hospital. Sleepy Hollow was located just 30 miles north of New York City, nestled along the east bank of the Hudson River. It was an historic area. Just south was Irvington, named after the noted American author and biographer Washington Irving, famed author of *The Legend of Sleepy Hollow*.

I was anxious to get a tour of the building and to get out of the car. I shut the door, immediately stepping back surprised and impressed by what I saw. It was part historic, part modern and whoever had renovated it had done an amazing job. It wasn't easy blending centuries-old with the new. Some of these once farming communities had turned industrial, from corsets to trains to cars, but factories had long since closed and many remained abandoned until someone came along with enough money to restore them. And Justin and his team had done just that.

"Holy shit. I didn't expect it to look that *that*."

"Wait until you see inside." He led us around back. We could see the river from where we were standing. Wow *was* right.

"Hey guys!" Justin turned his attention quickly to Maureen, smiling. "Hey, Maureen." My eyes couldn't help but roll themselves at the pep in Justin's voice or the obvious pleasurable response to his comment.

"Justin this place is beyond...*awesome*," she said. We followed him down the hall.

"How big did you say this place is again?" I was lost already.

"About 12,000 ft2, not including the basement. Here we have the main treatment area- six treatment tables, three triage stations, two dental suites..." he led us around the massive room.

I interrupted him, "my fuckin' dentist doesn't even have a dental suite as nice as that."

"Right?" he continued his tour, "we've got seven exam rooms and two consultation rooms."

"Plus, two diagnostic lab/ultrasound suites, one's for me, right buddy?" We stopped when we reached the reception area. Maureen and I looked at each other and chuckled.

"What?" Nate's hand was now on my arm. "What's so funny?"

Clearing my throat, I gazed at him half-apologetically. "Nothing, it's just that, you gotta admit that *does* sound a little bizarre- you having your own suite." He didn't answer but the semi-hurt look on his face said enough. "*Doesn't* it?" Still nothing.

"You know, Lea? Sometimes your sarcasm just isn't fuckin' funny." *What?*

"Sorry, we were joking. We weren't laughing *at* you, Nate." I sighed deeply. Then it appeared- that smile, so warm and cheesy it almost..."*Ouch!* What the shit, Nate?!" I held my arm, now stinging.

"Serves you right, Camioni. Now you owe me a drink." I leaned away, crossing my arms.

"*Really*? You're a real pain in the ass, you know."

"But aren't you glad I'm around?" I hardly agreed. "And look who's talking." I could see that Maureen and Justin were intrigued by our conversation. I caught their not-so subtle glares.

"Hey," Justin's loud voice sounded off like a foghorn, "if you guys are done with your little tit-for-tat, I wanna show you a few more things before we get outta here. There's a tavern down the street so we can walk over after we finish."

The Rip Van Winkle Tavern was the perfect place for such a brisk fall evening. Its dimly lit lanterns, once filled with candles, now flickered with electricity as they hung from low ceilings. Original long wooden tables still smelled and stale spirits from centuries past lingered in the air. Our table was in a corner near one of two original fireplaces. I stared into the flames, imagining what it had felt like for cold and weary travelers to sit in this very spot for a reprieve between long journeys.

I was excited for Justin- he'd worked so hard for this and his dream was actually happening. But I was a little jealous- okay, *a lot*, because while his dream was about to become a reality, I still wasn't close to doing anything for mine. I was doing what I loved but I'd wanted a place of my own and right now Maureen and I only had a very small piece of a very large pie, a piece so tiny it rarely amounted to much in the long term unless you got an opportunity to buy the whole place out.

"Is our food on its way? I'm gonna be drunk if I don't eat some real food soon." Nate passed some chips, our fingers momentarily brushing as he held the basket. I immediately took it from him trying to ignore the jolt. "Thanks."

"You're welcome." I smiled, our eyes locking for what felt like too long. Nate had always been a nice guy, a great guy, but that hadn't been the problem. I hated to admit (and had never told anyone) but sometimes I wondered maybe if things could've been different...

Besides, I thought, his kind would hardly last around here. I mean what Midwesterner would genuinely wanna surround himself with such a completely different lifestyle? I giggled inside. After all this time, after all the space between us, here he was: the tall, handsome, sweet-as-pie Iowa boy with the bewitching smile; the guy I was sure would never fit into a place like this or come to like it; the guy who would've stolen my heart all those years ago...if only I'd let him.

I was glad we'd reconnected, but today was the present and much like history had paved the way to this point, there were new memories to be made and a future to focus on. I had a budding career, hopes and dreams, my family and friends and Patrick, who meant more to me than almost anyone else ever had (present company excluded). Sure, we spent time apart, but we were both independent with our own goals and just because two people weren't together 24/7 didn't mean they weren't meant to be together at all, right? I just had to keep on telling myself that.

Chapter 26 ~ Child's Play

"Are we there yet?" my nephews asked anxiously.

"Not yet, buddy," my brother Anthony reiterated.

We were heading south on I-95 for some well-deserved fun, to a place I hadn't been to for years. The tantalizing smell of freshly baked bread from the Arnold Bakery wafted through the air as we neared the New York line, bringing me back. As kids we'd visit my grandparents in neighboring Westchester County, a short drive from where we used to live. Finally, the windy exit dropped us onto the Playland Parkway, which led not just to the beach but to a little gem known as Playland, one of the country's oldest amusement parks.

Located along the shores of Long Island Sound it had rides, a boardwalk, an ice rink and a decent stretch of beach, not to mention the Zoltar game from the 1988 movie *Big*. Playland held a lot of fond memories for me. We'd go on the rides in Kiddyland, hoping one day to be tall enough to ride The Dragon Coaster, which was itself a historical landmark.

As we approached the entrance, I looked up at the first roller coaster I had even been on. Built in 1928, The Dragon Coaster may not have been the tallest or the fastest of roller coasters, but it was one-of-a-kind. Standing high and majestic above the park, it may have appeared innocent with its old wooden frame, peeling paint and cartoonish artwork but that all changed when you got onto it. People were warned, it was no kiddy ride. Frightening screams from adults and children could be heard from the parking lot. I watched its wooden cars race up to nearly 50 mph around small turns, then hurl its passengers into the mouth of the dragon before dipping down a steep drop. People never stood because due to its uniquely compact and windy layout if they did, they'd get decapitated by one of the rickety tracks or the dragon's fangs that loomed overhead (which had, in fact, happened once).

I had many favorites. Some had been replaced by newer (and much safer) versions while others had been taken away, probably to some amusement park graveyard or to a land of misfit/not-fit-for-today's-safety-conscious-crowds toys. Just inside the entrance was Ye Olde Mill. The long stretches between boats leading you around a dark tunnel made for good make-out sessions. Of course, *that* ride wasn't totally safe, either, since years earlier someone had drowned.

Fast or slow, dark or creepy, nothing had ever frightened me more than The Salt n' Pepper Shakers. Built after a classic 1920s loop-o-plane, it had two long arms, each with an 'enclosed' car at one end and a counterweight at the other. Each car held two pairs of riders and its arms swung and looped you around. Sounds harmless, right? Wrong. We were given loose-fitting belts and when we rotated upside-down we'd come out of our seats, our hands and faces pressed up against the metal cage that was supposed to keep you from falling out. You were like a rat in a cage turned on its head, trying not to get smashed, while screaming frantically.

The Flying Witch, The Scrambler and The House of Mirrors felt practically unchanged but as I looked around, I noticed obvious differences. In front of one of the arcades was a funnel cake stand, which had replaced fried dough or pizza fritta, as us Italians call it. Right after that it started happening: ice cream became Carvel; the burger joint became Burger King and the pizza place became Pizza Hut. Just kidding on the last one- that shit would *never* fly in New York.

But even with all the changes Playland still felt the same. Playland was the happiest place on earth for me and right now it was gonna make me even happier because I knew they had at least one thing on old Walt Disney- they served beer. The smell of churros, hot dogs and cotton candy was already making me drool. Halloween décor covered the park and employees in costume meandered around for photo ops.

I approached Anthony and Erin, proud of my three-beer balancing act and watched as Luca and Owen moved up in line. Teenagers worked most of the rides and it was a frightening thought for ones like The Dragon Coaster, whose breaks were still manually controlled, to have your life or your kids' lives in their hands.

"Thanks." He took it from me and chugged almost half. Erin and I couldn't help but laugh.

"Sure," I responded. "So, you ready to go on next?"

"Oh, hell yeah," Anthony said.

The next few hours were a blast. We hit every ride at least three times and I'd even won a prize on the water balloon games. I still had the *Chucky* doll I'd won years earlier. He stood over two-feet tall and looked close to the original, only he didn't speak. If only he *had*...

Chapter 27 ~ An American Werewolf in London

Monday October 31st

I couldn't wait for this month to be over. Not only had it started out badly, these moon cycles were turning out to be a real doozy. The other week during the new moon I'd been coerced into an adult field trip which had felt like some kind of set-up. And this week was gonna be even worse with one hell of a double whammy: a full moon on Halloween, which meant only one thing- expect anything and *everything*. Monday had come too soon. I was at the bakery so at least I could avoid any potential disasters with pets or their owners for at least another 24 hours.

"I gotta admit, Lea, you do a good witch." Rachel stood next to me, mixing more royal icing. She had just finished a tray of ghosts.

"Thanks. Your Caspers came out well, too," I continued to pipe. "Whelp, that does it for this tray." Damn were my hands tired. I felt a cramp in the palm of my right hand.

"What's up, your carpal tunnel acting up?" Her giggle nearly made me drop the entire tray.

"I don't have carpal tunnel, asshole," I joked.

"Just kidding. So," she added, covering the bowl of icing with plastic wrap to prevent it from drying out, "what's next on the agenda?"

I finally spotted the parchment paper as I looked around the kitchen, "oh, I don't know, maybe some more pretzels. They're almost gone. We still have that white chocolate?"

"Yeah, think so. I'll finish these two trays if you wanna start melting. So, how was Playland? I wish Tom and I could've joined you guys. Is the haunted house still the same?"

"Kinda, but it ain't so scary anymore. When's the last time you were there?"

"Shit, probably at *least* seven years ago."

"You definitely need to go back. The people watching alone is worth it. Plus, the Thunderbolt still plays kick-ass hip-hop. I just hope they never close." Rachel and I both knew some things were inevitable, that one day it *would* close. Amusement parks would always be around, but smaller ones like Playland wouldn't last forever. For now, at least, it wasn't going anywhere.

And neither was Patrick. He'd been in London for over two months and I was beginning to really miss him. Maybe it was because London seemed further away or because he was off the continent. I was anxious for Thanksgiving and wished it'd come sooner. I stared off briefly as I waited for the double boiler to warm, wondering what he was doing right about now. Was he on set, hanging out with other cast members or training? Was he feeling the same way I was?

"Yo. That water's gonna evaporate if you don't add the chocolate soon."

"Oh, shit." Quickly I dumped the one-pound bag of chocolate discs into the stainless-steel bowl and set it over the simmering pot of water.

"What's bothering you, or shouldn't I ask?"

"You can ask, you're my best friend. It's...Patrick. This whole thing with him being far away is kinda beginning to get to me more than I expected."

"Of *course* it would, how could it not? You *miss* him. But you'll see him soon. Isn't he coming home next month?"
"Briefly, but it's gonna be kind of a whirlwind."

"Is there any other way with you guys?" she laughed.

"Not really," I answered, continuing to stir the chocolate. Rachel was already dipping pretzels and laying them on wax paper-lined trays.

8:00 pm that night...

I'd just walked in from my pilates class and had set my stuff down when my phone rang, or I heard the familiar ringtone, as we say these days. Most people I knew didn't even have landlines anymore except my mom and a few relatives who were either just old or insisted on clinging to aging technology for as long as they possibly could. Like my Aunt Ginny for example, who still had the most 'basic cable', only 21 channels. I hit the 'answer' button on my cell phone.

"I was hoping I'd catch you. I wasn't sure if you'd be out trick or treating." The familiar sound of Patrick's voice was soothing.

"Nah, wasn't done in time. You know how it is, they have to go before it gets dark, unlike when we used to go. I just walked in. How's things going? Is it cold there? I heard it can be pretty shitty in October."

He chuckled on the other end. "Actually, that's one of the reasons I'm calling well, other than to talk to you.

"*Oh?*" I asked curiously, getting some water.

"The weather's been shit. In fact, it's expected to remain shitty for at least another two weeks so we've gotta hold on filming."

"Oh, I didn't realize they'd do that. So, like what do you do then?"

"Some more training, but other than that not really much and I can't exactly leave either so..." I heard a long pause. "So, I was wondering, what do you think about a trip to London for your birthday?"

The shock made me suddenly unsteady, *"wh...what*? You mean like this *weekend*? I..."

"It *is* your birthday, isn't it?" he joked.

"Um yeah, but..."

"But *what*? I thought you said you'd love to see London sometime, well, now's your chance. And not that I'm a local, but who better to be your tour guide than me?"

"What are we gonna 'sight see' if it's gloomy, rainy and cold?"

"I guess *some* of it will have to be indoors," he flirted.

I shook my head, enamored. "Ah *ha*, ulterior motives. I see, Watson. I *did* and I'd *love* to- it's just that, well my brothers sort of planned this thing for me this weekend."

"Can't they reschedule?" He sounded disappointed.

"You want me to reschedule my *birthday*? I kind of can't, they made reservations and..."

"Can't you just do dinner when you get back?"

"I would, but it's not just with them- it's with the *family*."

"So?"

"So...I can't ask 30 people to rearrange their schedules. You know how important family is to well, my *family*."

"Oh, okay," he said disappointedly. "I really wish you could come. You'd have a first-class ticket, you know *and* me."

"I know- and I miss you so badly I almost can't stand it. I'm sorry. The timing is just...I *so* wish I could come, you know I'd be there but even still my job, or jobs I guess and well, it'd be hard to leave last minute."

"It's okay, I understand. I just want to see you. But I guess Thanksgiving isn't too far away. Once we start back up again I'd be busy even if you could weasel your way out in a couple of weeks."

"Yeah, I'm sure you'd be way too busy for me anyway."

"*Me*? You sound like *you're* the one who's always busy. Just what exactly have you been doing over there?" he laughed. "I feel like half the time I can't get a hold of you."

"Oh, I guess between the hospital, the bakery and the holidays coming up it's been overwhelming. I'm glad to be home it's just that some days I feel like I'm running around with my head cut off. Right after I got home that stuff happened with Evan, then work blew up, there's always family stuff and right about now is when the bakery gets busy and I can't leave all that load on Rachel. So," I paused, "to sum it all up, I've been spread a little thin lately, but don't worry I've got it all under control."

"I know you do," he laughed. I could sense his mood lightened yet I still had the feeling he was unhappy about me declining his invitation.

"You're not *mad*, are you?" I waited impatiently.

"*No*, not at all- I just wanted to see you. And I'm not worried about you, Eleana- I *miss* you."

"I miss you, too. Patrick, I'm really sorry I can't come to London. You know I'd be there." I gazed up at the sky. It was a clear night and only a few clouds were scattered around a very full moon. It shown bright, almost bright enough to light up the street and I wondered if he had the same view.

"I know. I'll just have to wait a little longer to see that beautiful smile." I blushed but since we weren't Skyping this call, he couldn't see it. "And...Lea."

"Yeah?"

"I'm sorry again what happened to your friend. I wish I could be there to help."

"Thanks, and thanks. I'm doing...better, I guess. I guess it'll just take time."

I was so looking forward to seeing him and on a screen was the closest I was going to get for now. I was sad about turning down his offer to go to London because the truth was, I really wanted to go, but something was telling me it was good I was staying. Yes, my brothers *had* planned some big family dinner, but my family would understand. And God did I wanna see him and hold him and do all kinds of shit I won't tell you, but for some reason I couldn't tell him about my intuition, or I didn't want to- I wasn't so sure.

As I settled on my couch for some TV, I noticed the moon gleaming down at me, as if it were trying to tell me something. Was it affirmation of my decision? A warning? Whatever it was almost sent a chill down my spine and for a moment I panicked. They say Scorpios have the most powerful intuition of all the astrological signs and I wondered if that's what I was feeling. Or was I feeling something else, like a transformation coming over me? Either way, something inside me felt different and I wasn't so sure if it were good or bad.

Part Four:
Mouse Trap

"No! Try not. Do...or do not. There is no try."

-Yoda,

The Empire Strikes Back

Chapter 28 ~ Goodfellas

"What do you *mean* you're not going to London?" Rachel clearly hadn't been in favor of my decision. I'd texted her that same night. "Your *boyfriend*, who's Patrick Thomas by the way, asks you to go to London while he's in the middle of a huge movie, and you say *no*?"

"My brothers planned this big dinner for me this weekend. You should know- you're *coming*."

"Oh yeah, I forgot."

"And they made reservations over two months ago because the place books up fast. I can't cancel on that many people just to be whisked away to European vacation."

"Why *not*? That is what most *normal* girls would do, ya know. Who doesn't like to be whisked away on a romantic weekend with a hot guy?" she pouted. I didn't have to be in the same room as Rachel- I knew every single one of her expressions by the tone of her voice. After all, we'd only known each other our entire lives. "Whatever. Anyway...*shit*, can I go? Maybe he wouldn't mind- he *does* like me."

"Bullshit. If I'm not going, neither are you." I laughed, fumbling through my bag. "Where the hell is my pen light?"

"Fine. He's still coming home Thanksgiving, right?"

"So far, yeah. I guess they're just holding off shooting for a bit then things should be back on schedule. I don't know though..." I hesitated. "Something...as much as I miss him, and believe me it's not that I don't, I sort of feel like I'm not supposed to go."

"Hmmm. I take it you don't just wanna be around your brothers," she added.

"*Fuck* no."

"You gotta admit, though, Anthony and Donnie aren't bad guys. I wish my brothers were that cool. Although I'm still not sure why the government ever thought it was a good idea to leave people like Donnie in charge of national security. You know you should've pitched that TV show idea a long time ago."

"No shit. They should have one with all their shenanigans. Unfortunately, their 'shenanigans' aren't exactly TV audience friendly."

"Yeah, it'd be bleeped out for damn sure. I wonder what we'd call it..."

"Probably *Goodfellas*."

"I was thinkin' more *Men at Work*." We busted out in laughter.

"So," she continued, "where's dinner again?"

"Fratelli's. Where else? We've been going there since I was little- still amazing. And they have those butter mints at the door."

"Ooh I *love* those." There was a slight pause across the wire. "Patrick's gotta be bummed not to see you."

"He is and so I am *obviously*, but you out of anyone knows how important family is."

"I definitely feel that Italian curse shit, too. Family never lets anything go. I love them but sometimes I wish I only had two cousins who lived across the country like my husband does. Do you know how hard it was to convince Tom I wasn't in the mafia?"

"No shit." We cracked up. "Patrick *still* doesn't believe me."

"I mean don't they realize that if we *were*, we'd be fuckin' rich? If I was I sure as hell wouldn't be livin' where I do."

"And we'd have our vacation homes in Hawaii," I giggled.

"Fuck that- I'd be *living* in Hawaii with a vacation home here and if my husband wanted to see me, he'd have to come visit." She was also right about that. Who wouldn't want a house in Hawaii? "I'll see you at the bakery Friday."

"Sure. Let me go- they're calling me." Six o'clock couldn't come soon enough.

Chapter 29 ~ The Holiday

Sunday November 20

I couldn't wait for Thanksgiving: stuffing, mashed potatoes, gravy- not to mention the desserts. It was the biggest feast of the year besides Easter in my family (because for Italians everything revolves around Jesus). Even more so, I couldn't wait for Patrick, who was arriving in New York in two days. It'd been 99 days and counting, literally, since I'd seen him in the flesh and boy could I use some of that flesh right about now. Technology was great but it had taken some adjusting- the texts that sometimes didn't go through, the missed calls, the wannabe skype dates...the not actually having him around. It was almost reminding me of my last 'long-term' experience and not in a good way, because the longer I went without seeing him the more my mind was beginning to wander.

Before this film Patrick had been at most a three or four-hour time difference away and for no longer than two months. Last year he'd gone to Minneapolis over Christmas but had stayed in Vancouver for Thanksgiving to work. This was going to be the first Thanksgiving we'd see each other, but we would hardly be alone. I was going to see his family *and* my own, *all* on the same coast. With the exception of Donnie's wedding two years back, few of my relatives had ever met him and even fewer had actually gotten to know him.

For two years I'd been living bicoastally and as funny as it sounds, I'd been far more used to the 'west coast' version of 'us' than any east coast version. I was in L.A., while he spent his time between L.A. and Vancouver and that'd been working well for the most part. The added bonus? Not having to be a serious couple around family or friends. But this holiday that'd be impossible to avoid.

I was nervous because although Patrick and I had been dating a while we hadn't actually attended any family functions together. Being anywhere near the distorted reality of L.A. it was easy to get lost in Hollywood, where things may not be what they seem, where people don't necessarily care. But if you moved away from all that, things became entirely different. And there's no better place to wake you up to reality than New York, nor are there a more qualified group of people to tell you how it is than New Yorkers- *especially* when it came to my family.

Acting was generally considered a joke in my family, with few exceptions. I had to work extra hard to convince them (especially my dad who'd called him a pussy the first time I'd even mentioned his name) that he was more than just a pretty face. In general people where I'm from don't typically care about what celebrities ate for lunch or where they bought their dog's clothes, and except for the rare Madonna or David Bowie siting they'd rarely blink if they walked by one and that's even *if* they noticed, which they usually don't because they're too busy.

My aunt had a vacation home about an hour from Patrick's family in Rhinebeck (where he was planning on staying) and this year was her turn to host Thanksgiving, which meant that I was going to have no choice but to bring him by. Except for Kevin, I hadn't seen any of Patrick's family for months. His sister Kelly and her husband Dylan were flying out from Chicago and his parents were flying in from Minnesota, making for an interesting mix of the Thomas family plus me. Although Patrick's family was much smaller than mine I was still nervous for this long-awaited weekend.

Between his parents Patrick only had one aunt and two uncles, all who still lived in Rhinebeck. He had a grand total of six cousins. My ten first cousins, 20 second cousins, 35 third cousins and God-knows-how-many fourth cousins added up to a small army, and most all lived within a 60-mile radius of each other, which isn't as great as it sounds. Because everyone knew everything that was going on with everyone else, even you swore them to secrecy; even if they bet their lives on it. Somehow, some way, word got out at exactly the time when you *didn't* want it to.

Patrick was jealous but I insisted that large families weren't all they were cracked up to be. Still, I felt bad at times because he didn't really have his cousins on speed dial, while I couldn't stop the ridiculous group texts from blowing up my phone. Patrick's support system seemed more like a skeleton crew, while I couldn't imagine my life outside the Italian Brady Bunch; even if some were off-the-wall or bugged the shit out of me.

As usual, I had gotten volunteered to bring dessert. Normally I had no anxiety in the kitchen but when it came to cooking for someone else (namely your boyfriend's family) I couldn't help it. I was already apprehensive about being around multiple family units and the fact that Patrick had invited me to stay with him the weekend had *seriously* bumped up the anxiety factor a few notches. Add in that I hadn't laid one finger on Patrick for ages and I was gonna have to work extra hard just to keep my hormones in check...can we say *awkward*?

Chapter 30 ~ Rocky

It was an unusually warm week. Patrick was due to land any minute but I wouldn't be seeing him until tomorrow, which was good in a way because I still had a lot to do. I called into work to check on patients before getting on with my to do list. Later on, I'd be meeting my brothers at my dad's for an early dinner.

It was still weird, my parents not being together. It had taken all of us time to get used to the new normal this past decade. We used to spend almost every holiday in a mass group of people: cousins, grandparents, aunts, uncles, great aunts and uncles...but that had all changed. Traditions had been reinvented, holidays rearranged...which hadn't been too bad I guess- because for *most* of us, the holidays were still somewhat enjoyable. But my dad's family wasn't as tight as my mom's, which meant that lately he'd been spending most of his time alone during holidays. It was hard this time of year not to think of the past, especially when the past held such fond memories. I was well familiar with that one.

The first Christmas without dickhead had really sucked, to say the least. For almost four years I'd spent Christmas week running from house to house, visiting his family and mine, even when he *wasn't* around. I remember being so happy. But then just like that it was gone and I didn't enjoy a Christmas after that for a long time. I didn't blame my dad for being a Grinch as soon as Thanksgiving neared and I didn't blame him for being bitter at his own family because of the way they were. I certainly wouldn't be singing *White Christmas* like I was Rosemary fuckin' Clooney, either.

I placed the last of four pies in the oven and put on a yoga video. I was gonna need it to get through this week (in addition to an alcoholic beverage or two). The simple 'core' workout had turned into full-on 'hard-core' with the instructor I had mistakenly picked. Thanks again to modern technology, 'streaming' programs through YouTube on your TV was a breeze. YouTube, launched in 2005, was the first video-sharing website that allowed users to upload, view, rate and share-anything from how-to videos to movie trailers to Hollywood mishaps. Then they began free-streaming more stuff like sports and now, it was watched more than two billion times per day. It wasn't until later that futuristic smart phones would replace BlackBerrys, tablets and downloaded apps (short for applications) would replace most laptop computers and peoples' faces would be glued to electronic screens nearly 24/7. And even better than YouTube was Netflix.

Netflix had come onto the scene about four years ago. It had started with mail order DVDs, making it the first big-time competitor of Blockbuster Video. Yes, sadly the days of going to the video store and renting movies and video games were over. You used to go to the video store and pick out VHS, then DVDs, to take home. If they were out of copies you were out of luck. Netflix made it not only easier and more convenient (but less fun, because it *was* fun walking around Blockbuster), but less expensive to watch your favorites movies at home. In the next year, Netflix would begin a new trend- original, streaming TV series and its first *House of Cards* would become a huge hit and set the stage for a whole new revolution ending with the near-extinction of cable TV.

Speaking of the upcoming year, tomorrow being Thanksgiving suddenly reminded me of yet another reunion only it didn't involve family- my twenty-year high school reunion. I wondered who was planning it and where it was gonna be. It was tradition in my town to have class reunions around Thanksgiving, the long weekend jam-packed with college kids- you never knew *who* you were gonna run into in the local bar. Who was doing what; who looked good and who didn't; who was married with kids; who had become successful or perhaps famous...

I wasn't a millionaire nor was I famous, but at least I was successful, one of only two doctors in my class which made me stand out, something I hadn't exactly done in high school. Not that I really *ever* cared, but let's face it- doesn't everyone wonder what it would've been like to go to all the cool parties or date the captain of the football team? I guess I *had* done a little better than that, though.

I finished getting ready, turned the oven off and called my brother to see where he was at.

"Yo, pickin' up Anthony. We should be at dad's in an hour," Donnie's cool voice reassured me.

"Ok, cool, see you soon."

I pulled into my dad's driveway, a different feeling than years past. I went around the house and entered through the back door. I walked up the flight of stairs and knocked. The smell of smoke exuded from underneath the door, making me cringe. Despite numerous attempts to quit my dad continued to smoke, although he did smoke far less than he used to. I guess given all the other shit people could get themselves into like drugs or alcohol (especially after having gone through what he had) smoking was the lesser of the evils, unless of course it gave you cancer. Still, it was fucking disgusting and every time I left his place I had to wash everything I had on *and* shower.

I could hear the TV from where I was standing it was turned up so loud. It wasn't because he was hard of hearing, he just liked it that way. I knew the scene well. How could I not, after having seen the movie about a zillion times?

"I got all this knowledge, I got it up here, now I wanna give it to you. I wanna give ya this knowledge, I wanna take care of you, I wanna make sure that all this shit that happened to me doesn't happen to you, you know what I mean?"
"Like I said, I don't need no manager."

It was probably one of the best and most underrated scenes in the entire movie, where Mick tries to convince Rocky Balboa to be his manager. I was two years-old when the first *Rocky* came out. It was one-of-a-kind and a no-brainer that every Italian on the planet would love that movie. By the time I was eleven, four *Rocky* movies had been made and every Thanksgiving since I can remember we watched the *Rocky* marathon on PBS. He'd probably been up all night watching them and was now on his second round. I noticed the door was unlocked so I turned the knob and walked into the kitchen.

"Hey, sweetheart, in here." *No shit, dad.* I set my bags on the counter and went into the living room.

"Hey, dad, happy Thanksgiving," I said, bending down to kiss him.

"Yeah, yeah," he uttered. "Happy Thanksgiving, honey. Where's your brothers?"

"They should be here any minute. *Rocky*, huh? Haven't seen this marathon for years. Sometimes I wish they'd make another one, ya know, while Sly is still walking. I don't know about that last *Indiana Jones* movie- Harrison Ford didn't look so good in that one."

"Yeah, well, *Rocky Balboa* was okay. He's always been in better fuckin' shape anyway so..." The sequel to *Rocky V* had come out five years ago and we'd been excited but that was only because we all missed seeing Sylvester Stallone on the big screen and to be fair I think everyone agreed that *The Expendables* had been a much better movie. But I had a feeling Stallone wasn't quite done with the *Rocky* franchise or *The Expendables*.

"Well I'm gonna go put the water on. Be right back." I found a large pot, filled it with water and set it on the stove to boil. I'd brought over some penne and sauce, a roasted turkey breast and some fixins' from Shop Rite because as much as I hated precooked food, this week I just didn't have the extra time. Donnie was supposed to bring some sausage, cheese and wine- not *too* typical of an Italian Thanksgiving...

This kitchen was far better than the last one he'd had. At least this one had a working oven and a stove top that didn't always crap out.

I poured myself a glass of water and went back in the living room. It was a small apartment but with two bedrooms, one which he used for an office, it was quite cozy. It's not like he needed that much space; as long as he had room for his safe and his weapons he was happy. I looked around, shocked to see my dad had actually cleaned. He'd even dusted off his prize collection of toy trains.

"So, what's on the menu? You bring any of that chocolate cake I like?"

I smiled lovingly at him. "Yup, and some Cool Whip."

"What? I wanted the *real* shit. It's almost my birthday- you're supposed to do nice things for me," he commented.

"And *you're* supposed to be on a diet," I retorted. "And since *when* don't you like Cool Whip? You eat that shit all the time."

"That's cuz that's all you get me," he laughed.

"I brought some low-fat ice cream too and some frozen yogurt to try."

"Like those fake fuckin' cigarettes. I tried those, too, and look where that got me. It probably tastes like shit but if it's Stew's, I guess I can try it." He wasn't wrong about frozen yogurt- sometimes it did taste like shit. *Stew Leonard's* frozen yogurt, however, was different from most.

Stews was a landmark where I grew up, sort of like the Disneyland of dairy stores, even making onto *Ripley's Believe it or Not!* and was known for its dairy. But that wasn't what made it unique. Hardly set up like a traditional grocery store, you walked through a winding maze of aisles, greeted by employees in animal costumes while up above animatronic characters like milk and juice cartons danced and sang. We used to watch conveyor belts of milk cartons being filled with milk, then go outside to the petting zoo and see the cows and chickens.

I heard my brothers' voices as the door opened. "Yo, Happy Thanksgiving." They busted in like they'd already had a few.

"Yo," my dad shouted back, even though we were just a room away. They threw their stuff on the kitchen table, laughing. I got up to greet them.

"Yo, pops, how's it goin'?" Donnie asked, hugging my dad as he got up from his chair. "Oh, *Rocky, nice.*"

"Good, good. I was waitin' to hear from you about that mag cartridge, found an extra one for my M16 if you want it." Those two couldn't be in the same room for more than 30 seconds without weapons coming up in conversation.

"Oh yeah sorry, yeah I'll take it. Anyway, we got some suprasod and parm. Anyone want wine? I know I'm ready to open that shit." Of course, what he'd really meant was Soprasetta and Parmigiano Reggiano; it's just that in Americanized layman's terms, that's how we'd all learned to pronounce it. Italians would probably curse us for ruining their language and dissin' the homeland.

"Sure," Anthony and I agreed.

I was already feeling the wine after a half a glass. The food smelled and tasted good, but I had to keep my eating to a minimum because tomorrow I'd be seeing Patrick. I also had several days of eating and drinking ahead of me before it was back to the dieting. I'd been doing well the past month. Not having your boyfriend around had some benefits, like eating whatever you wanted and not having to worry about looking or feeling fat, but the weeks leading up to his return I'd been strict.

"Dude, you gonna eat or what?" Donnie and Anthony kept asking me.

"I'm *eating*, *Jesus*, leave me alone already, will ya?"

"Yeah, like a fuckin' bird." Anthony continued eating pasta with some sausage.

"You on one of those L.A. diets? Don't let 'em brainwash you. Those broads were always like that- could almost snap 'em like a twig if you laid on top of 'em." *Jesus is right.* It's no wonder I never brought my girlfriends around my dad- he had a certain 'knack' for saying the wrong words at the right time. Lucky for me, I'd heard almost everything under the sun so there was little left in the world of 'inappropriate' language that could ruffle my feathers.

"*No*, dad, I'm *not*. Patrick's coming home tomorrow and I don't wanna look like a fuckin' cow."

"You don't look like a fuckin' cow, you look fine."

"Yea, you know if you looked like shit we'd tell you," Donnie chimed in. *Really? No shit, you do it all the time.*

"So, the *big shot's* coming home, huh? You gonna bring him by or what? I wanna see if he remembered any of that shit I showed him." *Fuck no.*

My dad had obviously met Patrick more than once and had taken the liberty of giving him some pointers with weapons this summer for his new movie role, *way* more than he'd asked for. I'd taken my last boyfriend to visit him plenty but that was *different*. My dad already knew him *and* his family, he was a Marine *and* he was Italian. My dad had this habit of not only getting to know any uy in my life, but his social security number and family history, just in case he had to take him down.

"I don't think so dad, he'll be upstate NY with family. I'm gonna meet him up there." I felt sad for a moment, because my dad actually liked Patrick, despite the fact that he was a 180 from my last boyfriend. I never had to worry about my dad being inappropriate or pulling out weapons because the guy had been familiar with all of that. We'd also come from similar backgrounds.

Patrick was what my dad liked to call a 'good-old boy': polite, a little *too* proper, of pure Anglo-Saxon descent, unschooled on weaponry... you know, all qualities someone like my dad couldn't relate well to and that *didn't* exactly run in my family. Of all the guys I'd ever dated he was the most well-rounded and 'normal', and many guys in my family weren't like that. Someone like Patrick was just a little off the mark of what I'd been used to. And not that I really ever wanted to be married to some Italian Stallion from the Bronx, but I knew how to handle guys like that. Guys like Patrick however, were unfamiliar territory and unfamiliar could be scary. I was worried my dad wouldn't take to Patrick but he'd surprised me and had actually come to like him. Now likely, along with the majority of my family, he had serious doubts about any realistic future plans with such a guy, but I chalked that up to him being a dad and not just any dad, *mine*. But I gave my dad credit where credit was due- he looked at Patrick as a regular guy and treated him with respect, *sort* of.

"Oh, okay. New York, huh?" He turned to Donnie and Anthony, "you going up there tomorrow, too?" They nodded agreeably. "Well, tell your mother I said hi," he continued, an obvious change in his tone.

"Yea, okay, sure." Then men on both sides of my family were of few words when it came to emotion. My brothers saw what I had- the disappointment and sadness on my dad's face. It *was* disappointing and we were *all* sad in a way, but it'd been years since our family had been together and the truth was it would not likely happen again, even if I ever *did* get married. My dad had gone to both my brothers' weddings, but it'd been a little more than awkward because surprise, surprise, my family wasn't exactly normal.

My brothers and I stayed until *Rocky III* was over. I mean, could you blame us? Those movies are as notorious for sucking in Italians as *The Godfather*, plus we were having a blast with little drama. I couldn't recall the last time the four of us had such a good time or seeing my dad so happy, despite it being the holidays. We'd gone through two bottles of Moltipulciano, talked about guns (duh), grandkids, more guns and the family business, including my dad's future plans with it and the land it sat on, which had been in our family for four generations. I'd been helping to manage it but that was all about to change.

Since I'd been out west, I'd taken a step back. But I found it increasingly difficult to micromanage all my hobbies and work. So after dinner, I'd informed him that I'd be passing the reigns to the boys 100%. Now normally in the mob you might be knocked off for such an act of disrespect, but the car repair business wasn't exactly riddled with mafia (there were other businesses they considered far more profitable...) and my family wasn't in the mob. No, *really*, it wasn't.

Despite appearances, big talk and maybe a few pieces of military paraphernalia some *might* consider illegal, my dad was an understanding guy, unless of course you got on his bad side. I was his only daughter, so he felt the need to protect me. But he also knew to *trust* me. We set up a date to have some paperwork drawn up and that was that. In a couple of weeks, I wouldn't have to hear about paint or framing unless it involved one of those paint and wine classes at some bar. Before we left Patrick made a guest appearance via phone and I had no choice but to put the poor guy on speaker so all of them could say hi.

"Oh, hey Mr. Camioni, uh, Happy Thanksgiving," he said.

"So, how's that movie going? I hope you paid attention to what I fuckin' said. There's only one way to do things when it comes to a semi-automatic- the *right* way." I hoped Patrick hadn't heard me snickering in the background.

"Yes, sir, I, uh, yeah. The director actually asked where I got the extra training. I told him it was classified." We all but busted out in laughter at his comment, including my dad. "But good, hoping to be done by Christmas but we've had a ton of setbacks." *What?*

"We'll see you tomorrow, right?" Anthony asked.

"Yes."

"Cool," Donnie added. I think they were starting to really like the guy and my dad was behaving for once- it was nothing short of a miracle.

"Alright well, you better be treating my daughter right or I'll be seeing you, too." I slapped my head with my hand. "And that won't be *all* I fuckin' do," he added. *Jesus Christ.* So much for miracles.

I could only imagine the look Patrick had on his face right now. My brothers were clearly enjoying this. I was lucky Patrick had learned not to take much of what my family said too seriously, but my dad was another story. I knew full well that deep down he wondered if my dad would ever seek him out and find him if ever hurt me. I wish he would've done that shit with that *last* asshole.

Chapter 31 ~ The Shining
Thanksgiving Day

My hands were still firmly gripped to the steering wheel, shaking. *I knew I shouldn't have had that third latte.* It was gonna be a long day, one I had been anxiously looking forward to, but first there was one small hurdle to overcome- I had to get out of the fucking car. *Oh God, here he comes.*

You'd think we hadn't met before or just spoken yesterday. That all-too familiar nervous feeling, the one I used to get every time my boyfriend had come home from overseas. Seeing him step outside, I felt paralyzed and a moment from the past flashed through my mind: November 2008, Monterey, California. I'd gone wine tasting solo because my friend had bailed. The wine trolley had been...*interesting* to say the least, starting with my second run-in with Patrick's brother Kevin. Next had come the drinking. More drinking had ensued and I met Kevin's family, including his sister Kelly, who was getting married the next day. And as if that *hadn't* been enough, Patrick himself had appeared-a stunning vision right off my TV screen, just like now.

I remember it clearly (well, not *that* clearly because I *had* been drinking): we were about to board the trolley when Patrick had pulled up in his pickup truck, sans girlfriend. I'd seen him, coming towards me, a natural swagger only guys like him possess. He was a God in the flesh, hot as fuck and I'd looked like Baby in *Dirty Dancing* all doe-eyed like an idiot. It'd been so surreal I'd thought I was dreaming but it'd been real- every single bit of it. To find out the family I'd randomly befriended was related to a celebrity had been one thing; discovering that the celebrity was Patrick Thomas had been another; coming face to face with the man I'd not-so-secretly had a huge-ass crush on and dancing with him at his sister's wedding had pushed things into uncharted territory and *that* had only been the beginning.

Three years later he still had the ability to make me tremble. With a slightly bigger build he'd obviously worked hard to achieve for this movie role and shorter hair, he looked beautiful. He looked nothing, however, like someone who'd been working weeks straight or been up for nearly 24 hours. And here I sat, that same meek New England girl he'd somehow fallen for, shaking in her car, barely keeping it together. He was dressed in bootcut jeans, a blue plaid shirt and a North Face fleece. Clean shaven and smiling to the nines, he waved and winked at me. *Definitely not keeping it together.*

A tear formed in one eye then the other. I loosened my grip on the wheel, wiped my eyes and put my hand on the door handle. *Breathe Eleana, just breathe.* In what seemed like an instant Patrick was at my driver's side door. I thought I was gonna fall out. I pushed the fear and anxiety down and forced a smile. The wait was finally over.

"Well?" he asked. "Aren't you gonna get out?" His smile grew. No computer screen could compete with the real thing and I had to admit, it was pretty great having the real thing. His hand was held out waiting patiently. I nodded then unsteadily stepped out of the car.

Without a word I threw my arms around him, tears streaming down my cheeks. I'd forgotten the way it felt being wrapped up in his embrace, his strong, taught muscular arms and perfectly defined body, head to toe leanness beneath his layers. I missed him more than I had thought possible and his being here only made me more vulnerable. He loosened his hold and leaned back carefully, gently wiping the tears from my face before fiercely smacking his lips against mine. I could've flown to the moon and back with the jet fuel he put into that kiss. I had to stop myself from getting out of control. God knows who was watching.

"Wow," he said, "just...*wow.*"

"Wow is right and thanks for opening my door. Sorry I was really trying not to lose it...I can't believe you're *actually*, physically here. I *missed* you so much."

"And I can't believe you made such good time. What were you doing, 80?"

"*No,*" I protested, "I left early. Do you blame a lonely girl for wanting to see her man? I half thought your flight would get delayed and you wouldn't make it."

"Well I made it," he said, brushing away my hair, and yes, I'm here, *finally.*" The longing look in his eyes was something I had been looking forward to for weeks.

"What?" I asked.

"Nothing just...*God,* I missed you. You look beautiful. Give me another kiss, I'm *dying* here." And with that we were at it again, wrapped up in each other's arms, oblivious to anything around us well, for another few seconds at least.

"She's here!" Their timing was impeccably bad.

We stopped, turning around. "Nothing like interrupting my long-awaited passionate kiss from a movie star," I uttered in a allow voice. I noticed two lively individuals emerging from the house. "Aunt Jennie and Uncle Bob, I assume?"

"Ah, yep. They may be just a *little* more excited to see you than me, in case you couldn't tell. They're not normally that 'animated'." He kissed me once more on the cheek and took my hand. "We'll have to finish this later," he whispered.

"Well, well, if it isn't Miss Congeniality." *That doesn't sound like a 60-year old man's voice.* Just then an attractive, tall male pushed his way through the couple and over to us. *Of course.*

"Hey, Kevin," I answered, a wry look on my face. "I thought you'd be sleeping off a hangover. I didn't know you were coming."

"That's tomorrow sweetheart." Much to his chagrin he put up a good front, making a point always to annoy me. "Didn't know I was coming, huh?" I shook my head with a resounding 'no'. "Well, well, I can already see the next few days are gonna be fun," he added.

"Whatever, Kev," Patrick said before turning his attention back to his aunt and uncle. "Aunt Jennie, I'd like you to meet Eleana."

The woman's arms came at me like a set of claws as she walked down the porch steps. I braced myself for what was next. "Well, aren't you *adorable*," she shouted. *Adorable, really?* "Let me take a look at you." *Why do I feel like a turkey being sized up for Thanksgiving dinner?*

"Um, hi, nice to finally meet you." She stared me up and down, unsure if she was pleased or disappointed with my appearance. I had no idea how many of Patrick's ex-girlfriends his family had ever met but I was pretty sure none had been anything like me.

She turned back to Patrick, half-annoyed. "You didn't tell us she was so adorable." *There goes that word again.*

"Well, that's probably because he wouldn't exactly use that word to describe her," I heard Kevin interrupt.

I smirked at him, holding in the desire to punch him. As if two real brothers weren't enough..." I wouldn't exactly use that for word you, *either*."

Alright kids, enough teasing; let's go inside. You boys grab her bags while I give her the tour," she added so politely I could've called her Mrs. Cleaver. I followed her inside.

"Quite a pair, aren't they? You should've seen them when they were younger." Aunt Jennie asked, pouring us some coffee. "I hope you like your room. We added that part on about five years ago- perfect for you two since I know you'll be needing your privacy." I blushed uncontrollably. *I guess Italians aren't the only nosey ones...can we say awkward? Do I respond to that?*

"Um, yeah, it's great, really, but we didn't need an entire suite- thank you. So," I continued, "you've lived here twenty-five years, huh?"

"Yes. We came up to visit and kind of never left." She was the one who was adorable, if women over 50 could be considered that. Her blondish-grey hair was pulled back in a neat bun and she was literally *that* sweet- and pretty.

"My cousins live in the next county- same with them," we laughed. Finally, the boys had returned from their round of catch up- and they hadn't returned alone. In seconds Patrick's parents appeared.

"Eleana, sweetheart, how *are* you? So glad you could come. I know how busy you are." It'd been months since I'd seen them.

"I'm *good*, thanks. How about you guys? You both look great."

"Oh, you know," Sal chimed in cheerily, "enjoying the semi-retired life." What a 180-degree departure from my dad, this guy. No wonder Patrick was the way he was. Kevin on the other hand had to have come from different breeding stock.

"What time do you have to leave? Patrick said you were going to your family's? We should've asked you earlier, but they are more than welcome to join us." Little did Sal realize the number of people we were dealing with.

"Oh, um, that's very nice of you but, uh, I think we'd be too many," I politely declined.

"Thirty," Patrick added, "her family's a *little* bigger than ours, dad."

"Oh. *Oh.* I can't believe your aunt had to make food for that many guests." Bernie sounded disappointed- and impressed. I knew how much she'd been wanting to meet my mom.

"Oh, we're used to it," I smiled, "so it's really no big deal."

"That *is* a small army," Sal commented. "Do we know when Kelly's arriving?"

"Not sure," I heard Kevin say, "probably a few hours or so."

"Good, that gives us plenty of time to get things going for dinner. Eleana, are you *sure* you're going to be hungry later? That sounds like some feast you're having." Aunt Jennie had just pulled some pastries out of the oven. Meanwhile, I'm sure my family was already sucking down cheese and meat.

"Probably," I answered. "We eat early so…"

"You mean like three or four?"

"Try one o'clock." Their bewildered faces were now staring at me, except Patrick, who had yet to witness a holiday, but knew exactly what I was talking about. "Italians do love to eat and on holidays, as early as possible, that way they can get a second meal in. Speaking of, I brought you some sausage and cheese from the Bronx."

"Wow, I'm jealous," Sal said, "maybe I'll go with *you*. Where is your aunt's again?"

"About 45 minutes from here, over the river. Actually, we'd better leave by 11."

"11, huh?" Patrick quickly pulled me up from the bar stool by one hand, an eager grin on his face. "Would you excuse us for a sec?"

Awkward moment #2- check. What is he doing? "Then I'm gonna give Lea a tour of the barn and show her the horses. I think one of them needs to be checked, isn't that right, Aunt Jennie?"

He had me out the front door before I could excuse myself for appearing rude in front of such nice people. "Psst...I haven't touched a horse in like seven years," I uttered.

"*Shh,* yeah, I know." He kissed me behind the ear and we were gone.

11:45am

Patrick's family probably hadn't had to guess too hard where we'd disappeared to for over an hour. When we'd emerged from the backyard in different clothes that'd pretty much said it all. He'd insisted on driving and also bringing not one but two very good bottles of red for my aunt, white for my mom and a batch of Uncle Bob's homemade hard cider.

Set in the Catskills Tannersville was an easy ride. As we turned off the main road towards my aunt's, one place in particular stood out among the multitude of bed and breakfasts. Set off the beaten path down what looked like an abandoned road, was The Deer Mountain Inn, a rustic, turn-of-the-century estate set on 200 hundred wooded acres. I'd stayed there a couple of times while skiing. It was beautiful yet creepy at the same time and so was the inside, a mix of *The Addams Family* home and *The Shining*'s Overlook Hotel.

"Is *that* the place you were telling me about?" Patrick asked as we pulled in for a closer look. "People get *married* here? I keep looking for Jack Torrance to come running outside, half-crazed."

"You should see the inside. We should check it out sometime." I could tell he had no interest.

"No thanks, I'll stay at a bed and breakfast."

"Okay, fine, not-so tough guy."

When my aunt had told me about building a log cabin upstate, I'd pictured a three-room structure with an outhouse. But it was just the opposite- Custom built and furnished with nearly 100% local materials it was made to last *and* entertain. Finally, we reached their road and as we neared their driveway my nerves kicked in again. This was the first time Patrick was meeting half these people, I realized. It wasn't so much that my family followed Hollywood, but Italians were better than almost anyone at gossip, which meant we'd likely be walking into a feeding frenzy.

Patrick noticed my momentary hesitation getting out of a vehicle for the second time today. He picked up my left hand and gently kissed it before kissing me. "What's wrong *now*? This is *your* family," he laughed then quickly flattened his smile when he saw my lack of enthusiasm. "You okay?"

"Yeah, it's fine. Just promise me you won't drive off if they get too in your face."

"I'm not going anywhere. What are you even worried about anyway? Besides, if I was gonna run, I would've booked it after I met your dad the first time."

"Funny," I lovingly touched his cheek.

He placed his hand on top of mine and leaned in empathetically, his eyes full of intention. Then he pulled me into his arms and engulfed me in a rousing kiss. A little too rousing, apparently, because we both slipped and hit the steering wheel. The car's horn went off abruptly. *There goes that romantic moment.* We jerked back, both startled, and before I knew it my cousin Tara had opened the front door, boasting a huge smirk.

"They're here!" she exclaimed.

"And it begins," I said, disappointed in our all-too brief kiss. "Well, are you ready?"

"Of *course*. The smell is making me more starving than I already am," he answered assuredly.

He has no idea what he's in for. "I meant for *them*. By the way, I hope you know how to play cards," I joked.

"What, no Baci court? Your family should be called *Card Sharks*, never mind *The Sopranos*."

I watched as four more girls busted out of the house to greet us. "That's in the back and they're *sharks*, alright. Brace yourself." I reached over and planted another kiss on his cheek.

"I think I can handle it- I'm *used* to crazed women coming after me, present company *included*."

Within minutes the feeding frenzy had indeed occurred. The girls oohed and ahhed, drooling enough to baste an actual turkey, then dragged me into the kitchen to help (and get the gossip), while Patrick was snagged by my Uncle Tony to sample his latest batch of Merlot. He hadn't seemed to mind too much but when it came to Patrick, his acting was so good sometimes it could be hard to tell.

"So?" Tara asked anxiously. At least she held out until Patrick was downstairs before speaking. I put the olives on the tray, trying to ignore her.

"*Well*? You gonna answer?" My cousin Maria asked hurriedly in her thick New York accent.

"About what? We just got here. How's work going, Maria?"

"Fuck work- work's boring. We wanna know how it's going on the Hollywood front."

"Yea," Tara added. I saw Adriana and Toni instinctively homing in with peaked interest.

"Well, he's been gone for three months, I don't know when this film is gonna be done, he goes right into another project after the new year, which you *know* I can't talk about...what else do you wanna know? Where's my wine anyway?" I asked.

"Here, have mine," Toni said, handing me her glass. The similarities between my cousins and I were at times striking and when it came to Toni and I, we could be like two peas in a pod sometimes.

"Thanks, cuz," I smiled back.

"No problem. The rest of the bottle's right here when you want a refill."

"*Someone* sounds a little bitter," Adriana said.

"She *misses* him." Tara defended. "When's he leaving?"

"Monday," I sulked, taking a sip. "Grab me the roasted peppers." None of them had ever known the feeling of a travelling boyfriend, but they *had* known me throughout my lonely years with dickhead and so they instantly recognized the familiar hurt in my eyes.

"So, did you get any this morning or what?" Tara probed. My long face turned upward *real* quick. "I figured," she said, "I don't how you could keep your hands off him for even five minutes; I mean *look* at him."

Most people wouldn't get our banter. In fact, if anyone ever overheard us while out in a public place they'd stare oddly, shocked by our rough language and inside jokes. But in our family that was just the way we talked.

"So, Patrick, how's the movie goin'? You gonna be done wit dat soon?" My Uncle Tony's thick Bronx accent overshadowed us as the men walked back up the stairs. They'd been in the cellar checking out the wine.

Before Patrick could answer, in walked Anthony, Donnie and my two sisters-in-laws, Erin and Moira, raising the noise level up a few more notches. It was really beginning to feel like home. The Hollywood boyfriend addition to the mix? Well, that part I wasn't so sure about yet, although my brothers had certainly already accepted him into the family.

"Yo, Patrick, my man!" Donnie walked right up to him like it was nothing.

"Hey, man, how's it going?" I couldn't believe what I was seeing- a semi-bro hug between them. Anthony joined in and the three of them looked like B.F.F.'s from way back. *What the hell?*

It never got old, seeing girls *and* guys ogle over him. Truth be told my family would've set their attention on *any* guy I brought around, because over the past decade I'd hardly had any relationships worth advertising. Introducing a 'significant other' to your family was reserved for someone you actually had a 'significant' relationship *with* and let's face it- I had little to no experience with that one.

"Yeah, you, too. Happy Thanksgiving."

Moira interjected her arm in between them. "I'm Moira, Donnie's wife. Remember you crashed our wedding?" Instantly he recognized her.

"Oh yeah, right. Happy Thanksgiving, Moira, nice to see you. Where are the boys?"

"Happy Thanksgiving. Oh, probably outside *not* listening. You remember Erin?" She nudged my brother aside, pulling her over.

"Oh, hi, um, Patrick, how are you?" She asked, blushing.

"Good, thanks." His smile caught the eye of everyone in the room. My mother, her sisters, the cousins all came running over, anxious for their turn at petting him like some zoo animal.

"Geez, don't look *too* fuckin' obvious, ma," Anthony said, as she threw her arms at Patrick.

"Hey, watch your mouth," my Aunt Linnie barked. If Anthony was little, he would've been smacked upside the head for sayin' that but my aunt just slapped his arm and laughed.

"Sorry, Aunt Linnie," he apologized.

"Honey, you're *here*." I could always tell when my mom had alcohol in her system.

"Look," Toni said, "she treats him better than your brothers."

"No doubt he's more charming," I said.

"I think in her mind she's already got a third son."

"Oh, let's not start with that shit..." I knew better than anyone how to not keep a guy around. Eventually I figured, Patrick would realize none of this scene was for him and jump ship.

"Oh, shut up, Lea. He's a keeper and you know it." *Hmm, maybe.*

I was never going to feel calm with the idea of marriage, no matter how perfect a guy came along- and he'd come along, alright; He just hadn't come to his senses yet, I kept thinking. I smiled at him across the room, discreetly mouthing the words 'are you okay'. Spotting me, he curled up his lip and nodded.

"Didn't you say he has a brother? *I'm* single." I shook my head at Toni, giggling.

"I don't think he's exactly your type."

"If he's as hot as Patrick I can *make* him my type. You should've invited him, too."

"Yeah well, he lives in L.A. anyway so..."

"That didn't stop *you*," she said.

"True, but living in different places isn't that simple."

Sometimes I really wished days like today could be longer so you could get more time together. My family enjoyed each other's company and I was sad to leave. We made the rounds and reluctantly accepted the oversized plate of leftovers. I hoped I wouldn't fall asleep on the way back to his aunt's house from all the wine because at party #2, *I* was the one who was gonna be put to the test.

Chapter 32 ~ America's Sweethearts

Back at Patrick's aunts Kelly and I had chatted a while. I still wasn't sure exactly how we'd hit it off so well from the get-go but nonetheless I was glad. She and Dylan had booked a hotel nearby so they could have their own space as Aunt Jennie's house wasn't big enough to accommodate everyone. It was a jam-packed day and by 10:00 pm I was ready to pass out.

"*Whew*," I said. I'd plopped myself on the lounge chair in the corner. "Am I the only one who's tired?"

"No," Patrick answered from the small hallway, "but maybe it was all that wine," he laughed.

"What are you a comedian now? Mr. 'Yeah, I'll try some more of that homemade wine, Tony', you should talk." The bedroom windows displayed a panorama of pastures and apple trees, more barren now than weeks ago. Leaves had long since changed colors and were dropping off trees.

"Okay, okay, maybe you're right," he said walking over, "but I couldn't *help* but say 'yes'. Your brothers and uncles are *persuasive*, what can I say. Plus, I was scared they might take me out back and so something to me..." he laughed again.

"You're probably right," I agreed, getting up off the chair. "So, what's on the agenda tomorrow? How long are Kelly and Dylan staying?"

"They fly back to Chicago Sunday."

"Oh, bummer. Well, I'm glad they were able to come – I missed them...*and* your parents."

"They missed you, too, but not as much as *I* did." The suggestive look on his face was almost sinister. His eyes darkened to a near hunter green as if commanding me and I knew immediately what he was after.

"Oh, *really*?" I asked, pausing.

"Uh, huh. Now, get over here."

"I need to wash up and change fir...."

"No, you don't," he answered astutely, motioning me to come over. I walked a few steps before he pulled me in close with force.

"Hmm, you feel just fine to me." I jumped as his hands rolled roughly over my behind.

"You're just saying that because you haven't seen me in 3 months. I feel like I put on about ten pounds today."

"*Still* not good on taking compliments, huh?" He kissed my neck from one side to the other. "When are you gonna get it through that thick doctor skull of yours- I only want you."

God he was hard to resist, not that that was anything new. "Anyway, what's the plan?" I tried asking again.

"The *plan*?" he asked, continuing to peck at my neck. "Well, I was thinking I'd kiss you a little longer, undress you, kiss you all over until you can hardly stand, lead you over to this *really* nice wooden sleigh bed, then drive you so crazy you won't know what hit you."

I was already unsteady on my feet. *Keep your balance, Eleana.* I could barely get out any words and I still had all my clothes on. "Um, in case you didn't notice, you already do. But I was talking about tomorrow, not now."

He paused, shaking his head. "For once can you leave tomorrow for tomorrow and just worry about today? You're off duty, you know." His right hand grazed my collar bone before sliding my shirt off my left shoulder, sending a tiny shiver down my spine. I tried to keep it together. "Besides, there's only one person you should be focusing your attention on right now." *Jesus.*

I could feel my heart flutter through my shirt under his warm hand, which rested on my chest. "Your heart's racing," he smiled victoriously. "So, the Camioni defenses *can* be weakened..." With his other hand around my waist he leaned in and kissed behind my left ear and I nearly went crazy, instinctively grabbing hold of his right hand as my breaths deepened.

"Maybe, with the right tactics," I said, trying my best to fight it. "Do you actually think you can make me *forget* what I was saying?"

"Maybe," he hinted moving his kisses nearer to my mouth.

"Okay, okay, I'll let you win," I admitted, "*this* time..." I shot him a suspicious look.

Before I knew it, he'd scooped me up in the air, still mostly clothed himself. Right about now I was grateful we were on the other side of the house because as tired as I'd thought I was, this was going to be one hell of a long night. So much for resting up for tomorrow.

Chapter 33 ~ A Miracle on 34th Street

Saturday, 10:00 AM

"That was *so* fun yesterday, Lea. You *really* need to come to Chicago," Kelly pressed. They were both seated across from us. Kevin sat between me and the window, probably to annoy me the entire ride down.

The train got more packed as we got closer to the city, which wasn't a total surprise being Thanksgiving weekend. New York was unparalleled in its Christmas décor and spirit. People flocked from all over the world to see parades, The Rockettes, walk its spectacularly lit streets, ice skate at Rockefeller Center or go for carriage rides in Central Park. I was lucky to have grown up so close and I truly loved the city, especially during the holidays. The only problem of course, was having to deal with and maneuver around the masses of people. It'd been a tradition in Patrick's family to go every year to the tree lighting at Rockefeller Center, making a whole day of it.

"*Definitely* the wineries," Kevin insinuated, a wise-ass grin on his face.

"Oh, shut *up*," Kelly barked at her brother. The wineries *had* been fun, though. I mean they were no Napa or Tuscany, but still, they were still beautiful.

"You're just jealous cuz you didn't get a massage and a facial…" I teased.

We'd spent the day at nearby wineries and a new distillery downtown Rhinebeck before hitting the spa. That'd been Patrick's surprise. Kelly and it was a much-needed relaxing day.

"Hey, whatever bro, you definitely missed out." Patrick picked up my hand and kissed it.

I don't think I'd ever be comfortable with public displays of affection, not that a peck on the hand qualifies as 'major' PDA. But Patrick had gotten me somewhat used to a hand hold and a brief kiss here and there which I didn't *totally* mind. I guess I just felt like people were always watching when in reality most hardly noticed, except now because I was pretty sure someone in our car just recognized Patrick. *That's right ladies, he's all mine,* I thought, smiling.

I laughed, my gaze fixated back outside. We were in Yonkers, with less than 30 minutes to go on what was nearly a two-hour ride. Bernie, Sal, Jennie and Bob had snagged the booth across.

New York was a completely different scene than L.A., *any* time of year. If we'd gotten off near Rodeo Drive it'd have been only a matter of time before someone recognized Patrick Thomas, formerly of *American Justice*. In a place like Grand Central Station however there were so many people arriving, departing or just bustling about, he didn't stand a *chance* of being recognized. George Clooney would get lost in this crowd of locals, obsessed tourists or these days practically anyone too busy staring down at their fucking phone to notice if a train was about to hit them, let alone if a movie star was nearby.

People came in masses for *far* more important reasons than to spot the random celebrity who might be in their midst. The Big Apple was undoubtedly known for its famed storefronts, from Fifth Avenue to South Street Seaport but come mid-November tourists and locals alike crowded sidewalks, hot beverages in hand, anxious for a thrill that required no money at all: *window*-shopping. Every year the lengthy lines along Fifth Avenue and beyond was proof of just how popular window-shopping could be if done right and for almost 150 years Macy's, the store who'd started the trend, had obviously been doing it right.

Originally a tactic to charm customers to shop, department stores had long since amped up the trend, transforming their windows into eye-catching, holiday-themed spectacles and inventive art exhibits. Nowadays many stores, from Macy's to Saks Fifth Avenue and Bloomingdales, carry on the tradition but Macy's Herald Square by far remains the most famous. With only six window displays, at its most crowded times (nearly 10,000 people a day passing by) you could hardly stand in front long enough to appreciate the amount of work and planning that went into their intricate design. Although the theme was ever-changing, Macy's devoted a set of windows every year to *A Miracle on 34th Street*.

Kelly and I stood there, admiring the wind-up corseted robot in front of us. This year's theme was steampunk and it was stunning- the 3D panels, animatronics and costumes; the colorful ornaments made by children from the Make-A-Wish Foundation. No matter how busy, it was always worth coming to witness such spectacular displays of love and hope, and it was heartwarming seeing people brought together by the holiday spirit, whether you celebrated Christmas or not.

We watched the gears and whirligigs move about the strange glittery figure in the window. She stood nearly 4-feet tall, a frosty-white-and-silver-animated Victorian-era marionette who seemed to come to life before our very eyes. We couldn't help but be mesmerized by the intricate scene and neither could the girl standing next to me.

"Damn, how do they do that? I've been coming every year since I was a kid and these things never cease to amaze me." I ignored her, assuming she was talking to someone else. Then out of nowhere she nudged me. "*Right*?"

Being in the holiday spirit myself, I refrained from biting her head off. I simply turned, nodded and smiled. Not that New Yorkers were as cold-hearted as many presumed, but it was not typical for someone to just make conversation with a stranger because, yes you guessed it, most New Yorkers were too *busy*. Was she alone, I thought? Whatever the case, I had to say something. After all, I didn't mind talking to the random stranger so long as they weren't creepy, and this girl definitely wasn't creepy; she was just trying to be nice.

"Totally," I finally said. "Haven't seen these for years. Glad I came before it gets crazy. Actually, I was wondering why it *isn't* that busy- it's the middle of the day."

"Me, too." Kelly caught on who I was talking to and smiled.

Then the girl continued, "maybe they're hitting the Black Saturday sales or some shit," she laughed. Her Staten Island accent was blaringly obvious. Brown hair flowing neatly around her shoulders beneath a woven hat, she stood in high-heeled boots, her skinny jeans stuck to her like glue. Her Staten Island boyfriend with the big wallet was probably around somewhere. "These are cool but I'm still trying to figure out what they are," She paused, thinking. *Hello- ever hear of Steampunk?* Before Kelly or I could answer, a male voice spoke from behind.

"Hey, I was *lookin'* for you. Hey, Steampunk- that's fuckin' *cool*." *Nate?* I looked down in Kelly's direction, my eyes wide with shock. She stared at me blankly. *It can't be...*

"*Nate*?" I mumbled under my breath, my head down.

"*There* you are." The girl whipped around, throwing her arms around the now not-so mystery man. My head and neck instinctively followed her. *What the hell?*

"Nate?"

"*Lea.*" Clearly, he was as shocked as I was.

"*Nate*? What are you doing here?" Our eyes locked bizarrely. He leaned away, momentarily ignoring the beautiful woman who was still clung to him, "I was about to ask you the same thing."

"Ah *hem*." *Oops- sorry, Staten Island.*

"Oh, sorry, um, Lea. This is...*Tina*."

"*Oh*." *Put on your best fake smile, Lea. Just fucking do it.* "Oh, Tina...right, hi." *Right.*

"Wait- you *know* each other?"

"Ah *hem*," Kelly tapped me on the shoulder. *Shit.* I'd totally forgotten she was even there.

"Um, Kelly, this is...*Nate*. Nate and I went to vet school together."

"Oh," she said. "Nice to meet you, *Nate*."

He stood there, unsure of what to say. "Yea, you, too."

Kelly held out her hand, "Kelly, nice to meet you."

Tina hesitated for a second before smiling back, "you, too. So," she paused, setting her attention back on Nate, "where *were* you, sweetie? I was waiting to show you the rest of these before we head over to the park," she winked, trying to show off before reaching up and kissing him. *Ugh- I think I'm gonna throw up- all over this fuckin' sidewalk.* Nate and I had never technically dated but seeing him kiss another girl this up close and personal still bothered me.

Freeing her hands, he stepped back, "I promised Tina a carriage ride in Central Park or whatever," he murmured. *How romantic- yak.*

"Yeah, in all this time, can you believe that?" she said, dotingly, "I think maybe he just never had the right company." *Oh, please.* "Plus, I told him he *owes* me after the other weekend." *And just what the fuck does that mean?*

Nate seemed suddenly uncomfortable and after looking at the two of them again, I was starting to feel the same way. The last thing I wanted to hear about was Nate Peterson's sex life. He'd made it sound like it was nothing serious with Tina and I knew Nate, at least I *thought* I had; He'd always been a typical guy: career-driven, into sports, women and a good time. Commitment had never been his thing. I might not have known all the little things about him but I had known that beneath that casual, sometimes flippant exterior was a terrific person. Maybe Tina had seen that, too.

"Oh, how *romantic*. We're all headed shopping after this. I can't wait to see what Bloomingdales has set up. Where's that husband of mine? He promised to take me to Tiffany's."

They both laughed. I didn't. "Sounds like you've got a great man. So far it's looking like I do, too," Tina beamed before planting another kiss on Nate's cheek. *Oh, for fuck's sake already. Is she trying to make me jealous? 'Cause if Patrick were here right now...* "Isn't he just the best?" Nate smiled, blushingly. Right about now he looked like one of the animatrons in the window, stuck between gears. "So, who are you here with? Do you work together?"

"Oh, *no*," Kelly eyed me. "My husband and I are here visiting family *and* Eleana, who may as well *be* family at this point," she winked cutely, wrapping one arm around me. "Speaking of which, I wonder where they are." She looked around.

"*They*?" The curiosity on Nate's face was unmistakable.

"The *boys*, and don't give me that look Lea, you *are*. My brother's wasting valuable time being away from you. Knowing those two they probably dragged my poor husband to some pub. My parents? Who knows."

"Um, Nate," I said, "Kelly is...*Patrick's* sister." *I don't know why that was so hard to say.* He lifted and lowered his head in response, pursing his lips. "We all took the train down from upstate for the day." Our eyes remained static. Tina, now perturbed, gave him a witchy stare.

"*Oh. My. God*?! Please tell me I'm not seeing what I think I'm seeing." Shocked, Tina grabbed Kelly and I abruptly, turning us to face the street. "Oh my God it *is*, and he's coming this way!"

Kelly and I giggled to ourselves. "And...here they are-*finally*. What were you guys doing?"

Tina gasped at Kelly's calm demeanor. "Wait- *that's* them?"

Unimpressed, Nate rolled his eyes, "don't tell me, you're a fan, too. I don't get what all the hype is about," he almost pouted as the guys got closer.

"I *loved* that show." Tina paused again. Wait- they're headed here and...*that's* the Patrick?" she looked back at me.

"Ah, yep." Before I could say anymore, three tall attractive men stood before us. Luckily the bustling crowd was too preoccupied with the holiday spirit to notice what Tina had.

"What *took* you so long? Lea and I have been waiting." They just stood there, shrugging their shoulders. Typical.

Dylan apologized, kissing his wife on the cheek. "Sorry, babe, we couldn't help ourselves. We just stopped for a beer. Wow," he paused, noticing the windows behind us, "these *are* awesome."

"Awesome is right," Patrick stopped, noticing Kelly and I had company.   "You can't go anywhere without making friends, can you sis?"

"Guess not," she answered, quick to point out Nate, "except he's not my friend. He's Lea's."

"Um, yeah. Funny, right? Midtown on a holiday weekend and we're here at the exact same time." *Great. The moment I haven't been waiting for: the sort-of-but-not-really-ever-happened meets current celebrity boyfriend.* I hung my head slightly. It was weird standing in the middle of the two of them right now. My mind went blank. Thankfully, Nate stepped in.

"So, the infamous *Patrick*." I observed the watchful look on Patrick's face. "I've heard nothin' but good things."

"*Really*?" He squinted at me, a smirk at the corner of his mouth, before turning his attention back to Nate. He'd had a beer, alright. "Uh, thanks, man appreciate it. And you are..."

"Nate."

"I'm Tina." Whatever nerves Tina may have had hadn't stopped her from forcefully pushing herself into the middle of a conversation. Patrick barely looked at her, still sizing up the stranger in front of him.

"Uh, Tina's a fan, too," I said trying to break up the sudden uncomfortable silence. "And, um I told you about San Diego? Nate was lecturing."

"Oh, right, yeah, sorry," he finally answered. "So you live here, then?"

"Jersey."

"You don't sound like you're from Jersey. Hey, I'm Kevin." *Apparently, I don't need my brothers around to grill every innocent guy who comes near me.*

"Oh, hey man, how's it going? That's 'cause I'm not- I'm from Iowa."

"So, Vikings, Packers or Bears?" *What is it with guys that they always need to bring up sports?*

"Kansas City." This was oddly reminding me of those cowboy stare-downs before a shootout.

"I hate to break up this little Midwest reunion," Dylan interrupted, "but we better get going. The in-laws just called my cell because none of you were answering."

I spoke up, eager now to remove myself from the situation. "Yeah, we've got some, uh shopping to do, right Kel?" I instinctively took her arm for support.

Patrick, unconvinced by my sudden enthusiasm for shopping, crinkled his eyebrows. "You *hate* shopping."

"I know, but it's *Christmas*- it's different," I insisted. "Uh, Nate, it was *great*, uh, seeing you. And it was so *nice* meeting you, Tina. Maybe I'll see you around sometime," I added awkwardly.

Nate's grinned wickedly. "I'm sure you will. That CE meeting is coming up next month."

Shit. I completely forgot. "Oh, yeah, almost forgot." I smiled at the now curious faces around me except Tina's, who I could tell was resenting initiating a conversation with me in the first place. We parted ways, Kelly and I off to meet the parents with the boys, while Nate and Tina headed to their stupid carriage ride. I never wanted to go shopping so badly in my entire life.

One hour later...
Starbuck's Coffee, 6th Avenue

"I *sooo* needed this," Tina said, sipping her café latte. "I was getting chilly."
Nate took a sip of his own before speaking. "Yeah," he smiled.

"I hope we don't have to wait long for a carriage." He didn't answer, his attention on the crowd outside.

"*Nate?*"

"*Hmm?*"

"Did you hear me?" she asked, annoyed.

"Uh, what?"

"Looks like someone didn't have enough caffeine this morning. Late night?" she asked flirtatiously.

His eyes gazed into hers with equal heat, "you *know* it was."

"Yeah, well, that's what you get when you break into my stash of tequila. So, Lea. Do you two *work* together?"

"Something like that," he uttered, breaking eye contact.

"Oh, I just never heard you mention her."

"I didn't. You know I don't usually talk about work."

"Since when do you work with her?" Tina pressed.

"She's an old classmate and a colleague. I wouldn't worry about it," he said, bothered by her questions.

"It just seemed a little weird between you two. Anyway, I still can't get over who she's dating- that' s so fucking *crazy*. How long has she been with him?"

Nate's left hand began to quiver, "I'm not sure- a while."

"Must be nice," she added.

"Yeah."

7:30pm Keens Steakhouse
72nd W 36th Street

"I've gotta use the ladies' room." I watched Kelly get up from her seat. "Lea, wanna join me?"

"Why do girls always have to go to the bathroom in pairs? I don't get it," Kevin garbled while tossing around a piece of steak in his mouth."

I rolled my eyes as the rest of the table laughed. I set my wine glass on the table, scooted my chair back and stood. "Sure, let's go."

Unlike most restaurant bathrooms I'd seen this one was by far one of the nicest. I checked my hair in the mirror. Most days I could care less what I looked like (because let's face it- no hot guys were coming into a veterinary hospital *or* a bakery), but I did enjoy a little primping every now and then. I borrowed some of the lavender hand crème from the bougie basket and slathered it all over my hands, enjoying its fresh scent. I saw Kelly emerge from the stall and stand next to me.

"So, I still can't get over us running into your *friend* earlier."

I observed her reflection in the mirror as I reapplied my lipstick. "Yeah, I *guess*, what are the chances, right?"

"With *your* track record? Pretty good, I'd say," she smiled amusingly. "So...you two never dated, huh?" *Where the hell did that come from?*

"Me and *Nate*? Oh, *no*, no, no. *No.* We're just friends. Uh, why?" *Fuck.*

"I don't know," she said, "I just assumed you guys had a history." *That's one way to put it.* "Huh. You could've fooled me. The way he kept looking at you...it was like his girlfriend wasn't even there," she mumbled. *Really?*

"Really?" I asked, a little uneasiness now in my voice, "I didn't notice."

I wasn't totally lying; running into Nate then having to field the incoming troops, including my own boyfriend, had thrown me, but she hadn't been that far off- we *did* have a history, which I sure as hell wasn't gonna elaborate on. There were things some people just *didn't* need to know, especially the sister of my current boyfriend.

Monday, November 28th

"*Ugh*, I don't wanna get up," I said groggily. The clock flashed- 5:00 am.

Patrick stirred next to me, awoken by my alarm. "Then *don't*."

"What do you mean? I have to."

"No, you *don't*. My bad, I forgot to shut off your alarm," he added, kissing my arm. I looked at him, tired and confused. "It's okay, I cleared it with your boss," he smiled.

"What do you mean you cleared it with my *boss*? *I'm* the boss. Well, 50%."

"I called Rachel."

"You *called* Rachel?" He nodded suspiciously. "Wait. You have her number?" He nodded again. My eyes furrowed as I awaited his explanation.

"Uh, huh." His kisses were becoming irritatingly tantalizing. "She gave it to me last time I was here, in case I couldn't get a hold of you."

"Oh, she did, did she? So, my best friend is cheating on her husband with *my* boyfriend," I giggled.

He pulled me on top of him. I leaned down to kiss him, trying not to laugh hysterically, "So," I said, now kissing his neck, "what did the 'boss' say?"

"She gave you the day off and wished me a safe flight back tomorrow."

"Oh, well in that case, what did you wanna do on your last day here? Hey!" In mere seconds Patrick had rolled us over, pinning me on my back. "*Oh*, okay. This is good. But wh..."

"Lea..."

"Right, shut up."

Chapter 34 ~ The Good, the Bad and The Ugly

I was sad that Patrick was gone. He'd left over a week ago and his smell still lingered on my sheets. I wished I didn't have to wash them. Our time spent had exceeded my expectations and although it wasn't Christmas, it was the best I was gonna get, for now. Patrick and I had visited my dad that Sunday before going to my place. It was more than just seeing a beaming smile on my face that had made my dad happy. After having gotten to know Patrick some, he'd warmed up to him and he knew as well as I did how good a guy he was. He'd never said anything like that to me when I was with dickhead. Maybe deep down he always knew I'd find better.

It hardly felt like Christmas was less than three weeks away with the warm December weather- unless you looked around. Decorations were in full effect, getting earlier every year. As soon as Labor Day ended people rushed to get to the holidays while I on the other hand, had every intention of soaking up as much sunshine as I could. Halloween décor was out on Labor Day, Christmas trees were up the day after Thanksgiving and of course Valentine's Day shit was practically plastered everywhere New Year's Day. I mean, let's make everyone wanna vomit, shall we?

Last year at this time, Patrick and I's schedules had prevented us from being together except for New Year's. Not only that, we each had our own traditions; our families also lived nowhere near each other. Another year later and we were back in the same place because as of now, it didn't look like he was even gonna *be* home for Christmas. We'd tentatively planned on New Year's together but seeing as reservations anywhere usually sold out months before I wasn't getting my hopes up. He'd broken the not-so good news about his up and coming project which I know I should've been excited about, but I wasn't- because it meant that not long after the New Year he'd be travelling again- not exactly what a girl wanted to hear.

Things were going well but this newly ever-changing schedule and Patrick's increasing popularity were about to put more strain on our relationship, which had planted a paranoid seed in my brain. Would this relationship end up doomed like my last long-distance one? Had I thought wrong about this working out? Would he get bored of me and decide to trade up for someone better and let his career get to *both* of his heads? I worried it was only a matter of time before things went bad and he decided he was through with the minor leagues and a girl like me.

I can't remember at exactly what moment I began questioning everything, only that it wasn't long after Patrick had gone back to Europe. But I guess that's what you do when your world gets turned upside-down: you panic, you feel lost, so lost that you forget where you are or what you were supposed to be doing. You lose sight of what's right in front of you and sometimes instead of turning to the people you need the most, you push them away, *far* away.

Looking back, I'd had no reason to doubt Patrick; all he ever did was treat me well and reassure me that everything was gonna be okay, even when it wasn't. But you know us girls- deep down we never believe what a guy says, especially if we've been hurt before, because we fear they're going to do us wrong or leave and all it takes is one monkey wrench (or a few) to push our paranoia over the edge. But it wasn't Patrick who I should've been worried about. In the weeks ahead there was going to be far more to worry about than the questionable dependability of a boyfriend. Things were about to go from good to bad to *really* ugly.

Saturday, December 17th

I was half asleep when I got the call. I'd been so out of it that for a minute I'd sworn it was Patrick. Europe was after all, six hours ahead. Sadly, it wasn't- it was my brother Donnie. My dad had him to take him to the hospital because he thought his cold had turned into pneumonia. Well his 'cold' actually hadn't been a cold at all. Turns out cancer can masquerade as almost anything, which unfortunately I'd been well familiar with. I'd also been familiar with the potential outcome, which was hardly ever good.

I won't get into the details or the crazy freaking out that I did in the immediate days after I'd hung up that phone because to be honest, I blocked most of it out. Because that's what happens when you get shocked like that- your mind goes blank and then you go numb. After that come the mounds of tears followed by anger; anger for not understanding why something so bad happens to someone you love or for not being able to change it. When I was in college my grandfather died. He was old and sick and I hated to see him leave this earth. That was the first time someone close to me had died. I was sad to lose a grandparent and I loved him a lot but I was never angry and it hadn't left any permanent dent in my heart, just lots of great memories that would eventually fade to the point where I barely remembered the sound of his voice, just a bunch of little things like the smell of his pipe and his favorite gum, Juicy Fruit. I couldn't imagine forgetting anything about my dad or anyone else in my family- it's something you always think is so far away, until it isn't.

The ten-minute drive to the hospital felt like forever. When I got there my brothers were both waiting for me. I rushed inside, walking so fast I'm sure the nurses' station knew where I was going. I imagined how often they witnessed frantic families in times of sickness or tragedy. After talking to my brothers I went in my dad's room and the look on his face was one I'll never forget. I could see it in his eyes- the shock, the terror of what could come. This man who I had idolized my entire life had suddenly become so fragile. The oxygen tubes (that he didn't think he needed, of course) stuck out of the wall behind him, his labored breathing apparent even from several feet away. *Severe pneumonia could do this,* I thought. And I hadn't been wrong. Animals got chronic airway disease and secondary infections all the time and it could be life-threatening. But so could other things.

I could tell my dad was pleased to see me. His smile, although stressed and hurting, had told me so. The doctors had come in and explained everything and had laid out a plan- in gibberish, of course. It's times like these that being a doctor comes in handy. After a few minutes into their spiel, I'd asked many questions, leaving a surprised look on theirs and my brothers' faces. When I told them I was a vet they looked at me with skepticism, until I'd spouted back at them in such detailed medical terminology I'd almost confused *them*. After that I had earned their respect but I wondered if these fucking people treated every family like this.

I guessed family members went through this every day, not understanding or being able to make the best-informed medical decisions for their loved ones. Doctors could be so high on their horses they never explained things in plain English. Most people wouldn't understand me if I spoke only in medical jargon. People need to understand and unfortunately, I'd understood- *perfectly*. My brothers hadn't, so I had to break it down in the easiest way I could, not that it'd been easy.

I wanted so badly for it not to be true. I wanted them to be wrong. After all, doctors make mistakes all the time; I know I have. But it *was* true, and they *weren't* wrong. I may not have gone to medical school, but I knew what I saw and it wasn't good. The doctors had shown me the x-rays and CT scans up close and I didn't have to be their colleague to see what they were seeing. I took one look at them and then at my dad and I knew; a year from now he wasn't going to be here. If he was lucky, he'd have six months.

Part Five:

Ouija

"Forgive. Forget. Life is full of
Misfortunes."

-Marlon Brando, The Godfather

Chapter 35 ~ Die Hard

Christmas Day

I'd dreamed for a long time what it would be like spending the holidays with my whole family again; everyone getting along, all forgiven and forgotten...I'd hoped that someday it would happen and now, thanks to the little friend I'd become uncomfortably close with it had, only it wasn't exactly something to sing about. Yes, it was *almost* like the dream I'd had with a few notable differences: like the lack of a cozy fireplace or spiked eggnog and the overwhelming smell of terrible food and disinfectants mixed with bowels, illness and death. My job was far from easy and there were days when the shit could literally hit the fan, but even an animal shelter smelled better than a hospital ward and as many diseases that could storm through a shelter, hospitals grew far more bugs and it's no wonder MRSA had learned to thrive from the moment it was born. I couldn't wait to get the fuck away from all the pathogens.

The weather had changed over the past week, making it really feel like Christmas. We hadn't seen snow on the ground Christmas Day for years and 2011 was no exception. I thought at least if we'd had something peaceful to look at through the hospital's mundane, prison-like windows we'd feel a little more of the holiday spirit. Plus, the sight of cards, medication charts and bed pans was getting old. I'd stayed all night after coming straight from work, sleeping (or trying to) on one of those cots. Not the most comfortable, but it served its purpose. I could've left I suppose and returned in the morning but I didn't want to leave my dad alone. It was, after all, Christmas Eve.

We used to spend it with my dad's family, a fun night of festivities (minus the Feast of the Seven Fishes because thank *God*, they didn't like fish). I remember listening to the Oldies' on the way to my grandparent's house: Brenda Lee's *Rockin' Around the Christmas Tree* and Elvis's *Blue Christmas* forever standing out in my mind as two of my dad's favorites. My brothers had come by during the day then returned to their own families for the usual tradition of opening presents around the tree. All I had to go home to was myself, so I had no reason to leave.

I'd brought over my DVD player, movies and homemade lasagna. I'd handpicked a decent selection from Elvis to Steven Segal to *The Godfather* but being Christmas, we'd chosen a trusty old favorite. Overlooked and too often scrutinized by many as a holiday classic *Die Hard* was a Christmas film in the eyes of most people I knew and in my family the holiday just wasn't complete without it. I mean, what could possibly put you in the holiday spirit more than a dead man with the words "HO, HO, HO" written on his shirt in his own blood? I love *A Christmas Carol* and the *Grinch* as much as the next person, but *no* one trumps an angry Bruce Willis running around barefoot with a machine gun and a lighter, not even Santa Clause himself.

It might be wrong to say but despite everything that was going on, Christmas didn't actually turn out so horribly. Yes, it was true that the circumstances sucked, that the outcome of all of this was more than likely to be bad and that there was absolutely nothing I or anyone else could do to change it. But what I knew deep-down was that no matter how bad things seem, it's always possible for a light to shine through. And it had. A few days of aggressive treatment and my dad was feeling a little bit of relief, which we could all see by the harmless yet distasteful comments he'd given to nearly every nurse who'd taken care of him. Once a Camioni, *always* a Camioni.

My brothers, my sisters-in-law and my nephews had brought my mom, too. It was a rarity seeing my parents together because they never *were* and that reality was still hard to get used to. The last time they'd seen each other was at Donnie's wedding two years ago and it hadn't exactly been unicorns and rainbows. For ultimately what reason they'd gotten divorced I wasn't sure, but I *was* sure about one thing-a lack of love *wasn't* one of them, and it was obvious from conversations we'd had that he never really got over her.

In all the years my parents had been married I don't think I'd ever seen my dad eye her the way he did that day in the hospital; it was like they were meeting for the first time. He'd been so excited she was coming. I remember his slick, dark hair and the smell of aftershave spilling out into the hallway. When she'd arrived, his face lit up like I had never seen, as if an angel had walked into the room, and I could sense the love still in the air. I wondered if anyone had ever looked at me that way.

If that hadn't been weird enough, the five of us were in the same room at the same time, and being together at Christmas? Well that was a phenomenon that hadn't occurred for nearly 13 years; you know, kind of like a meteor shower. When the three of us kids looked at each other at that moment we'd felt it and as quickly as the weirdness had set in, we'd left the two of them alone to talk or do whatever it is that two estranged people do when they haven't seen each other in years. The day had gone by too fast.

Chapter 36 ~ True Lies

We all want things to be sugar-coated sometimes to make us feel better or give us hope perhaps, in the face of challenges and obstacles. We'd rather hear a few white lies than the cold, hard truth because we think that for some reason they'll sting less, which initially seems like a good idea, but in the end the reality and the hurt will still be there, waiting. My dad's initial response to the treatments had given him a reprieve. I knew how skeptical the doctors were, but of course they hadn't exactly been clear. I knew the feeling; I had been there, *many* times- having to break bad news to people about their pets and then being asked about exact timelines of survival. How much would it cost and how sick would it make them? Were they being selfish keeping them alive? These were all valid questions and ones that I hated answering every single time I was in that situation.

I knew all too well in my profession the difference between being able to save someone and not. The guilt of not being able to fix someone despite any and all resources (or, sometimes none) followed me outside of work and pretty much everywhere I went. Each patient was like a wound, some deeper than others; it never went away and eventually faded into one of many scars, and I had *a lot* of scars.

As a doctor I understood the pathology of disease, the toll an insidious progression one could take on a body *and* an entire family. As a pet owner I understood what it was like to go through that process but I had yet to experience it with a close relative or friend and if this is what getting older was all about, watching the people you love get ill while you sat back completely helpless, I wasn't so sure how long I wanted to live. But for right now, I had to stay focused and be strong.

As hard as it was seeing my dad ill, it was almost harder watching my brothers. Seeing a grown man upset could destroy my composure in a second. Anthony hadn't been taking it well and like many guys in my family his emotions presented as anger and hostility, which wasn't making anything easier. He and my dad hadn't been that close in recent years. I guess when two people are that alike that tends to happen, and pride can be your worst enemy sometimes.

But as much of an asshole as pride can be, I think guilt can be far worse, able to slowly eat away at your core and make you miserable for as long as you let it. Although neither would admit it, my dad and Anthony had wanted to forgive each other for whatever it was that needed forgiveness; they'd just been too stubborn. Donnie and I knew Anthony had been on edge because he was angry at himself for not having tried harder sooner and even though he wouldn't say it, he worried he wouldn't get the chance. Time was something you just couldn't get back.

"Hey, sorry I couldn't answer earlier, I was with the doctor." I picked up my phone as soon as I stepped out of the elevator.

"It's okay. So, how is he?"

I looked around the lobby, finally spotting a chair over by its entrance. A hospital lobby was a busy setting, depending on the time of day. People walked in and out of its rotating doors with flowers or stuffed animals. There were lots of happy moments that came out of a place like this but for each one of those moments, there was a sad one; someone who *didn't* get to come home in the arms of a loved one. The smell of coffee beans caught my nose and pulled me towards the coffee bar. I needed something stronger than the watered-down mud from the machine upstairs.

"Well, *okay*, I guess, for now."

"Better than expected...or?"

"I don't know. Honestly?" *Probably not.* "He's putting up a good fight, just like he knows how."

"I wouldn't expect anything less." I could hear the sadness in Patrick's voice about as much as he could hear it in mine.

"That's true," I said. "And sorry if I don't feel like video-chatting right now- to say I look like shit is an understatement; I haven't slept well lately or, since you left, actually."

"I'm sure you look just fine, babe. I just wish I could be there. This sucks. And on top of this stupid-ass strike some of the set crew have started, we've had to move the location three times- it's bullshit, not that any of that compares to what you've got going on..."

"It's okay."

"No, it's *not*. I *know* you; you're just acting tough because you have to. Right about now I'd love to see the ringer you've been putting all the doctors through; I bet half the staff thinks you work there," he laughed.

"Ha, well not *exactly*, but one of my dad's doctors said he was gonna get me a badge."

"Because you're there so much?" he asked.

"No, because I ride peoples' asses. It really amazes *and* disappoints me how much you have to do yourself around here and I'm not talkin' about getting extra chocolate milk sent up. I mean, do I *really* have to ask about ordering a simple *blood* test? Ya know, sometimes I feel like I'm talking to some idiot intern...oops," I quietly caught myself as a group of interns walked by. "The way they run shit here I wouldn't want half of this staff, *including* the doctors, to work on a stuffed animal, let alone one of my patients."

"I'm guessing someone just heard that."

"Oops- yeah," I answered. "Seriously, a dog in I.C.U. probably gets better food, too."

"Did I tell you how much I miss you?"

I shook off my annoyance, grabbing my double espresso off the counter. "*No*. I miss you, too. Wait a minute," I said, taking a sip, "I guess I'll take that back."

"Take what back, that you *miss* me?"

"*No*, silly. About not wanting to hire anyone. I'd hire the barista- at least *he* can do something right around here."

"Well, when you go back up, tell your dad hi and no, I didn't finish that novel he lent me yet."

"I didn't know he lent you one of his books. Now I *know* he likes you," I smiled to myself.

"*The Hunt for Red October*. He said it would help me get into character. He also said I was a fucking idiot for not ever having read one of Tom Clancy's novels."

"I figured that wasn't all he said. Wait till he lets you into his secret stash of porn."

"*What*?"

"Just kidding."

"Oh. You know, I *still* can never tell when you're messing with me."

"I'm not. Well, I guess they're not *that* impressive. Plus, I think he gave them to my brother."

"Wait, *what*?"

Chapter 37 ~ When Harry Met Sally

Friday, December 30th

It was inevitable. No matter how badly I wished for it not to be true, I was gonna be spending the night solo. I wouldn't normally mind but due to recent events (and the fact that my boyfriend was out of the country) I didn't wanna be alone. I'd spent many years home on New Year's Eve, rarely staying awake long enough to watch the ball drop and even if someone *did* have a party, I didn't want to be on the road. I'd done the whole Times Square thing and was over it: jam-packed trains full of drunken idiots; the mosh pit-of-a mob scene they *don't* show you on TV, the miserable weather and lack of accessible restrooms...In the end, it just wasn't worth it. Unless of course you could afford a penthouse suite with a killer view and any hopes of that had gone right out the window this year.

I've always been a little harsh in my opinion of New Year's Eve, but the truth is that night hasn't ever been anything special. Maybe I just assumed it was too extravagant, flutes overflowing with champagne and plates of caviar, or maybe it was just because I'd never been invited to a ritzy party. I pictured a ballroom filled with a bunch of snooty rich people, hardly a scene I'd want to be in. But despite all that there was something special about it, the idea of being with that special someone (or finding one, perhaps) when the clock struck twelve that I hated to admit, intrigued me. Whoever came up with the idea that one night of the year could entail such mystery or magic even, I don't know, but people bought into its hype and it seemed it was getting crazier every year.

And if that's what most people liked to do, that's fine. Me? I'd rather sit home in my PJs eating a bowl of popcorn while watching *The Twilight Zone* marathon. I could live without the dressing up, champagne toasts and streamers; the thought of caviar made me wanna vomit. But kissing some mysterious, perhaps masked man at midnight?

Well, *that* sounded worth trying. Sadly, the only thing I'd be kissing this year was my pillow.

It was almost three when I'd gotten home. I'd gone into work for a few hours before heading to the hospital. Right before I'd left, my brother Donnie had arrived. He, Anthony and my cousin Joey had plans to hang out and seeing as I'd clocked my share of hours for the week, I'd declined their offer to stay. Also, Patrick and I were supposed to Skype. But instead of walking into a quiet apartment, I found Rachel standing in my kitchen wearing a make-shift apron. My stovetop was covered in pots and pans- she'd clearly been in the middle of something.

"Um, hello?" I asked, walking around the hallway corner into the open living space.

"*Shit*, you fuckin' scared me." She jumped as she looked up, "thought you wouldn't be home for another hour."

"Scared *you*? It's *my* fuckin' place," I laughed, hanging up my keys. It smelled good. "What are you doing, Tom kick you out?"

"No. I thought I'd make use of my key and surprise you with a home-cooked meal. You could probably use it."

"That's *not* why I gave it you," I said, shaking my head. "Anyway, turns out I didn't feel like being alone so I'm kinda glad you stopped by. You didn't happen to bring any *dessert*, did you?"

She stopped stirring and paused. The scent of sautéed vegetables floated through the air. "What kind of question is that? Of *course* I did. Now take a load off and have a glass of wine."

"I've been having a few too many of those lately. I really need to restart this diet. Maybe *I* should be in the hospital- God knows that shit they try to pass off as food will curb anyone's appetite."

"I don't think the holidays is the best time for that."

"I've just been off these past couple of weeks, like everything's just gone off the track. And now to top it all off, Patrick's stuck in Belgium until next week and as soon as he gets back he's got practically no downtime before he starts back up again."

"Oh. I'm sorry. Belgium, huh? Then he's headed back to Cali to film?"

"Yeah, *figures*. He's finally gonna be filming on the west coast and *I'm* stuck here. We were supposed to have plans for New Years and not only are *those* plans now shot, because of all this other shit I'm not even sure when I'm getting back out there."

"I'm really sorry, Lea. You're still welcome to join Tom and I tomorrow night. I know those kinds of things aren't normally your scene, but it might be fun. Shit, *I* didn't even wanna go but he talked me into it."

"Thanks, I appreciate it, but I'll probably just stay in, watch a movie and order takeout," I smiled regretfully. I was lucky to have Rachel in my life- she was my oldest and dearest friend and with everything going on with my dad I was glad she was around. Mac and I were close, but she lived in another state, another country half the year. Normally she'd be home on break, but she was away this week so seeing her was out of the question and other than Patrick or Rachel, she was the only person I'd even entertain spending New Year's Eve with.

"Ok, but just in case you change your mind, I'll forward you the evite."

Rachel was gone by 6:30. She would've stayed longer, but she knew how tired I was. We watched *Elf*, agreeing on Will Ferrell as a sure shot for laughs. I insisted on seeing her tomorrow at the bakery before visiting my dad. Now that I had no plans, I figured I should spend some time with him before sitting on my couch all night curled up with a blanket and a bottle of bubbly.

I'd just put the last of the dishes away when I heard my phone buzz from the living room. I instinctively rushed over to it, expecting a message from one of my brothers or Patrick. After all, he was supposed call and often he texted me first to make sure I was free to Skype. It was neither.

'Lea- it's Nate. I heard about your dad. I'm really sorry. Just checkin' in on how you're doing. I'm around if you need anything.

Did I even feel like responding? *Not really.* I knew he was just being a good friend. Maureen or Justin had likely told him. I wasn't in the mood to answer him nor did I feel like ruining the wine and Will Ferrell buzz I had going.

I stared at my phone- it was almost 8:00. *Patrick should have called or messaged by now.* I had talked to him earlier, but I was really looking forward to 'seeing' him. *Great.* I didn't feel like calling so I sent him a message. *I'll try him tomorrow.* I searched the TV for something to take my mind off things, now feeling the sudden urge for some old school, high school drama, and why not start where it all began? Yes, it's true- I owned all ten seasons of *Beverly Hills, 90210* and I was proud of it. I changed into my PJs and threw in season one.

New Year's Eve

When I got to the hospital my dad was asleep. I set a box of cannoli cupcakes next to his bed and walked to the lounge for some shitty coffee. I sat down and logged into Antech Imaging to review some of my patients' lab results while I waited for my dad to wake up. The clinic had been great about the extra time I'd been out. Bosses could be real assholes, but mine had been decently understanding. The week before Christmas I'd missed a lot of work. I needed to be there for my dad to ensure he was getting the care he needed. The digital world made it convenient for me to get stuff done outside of work. I could review lab results and x-rays, email my staff, my clients and specialists...everything short of a phone call or surgery.

"There, that's that," I said aloud, proud that I had accomplished something other than decorating some desserts today. I closed out my email and opened my Kindle e-reader in search of some juicy novel to read. Scanning through lab reports and sending a few emails hadn't passed much time. I looked down at my phone and saw I had missed a call from Maureen. *I bet she has some nice plans for tonight and with Justin, no doubt.* I was about to dial her number when my Skype began to 'ring'- it was Patrick. It was now after 1:00 pm, which meant it was around 7:00 pm in Belgium.

Since 2006 Skype's video chatting had made it a little easier and last year's mobile app made it even more convenient to talk to your loved ones from almost anywhere in the world. What had started as video conferencing had turned into something far more versatile and the possibilities were endless well, *almost.*

I wasn't quite sure how long I was gonna need to stay home, but there was no question-my family needed me, and I couldn't just up and go to L.A. the minute Patrick got back. The amount of responsibility was too much to ignore and as much as I wanted to escape, this was no time to flee to the beach. With a click Patrick appeared full-screen, crystal-clear, as handsome as ever. Seeing him always brought a smile to my face. He quickly saw where I was and asked me about my dad.

"Hi, babe, at the hospital?" I loved the stubble on his face. I knew all too well the feeling of his rough hair against my skin, but it did look awfully good on him. Of course, he looked good in almost anything, at almost any hour and for *that* I hated him.

"Hi," I smiled back, "my dad's sleeping so I was just doing some work. There's only so many *Golden Girls* and *M.A.S.H.* reruns I can watch.

"Gotcha. I'm really sorry about yesterday. By the time I got around to calling you, it was already late so, I hope you're not mad. I should've known when they said we only had a few things to 'wrap up' that'd be bullshit. They had us there 'til after 10."

I understood that. After all I was a patient person- I *had* to be, with my job and my family. Not that it came easy. "No, it's okay, I understand. Rachel ended up coming over well, breaking in actually...we had dinner and Will Ferrell," I laughed. "So," I continued, "are you ready to come back to the states?"

"*Am* I? Like a month ago," he answered. "I mean don't get me wrong, it's been an experience and Belgium's a cool place, but sometimes there's just no place like home. I can't wait to see you, too. I just...I'm just sorry about New Year's."

I sulked, frowning. "Me, too, it's okay. I'm not much in the mood for champagne toasts and parties anyway. Honestly, I can't wait to plant myself on my couch tonight. It'd be better with you here obviously, but..."

"No parties? Not even one? What about Rachel or your brothers?"

"My brothers are doing their own thing and...Rachel and Tom are going to *something*, but I can't remember what. Anyway, it's okay, really."

"Okay, if you're sure. A few of us are gonna hit a nearby taverne later but that's about all the excitement here. If only I could deliver a midnight kiss over Skype..." he winked.

"If only you could *deliver* more than that," I teased, winking back at him.

"I like the way you think, doc. Did I tell you how sexy you are?"

I giggled, my cheeks full of color, "*shhhhh*," I said just before turning down the sound and connecting my headset, "I'm in a *hospital*."

"I should be back in L.A. the end of next week. Any ideas on when you might fly out? No pressure, I was just wondering. I know you've got a lot to deal with right now."

"Not sure. My dad's got some tests next week so...I don't know."

"Well, let him know I'm thinkin' of him and I'll hope for the best. I was thinking, though, maybe you could fly out for a week or so you know, until you figure things out. We could spend some *quality* time- I *miss* you."

"I miss you, too." A decade ago I never would've pictured myself gazing into someone's eyes through a computer screen or a cell phone, nor would I have imagined it'd be the man before me now. I wished so badly that I could pull him out of the screen and kiss him passionately. I guess I'd have to wait a little longer. "Actually, that's kind of what I wanted to talk to you about. I've decided to sublet my apartment for a little longer if I can; that way I don't lose more than I have to."

There was a long pause as Patrick's gaze waivered off to the side. I could sense his disappointment, but I'd made up my mind and not that I'd said it aloud, but I'd already been able to extend the sublet and I couldn't go back on my word.

"Oh, *oh*, okay. Well, you can stay at my place then. You *did* leave a toothbrush laying around ya know. Plus, Fenway and I'd love to have you. Kevin *better* be taking good care of him. I make him Skype, too," we both laughed.

"Oh, I'm sure he *loves* that. You should make him do it in a public place," I added.

"I might take you up on that. I just can't leave right now, at least for the next couple of weeks. I *promise*- as soon as I get a better handle on things here, I'm comin' out full-speed right into your arms."

"You better," he sighed again, "I'll be here I mean, *there*, waiting. It's an open invitation, Lea, I *mean* it. But you're right- no matter what, family comes first. I wish this damned shooting would be pushed back so I could come there but...I'm barely gonna have any time to readjust back home as it is. Look, the first chance I get we're going away, and it'll be worth your while- that's a promise."

"I'm holding you to your word, Mr. Thomas." We smiled longingly at each other.

No matter how far technology advanced there was never gonna be any substitute for touching someone's flesh or getting their familiar scent on your clothes or caressing them...Patrick and I had just spent the better part of four months apart but we were gonna have to wait a little longer- there wasn't anything either of us could do about it. I had more to worry about and as much as I was missing Patrick and wanted desperately to see him, I had to focus on my family. Had I told him in so many words? Not *exactly*. Should I have? *Absolutely*, but if it's one thing Skype made *more* difficult, it was sitting face-to-face with someone while trying to bend the truth, something completely avoidable with a simple phone call.

We all know relationships are no guarantee, but Patrick was important to me and the last thing I wanted to do was screw things up. I'd go to California the first chance I got but as for the *next* four months? Well, I was just hoping my dad could hold out longer. Then maybe all this shit they were hammering him with would have a chance to work. I knew that might take a miracle (or two), but I was all for miracles right now- even if that meant I had to trade some of my happiness for someone else's. I hoped our relationship would continue to hold up, too, or at least that I would, and that Patrick's patience was as steadfast as I'd originally thought.

After our call was over, I checked my phone and saw that I had a missed call from Maureen. Figuring I'd give my dad a little more time to rest I dialed her number.

"Hey," she answered, "you at the hospital?"

"Yeah. Just finished looking through some bloodwork. You know," I added, "I had a feeling 'Pikachu' Platt was gonna have a low thyroid, maybe Cushing's. Hopefully they'll do the ultrasound."

"Oh, right. I think I saw his owner today. So, how's it going? Anyone else there?"

"Nope, just me. They're coming later. It's pretty dead here, no pun intended, because of the holiday." I caught myself laughing as two nurses walked by.

"You mean no one's walking around with confetti and horns to toot?"

"Nope. But I bet any amount of money my brothers will sneak in booze. You know they *don't* follow rules. When my dad wakes up I'll tell him you said hi. How was work?"

"Sounds like you'll have your own party going on." She giggled. "Not too bad, people are probably away or stocking up for parties speaking of which, what time are you staying there 'til?"

"I don't know, probably at least five."

"*Hmmm...*"

"I know that sneaky voice."

"*What* sneaky voice? My voice isn't sneaky. Okay fine, fine. Justin and I are going to this party tonight. One of his friends is throwing it. It's at Pier 17 on the west side- bands, open bar, food...I'm sorry. I know you're bummed Patrick isn't able to come and it sucks being in and outta there so much; I know how depressing it can be."

"No, it's okay really, I guess. I don't really have a choice, do I? Neither does he," I mumbled.

"I *guess*," she continued. "Anyway, I really wish you could come."

"That's okay, you know those big things aren't for me, except the occasional Hollywood party, but I hate most of those, too. Pier 17, huh? Isn't that where they do that NYC Food and Wine Fest? And what the hell kind of a 'friend' is this? A Rockefeller?"

"Something like that and ...yeah." There was a long pause on the other end. I glanced up at one of the monitors in the lounge. Old men running around in underwear advertising some new medication. It suddenly made me sad; my dad was never going to grow that old or even grey. At 60 he barely had one grey strand in his full head of hair.

"Oh, well have fun. I'm gonna chill on the couch later and find something decent to watch."

"You mean *other* than *Dick Clark's New Year's Rockin' Eve*?"

"Yeah, *if* I even stay up that long. God knows what lame-ass performers they have lined up for this year and am I the *only* one who thinks Ryan Seacrest is a fucking tool?" Just then a young couple and their children passed by. *Oops.* "I am looking forward to seeing Drake and Lady Gaga though. Justin Bieber? I don't know..."

Her cackle almost made me drop the phone right out of my hand. "Ha, ha. Well Dick Clark don't look so good. I swear every year I think it's his last."

"I don't know if I can imagine New Year's Eve without him. I've been watching him since I was born. It's like listening to American Top 40 without Casey Kasem- I just can't do it."

"You *sure* you don't wanna come? We have an extra ticket," she paused again, instantly making me suspicious. "Well, *Nate* does, actually. That's why I'm asking if you want to go." *What?*

"His date flaked on him or made other plans or I don't know, but he seemed kind of upset. I thought maybe you two could both use some cheering up. It's New Year's Eve- you're not supposed to be alone. Nate wasn't even gonna come until Justin threatened to drag him."

"His *date*...as in his *girlfriend*? What does that have to do with me? Besides, he doesn't *need* me to cheer him up; there'll be plenty of women for him to *bury* his woes in," I laughed. "Wait, does he know you're calling me?"

"Whatever, yeah, and not exactly. Anyway, it'll be more fun if you're there. Come *on*. Don't you wanna get all dolled up for the night, ride in a limo, dance in really uncomfortable shoes and sip on expensive champagne you don't have to pay for? These kinds of parties don't come along very often, unless you're dating someone like Patrick *Thomas*, I guess."

"I don't think so. Besides, I don't have anything to wear on such short notice." Part of me was curious about Nate being dissed on New Year's but part of me didn't really care; and part of me was curious about this party, which was probably gonna be awesome, while the rest of me just wanted to wallow all night in sorrow.

"Yeah, right you don't. Do you want me to come over there and drag *your* ass out?"

"Okay, *fine*, fine. I'll go," I said reluctantly.

10:00pm
Pier 17, Seaport District

"So? Are you having a good time so far?" I could feel Maureen's eyes prying. "Isn't this place *amazing*?"

It was cold outside but not freezing. We were standing outside on a sectioned-off part of the outside deck. The colorful strings of lights and lanterns surrounded the perimeter and the heat lamps and firepits made it warm enough to enjoy being outdoors. Hollywood parties were a dime a dozen and although some had great views of downtown or the Hills, none had a view of the Hudson River or Manhattan's towering buildings that stood behind us right now.

I stood next to Maureen, one hand holding my shawl around my shoulders, the other holding a drink, gazing out at the water. I turned to her smiling, grateful that I had braved it tonight.

"Yeah, maybe a *little*," I smiled again, nudging her. "This really is some shindig," I said, turning around. "Where's Justin?" We hadn't seen him or Nate for over an hour. Maureen and I had been so busy listening to the DJ and chatting, we'd almost forgotten about them.

"Who knows? It's not hard to lose track of him at something like this. I bet he knows at least 50 people here. It's that charm of his," she winked playfully.

"So, what's going on with you two anyway? It's been what, a couple of months now? You guys seem kinda serious."

The grin alone on her face hinted at a confirmation. *At least one of us will have a Happy New Year.* Seeing people you cared about so happy somehow took the sting out of things. For far too long Maureen had been dating a string of unmotivated losers and I was so over seeing her repeatedly disappointed. Up until a few months ago I hadn't been so sure, but this whole Justin thing had made me more optimistic, for *her*. My life on the other hand, was a completely different and complicated story that was seriously lacking optimism right now. Before I could get any juicy details out of her, two attractive men walked through the doors and were closing in on us. Talk about complications...

"There you guys are." For a moment it seemed like Justin was the one throwing the party. At least five people nodded and waved to him. I half expected them to start clapping. "I was looking for you," he sauntered over to Maureen. She looked at him, a glimmer of adoration in her eyes.

"Hey," she leaned in, pecking him on the cheek. It was a little odd, seeing Justin hold his attention to one woman. For far too long I'd seen *him* 'date' strings of girls, none of whom were anything serious. "We were just getting some air, enjoying the view. What have you two been up to?"

"Don't you mean...who?" I snickered, directly aiming that at Nate who acted innocent as usual.

Justin caught on, "who, *Nate*? Well, he has had some *serious* eyes on him tonight. I've had to fight off at least five," he laughed. "It's a good thing Tina isn't here."

Nate nonchalantly shrugged his shoulders. Back in our island days he and Jordan were two of the hottest guys in school and the way girls constantly gawked at them had been at times nauseating. Judging by the way I'd just seen two women eyeing Nate and his new partner in crime, it was clear times hadn't changed that much, for him *or* for me.

"Speaking of Tina, where is she?" Justin and I looked away, pretending not to hear Maureen.

"Bermuda or The Bahamas or some shit. Her family has a house there," he answered somewhat agitated, sipping his martini.

"Oh. And you didn't go because..."

"I lived on an island for three years. I'd rather fuckin' ski, plus we wouldn't have been alone." *Someone doesn't sound happy.*

Anxious to change the subject, Justin jumped in, "I wouldn't wanna go with her whole family either, man. What kind of vacation is *that*? You made the right call. Anyway, ready to head back in?"

"Sure, why not?" Nate said. "I need a refill though. How about you, Lea?" I looked down at my watered-down drink. Technically 'yes', I thought, but I didn't exactly wanna get hammered, even if I was secretly hoping the alcohol would make me forget the last couple of weeks. Noting the mostly melted ice cubes in my glass, he quickly swiped it out of my hand and put on the table.

I looked at him with surprise. "What did you do *that* for?"

"This looks like shit- how are you drinking this? Come on," he asserted, taking my hand, "let's go. We'll meet you in there," he said to Justin, leading me to the bar. "You guys good?" They nodded before disappearing inside. A few minutes later we had new drinks and were about to go in when he stopped me before the door.

"*Now* what?" I persisted, unsure of his intention. "We're gonna miss the fun stuff." He pulled me over to the side where a couple was obviously too busy sucking face to even notice us. *Of course- what would New Year's be without a very public make-out session?* I angled my head annoyed, then sipped my drink. Why these people couldn't wait to get back to their fucking hotels was beyond me. Sure, most of us had been there and done that at some point, but it'd likely been at some college bar or frat house, *not* an upscale adult party.

"I didn't really get a chance to talk to you alone tonight," he said, suddenly serious. "You sure you're okay? You didn't text me back." I was flattered by his concern, but I just didn't feel like getting into this right now. I'd managed to make it most of the night without thinking about cancer or the smell of a hospital. Patrick on the other hand had been a little more difficult to get off my mind...

"Oh," I admitted, "I'm...sorry. I must've fallen asleep. It's been a long week. I guess I'm just shot. I'm shocked I even made it out tonight. Honestly, I wasn't gonna come."

"*Really?*" he asked. I nodded 'yes'. "What changed your mind?"

"Maureen. I think she feels sorry for me because of...everything and..." He waited for me to continue. "...didn't want me to be alone and that since she, *you*, had an extra ticket and this was supposed to be a great party I shouldn't miss it. So, I caved."

"Ah, she thought we could *both* use the distraction." I nodded again. "Glad you came?"

"Sort-of," a tiny smile formed at the corner of my lip, "I *guess*. I don't normally come to things like this so..."

"Yeah me, neither. Totally not my scene," he said, looking around. "But it *is* kinda cool, isn't it? You look *great*, by the way."

I shied away, "um thanks, you, too and yeah, it is. So," I added, "how are *you* doing? Sorry about...Tina. I guess we both got the shit end of the stick tonight, not that New Year's is really that *special* anyway."

"That's nice of you to ask, but I'm fine. I just wanted to make sure *you* were okay. It's no big deal. Two people should...be able to have their own lives, right?" When had Nate become so mature and perceptive?

"Right," I thought. *Right.*

"I'm sorry, too." *Look away, Eleana. The night's almost over. Just get through it and don't confuse the power of alcohol and being lonely with real feelings.* "Alright, enough lame talk- let's enjoy the rest of this fuckin' party." *Now, there's the old Nate.*

Back inside, Justin and Maureen were at a high top by the room's sizable floor to ceiling windows. I glanced up at the huge wall clock- it was close to 11 pm already. Where had the time gone? As Nate and I approached them I looked over at him and wondered the same thing. Where *had* the time gone?

The music had been good all evening. Of course, in New York even the shittiest DJs kicked most others' asses when it came to a turntable. They'd played everything from classic rock to Brittany Spears and Jay-Z. But the 90s was the only music that really mattered, according to Nate. I was a fan of many genres, but he *did* have a point. Musicians like Louis Armstrong, The Beatles and Michael Jackson were unparalleled in their talent, but alternative and grunge blew up the 90s rock scene. Pearl Jam, Stone Temple Pilots and Soundgarden were in a class of their own and we all know there'll only ever be *one* Kurt Cobain.

Maureen and I had danced earlier. I had a hard time standing still to Bel Biv Devoe and Journey, but my feet were truly starting to ache and so I was pretty much done with the dancing shoes. Chalk that up to all those nights at NYC's clubs like The Limelight, Palladium and The Tunnel. And when I heard the tempo suddenly change, I *definitely* wasn't stepping foot back on the dancefloor. I recognized the familiar tune; I'd heard it a million times. They practically played it at every wedding and I'd been in my fair share. If Frank Sinatra and Tony Bennett couldn't make people fall in love, then Harry Connick Jr. could.

I watched as people covered in all kinds of '2012' accessories paired up and glided across the now crowded dancefloor. For some it was more of a stumble than a glide but still, it was quite the spectacle: young couples in love, people who'd just met and more than likely wouldn't remember each other tomorrow, older folks who'd been married for 30 years...it was the quintessential New Year's Eve. I'd had more fun tonight than I'd expected but the closer it was getting to midnight, the more I wanted to leave. Maybe it was because being among all these couples made me wish Patrick were here. Or maybe it was because in less than 10 minutes nearly every single one of these 'couples' was going to be locked in a kiss while 'Auld Lang Syne' blasted through the speakers and mounds of confetti covered them in celebration of the new year.

I wanted to make a beeline for the door and grab a taxi, but it was too late. Justin and Nate had already taken hold of us. There was no escaping and I knew it. Still, I did my best to avoid going out into the deep abyss of strangers. Nate saw my hesitation and waved them off. I smiled sheepishly at Maureen as she and Justin drifted off hand in hand.

"I thought you *liked* to dance. Don't tell me you're not a fan of Harry Connick Jr.," he said, baffled.

"I *do* and I *am* well *normally*, it's just that...I don't right now. Come on, don't make me go out there. Seriously, my feet hurt," I pouted.

"Like I believe that for a fuckin' second, Janet Jackson. Come *on*. One song." Nate was calm and charismatic by design; he had a way of making you feel instantly at ease. Somehow all the things that had been weighing me down lately faded into the background.

I gazed up at him. He seemed taller, more confident than I'd remembered a few months ago. He also looked damned good in that shirt and pants, a far cry from our island years. It was like James Bond himself had appeared before me martini in hand, his irresistible charm clouding my thoughts, but in reality, Nate and James Bond couldn't have been *more* dissimilar. Aside from their typical attire, accents and ability to jump out of a moving train, Nate lacked rhythm when it came to a dancefloor. At least, he *used* to.

"I don't know..."

"Come on, we don't have much time left. Here," he said, pouring me a glass of champagne from one of the tables. I reluctantly sipped it, shaking my head.

"Wait a minute. Since when can *you* dance? You could hardly keep up with me back at school, *remember*?" I teased.

He stood there, a brash chuckle escaping from deep in his throat. He stepped closer, "Yeah, I *remember*...but in case you hadn't noticed," he responded in a low voice as he leaned into my ear, "we're not in school anymore." *Gulp.* "Now don't make me carry you out there." He whisked me onto the dancefloor. Maureen and Justin were just a few feet away, dancing and laughing as Harry Connick Jr. belted over the speakers.

I was hardly Ginger Rogers, but I'd taken a class or two- still, I found it hard to keep up. At times I imagined myself living back in the days of swing, whimsically moving to uplifting music with a partner so debonair any girl would be envious. I'd been swept up in the moment and the song and before I knew it the next had started.

Studying me casually, Nate spoke up, "admit it, you're impressed."

Our feet moved with the music, shadowing the beat. "Hmm, maybe a *little*. I can't help but wonder though, *who* are you and just *what* have you done with Nathan Peterson?"

His grip tightened around my hand as the space between us closed in. "I'm still the same Nate, Lea..."

Our eyes locked and after several seconds I was finally able to look away. Neither of us had hardly noticed the music stop. Earsplitting voices around us counted down..."Eight, seven, six, five, four, three, two, one... HAPPY NEW YEAR!!!" Confetti rained down everywhere, creating a thick haze of paper specks and spirals. Finally, we stopped moving. The night had ended, the new year officially rung in. Our lips nearly touching we hesitated, motionless. My eyes involuntarily began to shut in anticipation of what might come next. He brushed the confetti out of my eyelashes before kissing my cheek, lingering for longer than either of us knew he should. "Happy New Year, Lea," he said.

He pulled back slowly, his eyes a mix of longing and disappointment. "Happy New Year," I repeated. As if on cue Maureen and Justin appeared as Nate and I ignored any uncomfortable air and quickly put on our game faces. Thankfully they'd been too caught up in the moment to notice anything out of the ordinary. I on the other hand, was feeling something all too familiarly *unordinary* and was now eager to get the hell outta there.

I was home before 3 am, almost unheard of after a New Year's Eve in New York City. I walked in the door, anxious for my PJs and a warm, cozy bed. During the car ride back, I'd noticed that Patrick had called. Apparently, I *had* been too caught up in the evening's festivities because I hadn't checked my phone but once since we'd arrived at the party. Part of me didn't want to seem preoccupied or desperate checking it constantly but also, I could barely fit the thing in my purse and every time I had to take it out I nearly jammed my fucking finger.

Advancing technology was great, but phones just kept getting bigger and the main reason for me even bringing a purse was to accommodate the humongous device. Phones weren't just phones anymore- they were a link to the outside world via email and social media. They were also most peoples' cameras. It was rare to even see anyone with a camera anymore unless they had a serious hobby.

Finally settled into bed I propped myself up and dialed my voicemail. Patrick had called just after midnight wishing me a Happy New Year and that he'd call me in a couple of days after he got settled back in L.A. I was glad he'd called. After all, it should've been us sharing a dance and a romantic kiss in the midnight hour, not me and some other guy. Hearing his voice not only put a smile on my face-it grounded me back to where I was supposed to be-but where was that exactly? Suddenly I wasn't so sure.

Chapter 38 ~ Groundhog Day

The definition of insanity? Doing the same thing over and over and expecting a different result. Of course, when you're in the moment your brain never sees it any other way, no matter what signs present themselves or what banner soars across the sky. It keeps going until it burns itself out, overanalyzing. I tried to stay focused, but it was no use- I kept ending up in the same spot and I was getting tired of it.

I'd hoped to be on the west coast already; God knows how badly I'd wanted and needed the break, not to mention Patrick. But the powers that be said otherwise. It was almost February and I was still amidst persistent stormy weather, inside and out. I hadn't remembered a winter like this since I was a kid. In the last two and a half weeks we'd had two blizzards and with temps still well below freezing, the mounds of snow had yet to melt. I doubted any groundhog was going to come out early this year.

On a positive note, my dad's initial tests had come back better than expected and not only were his spirits up he was feeling more like himself, which was good for him, but bad for the staff at the facility he'd been transferred to. I had to apologize on almost a daily basis for the shit that came out of his mouth. It's no wonder where I got mine from. He was a 'uniquely' comical (although often offensive) guy, making so many jokes half his wing would peer out of their rooms for the show. "Anthony? Oh, he's *fine*, girl. He's the life of the party around here," the aids constantly said.

'Rehabilitation' facilities, otherwise known as adult daycare, were sad places to visit. Some people were in fact there for in-house rehab because they needed aggressive physical therapy that couldn't be done at home. Others sadly, were rarely visited by family, seemingly left there to die. My father was somewhere in the middle. It smelled like a fucking nursing home and it didn't take long for it to depress you. I can't imagine how a guy like my dad felt staying there. The plan was to get him out and home as soon as possible, but he had a ways to go.

The place wasn't *too* bad, I suppose- it was clean, the people were caring and they were mostly on the ball with patient care. That didn't mean of course, that I didn't have to put *any* effort into making sure things went smoothly or that his belongings weren't stolen, which unfortunately did happen at these kinds of places. All in all, he'd settled in okay and with the constant visitors and field trips to various doctors, he'd been more active than he had in months.

The clinic had been unexpectedly busy for mid-winter, which was good, I guess. Being busy at work gave my brain something else to think about besides my dad and Patrick except of course, when I saw cancer patients- then I couldn't help it. Maureen had taken a much-needed ski vacation to Colorado. I would've loved to have joined her, but obviously I couldn't. Speaking of girlfriends, I was really hoping to see Mac more while she was home, but she was heading back down to Grenada in a few days for the next term. My dad had enjoyed seeing her. She'd always been 'one of his favorite girls', impervious to anything and everything inappropriate that basically came with knowing him. I called her to wish her a safe trip.

"Hey, there. All packed yet?"

"What's there to pack? I wear the same shit all the time. Most everything I need is down there anyway. I tell you what I'm *not* bringing- these fuckin' snow boots. I know I'm a New Englander, but enough of this shit." I didn't blame her. I loved snow, too, but four feet of the shit got old real fast.

"Totally. I could really use some palm trees right now, not that California is the Caribbean..."

"Damn *right* it's not. You know, you should've joined me down here, ya know, instead of running away to California."

"I didn't *run* away," I contested.

"Sure, you didn't." I envisioned her shaking her little blonde head.

"And if I'd done that, I wouldn't have met Mr. McDreamy," I laughed.

"What are you tryin' to say? You *don't* want any of these dark, handsome island men?"

"Nah, I think I'm good. Plus, Dengue Fever is one thing, Hepatitis and HIV are another."

"Ha, ha. Anyway, you should at least *try* to come down. I don't think I'll be home until Easter. You just take care of the old man and tell him he better keep on the right path so I can fuckin' see him when I get back. He promised he'd show me how to use that new Sig Sauer."

"Right, right, of *course* he did."

"And *you*, you make sure you keep *yourself* in one piece. You need anything, and I mean *anything*, I'll do my best to be here. They can live without me for a week," she said.

"I know, thanks. I promise, I won't hesitate."

"Speaking of dark and dreamy, when *are* you going back to Cali? Isn't Patrick back?"

"Yeah, about two weeks. He just started filming again, out there of course. I'm trying, I just need my dad settled in a little better. He's got a doctor's appointment Monday."

"Oh, that sucks. Which doctor?"

"The specialist at Yale. Hopefully he can start the next round soon. That radiation was fucking rough but at least that's done. Once we figure that out, I'm outta here."

"Okay, good. I'm sure Anthony and Donnie can handle things for a couple of weeks," she encouraged. "Maybe you'll see your valentine on Valentine's Day after all."

"One false move outta those two and I'm on the first flight back," I snickered, "and I *hope* so. You know it's my all-time *favorite* holiday."

"Mine, too. Isn't it *everyone's*?"

"*Totally*." I threw my eggplant parmigiana in the toaster oven to warm up and opened up a can of wine- another recent and very practical invention.

It was going to be another solo date night: a Turner Classic Movie marathon, starring one of my favorites- Roy Harold Scherer Jr., better known as Rock Hudson, one of the handsomest men that ever lived- so what if he was gay? Speaking of prince charming, maybe I *would* finally get to see Patrick soon. Between the months of phone calls and Skyping, I'd just about had it with long-distances and electronic devices- I was eager and ready to spend some time with my man and *nothing* was gonna stand in my way.

Chapter 39 ~ Working Girl

So much for wishful thinking. Why was it that every time I took a step forward, I got pulled back two more, despite my best efforts? When I wasn't busy working up cases or performing surgery, I spread myself thin elsewhere, and I mean *paper* thin. I'd scaled back at the bakery to make more time for my dad and had pretty much cut out the advice column. There were plenty of other people who could deal with cat piss and separation anxiety. I had *enough* shit on my plate.

And then...there was the volunteer work that'd managed to weasel its way into my life. I'd gone four years without stepping foot into a shelter and the second I did, it seemed there was no turning back. I may as well have signed my life away to fucking *Scientology*. Once you got into bed with them it was almost impossible to get out and every time you tried, you got sucked back into their shitshow worlds.

It'd started in 2008 with a harmless visit to the Santa Monica Shelter and before I knew it, I'd been voted in as the only veterinarian on their board. Then I ran into Ivan and my on-the-side volunteer work grew exponentially, to the point where I was basically doing it full-time when I was on the west coast. There was a part of me that'd come to thoroughly enjoy it; it was and wasn't what I'd expected and more than three years later it'd become intertwined with my life, a parasite using me as its host and whether I liked it or not, it was here to stay.

The amount of compassion in the animal rescue world was insurmountable, but it came with a catch (sometimes, four). The do-gooders involved were no doubt *unique*, meaning many were completely out of their fucking minds. We saw enough whackos in a regular veterinary setting to drive most people away- from the addicts and emotionally unstable to the obnoxiously rich and not-so famous- we didn't need anymore kooks. It was enough to drive most of *us* away but somehow, we always stayed. After all we *do* live for torture...

Our need to want to help animals and people is our weakness. We are all-too often trapped in this bottomless emotional abyss of pity and for many of us it becomes our downfall. We are extraordinarily dedicated, some might even consider us great warriors and healers, yet we can lose ourselves in it because our hearts are so big or we believe in not leaving anyone behind if there is a way to save them. So far, I was holding my own in the rescue world; I was still in one piece. But that didn't mean *that* didn't come without compromise. It was a difficult, but necessary requirement to separate emotion from work and not something everyone could do. There were days I wished I could unsee what I saw, erase the memory of the decisions I'd made, forget all the cruelty that was out in the world. But then there were the good days: saving a life, finding someone a home, a poor, abused little soul who only ever wanted to be a part of a family... that made it all worthwhile and I have never regretted my decision to help, except now.

"Maureen, I don't care *what* you're telling me- I'm not doing it, *no* way. Did you forget all the shit I just took *off* my plate?" I wasn't really that mad. After all, I knew she was just trying to help. Hmm, now where have I said that before?

"I'm just trying to help."

I stared her down with animosity before pouring us both some coffee. "Uh, huh, *sure*, like you *tried* to help me out on New Year's? I mean, *what* was that anyway?"

She half-ignored me, smirking. "I don't know what you're talking about."

"You know you're a shitty liar." I turned away for a moment to get some milk from the fridge.

"Why are you suddenly all shook up about this anyway? That was like three weeks ago."

"Because. *Because*, I didn't need any help. I *don't* need any help- I'm doing just fine."

Her face went straight. "What does *that* mean? I thought you could use the distraction and I thought you *liked* working with him. Plus he could really use you right now."

Still annoyed, I went on, "I *don't* work with him and I don't need a distraction. I've got plenty of those."

"Wh...What are you *talking* about?"

I looked at her again, puzzled. "Well, *Nate*. The whole 'come, don't be lonely on New Year's set-up gig' you pressured me into. What are *you* talking about?"

"Justin. *Pressured*? It looked like you had a good time to *me*," she remarked. "Anyway, I was talking about the *fundraiser*, you know the one you said you thought was a good idea and all I had to do was ask? Well I'm asking. Plus, I sort of already told Justin you had a knack for these kinds of things." Her sheepish grin said it all.

"Oh, sorry," I shook my head, sighing. "Okay, tell Justin to count me in. When is it again?"

"April. Wait a minute," she added, "*look* at me." She leaned off her seat and closer to me. "That really *bothered* you, didn't it?"

"That you committed me to something before asking? A little."

"No, not that- New Year's."

"Like, getting set up behind my back with someone who's already got a girlfriend because, I don't know, most people or their *boyfriends* wouldn't be too happy about that."

"I wasn't trying to 'set' you up- you both would've sat home and sulked and you know it. Admit it-you had fun. It was just a harmless night out with friends...we're all adults. I don't remember seeing anything mischievous." I didn't speak. "Or...*did* I miss something?"

"*No* you didn't." I felt fairly confident in that statement. I didn't tell her we nearly kissed though. So what if the bubbly had gone right to my head and brought back a few inconsequential feelings? That's what alcohol did. Just because you feel some of its unavoidable side effects didn't mean anything. "Whatever. Forget it. I'm not mad, sorry, it's everything else," I smiled. "Back to business, so April, huh? I'm supposed to fly out to L.A. soon. I don't know how much I can get involved."

Disappointed, she continued, "if you say so. Um, I get it. I think Justin is just happy to use some of your expertise." I wondered exactly what she was disappointed in- the fact that I was leaving or that she didn't get any juicy story. "They booked some country club in New Rochelle. You have Justin's number- call him. I'm sure you two can pow-wow via computer while you're gone- as long as Mr. Hot Shot doesn't get jealous that you're Skyping another man," she laughed.

"Ha, ha, very funny," we giggled, "but since I'll be at his place, at least I get to wake up with him every day."

She helped herself to a coffee refill, stopping mid-pour. "Wait-what happened to your place?"

"Didn't I tell you? I was able to sublet it for longer so I could stay here. So...Patrick offered for me to stay with him."

"Oooh...*this* just got interesting."

"*What*? I've stayed at his place before."

"Yeah, but he *asked* you to *stay* there. Hmmm...do I sense a slight serious turn of events here?"

"He asked me to *stay* with him, not *marry* him. Whatever you're thinking- *don't.*"

"Okay, sorry. I guess I just got a little carried away for a minute," she rescinded. "Hey, don't forget we have that quarterly meeting with the bosses March 1st. You'll be back by then, right? They hinted at some positive changes- that better be good."

Maureen and I were both anxious for more positive things at work, but we couldn't help but be a little skeptical. It seemed these days the words 'trust' and 'promise' were dwindling in the veterinary profession and hardworking, deserving people like ourselves were getting screwed more and more out of their dreams. Still, we remained hopeful our bosses hadn't turned like so many others in the business. I tried to remain optimistic, which for me wasn't the easiest thing to do right now. At least I could look forward to one positive thing in my near future, all six feet three inches of him.

Chapter 40 ~ Superman

Friday, February 10th, 2012

"Fenway, would you get out from under my feet?" I held onto the casserole dish, trying not to drop it.

Staying at Patrick's had its advantages, other than the obvious. My whole life I had wanted a kitchen like this, never mind the *guy* who was now in it. Why bachelors who hardly cooked had such modern and extravagant kitchens was an unsolved mystery. So was the fact that they liked to stock them with things like electric can openers and deep fryers, which were never used instead of the basics, such as the casserole dish I'd just nearly broken.

"Come on, dude, *move* it. You know you can't eat ziti." He continued to stare as if not understanding, which was bullshit because he'd understood every damn word. He just liked to play sad and stupid. "I promise I'll give you a really good cookie when I'm done, okay?" I swear the pitbull invented the sad puppy dog eye look. He reluctantly moved aside and let me work.

I'd been back in L.A. a little over a week and I was still adjusting. I should've had the moving back and forth down to a science, but it was a little different this time. For starters I was staying near Hollywood hills, hardly an oceanfront apartment. That alone was weird. I had also left more than my usual ongoing, unfinished 'business' back home: work, my dad and just recently-added, yet another fundraiser. I'd jumped right back into things, having to fill most everyone in on what was going on. Ivan and I had already touched base and all was good on the shelter/rescue front. My friend Sue and I had already gone wine tasting in Santa Barbara and Jamie had planned our workout schedule. It'd been good so far.

Although his days were super long, Patrick's shooting schedule was limited to weekdays. Between the shelter, Ivan's clinic and the fundraiser back in New York I had plenty to keep me occupied and even though Patrick came home late I still cooked because not only was it something I loved to do, it relieved stress and how the hell could it *not* relieve my stress cooking in a kitchen like his? The views alone were killer. To be clear, I was not trying to play the role of the housewife. It had reached the upper-60s today and although that was hardly beach weather it was a vast improvement from what I'd left at home. It was mid-February and already they'd forecasted a snowy start to Spring. I wasn't totally looking forward to heading back east, despite my missing my dad. The Skype thing was new to him but luckily my brothers had been able to help. Two things I never imagined would exist- online dating and talking to my dad through some gadget out of *Star Trek*.

A few minor setbacks had kept my dad in the rehab facility, and he was getting more frustrated, which made him even more difficult than he could already be. I couldn't blame him, though; *anyone* would want the fuck out of such a lackluster, depressing shit hole. He had this tendency to get a *little* out of control and there were few people who knew how to handle him. God knows it had taken me years to master what I called the impossible. He had a problem with following orders and trusting people *especially* the unknown; Once you got an ex-SEAL going there was no stopping him and as you'd guess, there was *little* room for compromise- *period*. I could understand where he came from, too. It wasn't easy putting your life in the hands of strangers even if they were doctors and especially when you'd seen so many in such a short period of time. And with me not there his anxiety over things had probably increased and that made *me* more untrusting and uneasy.

A month ago, I couldn't wait to get on a plane, surround myself with sunshine and palm trees, witness beautiful sunsets and above all else, be with Patrick. It seemed like forever since I'd seen him, and it'd been really great seeing him but now that I was here, a part of me was missing home. Ironically all this shit with my dad had brought my family closer and that was making me miss it even more. The arousing smell from the oven suddenly snapped me back to the moment and suddenly it dawned on me- I'd forgotten the garlic bread. I cut the baguette in half, doused it in olive oil and spread a paste of crushed garlic, parsley, salt and pepper. I put it on a sheet pan and set it aside.

"Alright Fen, let's go." Of course, every time you want a dog to listen to you, they *don't*. He'd sat like a statue watching me cook and just when I was ready to give him my full attention, he'd fallen asleep in the other room. "Dude, *seriously*?" He opened one eye, barely moving his head. "Fine, suit yourself. I was gonna take you for a *walk*, but..." Just then his ears perked up as if I'd said the magic words. His head lifted and after a quick stretch he got up and walked over to the front door.

We were gone for less than an hour when Patrick texted to let me know he'd be home around 8. I looked at my watch-it was only 6:15.

"Well?" I asked myself, "I guess that's plenty of time to call my mom and my brother." When we returned, I parked myself on the patio with my laptop and waited for the sun to go down. After sending Justin a quick email I dialed my mom's number.

"Hi, honey, I was just thinking about you. Your brothers and I just got back from dinner."

"Oh, nice. Where'd you go?"

"Pepe's. They wanted pizza and they opened a new one nearby. It isn't New York pizza, but…"

"Ma, *nothing's* New York pizza- you know that."

She laughed, "so, where's Patrick? Is he there? How's he doing?"

"Good, ma, good. He's still on set so I'm just hanging with the dog." The sun had made its way down quickly. I was an east coast girl no doubt, but there was just no beating a west coast (Or Grenadian) sunset in my book.

"Oh, ok, well please send him my love. How's the weather? We got some more snow today, but it's supposed to warm up this weekend."

"To what, 30?" I laughed. "Well, It was 67 today. And I will. He was just asking about you."

"So, do you two have any special plans for next week?" she asked.

"Next *week*?"

"For Valentine's Day." *Of course. How could I have forgotten?*

"Um, not really. He's working, ma. He can't exactly tell the entire cast and crew to take off."

"Oh, that's too bad…"

"It's fine, ma. You know I don't really care and don't worry- he knows how to make up for it. He's the romantic one."

"That's why I like him- he's such a good guy *and* a gentleman, too. There's not many of them left, you know. Good thing you found him."

"Yea," I uttered. "You know you should really come out here some time. I mean you gotta check out this view I've got right now. Even though I'm not on the ocean it's still pretty."

"I know. Meanwhile, aaybe your brothers can teach me that Skype thing so I can see it live."

"That would mean you *actually* have to get a smart phone with a touch screen, ma."

"Oh, I don't know how to use those," she answered.

"Exactly. Maybe your sons will get you an iPad for Mother's Day," I giggled to myself. "Those are easier to use. So," I continued, "anything else new? How are my boys? I miss them already."

"They're good! How *is* Patrick's new film going, by the way?"

"Pretty well. He's really enjoying it, plus I think he's just happy to finally be home."

"And be with *you*, I'm sure. You may have lucked out finding him, but he's one lucky man, Eleana." For most girls talking about boys with their mother was normal and commonplace but for me it'd always been awkward. I hadn't grown up super close with my parents-we were as far from the Cleavers as it got- and conversations like these? Well, they just hadn't existed.

"Thanks, ma. Speaking of guys, I promised Donnie I'd call him to see how dad did today, so..."

"Ok, I'll talk to you soon, honey. Love you."

"I love you, too, ma."

Despite the lack of sand in my toes, the sunset was enjoyable and peaceful; I realized I hadn't felt that for a while. I didn't speak with Donnie for long. Of course, it wasn't exactly easy having a conversation with an obnoxious little brother while his was out at a bar with his friends to begin with.

8:00 pm

"God, this is *so* good." Patrick barely took a breath as he shoved pieces of garlic bread into his mouth. "No *way* you'd be able to find bread like this out here. What's in it?"

"It's a secret, just like the vodka sauce," I answered. It was such a nice night we'd eaten outside. Then again, most nights were nice in Los Angeles. That was definitely an advantage out here-you could eat outside almost daily.

"Just make sure you save some for Kevin. As soon as he heard you were back, he was figuring a day to invite himself over."

"Is *that* why he comes over so much?" I asked flippantly. "Speaking of mothers, my mom sends her love. I talked to her earlier. She almost sounded like she missed you more than *me*."

"Aw, she's so sweet. I love her and I've haven't met anyone else yet who can keep up with my mother in the martini department," he smiled.

"Also true," I smiled back at him.

"So, what else did she have to say?"

"Not much, except she kept going on about how much she adores you. For some reason she seems to think you're a *great* guy, some kind of *'Superman'* or something..."

"And what did *you* say?" He angled his head at me attentively.

I just smiled glibly, "well, I *kind of* agreed with her...then I told her that beneath that very attractive Hollywood exterior, you're just a regular guy."

"*Really*? Well, I guess should take credit where credit is...wait-'*regular*' guy? So, you think I'm like everyone *else*? What happened to *Superman*?"

"You sound sure of yourself, Mr. Thomas," I eyed him adoringly. "You may have played a superhero once, but let's try to be realistic here...I mean, *Superman* isn't an easy act to follow and even *he* isn't perfect."

"I didn't say I was perfect and as far as the 'super' part? Well, you'll just have to stay tuned..."

"Whatever that means," I hesitated, "Anyway, she also said to tell you that you better be taking good care of me right now," I sneered.

"I hope you told her I was. And so *what* if I am? You need me to *prove* it to you, Camioni?"

"I don't know-*maybe,*" I answered, leaning forward to rest my chin on my hand. He leaned in, almost prowling.

"Is that a *challenge*? Because it just so happens you're in luck. How about next weekend? I know the *perfect* place."

I waited, visibly bedazzled by his charms. "Hmm, what did you have in mind? You know I'm *very* busy," I smirked.

"You're probably right, but I bet you're not too busy for this and I think you'll be pleasantly surprised."

I wasn't entirely sure what he'd meant. Patrick wasn't normally so secretive or creative with dates so that fact that he'd hinted at a surprise had thrown me. Still, if it involved whisking me away somewhere, I was all for it. Patrick and I didn't linger downstairs too long after dinner. I knew we were both tired from the long week we'd both had; I also knew I couldn't wait to get my hands on him.

Chapter 41 ~ Enchanted

February 17ᵗʰ

The warm breeze hit me like a ton of bricks as we stepped off the plane. I was no movie star or President, yet somehow disembarking a plane by aircraft stairs made me feel important. It'd been a nearly full flight, hardly a surprise for where we'd landed. The quick 2.5-hours to Cabo San Lucas from Los Angeles made it popular for west coasters.

It was 10 am and already the sun felt burning hot. Immediately I thought back to Grenada. Other than being a complete culture shock island life had had its advantages, including beautiful year-round weather. Compared to places like Baton Rouge, Louisiana Grenada's tropical climate was tame: less humid, breezier and far more bearable. Years later my body was definitely missing the sun full-time and *I* was missing my seemingly infinite tan but I sure as hell didn't miss those fucking disease-ridden mosquitoes. And what Mexico lacked in mosquitoes it made up for in mezcal and margaritas.

"So," Patrick asked as he snagged our bags off the counter, "you ready for some fun?" I took note of the customs agent eying us suspiciously.

"Absolutely," I answered all excited.

Esperanza Resort, Los Cabos

"I have to hand it to you, Mr. Thomas, you really know how to treat a girl- whisking me away to a tropical paradise, romancing me with your irresistible charms, surprising me with this gorgeous hotel...you've scored yourself some extra points."

"Honestly, I was kinda hoping to score in another area," he teased.

"I don't think that'll be a problem," I flirted back, grinning wildly.

"Besides, *you're* the one who's gorgeous...and we have a *lot* to make up for. Plus, you needed the break. I was tempted to force you to put on skis, but decided against it," he smiled.

"Hmmm...*wise* choice. You know I do love a beach, especially if it's close to the equator."

"Well I *was* being a little selfish- I figured you in a bikini on some beach would be a much better view, although questionably more enjoyable, than you tumbling down a mountain." His smirk began to grow annoyingly wicked.

"Very funny. I'm not *that* bad. I only fell once the last time we were in Whistler. Anyway, if I forget to tell you later, *thank you* for my surprise- I love it."

"I haven't given it to you yet." I titled my head.

"I thought *this* was the surprise," I insisted.

"Not *really*." Leaning towards me from his beach chair he gently kissed my hand, "like I told you before, you'll have to wait. Now let's go check out that water." He took hold of my hand and assisted me off my chair. "After that, what do ya think about walking the sunset before dinner?"

"Sounds great." I followed his lead inside.

By 6:30 the sun had gone down completely. I'd seen some of the best sunsets and night skies of my entire life in Grenada; after living there few could ever come close. If we were lucky we'd witness the 'green flash', that rare instance when the Earth's atmosphere causes the light from the Sun to separate out into different colors just after the sun dips below the horizon, appearing as a 'flash' of green off the ocean's surface.

Green flashes and stargazing aside, nothing was more romantic than watching the sun set with that special someone. For years I'd envied others: couples sharing a bottle of wine cozied up on their blankets at the beach, just like in movies. Patrick and I had been officially together almost two years yet surprisingly we hadn't had many chances to do things like that. We certainly hadn't vacationed beyond British Columbia or Catalina. This weekend was a unique and somewhat strange occurrence- as was Patrick's behavior, I'd just noticed.

I hadn't drilled him much about his taking me away; I just assumed it was his way of making up for our botched New Year's (and then some). I had no reason to think otherwise because he'd been right- we *did* have a lot to make up for, well *he* did technically, not that his work schedule had been his fault, just like my dad being ill hadn't been mine. But ever since we'd arrived in Cabo something about him seemed different and I couldn't put my finger on it, especially with all his constant doting.

I awoke the next morning feeling blissful and rested, not to mention lucky that I was even here- none of which I had been familiar with these past several months. With Patrick still asleep I walked out onto the expansive terrace and sat on one of the lounge chairs. I wondered why I had never been down here; it was so beautiful. The view from our room this morning was picture-perfect. I heard him stirring and immediately turned around, "hey sleepyhead, I was just gonna call room service for some coffee. Want some?" I winked playfully. Although I didn't actually *need* coffee to wake up, I was admittedly addicted to it in the morning.

"Sure, sounds good." He slowly made his way outside.

"Good morning," he said, kissing me on the cheek. "Pretty nice, isn't it?" He joined me on the oversized seat, gazing out at the water.

"Absolutely. So, where are we exactly again?"

"The Baja Peninsula. It separates the Pacific Ocean from the Gulf of California. Technically we're in what they call Baja California Sur, or 'south Baja California'." He pointed to our left, "The San Jose del Cabo Airport is that way, about 20 minutes north of here and down there," he turned his head right, "about four miles to Cabo."

"You sure you weren't ever a travel agent?" I asked, coyly, nuzzling up next to him on the chair. "You know, we haven't even *gone* anywhere yet and I already wanna come back."

"Tell me about it. Before I moved to L.A., I thought Mexico was made up of Cancun and that shithole Tijuana," he laughed.

"Yeah, me, too. So, what have you planned for us today?"

He put one arm around me, pausing in thought, "well...after a morning of love making I was going to take you kayaking around Lover's Arch, aka El Arco del...however you say 'lovers' in Spanish, followed by a private tequila tasting and lunch." He continued to kiss around the sides of my neck. I was barely awake and he was already driving me crazy. "After that, I booked us massages at the spa and *then* after *that*, dinner at a *very* romantic restaurant where we'll be served some of Cabo's finest local cuisine- *no seafood* for you."

"*Hmmm*," I said, "looks like you've thought of everything, and it's *del amantes* or, el arco del amantes, I guess." He stared at me. "What? I know some Spanish. So just to recap...you signed us up for sex, oh sorry, *love* making, kayaking, tequila tasting, massages, *more* sex and dinner." He nodded. "Wow- you went to an awful lot of trouble for some tacos and tequila. I would've been okay with San Diego," I giggled.

For a minute I thought he was gonna smack me with the look he had on his face. "I'll remember that next time," he said. "Well the tequila tasting alone is worth the trip. But you gotta admit it sounds good, right?"

"Definitely," I said, tantalizing him with a kiss.

"Yeah, I thought so, too. Impressed?"

"Oh, *definitely*."

LATER THAT EVENING...

"Oh my God- that was *so* good. I can't decide what my favorite part has been so far- the food, the tequila, the spa...and that Arco del Amantes? Wow, just *wow*. Did you see all those couples? I get why it's a popular engagement spot. There's probably a million pics up on Instagram and Facebook." *Yak...* I'd nearly licked my plate clean before noticing Patrick's unsettling glare.

"Yeah, well...wait- *what?"*

"What did I say?"

"Sorry if I forgot our ridiculously inappropriate couple selfie- we can go back tomorrow if you want. And...don't you think you're *forgetting* something?" The crease between his eyebrows scrunched.

"Like...what? And no, that's okay," I winked lightheartedly, "but we don't have that many."

"I guess you *do* have a point." He sat back in his chair stubbornly, angling his head, "but that's not what I was referring to," he added, boasting himself.

"*Oh,*" I realized, "and *you*, obviously, but I was thinking of activities *outside* the bedroom..."

"*That's* an activity." *Men.*

"You know what I mean."

"Of *course* I do, babe. It's just that I bring you all the way down here for some fun and you get all analytical when you're supposed to be *relaxing.* I'm beginning to think that's not in your blood."

He wasn't wrong. "I know, I'm sorry I can't help it. You're right," I snickered sarcastically, "and I'm not trying to analyze."

"Then why do you still look like you're pondering something?" he asked.

"I'm *not,*" I debated.

"Lea, you can't fool me- I know you too well. I can see your brain cells stirring."

I set my glass back on the table, "okay, okay. So...I've been wondering...this has been *amazing* and I can't believe we have two more days to enjoy all this...Seriously you didn't have to fly me anywhere I..."

He cut me off, covering my hands with his as his eyes narrowed, "You're probably right; we could've just stayed local, but where's the fun in that? Oh, *wait-* I almost forgot. Would you excuse me for a sec? Don't go anywhere-I'll be right back."

"Okay." I sighed deeply, resting my chin in my hands. *Now what the hell is he doing? We didn't even eat dessert yet.* Patrick returned and I noticed one of the waiters standing against the wall, smiling. I shook it off, envisioning a large scoop of Mexican fried ice cream.

"*Finally.* We're not leaving, are we? 'Cause I was really looking forward to dessert. You should see some of this stuff- banana tres leches, sopapillas, flan..."

"Ah, no." I looked at him quizzically. "There's this special dessert they make, but you have to ask for it. It should be out shortly."

"Oh, okay. I hope it's good."

"Don't worry," he smiled, "I got you covered. But just in case their infamous dessert doesn't sell you, I was kinda hoping *this* would." He pulled out a small velvet-covered box and placed it in front of me. You know how sometimes when something is right in front of you, you don't see it? Well I *didn't*.

"What...what is *this*? I told you, you didn't need to buy me anything, this trip was *plenty*."

"I *wanted* to. I know you're not into fancy stuff, so I chose something a little *different*. If you don't like it, you can pick out something else." *What?*

"It's not that golden shrunken head charm from the voodoo shop we stopped in, right? 'Cause I was just joking when I said it'd look good on my Pandora bracelet..."

He shook his head. "Ah no, not *exactly*."

"Then *what* is it?" I asked impatiently.

"Just open it, will you?" he demanded, anxiously leaning forward.

I picked up the box slowly. "*Fine*," I pouted, prying it open. *Oh, shit. That's not no shrunken head.* "Wait. What...what *is* this?" I knew nothing about diamonds; I hardly knew what a carat was. All I knew was what was in front of me *hadn't* been cheap. My eyes were so uncontrollably drawn to the squarish blue gem I hardly even noticed the diamonds. It was simple yet elegant, but at the same time could sink a small ship.

"What does it look like? It's a ring. *Surprise*."

I narrowed my eyes, "I *know* it's a ring which in case you hadn't realized, happens to be a *little* more than some small token of affection. Sorry, I'm...I'm just a little well, *surprised*."

"You're right- it *does*, that's kind of the point." I pulled my eyes off the ring and looked at him. *Gulp. Please tell me he's not doing what I think he's doing 'cause I'm so not ready for...* He paused, taking a deep breath, "I've been doing some thinking. Actually, I've been doing a *lot* of thinking and..."

"*What*?"

"We've been together what, two years now? *Us* two, lasting this long, who would've thought? I know it hasn't been easy, us being apart. But no matter how busy we are, I need you to know that I am completely, 100% committed to you, to *us*, and when I'm with you I don't know, it just *feels* right. These past few weeks have made me realize something."

"Uh, what's that?" I asked, my gaze steady.

"That I'm better with you than without you; that I'm tired of us being apart and...and I think it's about time we move forward- together. You're kind and selfless and beautiful...You're the only girl I've ever actually been friends with and I'm pretty sure you're the only one in my life I've never lied to, either," he reflected. "I know I never say it, but you mean more to me than anyone's ever meant." He took another deep breath.

"Patrick, what are you saying?" *Oh, dear God.*

"I'm saying I want to be with you."

"You *are* with me."

"Can you be serious for a second?"

"Okay, okay. Sorry, I'm listening."

"We need to take advantage of what's right here, right now and not worry about what anyone else thinks or what might or might not happen; I think we both know how short life can be. I don't want to look back with any regrets. Look," he said, taking my hand, "I don't know what the next two years ahead will hold; I don't know about the years after that, but what I *do* know is how I feel; I *love* you, Eleana."

He was serious. It took everything in me not to break down in the middle of the restaurant. I tried to think of the right words to say. I mean, what *do* you say when the man of your dreams tells you he loves you and then basically proceeds to propose to you in such a romantic place? I'd seen it played out in hundreds of movies, but not once had I ever believed that'd be me, especially with a guy like Patrick Thomas. Hollywood or not, my skepticism on true love remained steadfast, the Ms. Hyde to my Dr. Jekyll. It wasn't that I *didn't* feel very strongly for Patrick or want to be with him because there was no question- he was probably the best guy I had ever known. But deep-down I could feel myself holding back. Why the fuck I'd want to hold back at a time like this with a *person* like this was beyond me, but this tiny voice in my head kept hesitating.

Still speechless, I stared back down at the ring. I couldn't believe what was in front of me right now- this unbelievable ring and Patrick; they had both caught me completely off guard. Now I finally understood it; how girls just totally and completely lost it when their boyfriends proposed to them in public. It was an overwhelming feeling that was hard to describe.

"Eleana? *Hello*, Earth to Eleana."

I awakened from my temporary trance, finally looking up at him. "I thought I lost you for a second," he smiled. "Are you gonna say anything?"

"Yeah, it's just...*wow*, I...is this..."

"This isn't to pressure you, or to scare you. Think of it as a...a...*promise* ring."

I looked at him with confusion. "Do people even give those anymore?"

"I don't know, maybe, I guess I am. Hey, this isn't funny."

"Sorry, it's just that this was the last thing I expected when you asked me to come down here and...and with everything going on at home and work stuff I...I...I just don't know."

"Hey," he continued, "it's okay-you don't have to give me any answer this second. I know it's a lot to take in. I just needed you to know how I feel; more than that, I wanted to *show* you. I'm not going anywhere, at least not until my next project, maybe," he smiled again.

"*Good*," I answered, somewhat relieved, "because I don't want you to...it's *beautiful*." My eyes gleamed with contentment as I leaned over the table to kiss him. Not the most seductive of kisses, but we *were* in a restaurant and nauseating PDA wasn't my thing.

Over these past two years, our feelings for each other had grown but I hadn't stopped to analyze it; I just kept living in the moment. I guess I hadn't realized how strongly he truly felt and, not that a girl like me wouldn't *want* a guy like him (or any guy, really) to feel that way about me, he was right- maybe it was time we communicated our feelings aloud. Here I was, sitting across from this incredible man who'd taken a big chance and laid his heart out on the line. He wanted a future with me and wasn't in a rush for an answer. I had an immense fondness for him, and my feelings were undeniably strong, but it suddenly hit me- was I in *love* with Patrick or just in love with *us*? I thought maybe I had been; I just hadn't said it. I'd only done that once in my life and it turned out to be the wrong guy. *I'll fuckin' say.* I mean, before you tell someone you're in it for the long haul, you better be *sure*, right?

Maybe it was because all the other stuff in my life being such a mess, or maybe it was that stupid fortune teller and her visions haunting me again. She'd already been right about *one* dark evil- it'd come full-force at my dad. Did all girls go through a mini mental breakdown before saying 'yes' to an unexpected (that's an understatement) marriage or promise proposal or whatever the hell it had been? I'd frozen-up and 'yes' wasn't the *only* word that *hadn't* escaped my lips. Patrick and I hadn't actually ever exchanged those three little words. Since *he'd* been the one to say them first, I only hoped he hadn't minded too much that I hadn't repeated them right back to him.

Damn these waiters and their timing, showing up with a flaming dessert at the exact same moment I had an open ring box sitting in front of you. As if caught in a spotlight Patrick and I both turned towards the waiter, who'd suddenly become uncomfortable with the moment he'd stumbled into. I closed the box and hid it beneath the tablecloth as he set the plate down between us. Patrick smiled and thanked him before sauntering off.

"Wow, this looks *amazing*," I said, my mouth beginning to water.

"Not as amazing as you," Patrick answered.

"*Or* that ring- Thank you- I love it. But just wait till we get back to the room, Mr. Thomas, *then* I'll show you amazing." I winked playfully, tilted my head.

"I can't wait."

Chapter 42 ~ Clueless

I wished we'd stayed in Cabo longer. Our three nights away had been amazing and jam-packed. Patrick had kept us busy, both in *and* out of the bedroom. He knew me well; I'll give him that. He also had no problem letting me know that despite all my degrees that when it came to relaxing, I had a lot to learn. He constantly had remind me to sit and do nothing sometimes, which had been especially difficult lately.

Now more than ever I was keeping myself busy so busy in fact, that if it weren't for Patrick and I sharing the same dwelling, the palm trees and warm Santa Ana winds outside my window I might not have noticed where I was. Our weekend away had been a lot to take in and my head was still spinning. I wasn't exactly ready to make that kind of decision, especially with everything else on my mind. That required some major thinking about the future and right now I was having a hard enough time looking three days ahead without giving myself a fucking panic attack.

The week was flying by and before I knew it, I'd be gone again. I didn't really have much of a choice on that one: I had to be back for a work meeting with the hospital board, one Maureen and I both had been anxious about. We were excited to see what they'd have to say but I had to put any thoughts about that aside because although I had big dreams of my own, they would have to wait and so would Patrick, at least for now, because I was only concerned with one thing: my father. Everything else unfortunately had to come second. I was beyond ecstatic over Patrick's promise/proposal, but the fact was making any rash decision without thinking it through wasn't in either of our best interests right now.

On the outside I was completely flattered and enamored, but inside I instinctively remained scientific and logical. Back in high school I'd faulted the girls who too easily put their trust in the wrong guy, whether he was a football jock or an unassuming nerd. I watched from the sidelines as they got hurt, even scarred, and my conclusion was it didn't seem worth it. Would I have felt 'better' about myself if I'd lost my virginity to the captain of the football team? *Unlikely.* Would I have *really* wanted to date him anyway? Probably not. Most high school couples never last and we all know high school boys only give a shit about one thing, so I was probably better off not even trying.

By the time I'd hit college, the budding scientist in me had perfected the use of facts and figures to build a wall around my heart- and it worked. I never let anyone get too close, even the quarterback of the football team who'd taken an interest, and I remained unscathed; I'd never end up like any of those *other* girls, crying or feeling used. We all know college relationships don't go anywhere either and college boys? Well, their priorities are the same as in high school.

After college, I'd finally decided to open my heart and fully trust someone and where did it get me? *Nowhere*, with a shattered heart that even by now hadn't been fully rebuilt. After the devastation I promised myself that from then on, *I* would be the one in control; that I wouldn't let anyone do that to me again. So, with my new evidence, I built an even bigger wall around my heart and that's the way I'd remained- until veterinary school where for the first time in my life, I'd been proven wrong.

Which brought me to my current situation and a man named Patrick Thomas: this utterly wonderful guy who nearly *every* girl would kill to have, and he was *mine*. Not only was he mine, he'd asked *me* to be a part of his future. Everything about Patrick seemed perfect, but was he perfect for me and could I really picture a future with him? The *fuck* if I knew- I'd never been able to picture a future with *anyone*. But maybe I thought, it was because I'd never really tried hard enough.

Stupidly, after all this time with him I still wasn't sold on the idea of happily-ever-after, even though there wasn't a more qualified prince charming out there. And was I *that* girl? The girl who jumped on the chance to say 'yes' *to* a guy just because of who he was, or because of a big, fat ring? I certainly didn't want him to think that. I wanted to say 'yes' for the right reasons. But before I went any further, there was one person I needed to let in on my little 'secret' and when I did, she was gonna flip the fuck out- just like I'd already done.

I leaned over the side of the pier looking north to Santa Monica. At home I'd grown up with views of Long Island's north shore, nothing like what I was looking at now. Staring out at vast ocean and miles upon miles of eye-catching shoreline took some getting used to and I would never get used to the water being on the wrong side. One thing that I'd *definitely* gotten used to was watching surfers.

"I was waiting for you to call me back." I'd had my eyes nearly permanently glued on a guy coming out of the water with his surfboard. His wavy blond locks and ripped physique had snagged my full attention as I'd dialed Rachel's number. I didn't even realize she'd picked up.

"What?"

"What? Dude, you *called* me, remember? What are doing anyway? Where the hell are you? It sounds noisy. Are those birds?"

"What? Oh yeah, birds. And waves, and men, *hot* men, half-dressed…"

"Is Patrick listening? Is he doing laps again? 'Cause I'd fly all the way out there just to see him do that, by the way," she joked.

"No, no. I'm at the beach."

"The beach? What beach?"

"Venice. I'm on the pier, hence the birds and all the bird shit. Apparently, they like it here as much as everyone else does."

"Let me guess-surfers."

"You know me so well."

"Is Patrick working?"

"Yea. I just left the shelter, so I figured I'd take a walk on the pier, do some people watching. Mike might meet me for lunch. So, what's up? I didn't listen to your message," I asked.

"Of *course* you didn't. Every time I leave you an important one, you don't fuckin' listen to it. You listen to all the *bullshit* ones though," she laughed. "Anyway, I wanted to ask you something."

"About?"

"When are you coming home?"

"I'm not exactly sure. I had this work meeting on the 1st, but it's apparently been pushed back so I was gonna stay longer. My dad's doing okay- I just talked to him a little while ago. Why? Is everything okay at the bakery?"

"Yea. Yea, everything's fine, except it's not."
"What do you mean?"

"I *mean*, while you're out there living it up with L.A.'s most *ineligible* bachelor, gawking at hot men, in the *sunshine* mind you, *I'm* staring out at yet another five inches of fucking snow, stuck inside yet *again*, and although I love my husband, if I have to be stranded in this fucking house for one more day with him I'm going to die *or* kill him."

"Oh." See what I mean about people in love making each other miserable? When I heard Rachel talk like that, it kind of made me wonder if there was something wrong with me and Patrick, like we were *supposed* to argue about stupid shit like Rachel and Tom sometimes did. I wondered if maybe when two people really went at it like that, that showed their passion for each other. And Rachel and Tom by no means argued often- they were a match made in heaven- but when they did, even *I* didn't wanna be around them.

"Sorry," I continued. "So, what did you want to ask me?"

"Well for one, I miss my best friend. Two, I desperately need a fucking vacation. So, I was thinking that maybe if there's room out there in the love nest, I can come visit, ya know, see some palm trees and surfers, do a little shopping, maybe catch up with Paige…"

"Ha, ha, ha. Okay, *one*, Patrick's house is *not* a love nest," I said vehemently, and *two*, of *course* there's room. Actually," I continued, finally looking away from the hot blond, "that's funny you ask because a visit from someone from home sounds perfect right now and it just so happens there *might* be an even better option...my apartment." Silence took over the other side of the phone.

"I thought someone was sub-leasing it."

"They *are*, or at least *were*. The lady who's been there, her work contract ended early, so she's headed back to Hawaii."

"Maybe I should join her," she laughed. "How early?"

"Two days. So I've got to get in there and do some cleaning."

"Need any help?"

"What?"

"With the cleaning. 'Cause I'm checking flights right now and Thursday looks good for me."

I pulled the phone away from my face momentarily staring at its screen. "You're fucking crazy. On the other hand, that sounds great, although you know it's not exactly beach weather right now."

"Whatever, it beats the shit out of *this* weather."

"That's true. How long you think you'll stay? Does Tom know this yet?"

"No, but he will as soon as I hang up. Fuck that- he went away for some *Nascar* thing with his buddies- now it's my turn."

"What about the bakery?"

"I think they can handle my being absent for a few days," she laughed.

"Tom, on the other hand...You know how guys always think their woman is having a threesome when they go away..."

"I'm flattered you'd share Patrick with me," she added.

"Maybe. Anything *else* you wanna do while you're here besides boy watch and shop? And don't think I'm walking around Beverly Hills 'cause you know how much I hate it. Plus, I really don't feel like watching that TMZ bus constantly drive by looking for a Kardashian."

"It's not like either of us can afford anything on Rodeo anyway," she giggled, "although it *would* be pretty fun to walk into some bougie store like Julia Roberts..."

"Totally," I agreed, "and then when they try to kick us out because we're dressed like hookers, I'll tell them who my boyfriend is, and they'll be sorry."

"Or better yet," she interrupted, "we'll walk into some ridiculously overpriced, tasteless art gallery like Axel Foley..."

Immediately one of my favorite scenes sprung to mind. "Right and inquire about some ugly-ass dining room set with a rotating head centerpiece."

She caught on and began reciting from *Beverly Hills Cop*, word for word, "I see you look at this piece," she said, playing the part of Serge.

"Yeah, I was wondering how much something like this went for," I answered in my best Axel Foley voice.

"One hundred thirty-thousand dollar."

"*Get* the fuck outta here."

"*No*, I *cannot*, it's serious though because it's very important piece."

"Have you ever sold one of these?"

"Sell it yesterday to collector."

"*Get* the fuck outta here,"

"*No*, I'm *serious*. I sell it myself." I almost fell over the railing I was laughing so hard.

"Jesus," she said, "I *love* that fucking movie."

"Me, too. Besides, who doesn't *love* Eddie Murphy? I think we need to watch that when you come out."

"Definitely."

Part Six: Sorry!

"What's right is what's left after you've done everything else wrong."

-Robin Williams

Chapter 43~ Diamonds are Forever

Two Days Later...

"So, what time's her flight land?"

"An hour." I watched Fenway jetted after the ball. "I made reservations for 8:30. That should work."

"Yeah, if your brother shows up on time. I can never figure out why he's always so late."

"You know Kevin's all about appearances *and* he likes to make an entrance."

"Funny," I said, "I thought *you* were the star."

Patrick laughed, "True. I hope she likes the place."

"Rachel just cares about palm trees and sunshine. I told you we didn't have to go out-we could've stayed in. You impressed her a long time ago you know," I laughed.

"You sure you two weren't separated at birth? Anyway, I *insist*. Hopefully she won't mind Kevin's coming."

"Nope, I'm sure she'll be entertained."

"So," he continued, "what are you guys gonna do while she's here? Sight-see?"

"Nah, she's done all that. Plus, you forget her sister-in-law lives here. Maybe some shopping and just hanging out and she's gonna help me clean the apartment."

"Oh, right, I forgot. You gonna head over there tomorrow, right?"

"Yup. So you can have your boys' night or whatever," I said.

"Kev's already got the night all planned out...bar hopping, strip clubs, all-nite parties..." I remained silent. "Lea?" I glared at him. "Just kidding."

I smirked at the camera. Just because Patrick and I were in the same city didn't mean we didn't still Skype; just because we were staying in the same house didn't mean I didn't want to see his handsome face as much as possible, either.

"It's fine, really, I don't care; I trust you...unless you bring a bunch of whores back to the house. Then there's a *small* chance they'll mysteriously go missing. I can probably get my hands on some mafia blocks if I ask the right people..." I glanced up in thought. "If you're lucky, I just *might* let you live."

"*Mafia* blocks?"

"Yeah, *mafia* blocks," I repeated. "Oh, *right*, they don't have those out here, either. They must be hidden away with all the good pizzerias, delis and bakeries..." He continued staring at me. "*Mafia* blocks uh, cinder blocks, you know, the heavy things you tie around someone's waist after you've beaten them to a bloody pulp just before you drop in the river."

"I thought your family wasn't in the mob and why am I not surprised at your already-hatched plan?" he laughed. "Anyway, you don't have to worry. You know there's only one woman I really want to put my hands on." His charm never got old, that's for sure.

I blushed uncontrollably. "They're *not*," I insisted, an evil smile creeping. When it came to Patrick Thomas, there was little he had to do to make me blush. "Wow- you really *are* still that oblivious, aren't you? It's your handsome face I don't trust, not *you*. You know those chicks swarm all over you any chance they get. Next thing you know one of 'em'll try to steal you away."

"Never happen."

"I'll remember that, Thomas."

"You better."

"Anyway, let me go. You're busy and I've got a couple of calls to make before Rachel gets here so, I'll see you soon. Muah." I puckered my lips at him.

"Since when are you into the mushy stuff?" he asked.

"I'm not..." I noticed the doubtful look. "Okay. Maybe it's growing on me a *little*..." I smiled.

Two hours later...

"I thought you said this place wasn't that big," Rachel asked as we walked up to the roof deck. She paused as we stepped outside. "What the *fuck*. I have no words."

"Pretty sweet, huh?"

"Sweet?! I would *kill* for this view and I hate L.A. as much as you do," she pressed.

"I know, right? There isn't even an ocean view but the first time I saw it I loved it anyway. That's what sold Patrick, too."

"How much did you say he paid for this place?"

"1.9."

"That's it?" she teased.

"Yep, a real steal."

"So, what's the plan for tonight?"

"Patrick is taking us out. Guess he couldn't wait to have *two* beautiful girls on his arm," I said.

"Oh, nice, but you're right-I would've totally been cool with staying in. Anywhere good?"

"Knowing him, yes."

"Oh, so we're *not* showing our hot boyfriend off around Beverly Hills then?"

"No, Los Feliz," I answered. "You'll like it- it's laid back and *so* not Beverly Hills. There's...just one other thing."

"What do you mean?"

"There's another dinner guest- Kevin's coming."

"Oh, I remember him-he's cute, right?"

"Yeah, so?"

"Well, I was just thinking. I should keep my options open in case I decide to leave Tom and move out here with you. *Obviously* it's no New York, but I think I could make it work, especially if I had this back yard."

"Oh my God, can you imagine?"

"What do you mean, *might*? He's been pissing me off lately."

"Oh come *on*. You guys are a match made in heaven, whatever the fuck that is, but anyway... I'm pretty sure there isn't anyone else out there..."

"Hmm, I guess you have a point, a *small* one."

"But if I were you I'd choose Adrian over Kevin," I joked. "Patrick said he might be around this weekend."

"*Adrian*, as in *Entourage* Adrian? Are they really friends?" she asked.

"Yeah, and neighbors, kind of. He lives nearby."

She turned to me in thought as if studying me. "Look at *you*, Ms. Hollywood, *Doc Hollywood*, more appropriately, down with the rich and famous, still managing to hold on to this gorgeous guy and be surrounded by a steady *stream* of gorgeous guys..."

"You *have* your own, or did you forget him as soon as you stepped off the plane?" I laughed.

"*Maybe*," she teased, "and I *know* but..."

"Half of these guys out here are tools anyway, you know that."

"True, except all the ones *you* happen to know," she added.

"Which reminds me, did you ever get a hold of Paige?"

"I tried," she said, "but she and Derek are away- Mexico I think, speaking of which, you never told me how Cabo was."

"Oh, too bad. I haven't seen them in a while," I said. There was no skirting around big questions with your best friends- they picked up on *everything*.

"*Well*, how *was* it? I bet the weather was nice." I guess I hadn't realized how wide my eyes had gotten because Rachel immediately sensed my anxiety and grew concerned.

"It was...*good*. Actually, it was *great*," I felt my voice trail off.

Rachel continued to probe, "hmm," she said, "then why don't you sound like it was? Is everything okay, I mean, besides the obvious?"

A deep sigh escaped from my chest. It really had been amazing and so had Patrick. There wasn't one negative I could think of other than...*that wasn't negative and you know it, Eleana.*

"Well, are you gonna answer me? Or are you still flying high from all the wild and crazy sex on the beach that you haven't returned to Earth yet?" If it's one thing Rachel was good at, it was digging up dirt. Fortunately for her she was gonna find some. "Come on, spill it, lovergirl."

"What?" I blushed. *Well, maybe...* "Yeah, yeah, everything's fine." *I think.* "It's uh...okay, there's just one *small* thing I forgot to mention."

"What?"

I hesitated briefly, another sigh sneaking out. "*Promise* you won't tell anyone, okay?"

"Sure, of course. Lea, seriously, *what's* wrong? Does it have to do with Patrick?" I nodded 'yes'. "Did something happen with you two?"

"Well? *Sort* of, I *think* maybe or, I'm not sure..."

"What does that mean? Did he cheat on you? I don't care how many dumb, hot blondes are running around out here- he better stick with the brunette he's got or else his balls will end up in a vice faster than..."

I stopped her, "*no.*"

"Oh, okay, just checking," she paused pensively. "Wait. You didn't..."

"Of *course* not."

"You're not pregnant, are you?" *God, I hope not. That's a road I'd prefer not to go down right now.* I was baffled yet impressed with her suppositions. She wasn't far off; I mean at our age, there weren't many surprises lurking around corners but getting knocked up was one of them. Shaking my head, I chuckled.

"No. *Seriously?*"

"Then *what*? Don't tell me after two years with the man of your dreams you've decided you're gay and don't wanna be with him anymore." We both laughed loudly.

"Another point for creative thinking but, no. Actually, it's uh...*ugh*. It's easier if I show you," I huffed.

I led her back inside to the master bedroom. I walked over to one of the dressers, opening its top drawer. I ran my hand beneath the row of bras and pulled it out, walked over and handed it to her.

Perplexed, she inspected it before looking back at me as she sat down on the bed.

"Wait- are you *proposing* to me? I'm really flattered but..." My smile flatlined. I shook my head painstakingly slow and hers did the same as the air between us went silent. Not saying a word, she opened the little box and gasped. "I guess diamonds *aren't* a girl's best friend after all," she said to herself. "Is *this* the 'little' thing you were talking about? If this is *little,* then what *I'm* wearing is fucking *microscopic*! When were you gonna *tell* me about this?"

"You asked me how Cabo was. Well? *That's* how Cabo was." The corners of my lips raised.

"Okay, then I'll repeat my question. *How* was Cabo, Lea?" I could tell she was a little miffed but at the same time so drawn to the damn ring she couldn't take her eyes off it.

"It was great well, *sort* of," I sulked. She motioned for me to sit next to her.

"What do you mean, *sort* of? This shit is serious. When Tom proposed to me I..."

"Whoah, wait a minute, wait a minute. *Who* said it was an engagement ring?"

The look on her face turned sour, "*you* did. You said..."

"*No,* I didn't. I said *this* is how Cabo was," I pointed to the open box.

"Okay, *what* the fuck is this then?" she urged.

"It's a...*promise* ring. There *is* a difference, you know."

"*No* there is...*what* the fuck did you just say?"

"You heard what I said," I pressed, "don't you know what they are?"

"I *know* what the fuck they are. I know that the last one I saw was given to me in the 3rd grade so again, what *is* this shit? Actually, I take that back- it's *not* shit; it's the nicest 'non-engagement' ring I've ever seen. Did you look up close at this sapphire? Damn he's got good taste *and* a good jeweler. Anyway," she continued ranting, "a *promise* ring is what a boy gives his first girlfriend. It's not something a guy like *Patrick Thomas* dishes out casually, to just *any* girl, on a *romantic* weekend, in *Mexico.*"

"You're right- it's *not.*" I paused, breathing deeply, "it's totally not," I trailed off.

"What are you not telling me, Lea? And why the *hell* do you look so sad? If I were you, I'd be jumping up and down right now. I mean it's not every day that kinda shit happens- to *anyone.*"

There was no other way to say it- I felt kind of silly and embarrassed about that night in Cabo. She was right- any other girl *would've* been over the moon if Patrick Thomas had said to them what he'd said to me, and I hadn't exactly jumped up and down, then *or* now. Chalk some of it up to being completely caught off guard, but the rest I blamed on myself. "I'm *not*. It's just...I don't know," I huffed, "there we were in Cabo- kayaking, tequila tasting, massages, the whole nine yards...then he takes me out to this amazing dinner. You should've seen the place..."

"And?" Rachel had pushed herself to the edge of the bed, anxious for more.

"And...just before dessert's about to come out, he lays this on the table."

"*And?*"

"He says he's doing a lot of thinking. He seemed nervous-it was *weird*. He was so *sincere,* so *sure* about us, about everything- the way he felt, wanting to spend more time together a...fut...*future*..." I huffed again, barely able to spit out the word. *Fuck it- just say it, you wimp* "...with *me* and that this was his way of showing me his commitment."

She stared at me, waiting. "No shit, Sherlock." I shrugged my shoulders. "Okay so, let me get this straight. Mr. 'dark, dashing and debonair' basically proposes sorry, *promises* you, with one of the most gorgeous pieces of jewelry I've ever seen and...what am I missing? I don't get it, *what's* the problem?" She thought before continuing, "wait a minute. Please tell me you said 'yes'. You *did* say *yes*, right?"

"Not exactly, no."

"What do you *mean*?"

"I mean, I didn't say yes. I didn't say no, either. I just wasn't expecting him to..."

"Lea, *most* girls don't expect it when it happens. So, what *did* you say? I mean you had to have said *something*. You can't just leave a guy hanging like that."

"Of *course* I said something- after I got over the initial shock. I just *freaked* out a little; okay a *lot*. I mean, what do you even say to something like that?"

"Well, for one thing, *most* girls would say 'yes'." I could see her wheels spinning. Then she did what all best friends do at a time like this- they try to make you feel better, even if they think you're a fucking idiot, which clearly I was. "Ok, so you *freaked* out, understandable given the circumstances *and* the guy I guess, but things couldn't have gone nearly as bad as you're making them out..." I remained silent. "How much more could there be?" she pressed.

"Well? He just...said something else that kind of freaked me out even more. I...Well, Patrick and I aren't that lovey-dovey couple and...you know I'm not good when it comes to *feelings*. And when someone says stuff like that to me, it makes me wanna run for the hills. It's like some genetic defect or something," I stopped myself.

"Well at least the 'hills' are close so you can't go that far," she stopped laughing the moment she understood. "Oh, you mean he told you he *loved* you." *That's right- Eleana, wanting to run from a good thing the moment it gets down, dirty and real.*

"Uh huh, exactly," I sulked. She put her hand gently on my shoulder.

"You should be thrilled. You just landed one of the *hottest* stars in Hollywood. How many girls can say that? That's an accomplishment in and of itself."

"You know I don't care about that shit. If I *did*, I would've gone after one of the filthy rich, preppy assholes I grew up with."

"So, what's *wrong* then?" My head remained low. "*Ohhh*," she realized, "you mean you didn't say it back."

I shook my head a resounding 'no', unable to speak. "*What* is *wrong* with me? Patrick's this amazing guy. He like checks off every single thing on a girl's list, even *mine*. He's intelligent and funny and understanding. He looks like a fucking Disney prince- he probably *is* one, for all I know. I mean he's practically the perfect man and I'm just...what if..."

"Wait a minute. Are you still hung up on that whole 'he's famous and I'm not' shit? Don't be ridiculous-if he *really* didn't want to be with you, he wouldn't. Is *that* why you didn't say it back, because your warped mind doesn't think it could last? Jesus, give yourself some credit for once and for *once*, would you just pay attention to what's right in front of you instead of itching to run the second you get scared?"

"I *am* and I'm *not* I just, I don't know. Maybe my brain's messed up from being fucked over or...maybe I'm worried Patrick hasn't yet realized he doesn't belong with the peasant girl and can find better. A part of me feels like he will and when he does...*poof!* He'll disappear. You *know* how I feel about him...I just suck at feelings."

"If you sucked at feelings, you wouldn't have gotten this far. So, you pour out your heart- *big* deal. If not now, then *when*? Someday you're gonna have to take that chance again, Lea. If you don't, you'll end up alone with no ring at all- from anyone. Patrick is *real* and he's not going anywhere...unless you *want* him to. The sooner you realize that the better." Maybe she was right. Maybe deep down I *was* so afraid that if I took that leap of faith and let go of my fears, I'd lose control; that somehow things would go wrong...

"Do you honestly think that if you tell him you love him, that things will go south, that he's suddenly gonna *leave*? You need to stop torturing yourself for what happened with dickhead. That was a specific example of a low-life piece of shit."

"I'm *not*. And, that's true." She gave me a disbelieving look.

"If you say so. But you know none of that was your fault. That guy was gonna cheat no matter *what*. He deserves everything that comes to him."

"I know, but I can't help it. The one time I followed my heart without thinking it through and *that's* what ended up happening and now? I try to make sure I do things the right way and somehow I feel like I'm still gonna screw it up or it'll screw up itself."

"If that were the case he wouldn't be sticking around, would he?"

"No, I guess not. I mean, he *did* tell me to take all the time I need. I told you- it's like he's not real. I don't get it."

"Well, *I* do- he's in love with you and he doesn't want to lose you- this is his way of showing you that. He obviously knows a good thing when he sees it. The only question is...are *you* in love with *him*? Because if *you* are then you need to tell him and if you're not...you need to tell him."

I knew everything she was saying was true; I *wasn't* 100% sure if I was in love with Patrick. I did love him, but for some reason I still couldn't say it. And was he my future? That was something I needed to figure out; I just hoped he'd stay true to his word and be patient because I didn't want to lose him, either. Unfortunately, there was more to a relationship than love and the truth was, there were things in the works that might complicate us even more- I just hadn't found the right time to tell him yet. In order for me to give him any kind of solid answer, I had to be sure where my own life was going.

She studied the ring once more before handing back to me. "What about *this* then? You ever gonna put it *on* or are you gonna leave it in your drawer buried beneath all your bullshit excuses for not wanting to move ahead with this relationship and start planning your future?" she doubted.

"I *am* planning my future. I've *been* planning it, for a *long* time, in case you hadn't noticed," I retorted angrily. "Why do you think I've been working so hard at the clinic? You know that's always been my dream."

"And what about Patrick?" she insisted. "I thought *he* was your dream."

"He still *is*, Rachel, but that doesn't mean I have to leave my own behind."

"Just because you're with him, does *not* mean you have to leave your dreams behind and it *doesn't* mean you have to leave any of *yourself* behind, either. Why are you so afraid to commit to him? You think you can't do *both*? You've been doing okay so far and if anyone can do it, it's you."

"But what if I *can't*? What if we *can't* work around it? I start to panic the moment I look too far into the future as it is and right now the future, my *dream* future, may actually happen and I just hadn't planned on anyone serious being in the picture when that day came. And now that there *is*, it's like I'm drawing a blank on everything- I can't figure out how to work him into the equation."

"Are we back to the analytical Eleana now? Patrick is a *person*, not an element on the periodic table. You don't *calculate* your life or try to work things in or out of equations, *especially* love. You're a smart girl, Lea, and I love you, I really do but for fuck's sake, when are you gonna learn *not* to overthink and just go with your gut, your heart?"

Was she right? I sighed. I was beginning to wonder if I ever would, at least, fully. I worried that one day I *would* have to choose- between what I loved to do and who I loved. A part of me lived in constant fear of the day when someone I loved might leave me. I'd learned to overcome the past, adapt, be self-sufficient, to leave people *before* they left me so that I *wouldn't* get hurt. And it'd seemed to be working, until now. I'd never planned on someone like Patrick coming along and now that he had and had actually wanted to stay, I was having a small problem- I suddenly couldn't picture having it all- my dream job *and* the dream guy- without there being serious complications.

"Does Patrick know this?" she asked.

"Not exactly. I was gonna wait until after the meeting. For all I know, they'll pull a 180 on us and I'll be back to square one, or no square at all. And they're not excuses. Don't you think I *care* about Patrick? That I *know* how good a guy he is? The last thing I want is to lose him. I'm not running. Besides this," I said shaking the ring in its box, "is just a piece of jewelry."

"Just remember Eleana," she pressed, "diamonds and sapphires may last forever, but a guy like Patrick won't if you're not willing to give him what he needs, and that's you, and I mean *all* of you, not just the bits and pieces that you choose to give." I nodded my head 'yes', agreeing with her argument. "You don't always need a plan- if you really love someone then nothing else matters, it's like all the little stuff goes away. I am thinking though, that you should probably *show* him ya know, before you head back east, just so he *really* knows your serious." One look at her sly expression and I knew exactly what she'd meant.

"Actually, that's not a bad idea," I admitted. "I don't have much time, but I think I can conjure up *something*. Alright, what do you say we grab some bubbly and sit down by the pool?"

"Sounds good. I've got a few ideas we can toss around," she winked.

"Look, don't go getting any 9½ *Weeks* ideas, 'cause I am *not* dousing Patrick in whipped cream and cherries in the middle of the kitchen floor," I added, both of us laughing hysterically as we headed downstairs.

Chapter 44 ~ Swingers

"Lea, you were right- I like the vibe here," Rachel said as we left the restaurant. "And that place *was* decent."

"Well, you can't come to Los Feliz and not eat at Little Dom's," I laughed. "Patrick wanted to take us to another 'Italian' place, but I shot him down."

"Why?"

"Because I don't take anyone out for Italian here unless I taste it first. When he mentioned Little Dom's I said, 'stop right there. I know you mean well, but maybe we should steer clear of Italian. I don't think you realize what we're dealing with'. He asked me what I meant and I said, 'look, I know you guys have your own gastropub/wine country cuisine, but you always wanna *change* stuff, turn it into something it's not, just to be cool and different'..."

"Sounds like L.A. alright," she commented.

"Totally. I had to elaborate, 'I'm not taking my best friend, who's a New *Yorker* need I remind you, to a place where the chicken parmigiana is topped with avocadoes or the tiramisu is made with fucking tofu. And let's not get started on sauce and cappuccino'," we both laughed.

"Hey, what are you guys laughing at?" I heard Patrick's voice from behind.

"Oh, nothing. So," Rachel probed, "*then* what? I'm loving the background on our dinner, by the way."

"He just laughed, insisting I was wrong. I was like, 'I don't care how many celebrities stop in or what their opinion is because half of them don't eat anyway', and you know what he said? He said, 'well, Adrian likes the place'. Can you believe that?"

"Isn't he French?"

"Exactly, but after promising me we wouldn't be disappointed, I gave in."

"Well," she said, "I gotta say *this* time, I think he was right. That eggplant parm was pretty fuckin' good. New *York* good? Jury's still out."

"What was that?" Patrick and Kevin had caught up and were now at an ear's shot distance. "I'm sorry, did I just hear you say I was right um, *again*?" he asked, wrapping one arm around me.

I turned to him and smiled, "I *said*, you were *right*, about the restaurant."

"Uh, huh," he answered assuredly, "that's what I *thought*."

"So, you ladies ready for the after party?" Kevin asked.

"*After* party? You're lucky if I make it past 11:00. Plus we wanna get to the beach early," Rachel said.

"Did you just say *beach*?" he asked. We nodded 'yes'. "And *why* wasn't I invited to this?"

"Uh, because it's *girl's* only and...aren't you supposed to be spending quality brother time together?"

"Yeah," Patrick contended, "I was looking forward to our *brotherly* weekend of debauchery," he laughed.

Rachel interjected, "I mean you're *more* than welcome to come. So far our big plans include apartment cleaning and mani pedis. So, if you wanna throw on some rubber gloves, clean the shitter and sip martinis while getting pampered in some salon, have at it..." After no answer, she continued, "that's what I thought," she blurted.

The Dresden was over one block, about a mile away from where we'd had dinner. I'd never actually been there; I'd only admired it while strolling by. Since 1954 it had maintained that quintessential old school Hollywood lounge feel. It hadn't been remodeled since the 1960s, but its décor still drew in crowds.

Stepping through its doors was like stepping into the past. I imagined Frank Sinatra or Wayne Newton as regulars and it was no wonder a guy like Ron Burgundy loved the place. It was dimly lit with a dark color scheme and retro lounge chairs, tables and booths. Off to the side were its private rooms, reserved by the occasional celebrity. We sat in one of its leather semi-circular booths, checking out the scene- a mix of young and old, singles and couples, some dressed for current times, others who would've fit in better at an American Legion or some bar in Vegas.

"*Damn*," Rachel said, "this place is cool. Who are those people singing? They're hilarious."

I looked across the room, past the infamous spacious u-shaped bar, picturing Trent and Mikey desperately trying to grab a bartender's attention for a drink and any lady's attention for a phone number. Then I spotted them- the evening's entertainment, *unique*, to say the least. Marty and Elayne was a classic duo who'd been cranking out jazz since 1982; they must've been nearly 80 years old. Only in L.A., I thought.

Kevin couldn't help but butt in, as usual, "what *I* can't believe is how they haven't keeled over yet. They look like they escaped from some Beverly Hills nursing home, like a *decade* ago." None of us could help but laugh- their outfits were shabby-chic at best and it was obvious they did their own hair and makeup because it was horrible.

"Well," Patrick added, "at least they sing in tune..."

"I hear ya," Rachel said. "I mean they're certainly not the worst entertainers I've ever seen."

Kevin's head was turned towards the bar as he spoke. Clearly, he had his mind elsewhere- like on *any* girl. He excused himself and the three of us ordered another drink from our waitress. After Marty and Elayne's second set Rachel and I decided to go check out the bar for ourselves. Call me sentimental, and not that I'd never come back, but I wasn't leaving until I stood exactly where Vince Vaughn had stood and ordered a drink. I mean I'd finally made it inside- I wanted the full experience.

"You're back. We were beginning to wonder if you got lost. We also saw those two guys over there talking to you. You sure they weren't bothering you?"

Rachel's stare said otherwise. "Are you *kidding* me?" she asked. "We grew up going to New York City clubs. We can handle it," she smirked at Kevin.

"So," I said, "I see you've got your sights on some ladies tonight?" Kevin ignored me as he turned his attention back to some young prey at the bar.

"Absolutely," he answered, excusing himself again.

Rachel had been watching his every move. "You think he'll score or what?"

"Probably not," Patrick said.

"But it *is* fun watching him try," she answered. "Speak of the devil…"

"What, back so soon?" I asked, noticing Kevin's quick return. "What happened to your game?" Kevin stared me down, trying not to laugh himself.

"Funny," he said.

The duo was in the middle of a jazzed-up version of a Neil Diamond song. Witnessing two 80-year-olds play everything from ukuleles to drums while belting out the classics had definitely made our night.

I turned to Rachel, "You know, I really wish I could've been here when they were filming *Swingers*. Can you imagine that set?"

"Yeah, and I just love those two," she commented.

"Ah hem, excuse me?" Patrick asked. "I could do a good Trent."

"Yeah, me too."

Rachel and I both looked at them, faces blatantly incredulous. "Patrick, you may be tall and handsome and *kind* of funny, but you're no Vince Vaughn, I'm sorry babe."

"Wait a minute, wait a minute. *I'm* funny, I'm tall and I'm *definitely* good to look at," Kevin declared, feeling left out.

Rachel wasn't having it. "Now hold on a sec. First of all, you're not *that* good to look at and *second*, that's the third time you've returned to the table without a number- you don't even qualify as Mikey."

"Oooohh," Patrick commented, "that hurt."

Chapter 45 ~ Men at Work

Rachel and I sat at one of Fred 62's old and tattered checkered tables eating breakfast on our way to the beach. We'd left Patrick's house so early the guys were barely awake. The difference between true beach people and everyone else was that we didn't waste one second of a great beach day. The weather looked to be warmer for the remainder of Rachel's visit, with temps expected to hit the mid-70s, a rarity for late February, something I hadn't foreseen a week ago.

The other thing I hadn't foreseen? The text I'd just received. I looked down at my phone after I'd heard it buzzing. Usually I kept the ringtone off so I wouldn't annoy those around me. I hated people who had the volume up so fucking loud you could hear their obnoxious ringtone a mile away or even better, the ones with their Bluetooth permanently stuck in their ear.

Rachel noticed my confused look as I went to sip my latte, nearly dropping the mug. "What's wrong?" she asked. "Is everything okay?"

"Oh yeah, *yeah*," I answered. *Bullshit it is.*

"Then why do you look like it *isn't*?" she persisted. I took another sip, sighing deeply before I passed her the phone. "*Whoah*, can't you wait 'til I leave before the fuckin' love texting?" She reluctantly took the phone and I watched her eyes widen with shock and curiosity. "Um, are you *serious* right now? Did he seriously just text you?"

I shrugged in response. "Don't look at me like that- I'm just as surprised as you are."

"You told them where you live?" she pressed.

"Yeah, I told them. What's wrong? You know I only know like five people out here. Who cares anyway? They're old friends," I insisted.

"*That's* a fuckin' understatement," she argued.

"*Whatever*, anyway, I don't know. He's probably just saying 'hi'. I mean they *do* live out here, ya know. *I* don't know what to do with this..."

"Well, *I* do." I looked at her oddly. "I'm gonna text him back. We're gonna be at the beach anyway..."

I immediately snatched the phone back. "Oh no you're not, come on, now. Look," I said, "normally I wouldn't have a problem under you know, *different* circumstances. What if Patrick and Kevin decide to stop by? How the *fuck* am I gonna explain that one? You know I think they're cool guys but our 'fun' days with them were eons ago..."

"*So*...what's the issue then? Let's just see. Maybe it's nothing; maybe they're here for work. And why are you suddenly worried about Patrick?"

"Hey this is supposed to be *girl* time and...I don't wanna get into any...you know, *trouble*, with those two."

"*Trouble*? What kind of trouble could we possible get into?" I glared at her with skepticism. "'*A*', I'm married and '*B*', you're probably gonna be at some point...we don't know when but that's another story...anyway, let's just see what they're up to. It'll be *harmless*." Before I knew it, she'd already hit the send button.

We'd hit my apartment cleaning full swing and were nearly done by 11:30. We decided to take a break and sit outside at the expansive outdoor lounge area. The pool glimmered at us and Rachel was suddenly glad she'd brought a bathing suit.

I really liked my apartment complex. It sat on a dead-end street along the marina's canals. I was impressed the moment I'd seen it- its meticulously landscaped property gave it a private oasis-type feel. I knew I'd gotten lucky when I'd found it and for what I was paying it was a steal- you couldn't beat its location. We sat on a couple of lounge chairs soaking up some rays, watching boats head out of the marina.

"Remind me again why I don't live here?"

I shrugged my shoulders, a small chuckle escaping my throat. "I don't know; probably the same reason I don't- neither of us can stand these people or their environment full-time."

"I'm beginning to question that philosophy," she commented. "On another note, remind me why your boyfriend doesn't have one of those boats? Because we could be out on it right now instead of sitting here watching *other* girls sip champagne while blasting Snoop Dog."

"I'm pretty sure Patrick's 'boat', *if* he had one, wouldn't be one of *those*," I laughed.

"Ha, ha. But I guess I really shouldn't be complaining right now, because this view isn't bad," she added. "I could see myself working from home at a place like this."

"Now you're making *me* second guess my decision to stay the remainder of my time at Patrick's. I should make him stay here. It's more convenient for me but not for him so..."

"Speaking of guys, did Cal elaborate more on today?"

I pulled out my phone. "Uh, yeah, actually. I read it kind of quickly, but he said something about some promotional event for their clothing line. I can't keep track of all their artsy festivals, skate events and beach cleanups around here. Here, he said:

'Yo, Lea. Mark and I are in Venice all weekend for the Venice Entrepreneur Expo. We'll be near Muscle Beach so stop by if you're around.'

"Oh, cool. Is that it?" Rachel asked.

"No, he also said if I had any single friends to bring them along," I laughed.

"Of *course* he did. "Did you text him back yet?"

"Not yet, but I will. I'm not sure how long that thing is going on. Just wait 'til he sees who I'm bringing with me. That'll thrown him for a loop." I shot Cal a quick response.

"Totally. I also look like ten times better than the last time he saw me so this will be fun," she laughed, 'VA Beach: Take II'!"

We sat in our chairs hysterical, both thinking back to those summer days spent catching rays, bar hopping and guy-watching, among *other* things... "I hate to break it to ya, but Mark's not the only one whose looks have improved..." I winked at her playfully.

She shook her head, unable to stop laughing, "Oh...*shit*," she said, "this *is* going to be fun..."

The moment Rachel and I reached the pier, it was obvious something was going on. Not only were there more people than usual for this time of year, the crowd was different. Strangely, the amount of 'normal-looking' vastly outnumbered the typical skaters, stoners, muscle heads and homeless, who lingered despite the beach rules. Speaking of nonconforming rule-breakers, I was eager to see what the guys were up to and how their endeavor was going.

"Where'd they say they were gonna be again?" Rachel asked as we walked.

"By Muscle Beach. Look for a sign that says '51'."

We walked until we neared a black and white booth with American flags. "Wait, I think I see it," she said, grabbing my attention. "That it?"

"Probably," I said, slowing down. "And...there they are. I'd recognize that trouble anywhere." We smiled as our jaws uncontrollably dropped.

"Different coast, *same* hooligans," she laughed. "*Damn*, you really weren't kidding, were you?"

I looked plainly at her, "would I *kid* about that kind of shit?" Dating a total hunk and still I had to gawk. But I couldn't help it- they were hot.

I remembered it like it was yesterday. I'd been attracted to Mark almost instantly, not that that'd been too hard. His laid-back Northern Cali charms had pulled me right in. Cal, on the other hand was attractive, but far from my type: on the shorter side, louder and a little too full of Southern Californian machismo. Rachel had found him to be hot and entertaining, while Cal had been taken aback by her beauty, brains and a presence most men couldn't handle. Even the most highly trained men didn't have a contingency plan for girls like us and as for Rachel and I? Well, we hadn't exactly 'planned' on anything like *them*, either. And now, here we were years later, a different beach, a different coast, only *this* time we weren't single.

I wished I was back there sometimes, but not just because of the boys; I'd been there with my family many times before. SEAL reunions were in a word, 'unique'. They were everything you might expect (and much more, including the inappropriate) from a bunch of Team guys: booze trucks, bands and blowing things up on the beach. As a teen they'd been fun, but as an adult I got to partake in *all* the fun, including partying it up with hot young men, naval captains, my brothers *and* my dad. Whoever came up with the saying 'work hard, play hard' had never met a U.S. Navy SEAL; if they had, they'd have known that their version of *anything* took shit to a whole other level.

Speaking of hard workers, there stood Cal and Mark, sporting fitted t-shirts from their collection. Muscle Beach was some scene: a bright blue sectioned-off area of weight machines and adult-sized jungle gym toys. It was the perfect image of a beachfront gym and a Venice landmark. Arnold Schwarzenegger had even competed there years ago. Despite the important event going on, this *was* still California, the land of the show-offs and dying-to-be-discovered and so the gym was packed with people- few who were actually working out. But despite the show before us, Rachel and I couldn't help but keep our eyes on the two lean, well-muscled men who had now noticed us.

"Well, well, well. Look who decided to finally show up." The smirk on Cal's face was typical. He'd just finished talking to some skater, a dime a dozen around here. "Pretty fuckin' cool, huh?" He walked around to the other side of the table to hug me.

"Hey, Lea, what's going on?" Mark said politely. His smile scored him more points than Cal had. Then again, he never had to do much to score in my book. His sandy blond hair moved with the breeze, his dark blue eyes incandescent from the sun's rays. *If only,* I thought. He walked in front of Cal, lingering with his hug.

"Hey, not much. It is, I gotta say. Actually," I turned back to Cal, "we would've come earlier but we had some work to do at my apartment," I smiled playfully.

"*Work*?" Mark asked, one arm still loosely around my waist. *Oh dear God*. I remembered those hands and the chills they used to send down my spine, and up my spine and... *Shake it off, Eleana, shake it off.*

"Yeah, what kinda work? You see this? *This* is wor...*whoah.* Oh, hey, hey, who's this?" Finally, he'd noticed Rachel, who'd been eyeing him amusedly the whole time.

She shifted her weight to one leg, casually resting a hand on her hip, "who do you think, asshole?"

"*Asshole*? Ya see, normally I wouldn't get offended if some chick I didn't remember bangin' got pissed at me...God knows how many are out there...but since you're obviously a friend of Camioni's, I'll let that one slide," he said.

"*Really?*" she persisted.

I cleared my throat loudly. "Cal, you remember *Rachel*, *don't* you?" I giggled to myself.

He studied her carefully for a moment, "Rachel...no fuckin' way. *Huh*! Now this *is* a surprise," he smiled. "*Finally* came to visit me, huh? How you doin' since our last uh, *phonecall*?" he asked, winking openly.

"Nope, try again."

"If you say so. Anyway, you guys should hang out and shit. I may even have a shirt for you."

"How about for my *husband*?"

"Sorry we're all out of those. I got an XS for you, though." Mark and I couldn't contain ourselves. "What are your plans for tonight?"

"So?" Mark asked me, "'there's this beach bar nearby a bunch of us are going to in a little while; you should come," he insisted. We'd come all this way, now how in the *hell* could we turn that down?

"Of course," Rachel answered over me, "we just have to change first."

"Why?" Cal asked. "You look fine. Unless by 'change' you mean into a bikini, 'cause that's cool. *Ouch*! Fuck you do that for?"

"That's what you get, wise ass," Rachel had smacked him right in his rock-hard chest.

"Whatever. Where do you live anyway?" he asked me.

I pointed in the direction of Marina del Rey, "about a mile that way, on one of the canals."

"No shit," Cal said. "If I knew you lived *that* close we could've crashed at your place," he laughed. "Like old times."

"Yeah, right, I don't think so. One, it wasn't *my* place-it was Donnie's- and two, these aren't old times," I joked.

"Old times my *ass*," Rachel commented, "I *wish* I was livin' on the fuckin' beach."

"And a nice ass it is." Cal couldn't help himself with the comments- they kind of came with the territory and sometimes you just had to ignore them, as I had learned long ago. She gave him a callous stare, already smirking since she knew half the shit that came out of his mouth was sarcasm.

"You're welcome," he added just to annoy her. "And whenever you wanna ditch that 'husband' of yours, you're welcome in San D anytime you want." He really wasn't a bad guy- he just enjoyed messing around, especially with women. Mark on the other hand, was his opposite: calm, cool, polite, charming...it shocked me how close they were sometimes.

"Anyway, that probably wouldn't have happened," she said, referring back to the apartment.

"And why is that?" Cal questioned, disappointed.

"*Why*?" she repeated, holding up her left hand. "One, *married*. Two, Eleana's practically engaged so *no*, I don't think it would've been a good idea."

Cal shook off her reasoning, "you still married to that guy, seriously?"

"Ah yep, seriously."

"Well he's back in New York so..."

"Give it up, Wilson. Not happening."

"Can't blame a guy for trying," Cal said. "And who's this fuckin' guy you're *dating* Lea? He better have his head on fuckin' straight 'cause if it ain't I got permission to kick his ass. Just talked to Donnie last week and he made me promise to keep an eye on you while you're out here."

"How the *hell* are you doing that? You live in San *Diego*," I said.

"I know people," he hinted. If there was one thing about Cal, whatever he said, he was good for it. Never mind the *mob*; people like Cal *always* had connections and some of those 'connections' could set a plan in motion at the drop of a hat- legal or *not*..."He told me about your dad, too. Sorry. How's he doin'?"

I looked at them, saddened he'd brought it up but at the same time, grateful. "Okay, ya know. That shit is tough. I don't know."

"Okay, need anything let me know." Just like a SEAL to steer as far away from the emotional as possible. Like that, he'd changed back to the subject at hand- partying, not that I can't say I didn't appreciate it. "Anyway, *who* is this guy? He's not a fuckin' *actor* and shit, is he?" Cal laughed. I couldn't disagree with his assumptions. Before I'd met Patrick, I'd shared his pessimism.

Rachel and I shrugged our shoulders in response. "Well? Uh, yeah, *kind* of."

"*Seriously*, Lea? Don't tell me you got suckered into that whole fuckin' Hollywood bullshit. You need to watch out- they'll use you, abuse you, then lose you so fast you won't know what the fuck hit you."

"And exactly *how* is that any different than you guys?" Rachel asked on the defensive. We knew what happened to girls who attempted to stay with a SEAL for the long haul- they got left behind; not for another woman (although they *did* have a reputation for women-seeking), but for their love of country.

"Okay, okay, you *might* have a small point, *but*...one, we only use and abuse chicks who *ask* for it and two, we don't have a choice but to lose any attachments before we leave. It keeps us focused."

It might seem strange to hear two guys talk about leaving for missions when they had long since been in an active unit but once a SEAL, always a SEAL. My dad had always done that after he'd retired. I'd thought he was just rehashing the old glory days, but it was much more than that. It was an everlasting brotherhood few understood. It wasn't like belonging to some fraternity or even another military branch. They'd back each other up no matter what because unlike anyone who tried to mimic what they had, they were a unique *family-* and *nothing* got in the way of family.

"Okay, I'll give you that," Rachel said, "but trust me, *this* guy's not like the rest of 'em."

"*Really*. And just who is he anyway, a *prince*?" Mark asked.

"He may as well be," Rachel said, "You might have seen him on a billboard or two. His name's Patrick Thomas."

"As in the superhero dude?" Mark asked. I nodded.

"Hmm, impressive, Lea," Cal commented. "Not to brag or anything, but we've got a few celebrities of our *own* lined up as sponsors. Plus, *obviously* we're sort of famous ourselves..."

"*Obviously*," I said, laughing. "Like who?"

"Well, one of 'em was that dude you saw me talkin' to before."

"The one with the backwards hat and board shorts?" I asked.

"I didn't recognize him," Rachel insisted.

"Not everyone looks like Mr. GQ," he said, clearly referring to Patrick. "Some of us just have the swagger- we don't need to be all dressed up like a star to *be* one." *Spoken like a true Team guy.* "That was Tony Hawk." *What?*

The next morning...

"Hey, did you hear that?"

I looked at my phone. Finally, my eyes adjusted to the blue illuminated numbers. *What?*

"Shit- does that say 10:30?"

"Uh, yep," Rachel answered. I looked up to see her standing over me. "Did you hear that? I think someone's knocking on your door."

"What?" Now I heard it.

"And check your phone," she said pointing to it, "looks like Patrick's calling."

Still half asleep, I glanced at my phone. Shit, he *was* calling- but why? I answered it, confused. Was I missing something? It *was* Sunday, wasn't it? "Hello?"

"Hello back, babe."

"Um, aren't you supposed to be nursing a bad boy hangover right now?"

"Hmmm funny- I was gonna ask you the same thing," he said on the other end, "you sound tired. Long night?"

"Ummm…"

"I take that as a 'yes'. I'd ask if you got my texts, but obviously you were still asleep. What are you doing in there? We thought you were dead."

"Uh, sleeping in, apparently. I didn't realize it was so late." I heard someone else in the background. *We?* "If that's Kevin, you can tell him to keep his comments to himself," I added.

"Why don't you tell him yourself? We're outside." I stared blankly at Rachel.

"Outside, as in *here*?" I asked.

"Didn't you hear me knocking?"

"Um- that was *you*?"

"Uh, huh. Thought we'd take you to breakfast, but since I'm pretty sure that's over…"

"Alright, uh sorry, give us a minute."

"Sure. We'll just be out here waiting patiently." I hung up and headed for the bathroom to check out the disaster. *Not too bad, considering last night's body shots.*

Rachel followed me, "it's a good thing Cal and Mark *didn't* crash here. Now *that* would've been pretty fuckin funny."

I leaned out of the bathroom and smacked her arm, "Uh no, no it wouldn't have."

"*Yes,* it would. Can you imagine their faces if they'd seen two buff, half-naked men here, one of 'em tattooed to the hilt?" she asked, amused.

"I would've been toast. It wouldn't have fuckin' mattered for *you*- your husband isn't here."

"True," she said, rinsing out the toothpaste. "I'm gonna go put something on before they really think we're hiding men."

A few minutes later I opened my door to see Patrick and Kevin standing there with a tray of coffee. "Hey sleeping beauty. Good *morning*," he said, leaning in for a kiss.

"*Morning*?! It's practically afternoon." Kevin said, interrupting my Folgers moment. "What were you two doing in there? You got a couple of guys stashed in the closet? What took you so long? This coffee's cold."

I gave him an evil eye, "oh shut up, Kev. Did you want us to open the door half-naked?"

"That wouldn't be a bad thing," Patrick added, laughing. I glared at him.

Rachel had snuck up behind me, "that's right, Kev, tied up and gagged, unless they escaped out the back…"

I shook my head at her inventiveness, finally pushing the door all the way open. "So," Kevin continued as he made his way inside suspiciously, "what exactly *did* you two do last night? Looks like you did a little too much partying to me."

"Well? That's funny you ask. Patrick, remember those guys I ran into last summer at that conference, my brother's friends? Well, it just so happens they were up in Venice for work so..."

"So," Rachel cut me off, "we kind of ran into them and ended up getting dragged to a few bars." *A few?* "But...don't worry," she smiled at Patrick, "Lea was a perfectly good girl."

"So...basically you spent the entire night with a bunch of guys you hardly know who probably tried to take advantage of you..."

"I *do* know them. And they're not just *any* guys, they're good friends of my brother's *and* mine- he knows that," I affirmed, pointing to Patrick.

Patrick leaned in towards us, "is that *right*? Oh, please continue. I wanna hear the rest of the story." I was hoping he was just acting entertained and not being jealous.

"Story? We were just catchin' up with Cal and Mark," I said. "They're cool- trust me."

"Who?" Kevin asked. What was it with guys and jealousy? I didn't get easily shook about all the girls *they* ran into. Patrick was probably proposed to on a weekly basis and still I trusted him. "And since when are crazy, hormone-driven dudes considered 'friends'?" Before I could speak, Rachel had my back.

"They're not crazy. Well, they're not *that* crazy, and I'm pretty sure *all* men are hormone-driven," she firmly stated, giving him the evil eye.

Patrick finally spoke up, "they're SEALs, as in the Navy..." he clarified to his brother, whose face lit up instantly. I swear guys got more hard-ons when you said you knew a SEAL than if they were watching naked women shower. Sometimes it was just fucking ridiculous, which is why I hardly ever told anyone about my family.

"No shit. Oh *now* I get it- oh, Donnie's friends." *Duh.* "So, they were pretty much all hot then," he winked. "Dude, you might have some competition for once," he said to Patrick.

"I wasn't worried about that. I trust you," he kissed my cheek.

"Of course you don't have to be worried," I said, "although your brother's right- they are good looking guys." *He doesn't need to know I used to hook up with one of them. Everyone's allowed to keep a small secret here and there, right?*

"Okay beach girls, what do ya say we go get some uh, brunch? I'm starving."

"Good idea. I'll grab my keys."

Chapter 46 ~ True Romance

Tuesday, February 28th

We'd gotten lucky with the weather *and* the company during Rachel's visit, getting our fill the beach *and* boys. After lunch, Patrick and Kevin had left, alleviated when we'd told them Cal and Mark had left for San Diego. It'd been some long overdue girl time, but there was just one more thing to do before she went back to New York- *shop*, except we weren't going anywhere near Beverly Hills.

Santa Monica's Third Street Promenade was an upscale adaptation of pedestrian shopping, dining and entertaining. Its easy accessibility from downtown L.A. made it popular among locals and tourists. Nestled between Wilshire and Santa Monica Boulevards, it encompassed several blocks. Rachel and I made our way through the usual and had just entered Madewell, one of many boutique clothing stores.

"I can't believe you have to fuckin' leave tomorrow," I said, a little sad.

"Me, neither. I wish I could stay. Then again, that might cut into the little alone time you have left with Patrick, so I guess I shouldn't," she laughed. "Speaking of which," she went on as she glanced through the sale rack, "have you given any thought to what I said?"

I turned to her, finally letting go of the shirt I was holding, "about what?"

"About...*you* know." Her eyes rolled cattily to one side.

"If you're talking about buying out Victoria's Secret and the Love Shack then, *no*, I haven't."

"Look," she said, "in case you've already forgotten, you've just been recently 'proposed' or *promised* to, by a *great* guy. Did you forget that?"

"*No I...*"

"*That's* a relief," she huffed. "Well, did you forget that you're leaving soon?" I shook my head 'no'. "And you still didn't decide to put that ring on yet." Again, I shook my head 'no'. "And since you're not wearing it *and* you're about to leave for God knows how long *and* you have no idea where your job's going at this very moment..." I looked at her strangely. "Don't look at me like that. Let me finish. As your best friend it's my duty to look out for you *and* make sure you don't fuck anything good up, like *Patrick*, for example."

"What am I fucking up now?" I asked, a little perturbed.

"All of the above shit I just said leads him to believe that you may not *want* to wear that ring, or stay here, to *be* with him," she said.

"But I *do* want to be with him. I *have* to go back, Rach, you know that. What am I supposed to do, tell my jib and my dying father to fuck off?"

"Of course not. You need to *show* Patrick that you mean what you say or, in your case, *don't* say, since you never say what you fuckin' feel."

"And what is that?" I asked snidely.

"*You* tell me," she glared. "Look, all I'm saying is that if you really want him to know how you feel, you need to *show* him. The last thing you wanna do is leave without doing that. Then you risk alienating him and having some fuckin' hussy come along and take advantage of him when he's vulnerable."

"And by show, you mean dressing up..." I rolled my eyes, "Rach, you know that's *so* not me. Half the time I wear boxers or one of Patrick's t-shirts to bed."

"Well if you really want him to stick around, I suggest you alter your thinking. It's not like we're talking whips and chains, Lea," we laughed. At that very moment, two older ladies walked by us and it was obvious they'd heard the tail end of that conversation.

"Okay, okay, I see your point," I admitted.

"Good, then let's get the hell outta here. The *fuck* buys some of this shit anyway? Did you see that shirt? I bet if they cut two holes in a potato sack and Paris Hilton wore it, they'd get two grand."

I looked at one of the store's associates, eyeing us snidely after hearing us. But she hadn't been far off, because not too long ago Lindsay Lohan had been spotted in West Hollywood wearing what looked like dress made out of a pillowcase. After tackling Santa Monica top to bottom, we were spent (and so were our wallets). Rachel had an early flight tomorrow, so we'd decided to put our feet up, order takeout and chill.

"Hey, I forgot to tell you- someone from the manager's office stopped by before. I guess there was a piece of mail that got stuck in the mailroom," Rachel said.

"Oh, okay. Thanks. It's probably junk mail," I said.

"I think it had your high school's name on it or something. Maybe it's important."

"Oh." I thought for a second. Then it dawned on me. I went back inside. A long white envelope with blue lettering sat on the kitchen counter. I unfolded the paper and read it:

"Dear Eleana,

You have been cordially invited to attend Darien High School's 20-year high school reunion on Saturday August 18th, 2012 at Burns Country Club, at 7:00 pm. We look forward to seeing you there! Details to follow.

Regards,

Christian Spencer

Class President"

Instinctively my eyes rolled back in my head. I remembered *Christian*. Class President, filthy rich, spoiled and a total douche who thought he was entitled to everything, including every pretty girl in school. I was never really friends with him; then again, I wasn't friends with *most* of the rich kids. My friends were more like outcasts- the Depeche Mode, Guns-N-Roses, Skid Row-listening and Z-Cavarricci-wearing kind.

After high school I remained friends with a select few but beyond that, I never really saw anyone else. It wasn't until our 10-year reunion that I reconnected with any of them and I'd surprised myself by having fun. But, like all shy teenage girls with mediocre looks and style, I had still held back; I had still felt like the same shy girl from high school, the one who never dated the captain of the football team, never wore makeup, was never skinny and was about as far from outgoing as you can imagine. Of course, compared to even 10 years ago I'd improved and wouldn't it be nice to rub it into some of their faces...

"Well?" Rachel was standing in the doorway awaiting a response. I carried the letter outside.

"It's an invite for my 20-year reunion."

"Don't sound too excited."

"Why the hell should I be excited?" I asked.

"Well, from what I remember, which may be more than *you* actually remember, you had a decent time at the last one. Think of all you could brag about at *this* one."

"Hmmm, that *is* true but still...I'm not even sure I'd go. All this stuff with my dad and...and I might even be back here."

"If you say so," she said, "but I still think you should go."

"I'll think about it."

The following week...

Rachel had left over a week ago and even though I'd see her soon I wished she was still here. My work meeting had been rescheduled to the middle of March, so I'd decided to stay until then. Patrick's filming was continuing to go well; six more weeks and he'd be done for a little while. I was hopeful he'd come out east coast and as for my high school reunion? I was doubtful he'd make it or even want to come. Hell, I was doubtful *I* even wanted to go.

I'd taken everything Rachel had said seriously (well, mostly) and she'd been right- I may have been a highly skilled doctor but if it had anything to do with emotions I sucked; and when it came to romantic shit? I *really* sucked. I really wanted tonight to be special so Patrick wouldn't and *couldn't* forget me while we were apart. Rachel had been dead-on accurate about my relationship shortcomings and the thought of some starstruck, fame-hungry whore going after my man irritated the hell out of me.

I'd never done anything like this before- it was more like what you'd find in a racy romance novel you know, the kind where you have to reread the sex scenes just to make sure you got all of it right. With Rachel's advice and some help from my friends at Hustler and Frederick's of Hollywood, I'd come up with something creative. I'd pulled out every candle I could find and placed them strategically throughout the house. It was almost 8 pm. The food was warm in the oven, the wine was breathing and the table was set.

"Hello?"

I smiled when I heard the front door close. The bubbles were nearly overflowing in the jacuzzi tub I'd put in so much bubble bath. I listened, waiting for him to continue.

"Eleana? Fenway? Where are you?" I knew the smell of the food and all the candles would make him suspect something.

I spoke up over the music, "Upstairs," I said loudly.

"What are you doing up there? And what's with all the candles?"

"Just come up, will ya?" I said louder, "I want you to see something. Shit!" I let out, as I almost slipped.

"Is everything okay? Hey, why don't you come down so we can eat? It smells amazing down here and I'm starving." I could hear his footsteps creeping up the stairs.

"Um, in a minute," I answered, "just come here," I insisted.

"Okay, I'm coming, but what is all this? Are you having a séance? You're not planning on sacrificing me, are you?" He'd finally made it to the top of the stairs. "Well, I guess I should change anyw...Lea? Where are you?"

"In here," I shouted from the master bath.

A mix of shock, surprise and intrigue towered over me, all 6 foot 3 of him, and my mouth watered at the anticipation. "What are you doing?"

"What does it look like I'm doing, silly? I'm taking a bath."

"But the food's gonna get cold."

"No, it won't. But can you do me a *huge* favor though, after you strip down, can you bring up that bottle of wine?" I smiled cutely.

"Why do you want it up here?"

"The candles, the steak and potatoes, the wine and...me, naked, covered in bubbles awaiting your arrival..." He stared blankly at me. "Séance and sacrifice...*really*?"

"Well, *I* thought it was funny...wait- are you trying to *seduce* me?" He smiled.

"Well, if you don't get in here right now it'll be the first and last *time* I do this shit. Do you have any idea how far out of my comfort zone I am right now?"

He laughed, taking off his shirt. "Seriously, I don't even know what to say..."

"You don't have to say anything- Just shut up and get in here."

The next day...

"I still can't believe you went through all that trouble for me last night. That was... fun."

I looked at Patrick longingly as we lay in bed. "Yeah, it was, wasn't it?"

He traced his fingers gently up and down my arm. "Hmm, we should do this more often," he said, gliding his fingers down towards my hip. "I guess I owe you a 'thank you' for last night, don't I?"

"Well, you've got about a week left- you can thank me every day until I have to leave," I smiled back.

"I don't think that'll be a problem," he leaned over and kissed me. "So, you got anything else planned? I'm all yours."

"Good," I said, running my hand his vast chest as I propped myself up against him. I'd be stupid to let a guy like him get away. He locked his right hand with my left and after gently sliding them apart he brushed one finger across each of mine, finally settling on the ring finger. I realized where he stopped.

"What?" I asked, a slight giggle in my voice. I sat up to face him. "You're thinking about the ring, aren't you? Promise you're not mad?"

"Of course not," he hinted, playing some more. "I thought maybe you hocked it," he laughed.

"*What*? *No*. Are you kidding me?" I got up and walked over to the dresser, pulling out its top drawer. I took out the box and turned to show him, "It's right here, safe and sound, see?"

He held his hand out, "Let me see that for a sec?" I handed it over, tilting my head in question. "Come here." I sat back down next to him on the bed. He took my left hand and placed the ring on my finger. Beautiful couldn't begin to describe it- it was soft yet bold, glamorous without being flashy and utterly unique. And Patrick had been right- I didn't wear much jewelry but I loved this ring.

"You know, you look good wearing my last paycheck," he said.

"Well, it *is* the only thing I'm wearing right now," I played with it a little, spinning it around. Even if I had been ready to wear it, I couldn't- it was too big.

"True," he uttered. "I still can't believe I screwed up the size." He lowered his head, embarrassed. Meanwhile, it was me who should have been embarrassed since it'd been almost a month since he'd given it to me.

"Wait- let me see something." I pulled off the ring and moved it to my right hand, flaunting it at him. "How about that? It fits this one."

"Don't be silly, Lea. Just wait for me to get it fixed. I'm really sorry I haven't had the chance."

"It's fine, really. I mean, you *did* just give it to me and you've been busy." He went to take it off and I stopped him.

"You mean, you wanna wear it on *that* one?"

"What if I did, like for now? When you come to New York we can resize it there?" My eyes batted at him playfully.

"Lea, I know it was a lot to throw at you and...and you've had enough shit thrown at you in the past few months, but when I said no pressure I meant it; when I said I'd wait, I meant it; and when I said I love you..."

"I know..."

"No, you *don't*. Look," he went on, "it wasn't to 'freak' you out or scare you; I could've just as easily gotten you a bracelet or another watch but...it's a promise from me to you and I intend to keep that promise. As soon as I can I'll be out to see you."

"Good- I'll be anxiously waiting." I moved my hand over his hip, nearly jumping on top of him, pulling one arm and then the other over his head. "Oh, I forgot- there's just *one* more thing we didn't get to try," I smiled evilly, reaching behind the bed post.

He looked suddenly lost, "wh...what? Are those *handcuffs*?"

Chapter 47 ~ Office Space

"Well, I didn't see *that* shit coming."

"*I* did."

I turned to Maureen blankly. "Seriously? You *saw* that coming."

"Not *really*, but I had a feeling. Frankly I'm getting sick of these old bastards and their bullshit," she said, "what happened to trust?"

"I know. I can't believe they did that even though they *promised* they wouldn't." I'd unknowingly drank most of my martini and had to stop and reach for a breadstick. "How long have we been at this place, six years?"

"About that."

"And in those six years, how much would you say we've raised their profit margin?"

"Oh, I don't know, about 50%."

"*Exactly*, and this is the fucking thanks we get." I motioned the bartender for another round. "You ready? 'Cause I'm already done."

"Might as well, since neither of us has to work tomorrow," she nodded in response.

"One cucumber melon martini and one grapefruit fizz. Don't worry, I got it." Sid was one hell of a bartender- not only did he make kick-ass drinks, he always remembered what we ordered, a main reason Maureen and I kept coming back, especially since their Happy Hour went until 9pm.

"Amazing, isn't he?" she asked. "Too bad I'm not available, unless Justin pisses me off." We laughed hysterically as our drinks arrived.

"Anyway, as I was saying, all our hard work and these guys just decide to up and change their minds," I said angrily.

"Yeah and *fuck* us over in the process. Is there no integrity left in our profession?"

I swiveled my stool around, "why are you suddenly speaking Shakespeare?" I laughed.

"I don't know, I was trying to sound proper."

I stared her down, "I think you surpassed 'proper' a long time ago, don't you?"

"Yeah, I guess. *So* did you."

"Tell me about it. So," I continued, "what do you think you're gonna do?"

"I'm not sure. They didn't give us a lot of time, but their offer to buy out our shares wasn't so unfair. What'd they say, 30 days?"

"I think so."

"What about you? What are *you* gonna do?" she added.

"The bakery and shelter stuff aren't full-time. I don't get it- we worked *so* hard, we did *so* much for them and they promised, they *promised* they wouldn't sell out; that we were two of the best, most talented doctors they've ever hired, that they were so lucky to have found us and now in an instant, they're willing to just throw *all* of that away- there goes our dream, right down the fucking toilet. So, I don't know; I don't *know* what I'm gonna do. Maybe it's just not meant to be," I sulked.

"Or maybe that *place* wasn't meant to be," she thought.

"What do you mean?" I asked.

"I mean, *maybe* there's something bigger and better waiting around the corner." She smiled as if she had something up her sleeve, not that I was seeing anything. My forehead crinkled.

"And what corner are *you* fucking standing on? Because the one I'm at says 'Better luck next time- you just got played, son'."

"And why are *you* suddenly talking Compton style?"

"'Cause I don't feel like being so fucking proper tonight."

"Haven't you ever heard the saying 'when one door closes, another one opens', Ice Cube?" I nodded, disgruntled. "Don't you see," she went on, "we should take our money and hit the road; it's time to find a greener pasture and leave those old bulls *and* their old balls to fend for themselves."

"I'm gonna start seeing double soon if we don't order an appetizer," I laughed, "but right now maybe I should focus on other, more *important* things." I instinctively looked down at my left finger, thinking back to a couple of weeks ago in L.A., but that faded quickly as my thoughts shot back to my dad.

"You're right- you should," she paused for a moment, "but when I find something, I'll let you know. I'm not giving up on us yet. But back other things, what's Patrick doing after he finishes this film? Does he have anything lined up or is he coming out east at all?"

"Um, yeah he…"

"And don't you think we should talk about the big, blue elephant in the room?" Her gaze had moved down and it wasn't for a menu. "Did you *really* think no one would notice that massive blue rock on your finger? What is that, like three karats?"

"I don't know- I didn't buy it," I said facetiously just to annoy her.

"No *shit*, you didn't buy it. You hardly wear anything but a watch. It's so big it could be its own planet. Wait- is that the gem from *Titanic*?"

"Funny."

"So what is that anyway, an engagement ring?" she asked.

"*No*, not *really*. I don't know..."

"What the fuck does that mean?" She pulled my right hand towards her to get a closer look. "Let me see that."

"Hey!"

"Hey, nothing. Then what is it, a going-away present?"

"It's a gift," I affirmed.

"That's some gift."

"He gave it to me in Cabo. It's sort of a...*promise*, I guess," I said playing with it.

"Do people still give those?" I couldn't help but giggle. "Seriously though."

"I *am* serious."

Her face went flat. "No, you're not." I nodded my head 'yes'. "You're *not* kidding." I shook my head 'no'. "You mean *promise* as in like, precursor to engagement or..."

"I just haven't said anything because...well I kind of told him I need some time. It's a lot and I just have too much going on right now and just...don't say anything, okay? I mean, if anyone asks, just don't...elaborate."

"Fine, fine, whatever you say," she paused, "but looks to me like maybe you won't have to worry about working after all..." she smiled.

"*Wrong*. I've worked my whole career for what just got swiped out of my hands; I'm not giving up, either. Plus, I'm not that kind of girl- you know that."

"Kidding, I know you're not, but *some* girls are." Her eyes rolled down and I noted the change in her voice, hinting at something *else* she wanted to tell me, something I wished she hadn't.

Chapter 48 ~ Under Siege

Maureen and I had had a good, long talk about work, men and the potential outcome of our current situation. I wasn't sure what I was going to do or where I was going to go, but Maureen had been right about one thing- we shouldn't be giving up just yet. And for the moment there were far bigger things to be concerned about, like families and futures. I guess sometimes you had to leave stuff behind and start a new chapter in order to get where you wanted to be, what you deserved- and what we both deserved right now was *way* more than what we were being offered.

As much as we both wanted to deny it, times were changing quickly in the veterinary world: trust, honesty and sealing deals with a handshake were long gone and it was becoming apparent that passing down a hard-earned legacy was less and less important, while the dollar was becoming *more* important; so important, that even veterinarians were willing to sacrifice honor and good medicine for a few extra bucks. I wondered if our kind would eventually become obsolete you know, the ones who actually cared more about helping others than driving a Mercedes.

With corporate takeovers, reality TV and the infinite amount of bullshit information on the internet, it wasn't too hard to imagine a more distorted, less compassionate future in veterinary medicine and *that* was something I wanted no part of. Years ago, our biggest challenge in this field was trying to stay sane while doing the thing we loved the most. Now, it wasn't just a matter of sanity, it was figuring how to stay in the game without getting knocked off the board by either some corporate asshole or better yet, a colleague who you thought had your back. But not all colleagues were untrustworthy or conniving.

Our 'meeting' had been eye-opening but still, it left me with a huge decision to make- Did I want to stay on with less power and more rules to follow, rules made by people who'd likely make my life miserable? Or was it time to look for something better and just how much 'better' would I be able to find? I could probably pick up some relief work, but that wouldn't amount to a big enough salary, and it wasn't really my thing- you never got to form any bonds with anyone;

you just flew in and flew out. I always dreamed about being my own boss and when I began working with Maureen, I'd thought I'd found a partner. Now that dream, it seemed, had just gone up in smoke.

After what we'd just been told, I found Maureen's uplifting attitude strange. What was even more strange was that it felt like she was hiding something and I wasn't so sure it had to do with veterinary medicine. Well, I guess in a roundabout kind of way it kind of *did*.

I sat next to my dad as he slept. He had changed a lot since the last time I'd seen him and suddenly I wished I hadn't left. I'd had such a great time with Patrick, maybe the best time ever and I still couldn't believe what he'd given me, what he'd said. But I would trade all of that now to have been back here with my dad. I had talked to him and Skyped him; my brothers and the doctors had said he was doing okay but sitting here right now, watching him as he attempted to rest, his breaths more shallow, I wasn't so sure I agreed. He was thinner and paler, which only meant one thing.

I heard him stir, a slight gasp escaping from his chest, and I gazed up at the wall, covered with pictures and drawings of battleships and guns, courtesy of my nephews. A tear snuck out of my eye as I smiled a little. In one sweeping view I could see memories from years past and more recent ones, too- the time we went to Grand Cayman all the way back to when he took us camping and made us eat M.R.E.s while everyone else got to eat hot dogs and smores- Those were good times and it hit me- there weren't going to be many more.

It was almost 7:00 pm. One of the doctors had stopped by to chat. These were the times when it was advantageous being a doctor because I could understand things, except in this moment- I wished I didn't know *anything* about medicine or oncology or lost battles, and I wished there was a way I could fix this. Some days I felt like a miracle worker, while others I felt completely helpless, like now. I kissed my dad goodnight and walked out the door, waving to the nurses as I left.

"So, how was he?"

I wasn't exactly up for going out, so I'd told Maureen she and Rachel could come over. I needed to get my mind off things. Besides, I was going to see my brothers tomorrow. I continued cutting up cheese while Rachel did the veggies. Don't get me wrong- going out was fun, but eating in with cheese, crackers, veggies and dips was sometimes better- and cheaper. Cher had it right in *Mermaids*, feeding her kids hors d'eouvres for dinner- I wished I'd had that six nights a week instead of spaghetti and meatballs.

"O-kay, I guess."

"That doesn't sound okay," Rachel said.

"Fine, I'm lying- he's not. In fact, he looks a hell of a lot worse than the last time I saw him."

Oh," she said, "I'm really sorry, Lea."

"Yea, me, too. Did they have anything new to say?"

"Other than the usual crap? No, not really. But it's obvious things aren't going well and I think my brothers are having an especially bad time. I'm just not sure...how long, ya know?" I heard a train go by behind my apartment building, my back door rattling slightly.

"I know how that is," Maureen added, "when my dad was sick it was my brothers who took it the hardest."

"Well, that certainly lightened the mood a little. Thanks, Maureen." Rachel poured us all some wine and brought the plate of cheese and crackers over to the island.

"Well, I *do* try," she smiled. "On another 'lighter' note," she added, "you never really commented on what I told you yesterday.". I knew what she was referring to; I just didn't feel like answering. Maureen smiled again, only this time more sinister. "You know, Nate?"

She's gotta bring that shit up again, now? Rachel saw my annoyed face and tilted her head. "*Nate*? What do you mean?" She turned back to me, "what does she mean?"

I was beyond irritated. After all what Maureen had told me was, in more than one word, pretty un-fucking believable. It was also upsetting on a deeper level because it just hadn't made much sense- at least to me. But who cared what *I* thought? Certainly, Nate Peterson didn't.

"Nate's engaged." Just hearing those words again made me physically ill. I could feel the acid creeping up my esophagus and into the back of my throat. I swallowed deeply a few times to push it back down and along with it, the urge to run to the bathroom to scream and vomit simultaneously.

As if Maureen had just spouted some form of gibberish, Rachel turned back to her in confusion. "Say *what*?" I shrugged my shoulders, nodding in agreement as Rachel went on, "when?"

"Don't look at *me*," I said, perturbed, "I just got back, remember?"

"About two months ago," she answered shyly. *What? But he acted so weird on New Year's...*

"Wait- *two* months? You made it seem like it just happened." *Seriously?*

"I guess he decided to wait a little to tell people."

"And by people you mean..." *Oh please do go on...*

"What's wrong? You're his friend- you should be *happy* for him," Rachel added, "You *are* happy, right?"

"Apparently not as close as Maureen...and sure, yeah, I can be happy; I'm *happy*. So," I continued, "you must've known about this a *while* ago then," I pressed.

"Okay *fine*, I've known, okay? I just didn't wanna upset you. You've got enough going on."

"*Upset* me? I don't know how much longer my dad has, my family's a mess, my *job* situation's a mess, I just left my boyfriend back in California...how could something as fucking miniscule as this *upset* me?" I then realized I was sounding like raving lunatic.

"Ah, gee, I don't know," Maureen said, rolling her eyes, "you're probably right I should've said something, but judging by your reaction..."

"I'm sorry. I didn't mean to flip out like that– I'm just under a lot of stress. Honestly I'm happy for him, okay? Although...not that it matters but, she doesn't seem...I just haven't gotten that chemistry vibe-they don't really seem to have that much in common and..."

"And?" Rachel was now into the conversation. I mean, she had known me a very long time, which meant she also knew all about Nate.

"Well? He just seemed kind of disinterested, unphased, annoyed even. I didn't think he was that serious about her, especially since...I mean it's like one minute he's cheek to cheek with someone else and the next minute he's asking her to *marry* him?"

"Cheek to cheek?" they both asked.

"New Year's," Maureen smiled, eyeing me, "and maybe he just figured it was time. I thought nothing happened..."

"It *didn't*- I was speaking figuratively. Time for what- to be with someone you might not even want?" I asked.

"He's a guy, Lea, more than that he's *Nate*. Maybe some guys just have their own way of showing they care, like Patrick, for example." *What?*

"Whatever. Let's just hope this engagement lasts longer than the last one," I uttered, not realizing they heard me.

"Wait- Nate was engaged? I didn't know that."

"A while ago, I guess. I don't think he likes to talk about it," I said to Maureen.

"Hmmm," she said as she got up for more ice.

"Hmmm...*what*? Go ahead, I know there's a snarky comment just waiting to come out of that big Long Island mouth of yours." The three of us laughed loudly.

"Oh, nothing, it's just...you may wanna save all your bottled-up energy for Monday."

Confused, I said, "Monday?"

"Justin and I are going out for dinner."

"So, what's that got to do with me?"

"Oh, maybe nothing; maybe everything. Nate's going, too." She nodded cunningly.

"What's this about?"

"You'll have to find out. Luigi's- 8:00pm- be there or be square."

"Sorry, I can't. That's my bedtime."

"Oh, shut up and dress nicely, will ya?"

Chapter 49 ~ The Dream Team

Maureen and I stood patiently at the bar while Justin and Nate checked on our table. I hadn't intended on coming but Maureen had stressed that not only should I spend some time *outside* the hospital, but that it'd be worth my while. I had no idea what the fuck that meant but I went anyway, figuring the worst that could happen was I'd have leftovers to take home.

It felt odd being out as if on some kind of quasi double-date, especially since the four of us had done this before, though that was *hardly* the case. Nate hadn't noticed yet but when he did, I knew I'd catch some slack- but so would he. Tina was irritating and difficult (not to mention haughty) and I was perpetually mystified at the thought processes (*if* there were any) of guys like Nate who could look past such negative traits and stay with (or get married to) a girl, even if they didn't really love them. I never pegged Nate to be that kind of guy, but I'd been wrong so many times in my own life, how could I really judge? Maybe Nate *did* love her, but just wasn't the jumping up and down type. Or maybe, I just didn't want to admit that Nate had finally found someone to be with.

It was a beautiful night. The restaurant was packed. Despite the cooler temperature, people vied for the outdoor covered patio with heat lamps and warm lighting. The bar decorated in classic Italian taste was bustling with people. Typical of a Westchester locale, the loud New York accents and overwhelming number of what looked like mobsters and their cutesy dates crowded the space.

The service was impeccable and so was the food. Maureen and I talked about everything from wine tasting to a trip back to Grenada but despite us veterinarians swearing up and down to never talk about work out of the office, it came up anyway. I was dutifully reminded of the upcoming rescue fundraiser. The next conversation, however, caught me off guard.

"So, Lea, Maureen told me about what happened last week. I'm really sorry- I know how much you two liked that place," he said.

"Yeah," Nate added, "I'm sorry, too."

"Thanks." I lowered my head, feeling defeated from nearly every angle. I hadn't brought up my dad, not that I'd wanted to- that new development was already beginning to eat away at me.

"What are you gonna do?"

I looked at my plate then back up at him. "Honestly? I have no fucking idea. Right now, I need to get a hold of the rest of my life. Maybe I'll just bake or plan fundraisers- at least I'm good at *that*."

"Oh, come on, you're a *great* vet," Maureen smiled, "and so am I damnit and you know what? I'm gonna find somewhere else that *appreciates* me. That place was starting to act corporate *before* they became corporate, *you* know that." She looked like she'd already thought long and hard about this. *And...hadn't told me? That's odd, although apparently she likes keeping secrets lately...*

I tilted my head curiously, because I *knew* her; there was a plan forming in that brilliant brain of hers. Justin and Nate both sat there silent-it didn't take me long to figure out something was up.

"Speaking of recently unemployed vets, I have an odd question for you," Justin said.

Maureen stopped him, "Hey, we're not technically *unemployed-yet*. Let me," she smiled.

A perplexed look took over and I panicked. *Oh no, not them, too.* "Wait, wait. Before you speak, can I just say that I really, *really* don't wanna hear about *another* engagement right now *nor* do I have it in me to be a bridesmaid..." I scanned the table, noting very quickly my assumption had been off- *way* off.

"We're not engaged," they laughed.

"Oh," I corrected myself, "w*hew*- I thought you were gonna say you were planning some couples' destination wedding..."

"Actually, it's not about us well, *sort* of. Justin has this great idea." I leaned back in my seat, confused.

"And tell me how you *really* feel, why don't you," Maureen added.

"I hear the four of you have been spending a lot of time together since I've been away- that's all so..." I commented snidely. The guys were now following our heated conversation back and forth.

"You mean Nate and *Tina*? If you've forgotten, *these* two work together, I'm dating *him*," she pointed to Justin, "and so...*what*? We've hung out; that doesn't make Tina my best friend and you know what? She's actually nice." Her eyes narrowed angrily at me. I had offended her- I don't know why I was suddenly lashing out as if she'd done something to me.

"Ah *hem*," Nate commented, now visibly annoyed himself. "Yeah, why *don't* you tell us?" I remained quiet. "We *all* deserve to be happy, Lea. It's not a big deal, really."

"Oh, don't let her fool you- she's *happy*." Maureen, clearly still feeling my sting, had felt the need to get back at me, attempting to open up a completely different can of worms.

I looked over at her in full-on cat mode and raised my right hand at her. Damn the Italian need to communicate with gestures- I probably would've been able to hide it. "What is *that* supposed to mean? I'm *happy*," I insisted, before turning back to Nate, "I'm *happy*, of *course* I'm happy for you; and I never said she wasn't *nice*," Maureen shot me a disagreeing look. I looked over at Nate again, "I...right- we *should* all be happy." *I'd be happy if that fucking waiter came by and got me another drink.*

If I could've captured the look on the guys' faces- shock, awe...jealousy, maybe? It was actually kind of funny. The look on Nate's face? Not so much. His jaw dropped as he reached across the table.

"Wait, let me see that," he said, grabbing my hand.

"What?"

"That thing on your hand- what *is* that?"

"What?" I repeated. "Oh, uh, it's...a ring."

"Ah, hem, from *Patrick*." I broke my gaze from Nate and evilly moved it over to Maureen.

Just then, Justin cut the three of us off, "Wow," he looked at Nate, "I don't think you got Tina's ring at the same place, dude."

"It was just a gift," I explained.

"It's a little more than that," Maureen raised her voice in disagreement.

"No, it's *not*. Can't a guy buy a girl something without it being a big deal?" I asked.

"*That* is *not* 'something'; it's a big deal and you know it," she persisted. "She's just waiting for the right time to say yes, which she probably would have already if she didn't have all this other shit going on." *Gee, thanks a lot.*

As if I'd somehow hurt his feelings, Nate looked at me sadly and I wondered- was he *really* happy with his decision? "Oh, that's uh...great, Lea, that's really great."

I froze, trying to think of what to say. I mean, there's not just a 'good' way to discuss commitment or love with another person in front of someone you still had feelings for because in that very moment, I realized something; I *did* still have feelings for Nate, not that I could tell him. We'd made our choices well, at least *he* had- I still hadn't set mine in stone.

"Well I uh," I looked down at the dazzling gem reflecting the candlelight in various directions, "thanks but I...I'm *not* getting married at least, not for a long time anyway." I cleared my throat, "so, any date set yet?" *That's right, Eleana, change the subject back to where it belongs- to people who have actually had the balls to decide on a future, unlike yourself.*

"Oh, well, it's a really nice ring," he laughed, "he's a good guy so..."

I nodded. For some reason I couldn't look Nate in the eye; it was like I was suddenly questioning myself- *again...*"Uh yeah, yeah, he is. So," I cleared my throat again, "Justin, what was it you were saying, about work?"

"Oh. Well, I've been doing some thinking well, *we've* been doing some thinking and..."

"*We* as in...you and Maureen?"

"Um, yeah well, no. Me and Nate."

"Huh?" Puzzled, I went on, "About..."

"*How* would you like to come work with me well, let me rephrase that; how would you like to become a *part* of the future of *The Veterinary Care Center*?"

I was confused, wait- scratch that. I was fucking *lost*. I knew Justin hadn't been able to open his state-of-the-art hospital on his own, but I'd thought he just had investors. Then suddenly, it hit me. "Wait- did you just say what I *thought* you said? Justin, I don't think I can't afford that."

He and Nate smiled and Maureen, who'd been sitting there silently, joined them. "Ah, yep."

"Wait. I thought...who else owns it?"

"Well, so far, me, Nate, a couple of investors and..."

"Wait- *Nate*?" I shot Nate a look, shocked. "You're part *owner*?" He nodded.

I watched Maureen's face go from happy to devious. "*You? You're* going in on this, too?"

"Uh, huh, and we want you to be the fourth. When I told Justin about our bullshit situation, he said they were looking for more to buy in- it's gonna be huge, Lea, even *more* than they expected."

"Did I mention that it's *outside* your noncompete radius, .8 miles to be exact?"

"Yup," Maureen added, "so basically they can't do shit to us, no stirring the pot."

"They can boil to death in their fuckin' pot for all I care." Did I mention Camionis and alcohol don't mix, that along with streams of bad language comes increasing volume? Wait a minute- that's just Italians in general.

"Anyone care for dessert?" *Shit.* Out of nowhere the waiter had appeared. We all giggled uncontrollably, shaking our heads 'no'. "Okay, then I'll just be back with the check whenever you're ready."

"Well said, Lea, well said."

"Totally cool," Nate commented.

"So?" Maureen nudged, "what do you think? You *know* we'll make one hell of a team."

"What do I *think*? I think you guys are *nuts*."

Nate looked first at Justin and then back at me, "yeah, but a bunch of *smart* nuts." Now, how could I argue with that?

Chapter 50 ~ Indiana Jones and the Last Crusade

Two Weeks Later...

"I'm sorry, but I just *can't*, not right now," I tried to quiet my voice as I walked past the nurses' station but as they were well familiar by now, there weren't many people in my family who could keep their voices at a low level.

I rounded the corner and continued walking down yet another seemingly endless corridor. Why is it that they had to make these places so confusing? I didn't care if it *was* Yale, they were all the same. Turn after turn the hall appeared to stretch longer and longer as if I'd never reach my destination or a way out and I'd forgotten how many doors there were, although I had been here so many times I should've had that memorized.

"Why *not*?" Maureen asked.

"Because I have to stay here until they come back. I don't want to miss them again- it's hard enough trying to get one of them on the fucking phone," I huffed. "Actually, I *can't* miss them- it's important." My stress had quadrupled over the past several days, but I couldn't fall apart now; not when people needed me the most, when *he* needed me.

"Okay, but I was gonna go see my accountant and I wanted you to come with me." I knew what she was referring to and I should've been on the same page, but I also knew I wasn't in the right mindset at this very moment.

"Oh. Well, there've been some...developments- I'll tell you more later, but..."

She'd immediately caught on. After all, she'd already been through this six years ago and was familiar with the drill. "Oh, okay, geez I'm sorry, Lea. Well, I'll let you know what I find out. If either of us are gonna move forward with this thing, we've gotta have all our ducks in a row."

Right, I thought. Meanwhile I hadn't totally decided yet, but it had nothing to do with my dad. *That* was gonna be a long conversation with someone who probably wasn't gonna be too thrilled to hear it. Justin and Nate were friends, so they'd been willing to give us both some time and space well, me really. But what was there to think about really? It was one of those no-brainers- I'd be stupid to turn this kind of opportunity down, the kind I'd been dreaming about for what seemed like forever.

"No worries, I got your back- always. You just do what you gotta do. Let me know if you need anything, okay?"

By the time I'd returned with my coffee the doctor was back. Why they didn't have vending machines with alcohol instead of caffeine was another unsolved mystery of our time- people needed way more than coffee in times like these.

I didn't have to be an oncologist to guess what the problem was. I could tell by my dad's behavior his blood calcium levels had spiked again, which meant one of two things: either their treatments had worn off or the disease had worsened. As a daughter I wished desperately for the first, hopeful for some better way to fight this son of a bitch; but the doctor in me feared what they did- that this was a battle we *weren't* gonna win. If only there were some magic cure or potion, a cup of everlasting life that I could seek out. But I guess if any of those *did* exist, then pigs would be fucking flying by now.

I stood there in nearly a state of shock after the doctor walked away, not that he could tell. He was a nice guy, the type of guy I would've liked, under different circumstances- a handsome, young oncology resident ready to take on the world of cancer. He'd shown me the bloodwork and the CT scan. He'd pointed out the large nodules and narrowed airways, the enlargement of the heart and its pericardial sac, filled with fluid, the severe compression of the main bronchus- all of which was making it extremely difficult to breathe. He himself was baffled how my dad was breathing at all. I told him that that's the kind of guy my dad was- the steadfast, do-it-until-you-can't, fight through it, kind of guy. He'd been shot, nearly blown to pieces and witnessed shit they don't dare show you in movies and so he'd learned to tough it out, because that's what you *had* to do, if you wanted to survive.

He was impressed and said that not many people would even be able to take the amount of pain he was in right now and he asked me how I was dealing with it. I told him I just kept going because I had to, because I couldn't let him see me break down. I needed to be there for him like he'd been there for me all these years. Then he said something I *hadn't* expected. Three years into his residency and he was already thinking of changing his specialty because he didn't think he could handle seeing people like this.

I had them all wrong, I'd thought, that they couldn't possibly go through the same kinds of things we veterinarians did; that when you *can't* help someone, when you *don't* possess some magic pill or potion, you feel helpless, worthless even, in a way that no one else can understand. Being around very sick animals or people could really get to you and I could see his point, even more clearly than I think he realized; that it'd all already gotten to him, so much that he wanted a way out.

After texting my brothers, I looked around for the DVDs we'd brought. I found the one I was looking for and inserted it into my laptop. I checked my email quickly and heard my dad stirring, finally waking up.

"Oh, hey, dad."

"Hey, sweetheart," he said softly.

"Anthony and Donnie will be here in a little while. Want me to have them bring you anything?"

He looked over at me, motioning for some water, trying to sit up some more. "No, that's okay, but do me a favor, will you, honey? Throw on *The Godfather* for me?"

"Sure, dad, sure." I smiled, a tear sneaking out of the corner of one eye. I was glad he didn't notice.

Chapter 51 ~ High Fidelity

I was beginning to hate these so called 'family meetings'. As much as I loved my family, dealing with them was *always* a pain in the ass and dealing with *siblings*? Well, let's just say it wasn't easy. We'd had many discussions in detail about the business, my dad, the future, or lack thereof at this point...There was no way around it- we all knew what was happening and the way it was looking right now, it wouldn't be long.

We'd moved my dad to yet another hospital only this time, it'd be his last. It was smaller and quieter. I'd never imagined the work that went into finding a place like this. It was like using a real estate agent to find the best deal around, an available apartment or house to use for a couple of weeks, until basically someone died. It was weird. And if there weren't openings in one of the 'nicer' places, your only option was to die in a shitty ward of some hospital, lying in a crappy bed that was probably crappier than one in a prison. Except we'd gotten lucky; we'd scored a suite in a small hospital, designed for families to spend time together.

I sat next to my father's bed, watching him sleep though at this point, he really wasn't. It was beyond difficult watching someone you loved so much wither away. Now I finally knew what it felt like, what people went through and there was no other way to say it- it *fucking* sucked- *big* time. You begin to realize how short life is and that every single moment matters. We were lucky that we'd gotten to spend quality time as a family together; we hadn't done *that* for years.

I'd been here a few hours, but I needed a break. I needed to unwind, to go home and bake a hundred meringues while guzzling sangria and watching an Adam Sandler marathon. I decided to leave and maybe come back later, maybe not. There wasn't much I could do, yet I didn't want him to be alone. He'd been here for two days and between my brothers and I we were pretty much here most of the time.

I'd been home for less than an hour. Despite having every intention of putting myself to work, about the only thing I'd been able to muster up was a batch of double chip cookies. I figured they'd go well with an adult milkshake. Why I was craving dessert at a time like this was odd, especially since I hardly had an appetite when I was this upset. I heard a knock at the door and walked over to the peephole to see who it was. It wasn't anyone I was expecting.

"Oh, hey," I sniffled, wiping my nose. "Um, what...what are you doing here?"

Nate stood there concerned. I gazed at him with saddened eyes, my face still a little puffy from last night. "Uh, Justin told me your dad wasn't doing too well. Maureen said you'd probably be either at the hospital or...I didn't wanna intrude, but she said you were on your way home so...anyway, I hope it's okay I stopped by," he added. "I figured if I called or texted you, you might not answer."

Well, that's one guy, I guess. Patrick hadn't been able to get away because of yet another filming setback, surprise, *surprise*. I was beginning to think that movies never finished on schedule. I also wasn't his immediate family and so there was no way in hell he even *could* be here, so I couldn't totally blame him.

"So...you figured if you just showed up, I couldn't say 'no'," I smiled. "Um, it's fine; it's okay," I answered. "Actually, I'm glad you're here. I could use the distraction." I let him inside.

"*Distraction*, huh?" He teased. "Wow, it smells *great* in here. Whatcha makin'?"

"Cookies. That's about all I could do. Want one? They're still warm."

"Sure, but I thought maybe we could go somewhere, or stay here if you want, or if you want me to leave..."

It's not that Nate had never been understanding *or* kind, it just felt a little weird and wrong, him being here for me when my own boyfriend wasn't. I snapped out of my thoughts, suddenly remembering it was Tuesday. "Wait a minute- aren't you supposed to be ultrasounding someone or...wedding planning or something?"

"I cleared my schedule. Justin's covering for me. Fuck it, I only had a few anyway. He can handle it. If he can't, I'm not so sure I wanna go into business with the guy," we both laughed.

"Funny, Peterson, *real* funny," I commented. "And what about the *other* thing?"

"You mean, wedding planning?"

"You *are* still getting married, aren't you? Oh my God, I can't believe I just said that. I'm...I'm sorry. I didn't mean..." *What the fuck is wrong with you, Eleana?*

"I'll give you a free pass *this* time. And I am. I mean, *we* are, I don't know. I'm not into details. Tina's handling it. Why? Wanna *help*?" *Of course she is. Guys never want anything to do with weddings. It's like they just wanna show up and party...*

"Well, I don't blame you, I guess- *I* don't even like flowers or choosing color schemes," I snickered. "Uh, no. Thanks- I'll pass." *Act happy, will you?*

"You sure you're okay?" he asked, "'cause if you want some time alone, I just wanted to make sure you were okay."

"*No.*"

"*No?*" he asked concernedly.

"Sorry, I meant 'no', I *don't* really want to be alone; I've been alone enough lately. Even when I'm with people I feel like I'm somewhere else." My head hung low and I looked away.

"Okay, so…what are you in the mood for- pizza, burgers, wings…I'm treating."

"Nah, but a margarita sounds good right now. There's a great cantina just downstairs."

"Whatever, you know I'm easy," he joked, "but don't forget- that just means we can drink more."

"I wouldn't say that too loudly around here- there's a lot of single ladies who'd *love* to take advantage of a tall, strapping successful guy like yourself," I laughed.

He paused flirtatiously in the doorway, "strapping, huh?"

"I was exaggerating," I smiled.

An hour later…

It didn't matter how much chips and salsa I ate– Cantina Mexicana's margaritas always hit me hard, which usually led to either one of two things: walking next door for karaoke or letting my emotions get the best of me. It was three in the afternoon, so that pretty much eliminated the first thing. Regardless of the time that had passed, what we'd been through or where we were in our lives at this moment, when it came to certain friends some things just never changed; and when it came to *Nate*? I wondered if anything ever *would*. Inevitably it *needed* to, right? We were in our mid 30s; certainly, it was time for us to grow up, make grown-up decisions and carve out *real* futures with someone we loved. And we *were*- just with other people. That's what made sense, right?

"Dude, I swear, if they play *La Bamba* one more time I'm gonna strangle them."

I looked over at Nate, who was clearly annoyed at Cantina's music choices. He'd never been a fan of 'international' music, although when we were in Grenada he'd never seemed to care what was playing. He even disliked country music, despite being from the Midwest, which I had always found amusing. The bar was on the empty side which was nice because once happy hour hit it became so loud it was hard to hear anything.

"Whatever," I said, "you won't like anything they play unless it's fuckin' *Pearl* Jam, so shut up." I laughed and ate a few more chips to try and soak up the tequila. One thing about Nate- we always had a good time, no matter where we were. We could talk and laugh for hours especially when we had nowhere to be, like back then- and now.

"Yeah, you're right," he smiled. "So," he said, "not to bring up work but, what do you think you're gonna do?" Although even many of his friends didn't get that first impression from him, Nate was quite serious and tactful when it came to medicine and business. He was also sincere, something I have to admit that I hadn't seen myself when we'd first met.

"*Seriously?*"

He turned towards me, leaning on the bar, "seriously. How long 'til you have to decide?"

"Two weeks. I'm not exactly a 'rule' follower so...as much as I don't want to leave, I don't think I wanna listen to anyone's bullshit rules..."

"No shit- I knew *that* the first day I met you."

I shook my head sarcastically, "gee, thanks."

"I didn't say that was a *bad* thing," he smiled. "Wanna know what I think?"

"Sure, why not?"

"I think you need a change. And you know what *else*?"

I rolled my eyes and sighed, playing with my drink. "What?"

"You're better than that, then *them,* and you can *do* this; and I think we're gonna be *great*. I know it's hard right now to see it, but I really feel that when you believe in someone or some*thing, fuck* it- you should stop being afraid and just..." he paused.

I looked up from my drink. Not only had his smiled shifted, his eyes were trying to say something more and I wondered- was he still talking about *work*? "Just...*what*?"

He backed off, clearing his throat, "just uh go for it, ya know? Take a chance, see where it goes. We could be great together you know, at work, at the hospital so...so you should really reconsider, 'cause if you don't, you might not get another opportunity." Nate had never been one to stumble on words so seeing him like this was unusual, even for him.

"Oh, right, right. I *am*, I mean, *really*? You think we'd be *great*?"

"I *know* we would. You just have to give it a chance." *Gulp.* "Which is why I told Justin that we should give you the time you need *and* a job, as soon as you want it."

"*Really*? You...would *do* that for me?"

"You *know* I would; that's what friends are for." His placed his hand on mine and held it there. Stunned by his touch I shyly pulled it out from beneath and sat further back on my stool.

"Right, um...thanks," I said lightly.

He motioned for another round, leaning towards me, "I just want you to be happy." *Gulp.* "You...*are* still happy, right, I mean with everything going on and..."

I eyed him cautiously, although right about now things were a little hazy. *Yes, I am,* I told myself. "You mean with...I...I'm sure you don't wanna hear about my boyfriend woes..."

"Why not? I thought we were talking about being happy, moving ahead. Can't friends talk?"

"Yeah, of course, you're right. I'm sorry."

"You sure you're okay? Woes? I thought you two were practically engaged..."

"Yeah I...I don't know I just...wish he was here, but he can't be so..." My head lowered and I set my sights on the menu for another distraction.

"Well, *I* am so if you need anythi..." Our eyes met in a standstill as our faces inched towards one another.

I barely noticed the bartender arrive with plate settings or how close Nate and I had gotten. He nodded. Confused, I asked, "wh...what about Tina?"

"What *about* Tina?"

"I thought you were...we shouldn't..."

"Shouldn't *what*?"

Our lips were now millimeters apart and I was quivering inside, so much I had to close my eyes. Sometimes a little tequila is all it takes for you to feel those old feelings with someone. We'd had a lot of good times together, but the reality was we just weren't meant to *be* together, not then, not *ever*. History had made that very clear. Too many years had gone by and to think that this could go somewhere now was just silly. I wasn't sure what the hell was wrong with me- all I knew was that it would be wrong- *so* wrong if we did this and we'd both regret it tomorrow.

I opened my eyes to find him still just as close, waiting for a reason why we shouldn't just head upstairs for the after party, but I knew where it would head- the same place it'd *always* headed with us- a dead end. The truth was, it could never work. We were already on different paths with different people, people who were counting on us to be honest and loyal. I swore I'd never be that person, the one who'd betray someone I really cared about, just as it had been done so thoughtlessly and recklessly to me. Because it *hurt*- and I just couldn't live with myself if I hurt Patrick.

"We should... we should order some food before...I'm *starving*," I said. *Before this goes where we both know it can't, Nate. You know it and I know it.*

He sat back, "you're right, I'm sorry. I shouldn't have..."

"Forget it. We've both had *way* too much tequila," I smiled.

"No, *you* have," he corrected me. "If *I'd* had that much, I would've already had you upstairs." *What?* "Anyway, how are the tacos here? You're right- I *am* starving."

Chapter 52 ~ Gladiator

Thursday, April 26th

The past few days had been exceedingly rough. Any amount of planning for someone to die had been easily surpassed by the amount necessary to deal with the aftermath including the wake, the funeral or being laid to rest, if you wanna call being buried less than six feet under as a measly pile of ashes 'rest'. We'd decided against the usual long, drawn-out Italian wake: rather than two back-to-back evenings of mourning we'd done one which had been more than enough, since we'd been by my dad's side nearly every day for the past month. Why people insisted on prolonging their suffering was beyond me, but I guess that's just what Italians liked to do. They had gotten a few things *right* in *The Godfather.*

I guess I should've considered us lucky: lucky that we'd spent time together; that my dad hadn't suffered for that long and above all else, that we'd gotten to say goodbye. Of course, it *wouldn't* be a Camioni event if my brothers hadn't snuck booze into the funeral home for one final goodbye. I swear I'd heard a proud laugh come out of my dad's coffin at that one...

Because of what we'd *all* been through, my dad wasn't the only one who was at peace. We'd spent the past several weeks watching him inevitably change; from the loving father, husband and warrior we once knew to a fallen hero who had finally lost his ultimate battle.

The church had been so packed they'd run out of seats. It was an abyss of sobbing faces- family, friends, war buddies, people from years past who'd shown up to pay their respects to a man who'd inspired them...It was impressively moving and overwhelming. I always knew the kind of man he was because he was my *father*; but these people, many who barely knew him or hadn't seen him in years, were still touched by what he'd done for them decades earlier because the truth is, you just never forget someone like that. And it was clear from the masses of people who'd shown up, no one had forgotten Anthony Camioni.

I'd done a good job of holding it together the entire day: from the ushering of my father's urn to my brothers' speeches, all the way through the hundreds of handshakes and condolences. Afterwards it'd been a crowded scene, but not because so many people had gone to witness the final event. Grove Cemetery was the oldest in the county, so old that its small and windy gravel paths were barely wide enough for a horse and buggy, never mind a car or a limousine. It was emotional seeing three generations of my family all in one spot and even more so now that my dad was to be added. But it wasn't being in an old cemetery surrounded by tombstones that had gotten to me. It wasn't the family and friends standing around us in tears because to be honest, I don't think I remember looking at a single one of their faces. And it wasn't hearing the priest say his well-rehearsed lines either, the same one he likely repeated week after week from his Bible.

I had never witnessed a military funeral before. It was far more consuming and emotional than they portrayed in movies. I guess eight uniformed men performing a 21-gun salute will do that to you. They stood silent and perfectly still, focused on the difficult task of laying one of their own to rest. My brother Donnie, who'd been in full dress uniform, stood quietly beside them unable to cry, though anyone who knew him well could see the sadness in his eyes. 'Their eyes always tell you the *real* fuckin' story', my dad had always said. Of course, I could never tell whether he was referring to guys or terrorists but nevertheless it was good advice.

Today may have been mine and Anthony's first military funeral but unfortunately it *hadn't* been Donnie's. At 30-years old he'd already lost three of his *other* brothers in the line of duty. It was a loss so great and so personal you couldn't understand. But the loss of a father? Anthony and I understood that completely.

The echoes of the perfectly timed and succinct gunshots resonated loudly through the air, making it known for miles that someone was being honored. Although referred to as 21-gun salute it was only three volleys of rifle shots, an adaptation of battle ceasefires, indicating that a deceased was cleared and properly cared for. But although witnessing that had been hard, I hadn't cried- not even after the flag detail had folded up the huge United States flag and the shell casings and handed it to the Captain, my father's longtime friend, who had then presented it to me while *Taps* played in the background. I'd looked him right in the eye, grateful and proud, because I knew how difficult it must've been for him, too. Later he'd told me that in the hundreds of times he'd done that, he had never, *ever* seen anyone, man or woman, hold it together the way I had.

Speaking of proud, I'd been proud of myself because at 3:00 pm I was still standing *and* sober (well, not completely). I'd paced myself, which was a miracle seeing as Italians were right behind the Irish in the amount of alcohol they consumed on days like this. I stood at the bar staring out at the water. The local boat club was no yacht club but it had what many yacht clubs *did* have- food, a bar and water views. I noticed

Nate walk up and stand beside me at the bar. He, Justin and Maureen had been some of my closest friends I'd invited. Mostly it'd been family, all 100 *plus* of them, but you know Italians like to do things...

"Hey," he said, nudging my right arm, "How you holdin' up?"

I shrugged my shoulders vaguely, "eh, okay."

"Just 'eh', huh?" He leaned in further, "you *sure*?"

A small smile formed on my lips, "okay, maybe...not really okay-you got me. Whatcha want?" I asked, referring to a drink.

"Whatever. What are you getting?"

"Actually, I was thinking of getting a shot."

He stared me down suspiciously, "*really*."

"Why not?"

"What's the matter, Camioni, not enough wine? I mean, *shit*, I thought I'd walked into a wedding with all this booze," he laughed.

I laughed along, "you're part Irish- you should know these things are more like weddings than funerals. The only thing missing is the cheesy DJ."

"Someone said they're doing karaoke tonight in the next room. We should go over there after. Seriously, I thought the slide show was great. Those were some great pics. You look exactly the same as when you were five."

"Gee, thanks. It came out well," I added, motioning to the kid behind the bar for a drink, "tequila okay?"

"Sure, whatever, you know I drink anything," he added with his signature wink.

I turned to him joking, "you really *are* that easy, aren't you?"

He shrugged, "um, yeah, pretty much. So, I was talkin' to your brothers; cool guys. I can see the family resemblance," he winked again more facetiously.

I ignored his comment. "So, what'd they do, send you over here to check on me?" I turned around pointing out Mac, Maureen and Dana.

He shrugged again, "sort of. We figured you might need a break from the family drama."

"Thanks. After today I just need to...I don't know..." I looked down, my thoughts trailing off. I raised my head back up to found Nate's gaze on me. There was something in his eyes, something other than friendly concern. "Nate? Earth to Nate."

"What? Oh, sorry," he realized after a few seconds. "I was just thinking." Everything around us seemed to fade slowly into the background.

"*About*?" I asked, curious.

"I don't know- *life* and shit; how suddenly it seems short- death, dying, past mistakes," he added. "You believe in second chances?" *Now where the hell did that come from?*

I gave him a confused look. "I don't know- *sometimes*, I guess. You mean like with...*Jenna*? Sorry," I quickly caught myself, "I didn't mean to..." I knew he'd had anger about that whole situation, but that's about *all* I knew- he'd never gone into detail.

"Hmm...*no*, not *exactly*," he answered, not looking away, "just- do you ever think about maybe doing something over or..."

"I think everyone does- about *something*. That doesn't mean that if you did change it your life would be any better though. Or maybe it *could*, I guess."

"What do you mean?"

"I mean like, what if you had a chance to go back and change one little thing and...you changed the whole future? Like, what if you did that and you take the chance of..."

"Screwing up the time-space continuum?" he mocked.

"Shut up; I'm *serious*." I giggled, unable to resist his smile. "I can understand looking back sometimes and wondering. In fact, I used the be the queen of that, but I've learned to focus on *today*. Besides, why would you *want* to? You're in a good place right now, for the better, so..." *Go ahead, Eleana, say it.* "Forget about the past. Look at you- all your degrees, the hospital venture...*Tina*..." *Yak...*

There was a pause as if he'd forgotten who I was talking about. "Oh, yeah, right, Tina."

"I mean, you *do* remember your fiancé."

"Uh, yeah, of *course* and she's *great*. It's just..." Our eyes remained locked as he pondered his answer, "I don't know..."

Instinctively my hand somehow found its way on top of his. Unexpectedly I was now consoling him. "*What?* What...don't you know?"

Here's the part where you say, 'but Tina's great and she's perfect for you,' Eleana. Bullshit she is.

He sighed deeply, "don't you just wish you could go away for a while like, take a breather from everything?"

"Everything. As in..."

"I don't know- life, work, funerals, weddings...It just feels like too much lately. Sometimes I wonder what the hell I'm even doing it for."

"Well, if you're talking about work, I'd say for *you*- you've earned it and the future is gonna be awesome. If you're talking about the *other* thing then...I can't really answer that for you but as your *friend*, I guess I should say, 'because you wanna be with her, because she makes you happy, because you lo...'" I stopped as if unable to say the word. His face was pensive, unenthusiastic almost. Maybe he *hadn't* been as happy as he'd let on. *And what are you supposed do about it anyway, Eleana? He's not your problem.*

"Right, right," he thought, "Just curious, though."

"About what? I'm giving you my advice here, Peterson; you're supposed to listen to it, not ask questions." I smiled, trying to lighten the situation, but this time he didn't follow my lead.

"I *am*. I know you, Camioni; you never say what you're *supposed* to say- you say what you want. So, what are you *really* saying?"

First of all, there's no way I'd say that, unless of course I were crazy, which I'm not. Just be a friend, Eleana. Stay focused and on point. Yeah fuckin' right. "I...just mean that you should be with someone because they make you better, because you can see yourself growing old with them and making a future, which I'm sure you are so..." I thought about what I'd just said- did that pertain to me at this exact moment?

He stopped, sighing deeply in thought. "Hmm, yeah, I never thought about it like that." *You haven't? Then what the fuck are you doing? No, don't say that.* "When you say it like that it sounds so serious."

"That's because it *is* serious."

"Yeah, I guess now's as good a time as ever to grow up, huh?"

"Ah, yup. Might be a good idea," I laughed.

"But seriously though, I really wish I could get away for a few months, take myself on some exotic vacation or some shit. What about you?"

I pointed to myself, "already did that, remember? Oh," I said in a more solemn tone, "you're not joking." He shook his head 'no'. "Why the hell would you wanna do that when things are going so well? I mean, they *are* still going well, aren't they?"

He hesitated, "I *guess* so, yeah. I don't know- for a change. It seemed to work out for you: you went to Cali, found a new lease on life, you're dating a movie star...stop me anytime here," he laughed, although inside I knew he wasn't.

"What are you saying- you wanna find some movie star to marry now?"

"Well I was thinkin' more *porn* star actually..." he laughed loudly.

"Funny. Anyway, when I went out there, things were *different*. I had a lot to figure out for myself and...and I didn't have someone great like you," I paused, catching myself, "you do...someone worth sticking around for, like Tina." I felt the taste of tequila creep up my throat.

He sat there silent enough I could hear the gulp in his throat. "Ah, maybe you're right. Maybe I should fuckin' follow through for once, make good on my promises instead of moving around or on to the next best, or *worst*, thing. That worked out *so* well for me the last time," he thought to himself.

Right. "Maybe everything isn't as 'scary' as you're making it out; maybe this one's worth it."

He looked me right in the eye, "yeah, maybe. Wait- who said I was scared?" *Really? Why the fuck does he have to always be so nonchalant about everything, including marriage?* "Speaking of promises, happily ever after and people worth sticking around for, I really hope you decide to stay- *this* time."

"*Stay?*" I asked. "Wait, *this* time?" What the fuck was he talking about?

"Yeah, *stay*, do what's best for *your* future instead of tagging along behind someone else's; not trekking the globe every other month trying to maintain some idealistic relationship." *Did he really just say that?*

I was angry. Where all this penned up shit was coming from, I had no idea. "I'm *not*; I *don't*. Wait- you think my relationship with Patrick is *idealistic*? For your information, he happens to be a *great* guy, who supports what I do 100%. No, scratch that- *110%*."

"Hmm," he answered snidely, "yeah, yeah, he's got a 5 million-dollar house- you don't have to remind me, but are you sure about that?"

"What the hell does *that* mean? Of *course*, I'm sure."

"Oh, nothing. Just that lately you don't seem so sure. Plus, you said it yourself- your family and everyone you care about is *here*, not out there. I thought family was always so important to you."

"So not only is mine and Patrick's relationship *phony*, deep down I don't really *care* about him, either *or* my family." He shrugged.

"I didn't say that- I said it's *idealistic*. I mean he *is* famous- that alone drives up the odds."

"Says the guy who isn't even sure he still wants to marry the girl he proposed to or wait, *did* you actually propose or were you just too much of a pussy to say how you *really* felt when she asked *you* to save her feelings? 'Cause we *all* know when it comes to relationships, you're a fuckin' pro." I was hurt by what he'd just said, the way he'd just suddenly decided to rain on my already rained-out funeral parade and dig way too deep into my life. For the first time ever, I was actually *angry* with Nathan Peterson. "And since *when* do I have to answer to you anyway?"

"You don't have to answer to anyone, Lea, least of all, *me*. I'm sorry. It's *your* life- if it works, it works and if constantly being on a plane is enough for you, then that's cool. It's just you talk about someone making you happy and I don't see how you're happy when he's not even here right now."

"I'm not happy because my dad just fucking died. And for your information Patrick's working. What do you want him to do, breach his contract, walk off set and go running to his lonely, sobbing girlfriend?"

"Hmm, maybe, yeah." *What?*

"Well, he *can't,* and I don't expect him to. Just like he shouldn't expect me to drop everything here and run when he needs me. Talk about unrealistic." My callous look said it all, not that Nate couldn't see through my walls and insecurities. And right now, that's exactly how I was acting- insecure. *Childish* and insecure- and I knew it.

"Well, I hope you decide what's best for *you*, not anyone else...unless your dreams aren't that important anymore. But since I know you so well, I'm not thinking that's the case." If it wasn't my father's big day, I would've punched him- *hard*.

"Hmm...you think you know me *so* well, Peterson? Well I got news for you- you haven't known me for a *really* long time."

"Is that right?"

"Yeah- it *is*."

"If you say so. Just answer me one thing. If you had to choose between your career and well, everything else, would you be able to?"

"If by 'everything else' you're referring to *Patrick*, then I...I don't...I don't think that's a fair question. Would *you*?"

"We're not talking about me. If you decide to join us on this little venture, and by 'little' I mean 'huge, kick-ass, bound-to-be-crazy-successful' venture, *what* then? I mean, what does Mr. *Hollywood* say about it?" He got me on that one. I sat there, dead silent- no pun intended. "You *have* told him, right?" I reluctantly shook my head 'no'. "I thought so."

I looked at him, having regretted starting this conversation. "*What*? I hate to burst your bubble, but even all your degrees don't make you Sherlock Holmes," I smirked annoyedly.

"You think I'm *wrong* on this one?" he asked. Some fuckin' day he picked for an interrogation. "Let me tell you why I'm right *and* how well I *know* I know you: You really like the guy; you might even *think* you love him. He's the picture-perfect guy you always dreamed of only now that you got him, you're worried it won't work out- deep down you're not really sure about your future, which is why you don't have that huge ring on right now. And just when *your* career's about to take off, you're not sure whether to go for it or to hang on the sidelines, while other people move ahead and become successful."

"No..."

"I'm not finished." I looked down, aggravated. "Which part are you denying, the undecided future part or the fact that you're not really in love with him?"

"Neither, it's..."

"It's what, Lea? This isn't you. You've always known exactly what you wanted- being your own boss. Why are you so willing to back down just when everything is falling into your lap?"

"I'm not backing down- I'm just undecided. I'm supposed to take advice from someone who's never finished anything in his entire life, the guy who's always been too scared take a chance on something good when it was right in front of his face?"

"Are we still talking about me here?"

"*Now* are you finished?"

"No."

"Fine."

"All I'm saying, as your *friend*," he paused, "is that after all this (he pointed around the room) is over, you need to seriously sit down and think about your future and I mean *your* future, *minus* the rest- the white picket fence, the fuckin' Hollywood sign, all of that shit. You need to think about what *you* really want and what's most important," he smiled. "Just please do me a favor- don't decide something for the wrong reasons; you've come too far. You deserve better than that. You deserve...don't change your mind because of someone else. I did that once and it was the biggest mistake I ever made."

"Change your mind about *what*?" My eyes widened. I recognized that voice- it was Patrick.

Chapter 53 ~ Something's Gotta Give

On the one hand, I was completely caught off guard by Nate. He'd meant well bringing up the hospital and for good reason- he was just as anxious for my decision as Maureen and Justin were. But somewhere in the middle of all that the conversation had shifted from work to significant others and life plans, a place I *wasn't* exactly in the mood to go. And then there was Patrick, who'd just appeared totally unannounced and had just happened to have caught the tail end of that conversation. Exactly what he'd heard, I wasn't sure, but the look on his face told me he hadn't been too thrilled.

Immediately I turned around, "*Patrick*?! Uh, you're...*here*! Wait, what...what are you *doing* here? I thought you said...you couldn't make it," I said, trying to ignore Nate's stare.

He paused for a moment, a smile briefly surfacing, "hmm, judging by the look on your face, I'm assuming you didn't get any of my messages," he answered dryly. I shook my head 'no', somewhat embarrassed. "Sorry, I hope I wasn't *interrupting* anything."

I quickly glanced back at Nate, "Oh, no *no*, of *course* not," I said uneasily. "You remember Nate," I added.

Patrick looked at him, trying to remember, "oh yeah, Thanksgiving, New York. You were with your girlfriend, right? She here?"

"Uh, no, no," he answered. "Anyway, I'll leave you two alone," he looked back at me a second time. "Lea, I'll, uh, catch up with you later." His eyes shied away as he walked off.

"Ah *hem*," Patrick said to regain my attention.

"Oh, sorry," I apologized, "spaced out there for a second."

"So...what were you guys talking about? It looked intense; I was almost afraid to interrupt."

"What? Oh no, no. Just uh...work stuff, that's all."

"Looked like more than work," he hinted.

"It's nothing, really. Do you mind if we talk about this later? I've just been so distracted with...everything. Let's back to me not having any clue you were coming. You...said you left me messages? Maybe my mailbox is screwed up or something. When did you call?"

"A couple days ago. And yesterday. And today- *twice.*"

"What?" I searched for my phone, realizing I didn't have it on me. "Oh, shit, I'm sorry. I must've left my phone somewhere." His skeptical look was killing me. I felt like kind of a jerk, especially after he'd just come over and found what may have looked to be something going on between me and another guy. He wasn't totally wrong- these days not having your phone attached to you was like leaving the house without shoes, but still- did he expect me to check my Facebook status in the middle of my dad's eulogy?

"Oh," he said, almost rescinding his comment.

"Honestly. I don't know where it is; I swear this morning I didn't see any new messages. Maybe the thing's overloaded."

"It's okay, really, babe. I was just worried and I'm sorry, too. It's been one hell of a week. My assistant decided to quit on me, I had to seriously weasel my way out of work *and* I made all my arrangements on my own," he smiled, "you just looked so surprised to see me."

"Well I *am*, in a *good* way, I mean. I'm glad you're here- I could use the support and...I missed you," I smiled.

"Good," he said, "because for a second there I wasn't so sure." Confused, I tilted my head. "I mean, I was afraid you were doing just fine without me." I had never seen Patrick as the jealous type. Then again, he never had a reason to *be* jealous.

"What?" I asked, even though I knew why he'd brought it up. "Oh, Nate?" He nodded. "Honestly- we just came up here at the same time." I paused before continuing, "anyway, he's *engaged.* Remember that girl from Thanksgiving?" *Whew.*

"Really?" he asked, somewhat surprised. "He seems like a decent guy," he smiled. I noticed his gaze drop and stay there. He lifted up my left hand, gently running his thumb over my fingers, stopping at the large piece of jewelry on my ring finger. *Shit.* I'd completely forgotten I had it on. "Or was I wrong and I've already been replaced by...*Donnie Brasco?*" he chuckled. I pulled back my hand. I guess it hadn't been too hard to notice the black, shimmery rock. "I gotta say, I'm surprised by your change in taste," he smiled.

"You have no idea how many gangsters I had to sleep with to get this."

"I bet," he said. "Where'd you get it?"

"I found it in my dad's jewelry stash. Pretty gaudy, huh?" I stood there admiring the two diamonds set outside the singular large onyx stone. Gaudy was right- I doubted even the most notorious of gangsters would've worn this fuckin' thing. "It's a pinky ring. I know, I know, don't say it- another Italian stigma," I added playfully.

"Okay, I *won't*," he answered lightly, both of us chuckling, "I thought maybe you were embarrassed to wear my ring."

"No, no, it's not that," I recovered, "it's just...I was afraid yours might get lost- it's a *little* looser now, stress I guess." He eyed me strangely.

"I *thought* you looked thinner, babe. You *sure* you're okay?" he asked concernedly.

I really did miss him and it felt good to have him here, but something was off. It might have been all the stuff with my dad or the huge business proposition looming over my head that I hadn't *quite* told Patrick about yet. Or? It had to do with something else entirely.

By the time everyone had left the boat club it was well after six. It's funny how the older you get you don't see certain people unless someone either gets married or dies. These things were more like reunions sometimes- you never knew who'd show up: long-lost relatives, old friends, friends of long-lost relatives, exes...the list went on. I had actually enjoyed seeing all the faces, but I guess that's because I'd already mourned. I witnessed tons of people crying all week and I felt badly, but I had gotten to say goodbye, to tell my dad how much I loved him.

Recent events had kept me distracted, which had led to procrastination, which was far from my norm. There was so much to talk about, things Patrick didn't know: like the fact that this potential business deal would mean I'd have to mostly live here. Patrick was an understanding guy, but what if he *wouldn't* be okay with that? I'd wanted to tell him for a while, but seeing as he was here now, I had no other choice- I was gonna have to bite the bullet.

Part of me thought I should care more about his feelings. That I shouldn't chance throwing it all away and losing him over some job. But the other part of me thought, 'too bad'- it *wasn't* just some job- this was my *future*, a future I had worked extremely hard at solidifying. Why should *I* be the one to compromise when *I* had gotten this far? After all, he'd done everything he'd wanted to do with *his* career the past few years, right? And if someone really *loved* you, they'd not only want to make themselves happy, but also be willing to sacrifice at least some of their wants and desires in order to make you happy.

"What's so funny?" Patrick asked, setting the large box on the kitchen counter.

Finally, I got up from the couch. "Oh, nothing. I just like watching you get tortured."

"It's not torture," he replied, shaking his head.

"Well, that's what *I* call it when I have to work with family," I uttered, "but maybe they like you better. You flew across the country to see me and you get coerced into clean up. Shit, Anthony and Donnie practically stole you away from me."

"Nah, they weren't bad and they didn't *coerce* me- I was glad to help," he added, closing in for a quick peck on the cheek. "Plus, I got to spend some quality time with your fam."

"If you consider hanging with them after they've been drinking too much 'quality', then I *guess*, sure," I laughed, putting away the food. Not that I had much of an appetite.

"Nah, it's all good, I promise. Besides, I'm used to the Camioni's when they overdo it, especially with wine," he said with a wink.

"Funny," I answered cutely, excusing myself to the bedroom. "You know, you could always switch places with Jeanine." Patrick's impromptu appearance had meant I'd had to ask Jeanine to go stay with my mom; she'd come to visit for a few days.

Not a moment later he spoke up, "speaking of stealing, I didn't realize you and 'what's his name' were so close. I thought you said you barely ran into him." *What?*

I peered my head around the corner, giving him a perplexing look. My shirt half-hanging from one arm, I covered myself, as if suddenly shy of showing flesh around my own boyfriend. "I don't." *Well, that wasn't a complete lie.* "We were sitting there for like 3 minutes before you showed up, don't be ridiculous," I insisted. "And you *know* his name- Nate."

"Right, Nate," he corrected himself, "and that's not what your Aunt Toni said. For some reason she felt the need to point out the fact that you two were getting chummy over at the bar, not that I took her seriously."

"Well, you shouldn't- she's a drunk" I persisted, a little peeved. "She likes to stir up shit for no reason, which there *isn't*, by the way." I emerged wearing a loose-fitting tank top and yoga pants.

"If you say so," he smirked. I knew he was kidding but still, I was on edge.

I joined him at the kitchen counter. "I *told* you- our class was really close; a few of us still are. With some people that kind of thing just never goes away." I smiled cutely at him, trying to win him over with charm, "it's hard to explain..."

"Yeah, I know, it just looked a little too close." Was he joking or not? I couldn't tell.

"Geez, you act like we were making out," I laughed again, this time more loudly. "He's engaged, remember? And FYI," I added kissing his hand, "he just lost his dad last year; sometimes it helps when someone else knows what you're going through."

"Oh, I didn't realize. I guess I got a little jealous there for a minute. I'm sorry, I'm just not used to having to share you with so many people or see you at the center of attention. I should've been more sensitive."

I paused for a moment, "it's not easy, is it? Seeing someone you care about so up close and personal with the opposite sex?" I winked. "Kind of like...*you*?"

After starting out confused, he understood where I was going. "You're right- it's not. I guess I never thought of it like that. Sorry to doubt you- you know I trust you," he smiled again, kissing my hand.

"Well, after seeing hundreds of women gawk over you and constantly having to retrain myself from strangling a few on occasion? You *better*," I smirked evilly.

"Ha, ha, funny." His grin faded. "*Seriously*?"

I slid one arm under his shirt- I hadn't realized how much I'd missed those muscles. I swear he'd grown a dozen more. "Scorpio, remember?" I reminded him.

"I thought you said you were one of the 'nice' Scorpios you know, the kind that *don't* kill its prey?" he asked, wrapping one arm around me.

"I *am* nice- I let you *know* when I'm gonna kill you. The other ones do it unsuspectingly. Hey!" Speaking of unsuspected, Patrick swooped me up off the stool and carried me to the living room. "Wait, wait- the bedroom's that way," I looked up at him from the couch, pressing my arms against his chest, not that I was a match for his strength. He held me down, answering me with a barrage of kisses, sending waves of trembling sensations through my body.

"Who needs a bed? I've got a few surprises of my *own*, Ms. Camioni."

"Is that right, Mr. Thomas?"

"Uh, huh," he said in a soft sexy tone, proceeding to lift up my shirt, "just wait." And just like that, we were in the throws of a total and complete old-school make out session only instead of being in the back seat of a Chevelle at a drive-in, we were in my living room.

Chapter 54 ~ Gone with the Wind

It was Friday and although I'd normally be at the bakery with Rachel I'd committed to..."Oh *fuck*!" I exclaimed as I closed the refrigerator, "how did I forget that?"

"Forget what?" I heard his husky voice from the bedroom.

I set two mugs on the counter in a slight panic. "It's just I had something *kind* of important to do today." *Kind of?*

Patrick, half-stumbling around the corner, immediately reached for the coffee pot. "God, that's good. Am I the only one who thinks Starbucks is overrated?" I shook my head 'no'. "Anyway, what were you saying?" he leaned in to kiss my cheek. God was right- he smelled even *better* than my latte- and I would argue he tasted better, too.

"Good morning," I smiled, "I was just talking to myself."

"So," he continued, "what did you forget?"

"Well?" I said, sitting on one of the counter stools, "remember when I said Jeanine was supposed to crash here?" He nodded as he poured some sugar in his coffee. "I promised to take her by work today to show her the uh, progress." I paused in thought.

"You mean the bakery?" I shook my head 'no'. "Oh, the clinic." Again, I shook my head 'no'. It was obvious he had no clue what I was talking about.

"To be honest, I haven't been there as much lately."

"The bakery?"

"No, well um, yes; not exactly," I squandered.

"Eleana, what does that mean? Either I haven't had enough caffeine or you're not speaking clearly."

"Uh no, I mean yes, but *no*- that's not it."

"Then *what*? You were acting weird all day yesterday. What's up?" *Besides the fact that I was burying my fucking father?*

I was sensing some hostility, an unusual trait of Patrick Thomas. In fact, I don't think I'd ever seen him get angry or raise his voice, but he was right- I hadn't been completely forthcoming.

"I haven't been at the bakery *or* the clinic as much, but there's a good reason..."

Patrick cut me off before I could continue, "your dad- I know, Lea; it's okay. I understand; it just feels like lately there's something *else* on your mind."

I sighed deeply, "you're right- there has; I mean, there *is*," I admitted. "my dad *has* been a big reason...but there's actually another. Patrick," I sighed again, "I haven't been completely honest with you and I wanted to tell you last night, but I couldn't find the right time and...actually I've been meaning to tell you that..." I lowered my head, ashamed that of all the people I *hadn't* told, Patrick was the one person I *should* have. I was doing it again- shutting out the people I needed the most. I wondered how mad he was about to be at me.

"What are you talking about?" he asked, more serious.

"Remember last night when you found me at the bar?" Quietly he nodded. "It's kind of funny uh, Nate and I actually *have* crossed paths lately," I defended, "but not in the way you might think, which you *shouldn't*. I've cut back at the other places, but not just 'cause of my dad- it's because...well, I've kind of got a new job." He looked at me, a calmer expression over his face.

The truth was, I was about to make one of the biggest decisions in my life and Nate had been right- it was time I thought about what was best for *my* future. The fact that Patrick hadn't been around meant I'd had to count on everyone else for my support system- So *what* if Nate had been one of them? He was going to be one of my potential partners *and* he was my friend.

"Oh?"

"Justin opened a new hospital- it's huge and pretty amazing- you should see it."

He put his arm around me relieved, "that's *it*? *That's* the big secret you had to tell me? I thought you were gonna tell me something bad." My face slightly sunk again.

"Well?" I said, "there's *more*. That's where I'm supposed to take Jeanine today for a tour."

"What's so bad about that? I'd love to check it out- sounds like a great place."

"Really? That's *great*! Because that kind of *is* my new job," I shrunk slightly in my seat. I could see his curiosity peaking. "I haven't signed anything yet, but I really think it'll be a great opportunity..."

"Oh," he said, "well, that's good. You've been saying for months how the other place might not work out. Maybe it was for a good reason." *You have no idea.*

"It's just been so much to take in with my dad and everything. I haven't had a chance to..."

"...*mention* it?" he asked, disappointment in his voice.

"I know, I'm sorry. I wasn't *trying* not to, it's just...the time has gone by so fast. It's a change I've been wanting to happen for a while..."

"Babe, I had no idea," he answered. "So, I'm guessing Maureen's gonna be there, too?" I nodded. "Well, that's cool. I know how much you enjoy working together. Maybe since you know the owner you might have even more flexibility than you do now..." *Hardly.*

I nodded, shrugging, "Well- that depends on your definition of 'flexible'."

"Huh?"

"You're right, about knowing Justin and yes, he *is* the owner but...Nate, he's actually a partner, too." I watched as Patrick's smile began to flatten. "So...so we'll all be working together, which is good because right now Justin needs all the support he can get."

"Hmm, didn't realize. Don't they have managers for places like that?"

When it came to veterinarians running a small business, Patrick (like most others) didn't realize the complexities involved. He probably assumed it was just a matter of a few signatures on a piece of paper, an investment, which I guess was true in certain circumstances- like corporate takeovers- but that's only because they had their little minions doing all their fucking dirty work. Owning, or partially owning, a veterinary hospital was a serious endeavor and a big deal, not just from a business standpoint, but from a medicine one.

As veterinarians, we took great pride in both the care and well-being of both our patients *and* our clients- we had *double* the work of a physician when it came to our daily routines. Some nights we were kept awake tossing and turning about a case or a patient we'd lost; others were due to the deteriorating condition of one of our clients, while others were because of some asshole who'd tried to make us feel like shit. The reasons were endless and at times tiring, which is why so many veterinarians *didn't* want to embark on the journey of practice ownership- the job was hard enough without having to deal with the business side.

Over the past several years the drive to be my own boss had grown and when Justin had asked me to be part of his venture, I'd been floored. The fact that he'd even thought to include me was incomprehensible. I wasn't about to throw that kind of opportunity away, especially since it may never come up again. Not that Patrick actually *knew* that yet.

"Um, I wish but unfortunately, I probably *wouldn't* be as flexible, at least for a while. I'd have to be here *more*."

His face turned a little sour, "more, as in...*how* much more? I hardly see you as it is," he smiled handsomely. *And that's all my fault?* "Did I forget to tell you how much I missed you?"

Now I was feeling even worse about all of this. "You know I miss you. And I'm not totally sure, but I *do* know I'd have to cut out a lot...there's just no way I'd be able to do it all."

"But I thought you *loved* multitasking," he commented. "I happen to think you've been doing a pretty damn good job *so* far," he smiled. "Why do you think this will be any different?" *Because it will be different, especially if I have to live here....* "I bet you in no time you'll be able to pick up and leave and they won't even know you're gone," he added. *Not exactly.* He really had no idea. As if I hadn't already said it a million times, Patrick was one of the most understanding people I knew. The only question was- how understanding would he be when he found out the whole story?

11:30 am
Veterinary Care Center

"*Jesus*, Lea, you weren't kidding. What is this, 20,000 square feet?" Jeanine was practically clinging on to Patrick as we walked around the monstrous facility. Thankfully due to his ever-changing appearance and the nonstop action of a busy veterinary hospital, people hardly turned their heads, except for the random female. Patrick may not have been recognizable, but he was still tall, dark and extremely attractive.

I laughed to myself proudly, nearly stumbling into one of the treatment tables in triage. "Thirty," I stated.

"Wow," Patrick interrupted, "impressive."

"So, Lea, any idea where your office will be?" she caught herself, "I mean, *would* be?" Jeanine had been well-aware of this opportunity *and* of how stressed I'd been the last few months, especially over telling Patrick. Looking back, I guess it really hadn't been that big of a deal but at the time, a lot of things were circling my mind.

"Oh, um, I...I don't know- I'd have to ask Justin, if I can find him..." As we approached the main office area, I peeked inside. A male with brown hair sat at a computer and had just hung up his phone. He didn't even have to turn around- I'd recognize Nate's sigh anywhere. "Hey," I called out.

Immediately he looked over and swiveled his chair around, smiling. "Oh, hey, Lea! What's up? You working today?" he asked, quickly taking notice of my guests. "Oh," he said, eyeing Patrick, "guess not. Hey, man; didn't know you were still here," he said to Patrick. "Jeanine, how long you in town for?"

"'Til Sunday. I was planning on staying longer for emotional support, but turns out I've been upstaged, literally," she said, smiling at Patrick.

"Anything for Lea," he responded, turning towards Nate. "Hey," he answered somewhat coyly, "how are you?"

"Good, good. Nice. Did you guys get a chance to see the whole place yet? If not, I got some free time. Did you see the new MR machine? Did you see Justin? I think he was just in there," he continued, "he loves that thing so much I think he wants to marry it."

"Uh, no, not yet."

"Want me to show you? I needed to talk to him about a case anyway so..."

"I didn't know M...R? machines were that exciting," Patrick commented in a low voice. Jeanine and I just smiled. *Of course, you don't- you're an actor.*

"These new models are so much faster, use a shit-ton less energy and give better results." Nate was clearly overenthusiastic about the new equipment, but he was right- it wasn't just state-of-the-art; it was almost futuristic.

Unimpressed, Patrick shrugged, "I guess so." I could tell his was feeling somewhat out of place. Either that, or he was annoyed that Nate was here.

"Anyway," Nate continued, asking Patrick, "how long you in town for?"

"Through next week, hopefully," he said.

Nate had been right- There sat Justin in one of the rooms, reviewing image after image. "I knew you'd be in here," he said, barging in. "We have some special guests."

Almost immediately Justin looked up. "Hey, Lea, I wanted to talk to you... Oh, hi...Jeanine, right?" he asked, now noticing Patrick standing there. "Oh, Patrick. What do you think?"

Jeanine nodded, hardly able to contain her own excitement, "I have to tell you, Justin, this place is...spectacular. If I didn't live so far, I'd be partnering up with you guys. Can you imagine us all on a board together?" It wasn't her fault. Jeanine's tendency to get overzealous made it nearly impossible for her to keep her mouth shut. *I'm in trouble now...*

Ignoring the newly sprung tension in the air, Justin answered her, "you would've been a *great* addition to the team. Hey anytime you wanna reconsider, let me know," he said.

"Thanks, I'll keep that in mind if I ever move to New York, but looks like you're gonna have an all-star team without me, especially when Lea joins you..." I watched Patrick's expression change.

"Nah, come on, J-Lo," Nate commented, "I've heard some pretty great things about you in the rehab department. We're adding that in the near future, FYI," he winked. Jeanine had never had a thing for Nate but still his charm got to her just like it had every other girl. There was no hiding the flush in her cheeks. My guilt on the other hand? Well...

Although at first disconnected from our conversation, Patrick had suddenly taken interest. He turned to me, "Partner? I thought you said you were *working* here."

I shrugged my shoulders, uncomfortable about being thrown into this discussion. *To the wolves is more like it.* "Um…well?"

Jeanine nudged Patrick, "pretty *cool*, right?" she asked.

He looked at her, trying to force a small grin, before turning back to me, "uh yeah, it's just…is *that* what you meant when you said you'd be working more?"

"*More*?" Justin jumped in, "try a *lot*- we're gonna need *all* hands on deck. We've got a long way to go before this thing is steady state, so I don't think she'd be going anywhere for a while." *Gulp.* Justin was right- it was a huge commitment for *all* of us.

Patrick looked at me curiously, "Wait- you've already *decided* this?"

I felt my stomach drop and my reluctancy to answer rise. I sighed deeply before finally opening my mouth, "Well, I've been thinking it over and…and I think…" It was amazing how deafening silence could be, even in a place as busy as this. The constant chatter and barking faded seamlessly into the background.

Noting our need for privacy, Justin spoke up, "um, I think that's our cue. I have to go check on a patient anyway so…" he paused, "uh, Lea, the meeting's been moved to Monday at 9- that's what I needed to tell you. Call me later or text me or Maureen- whatever." He grabbed Nate's arm and eyed Jeanine to join them, "Nate maybe you could take Jeanine for some coffee."

"But…" Jeanine apparently hadn't gotten the 'they need some alone time' memo. In a flash they yanked her out the door, leaving Patrick and I in a big empty room to hash things out.

Patrick looked at me, his eyes now casting more than a hint of disappointment, "So, I'm taking that as a '*yes*'," he said.

I grinned childishly, "uh…Wait- before you say anything, let me explain."

"Explain *what*, Lea, that you've been planning this for months and somehow forgot to mention it?"

"Patrick, it's *not* like that. You make it sound like I was scheming behind your back."

"Then what *was* it like?"

"Well, first of all, I didn't *plan* anything. It just kind of fell into my lap. What else? Let's see- overwhelming, intimidating, stressful…" He waited for me to continue. "But honestly also kind of exciting- it's the opportunity I've been waiting my *whole* life for," I said.

"What about California? And *us*?" he asked.

"California's a *place*, and this doesn't have anything to *do* with us- it's about *me* and my career, which in case you haven't noticed is *everything* to me- it's my life. I can't turn this away now, not when I've worked so hard and have the chance to finally make a difference the way I want."

"Lea, don't be silly- of *course* you make a difference. You think what you do isn't enough?" *Clearly you don't know that many veterinarians...* "And why did you think it was okay not to bring it up, not even once? Don't you think I might wanna know?"

"No, it's *not,* and I *wasn't* trying to keep it from you- things just happened so fast and I wasn't ready to tell everyone, not with everything else going on...I've barely had a hold on things myself..."

"And by everyone you mean...*me*..."

"That's not true- until last week it was only Mac, Maureen, Justin and..."

"*Nate?*"

I looked at him, anger and resentment coming on, "*yeah*, and *Nate*, who for some reason you wanna keep focusing on. I told you..."

"Yeah, right. There's nothing between you too, I heard you when you said it the first time," he sulked, "somehow that line's getting harder and harder to believe."

"You heard me, but you weren't *listening*." It'd been a long time since I had to defend myself to a jealous boyfriend and I didn't miss it one fucking bit. It was beyond irritating to be with someone who supposedly trusted you, yet suddenly wasn't believing a single word you said.

"I *was* listening, but maybe if you'd trusted me enough to confide in me instead of everyone *else,* I wouldn't be so upset. I'm just curious, Lea, when was it you exactly decided on this hospital venture thing- was it before or *after* you found out your old 'friend' Nate would be a part of it?"

That really struck a nerve. My eyes began to tear up from hurt and anger. "*What*? You think this has to do with *Nate*? Because I got news for you, Hollywood, it *doesn't*-I told you..."

"You *didn't* tell me, Eleana, that's the point."

"But I'm telling you *now* and I'm trying to tell you why," I defended, "that doesn't matter?"

"Right, let me guess, your dad. Is that gonna be your excuse for everything?"

I sniffled loudly, wiping my eyes and now my nose, "Jesus Christ- give me some fucking time to grieve over my dead father, will ya? And for your information, veterinary medicine has *always* been the biggest thing in my life, it *always* will be. There's nothing new about that."

Patrick stepped back, "*always*...right," he answered softly. "And what about the *rest* of your life, Eleana?" I sat there, unable to answer. "So...if California's just another 'place' to you then what was I, just another guy, or was it more of a game for you? See if the small-town girl can score the hot playboy then when the life she really wants shows up and she has no more use for him just discard him? I have news for *you*, Eleana, there's more to life than work and animals aren't the only ones who have feelings."

That pissed me off. "Don't you think I *know* that?" I replied callously, "if you think even for one minute that I could even be *capable* of that, then I guess you really *don't* know me."

He was sitting down now, a few feet away. "That's the thing, Eleana," he sighed, "lately I don't feel like I know you at all- these past several months it's like you've been somewhere else…" *No shit, Sherlock.* "You've been pushing me away. Your dad gets sick, you push me away even more, yet you have no problem confiding in other people. And then you decide to work with a guy who's clearly still into you and lie about it and not only that, you conveniently leave out the fact that you're gonna be *partners*. So *no*, Lea, I *don't* think I know you- these secrets, these lies, it's like there's this whole other side of you and I'm not sure I like it."

The last thing I wanted was to add fuel to the fire, but I couldn't just bend over and apologize because he didn't agree with my decision; the truth was in my mind I hadn't done anything wrong. "That's not fair, Patrick. You go off for weeks and months at a time, doing what *you* want, *when* you want, chasing *your* dreams. What about *my* dreams? I'm almost 40 years old- when do I get my chance, when I'm *dead*? What if this opportunity never comes around again? I'm supposed just to give up my dreams for…"

"I didn't realize you felt that way, Lea."

"Well, I *do*," I said adamantly.

"When I met you, you were passionate about your job, but you had fun; you never obsessed about it or let it take over your life." *You really need to meet more veterinarians…* "What happened to that girl; what suddenly changed?" I looked at him pensively. Was he right? Had I become some crazy veterinarian so obsessed with her job that nothing else mattered, even the man she loved? I felt my eyes water again.

"That's not fair and you know it, Patrick," I persisted, "Veterinary medicine may not be glamourous or important to people like *you*, but it *is* to me and it's *who* I am; it's *not* just some job. Look around you- it's a helluva *lot* more," I pointed at the door. "These past several months with you travelling, me losing my friend *and* my dad, have been the most difficult and challenging of my life, so tell me- how the *hell* am I supposed to 'confide' in you when you're off in Rome kissing Scarlett Johansen or…or London making out with Kate Bosworth? If you *had* been around, you would've *known* how lonely it's been and how much I needed you here. I can't help it if it's made me more driven and more determined to follow my dreams, dreams I thought were out of reach."

I continued my ranting, unable to control myself, "you know, maybe you're right- maybe I *have* changed- I'm finally becoming who I'm supposed to be. I thought you of anyone would understand that. I'm not the pretty, dumb model who sits around pining for you while I do busywork to pass the time. I thought you were different from the rest of the playboys, that you respected me being my own person. I mean, there *is* life outside of Hollywood, ya know. And maybe I was stupid to think I could ever fit into that world. So, forgive me for wanting something more fulfilling out of my life."

"I *do*," he pressed. "Lea, that's not fair and *you* know it. I've always supported you. I've *never* thought of you like that. I care about you. I *love* you for who you are- or *were*- that's why I wanted to be with you." *Wanted?* I remained silent. "I've treated you the best I could; *Jesus* I took you to Cabo, gave you this expensive ring, that took hours to pick out by the way, I poured my heart out but...that's not *enough* for you, is it? All this focus on me not being around and unreliable guys...those are just lame excuses, aren't they? It's *you* who doesn't know what she wants, who won't fully commit."

"Patrick, that's not true I..."

"You know, you keep filling your life up with nothing but work you won't have any left for anything or *anyone* else- or is that the point? Deep down, you don't really want someone to share your life with, do you? You're afraid they might get in the way of your big plans. You don't want love; you want a check list. You want a guy on the side when it's convenient for you and just so we're clear, I'm *not* that guy; I can't compete with whatever it is you've got going on inside your head which..." he paused, "just tell me one thing, honestly, Eleana- do you even *love* me? I mean, you've never even said it back."

He was angry and hurt- I had to do something. I mean, shouldn't the words have just come out naturally, like in all those lame-ass *Hallmark* movies? Sure, but that's not what happened and why? Because I was an *asshole*- I choked. I felt painted into a corner, afraid to make such a grownup decision on the fly. What if I turned down this opportunity only to regret it months from now? To complicate things even further, there was this part of me that questioned why Nate had been brought back into my life. Was there even a reason? Should I try to find out?

Sensing my uncertainty, Patrick took another step back and glanced down at the tile floor. I felt like I was under water, unable to get enough air to swim to the surface and cry for help. I inhaled deeply, about to speak, and then the loudspeaker came on with an announcement, interrupting my brave attempt at reconciliation. *Perfect fucking timing.* "Patrick..."

"You can't say it, can you?" he asked. A tiny tear formed at the corner of his left eye. "Maybe this was all my fault, coming out here and barging in on your 'other' life; It's obviously more important. Maybe I didn't realize how much all this and everyone *else* meant to you..."

"Patrick, I...I just...this is all so much I don't know what I'm supposed to do..."

"You're supposed to do what you feel is right, what you really want." He grabbed hold of me, desperate for an answer, "look at me, Eleana- *what* do you want?"

Tears streaming down my face, I sniffled, struggling to find the words. "I don't know..."

"Look, I think it's great that you have this opportunity I really do, and maybe you're right, maybe you won't ever get this chance again. If this is what's most important to you, then who am I to try and stop you? I love you and I meant every word I said, but if you're unsure, then I don't think I can wait around to find out if you *might* be someday. If what I said isn't enough for you, if *I'm* not enough, then maybe I'm *not* the right guy for you. If you're not all in, then what are we even doing this for? Look," he sighed, "I got a call from the studio this morning. I was gonna try to extend my stay, but I should probably get back. There's a 10 o'clock flight out of La Guardia."

He stood over me almost apologetically, tenderly wiping the tears away from my eyes, a slight smile on his face. "Oh..."

"I think it's probably best." All I could do was nod. I mean at this point, what else was there to say? A great man was standing before me, ready and willing to commit, every girl's dream, yet I couldn't give him a simple answer. What the fuck was wrong with me? Was there some other way to make it all work or did I absolutely *have* to choose? Was I just gonna sit here and let my potential future walk away without a fight?

"Oh," I sulked, "um, so where does this leave us?"

"Eleana, you need some time to...work things out and I wanna give it you; I just can't promise I'll still be here when you do."

And just like that the man of my dreams walked out of my life almost as quickly and abruptly as he had come into it. Suddenly I was transported back to that scene in *A Christmas Carol* where Ebenezer Scrooge is given an ultimatum by his girlfriend to either spend his life with her or work and he chooses work; in his mind, he had done right to secure their futures. Well of course that hadn't been the answer she was looking for and she bolted- and he didn't even go after her, even though deep down he really *did* love her.

And as the story goes, he became a crotchety miser, alone for the rest of his life but really...*had* he been completely wrong in that one small moment? And in this very moment, had *I* been wrong, too?

PART SEVEN: The Game of LIF

"Stop leaving and you will arrive. Stop searching and you will see.

Stop running away and you will be found."

– Lao Tzu

Chapter 55 ~ Back to the Future

One month later...

I sat at my desk staring aimlessly at the calendar, something I'd been doing a lot of lately. It's true what they say about time- it either flies by or stands still, but for me it had been a little of both. The past month had dragged yet it felt like just yesterday I'd been in this same room, forced to decide my fate. Well I hadn't exactly been *forced*; I'd just been given an ultimatum- either give up a comfortable yet unfulfilled life (to me) I'd built with Patrick or give up my dream job.

I'd been waiting and preparing for this kind of opportunity to arrive- the kind that opens new doors and has the potential to take you to infinity and beyond, a place many of my colleagues aim for, yet few actually near, whether it's because they never get the chance, lose their drive or burn out. I'd been lucky enough to have been given that chance, to be set up with the tools to go beyond anything I could've imagined possible and for that I was grateful. But Patrick and I had also been lucky; we'd had something few people get to experience and *that* had made my decision a difficult one.

I've believed for a long time that if something is meant to work out then it will, and if it's not...well? Either fate didn't want it to, or you fucked something up. Right now, I wasn't sure which was truer. I hated more than anything feeling cornered, having to choose between love and money. I guess I never thought that'd happen to me and if it ever did I'd always known *exactly* what to do: when faced with the opportunity of a lifetime or love, in my mind the answer had always been simple- take the chance, go for the gold, win big; *screw* love, because realistically what's more likely to take you further in life, a great career or some guy who might not stick around in the long run? At least my job (and my family) would always be there for me.

The problem was Patrick *wasn't* some meaningless guy and our relationship wasn't just some casual fling- or was it? Still, was it worth throwing away everything I'd worked for to find out? I kept wondering if it was too late. There hadn't been much of an argument; Patrick had pretty much told me to take the job. Had I *really* been too consumed by work to see the bigger picture? Or had *he* been the selfish one? Either way, he'd gotten on a plane and resumed his thrillingly famous life on the west coast, leaving me stranded in a place that suddenly didn't feel so homey anymore.

I was still trying to figure it all out, get used to my new routine, to not talking to him constantly, to being alone, although I wasn't completely- I had plenty of family and friends, not that any of them could really help. Because the truth was, this was a fire I had started all on my own and I was gonna have to deal with its backdraft *and* its scars. Right now though, the burns were still raw. In fact, they looked like they were beginning to necrose. I glanced down at my desk, loaded with crap: files, notes, flash drives, scientific papers to review for a new oncology study the hospital was looking into...and admixed the occasional condolence card. I swear if I read one more, I was gonna puke.

After Patrick had left all was far from quiet on the eastern front. I'd dove head-first into work: documents were finalized and submitted, old contracts were broken and new ones signed, and I was doing my best adjusting to a new role. Amongst all the craziness though, I still found time to ponder over my most recently broken contract and the impressive signing bonus I'd turned down- a 6-foot three dashing prince and his castle set high in the hills of Hollywood Kingdom. And despite the brave front I was putting on I still found time to cry over it. My dad had ingrained in me that crying was for pussies but no matter how hard I tried I just couldn't stop: I snuck away whenever I could to a bathroom, a supply closet, the morgue...you know, all those places the young medical interns on *E.R.* and *Grey's Anatomy* go to have sex, only that *definitely* wasn't happening. And *unluckily* for me, every now and then someone would check in and make sure I was okay at exactly the wrong time.

"What the fuck happened here?"

"Oh, hey," I answered, suddenly aware Nate had quietly snuck in.

"Lea, it looks like a fuckin' bomb went off in here. Everything okay?"

I let out a big sigh, quickly shuffling some of the papers before shoving them in a drawer. "Uh yeah. Why?" He was right about the mess- it was embarrassing as hell.

"You sure? he asked doubtfully, "'Cause for a second it didn't quite look that way. Oh," he stopped himself, "that's right, I forgot- Camioni's don't show emotion." His devilish smile was not at all what I wanted to see right now, but he'd had a valid point.

"Actually they do," I smiled back, "some even say they're capable of crying, but it's gotta be a special occasion, like when Sonny Corleone gets murdered or the store runs out of Capicola or fresh mozzarella."

"Hmm, funny." He pulled over a chair and leaned on it. "What about your dad's service? Even *I* teared up when your brothers did the eulogy. Funerals aren't considered a 'special' occasion?"

I rolled my eyes at him, "of *course* they are- we're just good at putting on a good front. Plus, your dad wasn't in the military."

"Let me guess- crying is a sign of weakness," he said.

"You have no idea. Anyway, I'm okay, but thanks for checking."

"If you say so." He was sitting down now, staring at me.

"Now what do you want?" I asked.

"Oh, nothing."

"Then why are you staring at me like that?"

He crinkled the space between his brows. "What makes you think I *want* something?"

"You forget how well I know you. You don't fool anybody with that smirk, Peterson." Rolling his chair closer, he laughed. "Cough it up."

"Okay, okay, you got me. It's about work."

"Of *course* it is," I chuckled to myself. "Let's hear it- when do you want me to cover for you?"

"I wanted to take Tina away this weekend. There's only one problem- I'm working Friday."

"Let me guess," I tilted my head, "no one else will do it so you figured the lame-ass single girl would be free."

"Kind of, yeah."

"Gee, thanks."

"I owe you big if you do this for me."

"You'll owe me *more* than that," I said. "I helped you out a few weeks ago, too, remember?"

"Okay- you're right. I promise I'll make it up to you." He laughed.

"I'm sure I'll think of *something*, but I'm always happy to encourage along a healthy relationship, even if it's not mine." I laughed to myself.

"Lea, you'll be fine. Don't worry, it'll all work out," he added, placing a hand on my shoulder.

"That's easy for you to say, Nate. Your life's looking a helluva lot better than mine right now."

He hesitated for a moment, letting out a huff, "hmm, yeah, I *guess* so."

"What do you mean, you *guess* so? What's the matter, trouble on the Jersey Shore I mean...*paradise*?" I joked.

He shrugged his shoulders nonchalantly and his cheeks, now red, meant something was clearly on his mind. "Really? You're gonna go and start that shit, too?"

"What?" I asked blindly. "Go where? Start...what?"

"Ever since Tina and I got engaged I've heard nothing but criticism- 'don't do it', 'stay single', 'you could do better than that', 'she's not the right girl for you'..."

"Like *who*?" I asked, still unsure what had spawned this sudden outburst from him.

"Everyone..." His eyes shot right back at me, "including you."

"*Me*? I never said that..." *although you obviously could do way better and everyone including me knows she's completely wrong for you...* "It's your relationship- you can do whatever you want. I thought things were going 'great'. And since *when* do you care what other people think?"

"I don't know- since what I keep hearing bothers me, especially when it involves people closest to me, people I thought were on my side. Why are you looking at me like you don't know what I'm talking about?" Now *my* shoulders were shrugging.

"You don't think I'm on your side?" *That hurt.*

"Come on, Eleana. You don't think I *know*? It's no secret how you feel about Tina."

"What?" I played, "I never said I didn't...*like* her." His disbelieving eyes saw right through me- "Okay, fine. It's just that...I just think that you..."

"That...what, I could do better? That she's not my type? Please enlighten me. If I can do *so* much better, than who should I be with...*you*?"

I couldn't believe he'd just said that. I felt my stomach drop- again. You'd think by this point I would've been well-adjusted to the sour feeling. In the past nine months my innards had nearly fallen out of my body at least a dozen times, like I was on some perpetual rollercoaster ride. "Well, no, but...wait. How did you..."

"*How*? A little birdie called Maureen can't keep her mouth shut." *Oops.*

"Nate, it just kinda seemed like you hadn't thought it through, that's all. I didn't mean..."

"Right; I've only been dating her for over a year- what the fuck would *I* know? Like you should be one to judge anyway," he continued. "Sorry. Look, I just...didn't come here for advice or lecturing on any past *or* present relationships, especially from you- no offense." *Ouch.* "Can you help me out or not?"

"Yeah, yeah, I can do it," I said bleakly, gazing down towards the floor.

"Lea, look at me." Just then he took hold of my chin and raised it so our eyes could meet. "It's not that I don't value your opinion. Trust me, out of everyone, I value yours the most- which is why it hurt that you never said anything to me. I care about you. Maybe you didn't notice, but I never *stopped* caring about you and I respect you- as a colleague and a friend- but the truth is I stopped caring about your opinions a *long* time ago- I *had* to." There was a break in his voice. *What?* "Things just are the way they are now. I've had to accept things I didn't like and now as my friend, if you truly want me to be happy, you're gonna have to accept certain things, too."

"Nate, I *do*...want you to be happy; it's all I ever wanted."

"Then...let me be...*happy*. This is the second chance I've been waiting for." *Gulp.* "I just wish you...everyone could see that it's what I want."

For a long moment I sat there, unsure of what else to say. Had he felt the same way about Patrick as I had about Tina? And why hadn't he told me? Nate was acting so unlike his usual calm, laid-back, non-worrying self and his angry, unforgiving words had thrown me. Now more than ever, I didn't want him to know that I never stopped caring for him, either.

But what good would it do? He'd already made up his mind about who he wanted to be with, and it wasn't me. It was déjà vu- Way back when, I'd kept my feelings for him bottled up and by the time I'd worked up the nerve to tell him, he'd already met someone else and anything I thought we'd had had fizzled back into friendship. But listening to him now, maybe there'd been more to it. Still, it didn't matter now and him dishing it out hard made me feel like I was under attack by *two* formidable opponents- the guy who'd just flown out of my life, possibly forever, and the one standing in front of me who I'd just learned had never left.

"Well, if it's what you *really* want, then you should do what makes you happy. And if Tina makes you happy, then I *promise*- I'll be happy, too." The corner of my lip curved up, forcing him to smile back at me.

The truth was, in the dozen or so times I'd met Tina I hadn't really thought much of her, and neither did anyone else. It's not that she was an evil bitch; she just tended to rub people the wrong way. It also might've been the fact that no one (including me) saw any compatibility whatsoever between them, not that that was my problem. He was right about one thing- he was a big boy and could make his own decisions. If he wanted to marry her, then who the hell was I to stand in his way?

"I know. I'm really sorry for getting all worked up. I haven't been feeling like myself lately." *No shit, Peterson. You think no one's noticed?* "You know I love you, Camioni. It's just between me being here all the time and Tina's wedding planning, she's been way more stressed *and* so fuckin' bitchy."

"It's okay- I understand."

"You know, it's funny- I feel like sometimes you're the only one who *does*."

"Anyway, so what's the big deal if she's stressed?"

"Because...she's fuckin' bitchy *all* the time. It's like I can't make her happy." *Again...is this a new thing? Guys are so stupid sometimes.*

"I'm sure it's just a passing thing...and don't you mean *your* wedding?"

"I fuckin' hope so- I don't know how much more I can take," he stressed. "Yeah, *our*, whatever." *Men.*

"Well I'm sure the torture will be over soon enough; just remember though, you got a *lifetime* to look forward to." My grin was now totally in his face and I was loving every second of it. "When's the big day again?"

"I don't know, September I think?" *Why am I not surprised that you have no idea when your own wedding is?*

"You *think*? Anyway, what are your big romantic plans this weekend?"

"The Hamptons- supposed to be nice weather."

"You mean you're *not* going to the Jersey Shore?" I snickered more obnoxiously.

"No, wise ass, we're not."

"That's too bad. Sorry, couldn't help that one. Well, have some fun for me anyway."

"I don't think that'll be a problem." His wink sent waves of jealousy up my spine.

"Yeah, I bet."

"Well, thanks again for working. I've got an appointment- I'll catch up with you later and Lea? You're *not* lame." There it was again- that damn award-winning smile.

I looked up at him and paused for a second, "is that supposed to make me feel better?"

"No. I just meant we've all been there."

"Thanks, but I hardly think you've *been* there. You haven't landed the man of your dreams, set the stage for a picture-perfect future and then somehow managed to fuck it up, all because of your own selfishness?"

"Hmm, you're right- I've never met the 'man' of my dreams," he chuckled, "but I have second guessed some decisions I've made, wondered if things would be any different. You'll figure it out- you just have to give it time."

"I hope so." I mean at this point, time was pretty much all I had.

"What do you *mean* you have to work Friday? I thought we were gonna check out that new *Beatles* exhibit at MOMA?"

"Oh, shit, I totally forgot," I said, trying my best to ease Rachel's disappointment. "I'm sorry- can we do it next week? I already promised Nate I'd cover for him."

"You promised me first, ya know, for my *birthday*," she said, knocking me as we neared the street corner. The Seaport was beautiful this time of day, despite the cloudy skies above.

"I know, but I can't go back on my word now- I don't wanna be the cause of a botched romantic getaway."

"If that shit's 'botched', I'm pretty sure it doesn't have anything to do with you. But out of curiosity, since when are you so involved in Nate's love life? And when did you become a fuckin' matchmaker?" she asked.

"I didn't- I'm *not*-I'm just…doing him a favor. Just because I can't have any fun doesn't mean he can't. And how exactly do you play matchmaker for someone who's engaged?" I grabbed the heavy door handle as two people stepped out to let us in.

"You know what I mean," she said. "So, I guess the wedding of the year is still on after all?"

"I guess so, yeah," I answered as we stepped inside the café.

We looked around for a table. "You sound thrilled. Come on, you see the guy every day; you also complain about that bitch almost every time I see you. I was just wondering why all of a sudden you'd wanna help out their relationship. I thought things might've changed, that's all."

"I still don't see what that has to do with me. It's none of my business, he made *that* pretty fucking clear," I remarked callously.

She stopped mid-walk and glared at me with mistrusting eyes. "Obviously there's more to *that* story- care to elaborate?" I shook my head 'no'. "Fine," she continued, "I'll have to get that out of you later. Hey, wanna split one of those spinach pies?"

I followed her gaze towards the display case, full of breads and pastries. "Sure." We put in our order and sat down. "Okay, enough boy talk. Let's try to enjoy our lunch."

"On that note," she said, taking another bite, "have you talked to Patrick lately?" Annoyed, I glowered at her as I chewed. "*What*? I can't bring up one without bringing up the other. As your BFF, it's my duty to perform a wellness check at least once a week. Plus, you may not think so, but your personal life is a lot more exciting than mine."

"A likely story. You asked me that the other day. What personal life? In case you didn't notice, I don't have one right now."

"It sounds like you've got a *lot* more going on than you're letting on. And *no*, I didn't," she argued, breaking into the side salad, "I asked you if you'd *heard* from him. That's an entirely different question."

My eyes rolled instinctively at her, "you're such a wise ass."

"I know- that's why you love me." The Grinch's evil grin came to mind as I watched her face.

"I know. I couldn't get rid of you if I tried."

"But would you want to?"

In 30 years, Rachel's smile hadn't changed one bit. We were six months apart and had basically grown up together. If I closed my eyes we were back playing Barbies, dressing like Madonna or seeing Motley Crue make their first come back. I wouldn't trade any of our memories for anything; she'd been the best friend I'd ever had and her smile wasn't the only thing that had remained unchanged. Our friendship endured and continued to get better with time. I wish I could have said the same about me and Patrick.

Chapter 56 ~ Just Go with It

June 20th, 7pm

I tried everything I could think of: going to the movies, watching local bands, letting friends drag me to boring fundraisers; I stayed late at the hospital and helped at the bakery; I even took up boxing lessons, but none of it worked- my mind continued replaying the same disastrous scene over and over. To most, what I'd accomplished was impressive but to me, it was just the opposite. I should've been happy and proud, but I wasn't because despite what I had gained, I'd lost something even bigger.

I felt like I'd made a deal with a genie or the devil even, so easily willing to trade my soul to further my career. Sitting here now, I wondered if it had been worth the price. People constantly reassured me I'd made the right choice and I tried to play along, telling myself that if I had turned down this opportunity purely for a relationship, a relationship with no guarantees, I'd potentially jeopardize my chance at a successful future forever. Patrick had already been successful before he met me, and his career continued to take off; he didn't risk losing any of that by being with me. My career on the other hand, could not go anywhere if I maintained my recurring role as the actor's girlfriend who just 'happened' to hold some medical degree.

From the very beginning I had feared my world with Patrick might end; that a time would come when I'd be forced to choose a certain path and that in order for big changes to happen even bigger decisions-and sacrifices-would ultimately have to be made. After all, *was* it really possible for something as good as what Patrick and I'd had to last, or had I just run into the inevitable?

Still, the weight of my decision tormented me constantly. I kept waiting for the uncertainty to dissipate and for happiness to take over, but several weeks later the sadness and regret remained- sadness for what I had lost and regret for both what I done and the hurt I had caused. Here I was for the first time - the dream job and the dream life I had always wanted...It's amazing how you can technically be in such a good place yet at the same time feel like you're not-like you've finally gotten into paradise only instead of being elated your life seems no better than *before*...

I absolutely loved these sunsets- they were one of the things I loved most about being out here. The miles of beautiful, flawless coastline and incredible, unobstructed all-encompassing ocean views were hard to beat, but my absolute favorite thing? The way the sun magically set in a perfect Pacific sky every single evening- now *that* was extraordinary. Unlike my life at the current moment, which was about as far from extraordinary as it could get.

As a people-watching magnet Venice Beach got easily crowded especially around sunset. It was just after 6:30 pm and everyone from couples to friends were scattered across the sand, waiting patiently for the large golden star to put on its show. The sun dipped down a little further, causing the gorgeous blue sky to change shades. I recalled the first time I sat on that same beach staring out at the horizon, wishing and hoping for a different life, a life I now had. It seemed like so long ago that I'd first come here and fallen in love with a marina so alluring, so different from the only home I'd ever known. But that hadn't been the only thing I'd fallen for.

I leaned over the semi-worn railing and peered down at the waves crashing into the pier's sturdy legs. An older man stood next to me, still hopeful for one last catch. I watched as three surfers effortlessly rolled into shore one after the next, carrying their boards. Although not nearly as clean or built-up as its northerly neighbor, The Venice Pier still jetted out well off the shore at 1300 feet, making it a prime spot not only to fish but to gaze at L.A.'s shore. It was splattered throughout with white droppings, evidence that humans weren't the only species who loved a good view.

Two miles to the north the lights of the Santa Monica Ferris Wheel and its sprawling pier began to glow more brightly against the backdrop of a slowly darkening sky. I laughed, thinking back to that bizarre night nearly four years ago, on a random blind date that I had heatedly protested. I remembered my legs shaking as I reluctantly walked across the street and into the upscale oceanfront restaurant, unprepared for what lied ahead. I remembered the hostess trying to calm my nerves as she led me outside to a reserved table where my date sat patiently waiting and when I saw who it was, wishing I could turn and run.

My eyes wandered up the shoreline towards Ocean & Vine, a mere speck in the distance. I wondered if Patrick ever thought back to that same magical night; at least, it'd been magical for me, and one I swore I'd never forget. But the truth was I *was* starting to forget; the magic spell once bestowed upon me by some invisible fairy godmother was beginning to wear off and I felt myself slowly turning back into the unworthy, lowly maid who'd never get that kind of chance again with a guy like that again.

"Or could she?" I said aloud. I could tell the man fishing beside me didn't understand English. The guy who suddenly approached me, however, did. I looked over and saw Mike, who'd obviously been close enough to hear me babbling to myself.

"Hey, cuz, talkin' to yourself again?" His fun-loving smile could always cheer me up.

I smiled back, stepping away from the dirty railing. "Yeah well, you know. Who else do I have to talk to?"

"No worries, it's a known fact that *all* Camioni's do it. Shit, I'm the only one who fuckin' listens half the time," he chuckled. "So," he continued, "what's on the agenda tonight? I see you checkin' out the pier. Wanna go on the ferris wheel, play some games?"

"Nah, nah. I was just uh...no. You tell me. This is more your hood than mine. I still think of myself as 'just visiting', ya know?"

"What do you mean? You have an apartment here; you spend at least 1/3 of the year here- which *practically* qualifies you for residency." *Ugh- don't say that.*

"Actually," I said sullenly, "I'm not so sure *what* I'm doing right now. Honestly? I'm not staying that long and..."

Noting the change in my voice, he tilted his head concernedly, "wh...what do you mean? I thought things were going great. You got that new practice which, in case I haven't told you, congratulations- that's fucking awesome; you've got a killer apartment in one of the most sought-after areas in L.A. which you can *afford*, *and* you've managed to singlehandedly do in a short period of time what most people who come out here can't do in 20 years."

"And what's that?"

"*Succeed*. Live out your dreams. And let's not forget landing the dream guy."

"That's not true; look at *you*. You've got a successful business going. Didn't your Instagram page just reach 300,000 followers? And you left out the part where I squashed any chances at a happy ending. What I've singlehandedly managed to do is fuck up, at least the last part and I'm pretty sure there's no fixing it."

"Yeah, I guess you're right. I'm no Patrick Thomas, though," he boasted. "And...how do you know that?"

"I just have a feeling."

"Have you talked to him since you've been out here?" he asked as we neared the boardwalk.

"No, not since...a while. One, he doesn't know I'm here. Two, he's been busy on his new project and he's not even in L.A. at the moment. Plus, I doubt he wants me bothering him anyway. I mean, haven't I done enough?"

"Oh. *Enough*? Come on, Lea. You know that's not true. Maybe he just wants you to have a chance at fulfilling your dreams and figured the only way you could is if you were freed up to do it, as in maybe he thought *he* was getting in *your* way somehow." Abruptly his feet halted, causing a couple behind us to nearly step on our heels. I shrugged my shoulders, hesitating. "Wait. I have an idea."

"I know that look. What?"

"I was just thinking."

"Should I be worried?" I asked.

"No, I was thinking...I know a great place nearby for happy hour..."

I looked at him, baffled. "I don't think we're gonna make it, Mike. It's after seven."

"It's never hurts to try. You know what else?"

"No, I don't."

"No matter how slim the chances, it never hurts to *try*. Come on, let's go, cuz."

I looked down at my phone. 7 am and already I had six text messages and far too many emails. I had to look out my window to remember where I was- I forgot I was three hours behind- *no fuckin' wonder.* It felt strange being back out here this time; not only was I on another coast, in another time zone, I was in another bed-*my* bed, not the one I had previously spent so much time in before I'd left.

The first text was from Rachel, asking me how L.A. was and telling me repeatedly how much she hated me for being out here. The second was from my mom making sure I'd arrived okay. The third was from Mike, making sure I as alive. After last night's prolonged happy hour, I couldn't blame him. We'd arrived at the taqueria minutes after their supposed 'happy hour' had ended but thanks to Mike's charm between the two of us, we'd finished two pitchers of spicy margaritas. Good thing my apartment was within walking distance. How he'd made it home in one piece I had no idea. The other messages were unimportant, so I ignored them and got up to make coffee.

After some much-needed caffeine, I turned on my computer to check my email. Nowadays, in addition to web-surfing and social media posting everyone used their phones for email, including me, but I still preferred looking at certain things on a big screen. As usual most were bullshit spam, and none of them were *that* important, so I quickly closed it out. I decided to check out flights back home. I had only planned on staying in L.A. for a couple of weeks, in time to be home for July 4th and just in time to *avoid* any possibility of seeing Patrick. I hadn't spoken to him recently, but I remembered he was away until sometime in July, which gave me plenty of time to check out the house. I wondered if Patrick had left things the way they were or got angry and threw everything I'd left there out. I also wanted to check on Fenway, not that I needed to- he'd probably been left in the capable (well, *semi*-capable) hands of his brother. And not that I didn't like Kevin, but I really wasn't in the mood to run into him.

Right now, though, I didn't have time to worry about the Thomas's disrupting my visit. I know that sounds harsh and looking back, it may have been, but I wasn't sure if Patrick had even *wanted* to see me or what negative things he might have told his family. Like my last relationship this one had gone sour but it'd been *my* fault, not his, and for that reason I was afraid that if I did see him whatever I said would be wrong; that no matter what valid reasons I might have had, he wouldn't see things my way. The truth was, I didn't have any regrets about wanting to achieve my goals; the only regret I'd had was not telling Patrick how much I really cared about him, how much I had wanted him to stay. I suppose thinking I could get everything I wanted had probably been unrealistic from the start. Maybe if he were here, I could apologize or somehow try to win him back...or maybe it *had* been too late and it was just better to leave things as they were and move on.

I scrolled down to another text message- it was from Ivan, who I could tell was both excited and anxious I was back, so I knew I'd have plenty to keep me occupied over the next several days. As much as I would've liked to have sat on some beach all day, I knew that'd never actually happen. I messaged him that I'd be at the clinic first thing tomorrow. Today however, I wanted absolutely nothing to do with shelter medicine.

"Good timing," I said, throwing on a pair of yoga pants. I hadn't seen my friend Jamie in months. She lived downstairs from me and was my workout guru, or should I say drill sergeant. Way back, I'd given her the key to my apartment so she could check on things from time to time. Right now, it was obvious who needed checking on and if there was anyone who could beat the stress out of me, it was her.

"Just how the hell are you even awake right now? You sure you're up for this?"

"Trust me," I answered chugging some seltzer, "I'm feeling it, alright. You can blame Mike," I laughed. "What I really need is for you to beat the hangover *out* of me." *And the memories...*

"Oh, I don't think that'll be a problem. What I got in store for you, oh boy," she giggled to herself. "Anyway, you leasing this place anytime soon? I haven't seen anyone here since Cheryl."

"Oh uh, I'm not sure, probably. I know I could really use the money, especially now since...since the new practice and stuff, but honestly I just haven't been focused. The last I heard from Cheryl she wasn't sure when she'd be back. Why?" I asked.

"Oh, no reason. Just that my lease is kind-of, sort-of up soon and I was just wondering..."

A lightbulb went on in my head, apparently the same one that had already been on in hers. "Wait- are you saying you might wanna take it over?" A smile came across my face.

"Well? *Kind-of*, yeah, I mean, it's just a thought. I mean your place *is* nicer than mine..."

"Done." I wrapped my arms around her so tightly she almost choked.

"But what about..."

"Forget about it. It'll be one less thing for me to worry about. Plus, I'll have somewhere to stay next time I visit, unless of course you're planning on leaving L.A. anytime soon," my smile faded just enough for her to notice. I hadn't exactly elaborated on what'd gone down with me and Patrick.

"Wh...what do you mean? Why wouldn't you stay with Patrick? Don't you have a key? I saw you so little the last two times you were here, I thought you were moving *in* with him and the last time we spoke, you said everything was fine."

"I still do and...I might've lied a little," I admitted.

"Apparently," she huffed, "so what happened?"

"Nothing." *Everything.* "Look, can we talk about this later?" I asked as we headed out.

"Hmm," she uttered, clearly bothered by my dishonesty, "yeah...sure- you can start by telling me what the hell is going on *after* you're done with the 25 extra tricep dips you just earned for this charade." *Charade? Well, I guess that's a good name for it...*

Days later...

"So, how's everything? You never called me back the other day," Rachel said on the other end. I ignored her as I stepped inside. "*Well*?" I listened for that familiar voice. "*Hello*. Are you dead?"

"No," I answered quietly crept around, "I'm just...looking for the dog."

"What? What dog? And why the fuck are you whispering? Where *are* you?"

"Patrick's."

"Why the hell would you be whispering at Patrick's? Did you break in?"

"I have a key, asshole." *Where the hell is this dog?* I set my stuff down in the kitchen as I eyed his empty bed.

"Then what's with the undercover mission?"

"I just came over to...use the pool and hang out with Fenway."

"Fenway?"

"The *dog*."

"Oh," she answered. "*Sure*- you were checking on how things looked since you've been gone."

"Actually, I was worried my stuff would be in a bag out front," I said, walking upstairs, "but also I really wanted my espresso maker. I'm dying without it."

"Wait- you've been out there a week and this is the *first* time you're going over there? And come *on*," she insisted. "He might be mad at you, but the guy *does* have a heart and if you ask me, he still cares about you."

"Honestly I was kind of avoiding it. And I'm not ask..." I paused at the master bedroom doorway. It was just as I'd remembered- a perfectly made California king covered in dark blue linens and a soft white comforter with simple coordinating drapes on the windows, little to no clutter and a spotless floor. Unlike most guys Patrick was extremely neat. Even the dressers and nightstands were covered with the most minimal of décor. My smile faded just as quickly as it'd formed as I glanced at the large dresser and noticed something missing.

"Lea? You there?" Rachel asked.

"Yeah, I'm here." My voice had changed.

"What's wrong?"

"Nothing," I sighed, "except I'm beginning to have serious doubts about your last statement."

"Why?" she asked.

"Other than the fact that he never returned my last call? It's gone." My hand ran across the now seemingly barren dresser. *Not even a speck of dust.*

"What?"

"The picture I gave him for Christmas- *our* picture. The one of us."

"Maybe he was just cleaning."

"Patrick may be neat, but he doesn't clean. He has a maid for that."

"Don't we all wish," she commented, "well, maybe she moved it."

"Or he threw it out."

"Stop being so paranoid, will ya?"

"I can't help it."

"On the other hand..."

I sat on the bed, ruffled. "Hey, you're supposed to be on *my* side."

"I *am*."

"Then why doesn't it feel like it?"

"Oh, chill out. Seriously though, do you *blame* the guy for being a little angry?"

I couldn't exactly argue with that but still, I hadn't been the only one who'd signed up for jobs involving long hours, lots of travel *and* working side by side with members of the opposite sex. "*No*...but I'm pretty sure I've lost track of all the time Patrick was MIA *or* the number of very attractive costars he's repeatedly made out with..."

"That's different; that's his job and you knew about it. You kept him in the dark about yours and correct me if I'm wrong, but I don't think I'm the only one who's noticed a change in you since you've been home, Lea." *Whatever.*

"I didn't exactly keep him in the dark- I just...*what* change? You mean as in working my ass off? Or are you mad because I'm not at the bakery anymore? Rach, I tol..."

"I'm not mad because of that," she insisted. "You're my best friend- you deserve to be happy."

"Then what? I was just doing what I thought was right, so I could have a secure future and *be* happy. You think I was wrong?"

"Not if you really believe that but..." she uttered.

"But *what*?"

"Nothing- it's just...you don't *seem* very happy, that's all." She had a point- ever since I'd signed those papers something inside me had felt off. I thought once some time had passed, I'd feel better with my decision but that had yet to happen and now I *wasn't* so sure it all had been worth it. Of course, I hadn't told anyone that.

"Rach, how am I supposed to get where I wanna go without taking risks? These opportunities don't come along very often; in fact, they hardly ever come along at all. What do you want me to say? I saw a chance and I took it; I can't change that now and I'm not entirely sure I want to."

"And Patrick?" she asked.

"It's not fair to ask him to wait around forever and how can I ask him to? I'm not sure *I* would. He's either okay with my decision or he's not- I can't *make* him be. I wish he'd answer one of my texts, though." I peeked down at my phone, disappointed. "Maybe he *has* made up his mind, just not in the way I'd hoped. I thought we were still friends, but maybe that's changed, too and this is his way of telling me."

"Hmmm...you may be right but...do you really believe that? I still think you should give it a chance. You're out there; why not try and talk to him?"

"Well for one, he's not around. Two, you got any great ideas? 'Cause I don't..."

"Lea come on, don't say that. And don't do anything drastic. At least wait 'til you talk to him," she said.

And what good is that gonna do? He probably hates me by now. "Okay, fine, but I'm still taking my jeans...*and* my espresso machine- I miss them."

After hanging up with Rachel, I went back downstairs and sat outside on one of the loungers, my eyes fixated on the scenery. Other than the beach, the view from Patrick's was one of the few I enjoyed in this city. Of course, it'd been better with him sitting next to me. My thoughts wondered off to the first time I'd seen this place, the first time I'd stayed in that gorgeous master bedroom…Then out of nowhere a goofy, four-legged beast with enough energy to pull a plow came flying at me, nearly bowling me over.

"What the…" *Patrick?* "Hey, hey, buddy. Where did you come from?"

"The park. What are *you* doing here? Aren't you supposed to be stitching something up or putting it out of its misery?" *I'd like to put YOU out of your misery right about now…*

I turned to see Kevin saunter through the sliding doors like he owned the place. "Aren't *you* supposed to be hitting on anything with boobs that breathes?" I laughed.

"Funny, but I'm a little pickier than that these days," he answered, smiling.

"My apologies," I smiled. "I had *no* idea you'd upped your standards- Bravo."

"And I had no idea you were in town." I stood up as he approached, giving him a brief hug. "When did you get here?"

"Oh, a few days ago."

"Cool, cool. Staying long?"

"No- I gotta get back…to the hospital."

He looked me over decisively, "ahh, the great responsibility, gotcha."

"Yeah, kind of. I just came out to check on the apartment and…"

"*And?*" he asked curiously.

"And…take care of some shelter stuff and," I continued, patting Fenway, "see *you*, you big goof." The tone in my voice made him even more excited and he ran around in circles waiting for me to throw him a toy.

"Oh," he said, almost disappointed. "Well maybe seeing him will change your mind. He won't say it, but I *think* he might miss you a little bit. I can see it in his eyes."

"Of <u>course</u> he does, don't cha, boy?" I said in a louder voice. Fenway barked in response.

"You know, for a doctor you're really not the quickest, are you?" he asked, shaking his head. "I was talking about my brother."

"Oh," I said, finally catching on. "I doubt it. I don't think he's very happy with me right now. Who knows *what* he's thinking. He hasn't answered me back. I just wish…I half-thought I was gonna show up to changed locks."

"Well *I* probably would've changed them but...I'm not my brother," he remarked, a slight snootiness to his voice. "Kidding. Anyway, instead of all this back and forth bullshit with you two, why don't you just *talk* to each other, face to face? Hey, I like Skype for video chats and sexing just as much as the next guy, but there's only so much that can do for you..."

Of course, you do. I looked at him and shook my head, "that's easy for you to say. Plus, he's not even here. I'll probably be gone by the time he gets back anyway so..."

"What do you mean he's not here? I just saw him this morning."

What? I nearly fell backwards on one of the chairs. "You okay there, doc?" he laughed.

"Uh, yeah...what? But he said he wouldn't be back in L.A. for another few weeks..."

Kevin shrugged his shoulders innocently. "Hey, all I know is he's here now. I think he finished up whatever he was doing earlier than expected...I can call him for you..." *And didn't feel the need to tell me?*

"Uh, *no*, no. Maybe just...can you do me a huge favor and *not* let him know I'm here? Just forget you even saw me."

"You don't think he's gonna notice the missing espresso maker?" *What? He never even uses that.* "And, I don't think so, Camioni. You do know aversion is not exactly the way to go here, not if you really want to make your case and apologize," he winked cleverly. "I tell you what- I'll promise to hold off on telling my brother that you're here for at least another 24 hours if *you* promise to set me up with that cute neighbor of yours- what was her name again?"

"Jaime. Hmmm, how did I know there'd be a condition like that? Wait- apologize?" I thought. "Okay, fine, fine, I'll ask her just *please*..."

"No problem," he said, "*trust* me."

Chapter 57 ~ Bad Boys

June 26th

"Do you have to leave so soon?" Mike asked. "I miss hanging out with my favorite cousin. What about that killer party this weekend at Drai's? Can't they survive without you a few more days?"

"It's almost a whole other week," I said, huffing, "plus, I was planning on spending the Fourth at home. I've never even heard of that place."

"You practically have to be a celebrity to get in and *we* got the in my band, that is. Why not stay and celebrate here? Aren't you the one who told me they nearly had to *force* you to take a vacation?"

"Yeah, I guess."

"So then, stay. I'm sure they'd be okay with it."

"Right, sure, 'Um, hey you guys don't mind if I stay in L.A. and party it up, bask in the sun a while longer, do you? You can just handle all my cases for me'...Mike, I..."

"Exactly," he said.

"Boy, you really have been living out here too long. You think everything's just a wink and a smile," I laughed, "that people don't really care who shows up to work or not."

"When it comes to *your* smile? Absolutely," he commented. "Oh, come on, Lea. They're your friends and aren't you an *owner*?" Mike could be quite persistent. Still, I hadn't intended on staying any longer than originally planned and now that Patrick was in town, strangely I was even more anxious to go.

"Well, I guess I could try...someone *does* still owe me a favor..."

"Great."

Three days later

"So, basically you used me as an excuse to avoid your boyfriend. I mean, he *is* technically still your boyfriend, isn't he? Can you explain why I agreed to help you *and* why you're avoiding the hot-as-hell celebrity most any girl would kill for?" I could tell Jamie wasn't entirely thrilled that I'd volunteered her services.

"Oh, come on. It's a date, with a nice guy who's totally cute, by the way. Who knows? You might even like him."

She stared at me with crossed arms, "Hmm...if he's so nice, then why do you always refer to him as a jackass?" *Because he is.*

"You know better than to listen to my snarky comments. He actually is a nice guy. I wouldn't have said yes if he wasn't." *I might have stretched the truth just a little.* "Thanks a lot, I owe you one."

"Damn right. So, where are we meeting again?"

"Some sushi place in Hollywood."

"But you don't eat sushi," she said.

"I know, but they have other stuff. I'm so nervous a drink is all I can think of right now."

"Have you talked to Patrick?" she asked curiously.

"The other day. He sounded preoccupied, though." *Or he's ignoring me.* "We didn't talk long. I don't know. He texted me yesterday. I was at the clinic. I called him back, but he didn't answer so..."

"Well," she smiled, "it's a good thing we're going as a sort-of a double date so I can be there for emotional support- I think you're gonna need it."

She was right. As much as I missed Patrick, the thought of being alone with him face to face felt strangely terrifying. Normally I couldn't wait to see him and I probably should've felt better that Kevin that thought he'd missed me, too, but instead I felt like the same selfish jerk from two months ago and now this whole thing just felt weird. I wondered if the reason I hadn't heard much from him was that he was brushing me off.

Had I surprised him by coming out here and spoiled his plans to break up with me? Had he intended on doing it tonight at dinner so we wouldn't have to be alone? What if seeing me would only reassure him he'd made the right decision leaving so abruptly or worse, what if he'd already met someone else? That was, after all, how the game was played out here and maybe after all this time, Patrick couldn't help but fall prey to temptation. I mean it's not like I really compared to even half the women he met.

Katsuya was one of Hollywood's more popular restaurants, its chef touted as a master of Japanese sushi fusion, not that that'd meant shit to me- I didn't even eat anything from the sea; I just loved to be near it. But to people who did, it apparently had some of the best sushi in Los Angeles. Its uniquely provocative lounge décor also made it a prime spot for Hollywood parties. Unlike Patrick, Kevin was all about the in places and so it'd been no surprise where he'd chosen to go.

"Wow," Jaime commented as we walked inside, "this place is ridiculous!"

"Totally," I agreed. "Who would've thought a ginormous set of red lips would look so good up on a wall? I mean who even puts something like that up?" Eye-catching was an understatement.

Just then a deep voice jumped out of the background, "Some guy named Starck." Apparently, Kevin had a new-found talent for shocking the hell out of me.

"Stark...as in *Tony*?" Jaime asked, laughably.

"No but...impressive answer," he flirted in his typical swagger. "You must be Jaime. I'm Kevin." It may have been the restaurant's glittery gold décor but for a second, I saw a hint of attraction there. Like most women in Kevin's vicinity, her words got stuck in her throat, turning her into the world's giddiest little schoolgirl. I would've almost done the same thing the first time I'd met him if he hadn't opened his mouth.

"Oh, um, yeah, hi," she finally said. *And another one bites the dust*...Their hands met and I nearly gagged, so distracted I didn't even realize Patrick wasn't with him. *Maybe he's parking.*

"Um," I said, clearing my throat loudly, "wher...where's Patrick?" I went into a slight panic.

Kevin snapped out of his momentary trance and turned his attention back to me, surprised. "Uh, he didn't call you?" Now beginning to tremble inside, I tensely shook my head 'no'. "Oh," he uttered, "I thought you knew. He had to stay in Vancouver longer- he's not coming. He really didn't tell you?" Suddenly feeling queasy, I instinctively put one hand across my stomach.

"Uh, no, he didn't." *He couldn't even text me? What the fuck? Was* there something going on I didn't know about? I wondered if Kevin did. I peered behind me for something to lean against. *In front of all these people is definitely not the time to faint, Eleana.*

The background noise of the bustling restaurant filled in the seemingly massive dead space between us and as I looked over at Jaime's face, I could see she was feeling the same amount of tension I was. "Maybe his phone died or something. I'm sure he didn't mean..."

"Shit," Kevin interjected, "I can't believe that. Honestly, that isn't like him..."

No shit, it isn't and who's fucking phone dies these days with batteries that last a week? I wanted to run out of there screaming. I had no idea what to do- go outside and call him? Did he even want to talk to me or was this the sign I'd been dreading, telling me how Patrick really felt?

Sensing my nervousness, Kevin pulled out his phone. "Want me to call him?" Reluctantly, I shook my head 'no'. "You sure? 'Cause..."

"No. That's okay." My heart sunk in an all-too familiar defeat. *Great- way to act the fool, Eleana.* As if on cue, a hostess came to tell us our table was ready.

"Kevin, party of four?" she asked politely, her skimpy outfit tightly clinging to her slim figure.

"Oh, um, yeah that's us," he answered before motioning Jaime and I to join him. As if planted in cement, my feet remained where they were.

"Lea, aren't you coming?" Jaime asked concernedly.

"Uh, no, um...I don't think so; I think I'm gonna...I'm gonna go....*and throw myself in front of a TMZ bus...*" I felt the surge of emotions coming on and not knowing if I'd scream or cry, I figured the best plan of action was to leave.

"Come on, Lea. Don't be ridiculous. We came all the way here," she said.

"Yeah, Lea. Why do you wanna go?" Kevin asked. *Seriously? Do you really think I have an appetite right now?*

"It's okay, really. You two enjoy your dinner. I'm not that hungry anyway." I headed for the front door.

As my cab went up Sunset, I noticed the people about, their nights just beginning while mine had come to a screeching halt. I felt my phone buzz. I looked down and there it was- a voicemail from Patrick, the same voicemail that hadn't been there earlier. *Well, at least he didn't break up with me in a text.* I noticed the time of the call- 7:30pm- just minutes before our reservation. Reluctantly I listened to it, afraid of what I might hear:

"Hey, Lea, it's Patrick. I'm really sorry. I thought I was gonna be able to make dinner tonight, but my, uh, meetings went longer than expected and I won't be back in time." *Really asshole?* "I'll explain later but I didn't want you to think I was blowing you off-I really was looking forward to tonight." *Could've fooled me.* "I promise I'll call you when I'm back. Hopefully you'll still be in town..."

Not even an 'I miss you'. What was it about guys and voicemails? Why couldn't they just spit it out and tell you the truth? Why did everything always have to be some mystery? It's like they wanted to keep you hanging just to torture you, while they threw you lame-ass excuses, one after another. I felt like the pathetic wife receiving a call from her cheating husband, except not only was Patrick *not* my husband, I wasn't even sure if he was still mine. It took everything in me not to ball hysterically on the ride back to my apartment- I sure as hell didn't need any more pity.

"What do you *mean* he didn't show?" Rachel's New York attitude was in full swing. "Where is that motherfucker? I swear, I'll fly up to fucking Canada or wherever the fuck he is and kick his pussy ass." I might've been crying on my end of the phone but still, it was funny listening to her rant. "You need me to come out there? Seriously- I *will*. I don't give a fuck."

"No, no," I said, "I'm leaving Monday anyway. I think I've had about enough of this place…"

"That's right- fuck. Okay well, let's just think about this for a minute," she continued. "Didn't you say you spoke to him the other day?"

"Yes."

"And he didn't say anything?"

I sniffled, calming myself down, "he said something came up and that he'd see me Friday."

"Well what the fuck does *that* mean? I thought he was better than that."

"That makes two of us and I don't know- the message he left said he'd tell me when he got back. I have no idea when that is…"

"I can't believe I'm saying this but, *that* asshole!"

"Maybe this is his way of breaking up with me. I should just cut my losses here…"

"No, you *can't*," she said adamantly.

"You just called him an *asshole*," I sniffled again, wiping my face.

"I know."

"Well did you change your mind?"

"No. I don't know just…give him one more shot before you decide anything drastic. I feel like you've been a little hasty lately, like you're not thinking things through or…or you don't *want* to. That's not like you."

"Maybe that's because I'm finally starting to see things a little more clearly."

"I thought the way he felt about you *was* clear..."

"So did I but…what if things have changed and he doesn't feel the same way anymore? This is just a sign that I don't belong here; I never did."

"You and your fucking astrology," she huffed.

"It's not astrology this time- it's my brain telling me to wise up."

"Well as your best friend, I think you need to get a good night's sleep, go to that kick-ass party with Mike tomorrow night and have *fun*. Who knows? Maybe things will settle down and you'll hear from him by then."

"Okay, fine. I don't know how much *fun* I'm gonna have at a Hollywood free-for-all though."

"Whatever. Just send me some pics." We hung up and within minutes I was asleep.

Chapter 58 ~ A Night at the Roxbury

Saturday June 30th

I really wasn't in the mood to be around people. And I wasn't in the mood to be in a *crowd* of them at a party, no less, especially one like *tonight's*. I'd been to Hollywood 'social' events before and although they may have looked all the rage on TV, they always ended up being the exact opposite. Everyone was more interested in talking about themselves than actually socializing like normal people. It got old- *fast*. But I'd promised Mike I'd go and so I put on my best game face. It was against everything in my being to try and fit in to L.A.'s fashion scene but I figured that for one night I could at least act the part. I mean it wasn't every day I got invited to a V.I.P. party. Earlier in the week Jaime and I had gone shopping and ended up with some cute dresses and shoes that were *more* than hard to walk in. I wondered how long I'd last...

"Ouch! Damn these shoes already!!" I exclaimed as Jaime opened her door.

"Whoah! Look at *you*, you hottie! They better watch out tonight! You ready?"

"Yep. You call a cab?"

"Nope."

"Then how are we getting there, by broomstick?" I asked curiously.

"Uber."

"*What*?"

"Uber." I tilted my head, confused, while she rushed me down the stairs. "Come on, they're gonna be here in like three minutes."

"What the fuck is Uber?"

"It's the new cab. Faster *and* cheaper. They have an app." *Hmmm*. "It just came on the scene here earlier this year. I'm surprised you haven't tried it yet." She was right. By the time we'd made it down the stairs a car was already waiting.

'Uber', launched in San Francisco in 2009, had become so popular its demand was growing exponentially. It was now in New York and Los Angeles and was quickly replacing classic 'taxi' service. From inside a restaurant, a hotel or your house, with the push of a button you could find a ride, pay and track the car that was on its way to get you and you rarely had to wait more than five minutes. It was revolutionary and the bonus? It gave thousands of people a way to make extra money. The negatives? Well, you never knew who you were gonna get: the weird Middle-Eastern guy with a heavily perfumed vehicle playing loud music or the girl who barely looked old enough to drive, with a baby seat in the back. Still, people loved it and with time, things would only improve.

Drai's was located atop the W Hollywood Hotel and at over 20,000 ft2 its indoor/outdoor footprint made it the ultimate rooftop party spot, one that celebrities and production studios fought over. We arrived around 9:45 pm, still early by club standards. The place had obviously been decked out for Independence Day. From the red, white and blue décor and signature cocktails, to the light-up pool floats and sparkly waitstaff, it impressed even me. Once we stepped outside all negative thoughts went out of my mind.

About an hour into the party things had really picked up. The music was pumping (although the quality of the DJ was debatable), the dance floor was packed and the drinks were flying out of the bars at record speed. Maybe it was the fruity, bubbly cocktails, but I was actually having fun *and* I'd managed to move decently in my heels. Back in the day we used to go to clubs in sneakers. I mean, how else were you supposed to move to Nice n' Smooth and Biz Markie?

"Hey, cuz. Looks like you're enjoying yourself. Not bad for your typical Hollywood party, huh?"

I barely heard him over the music, "huh? Yeah. I can't believe I'm saying this, but I'm glad I came. In case I forget to tell you later, I had a good time. Thanks for dragging me out," I smiled.

"That's what family is for. You know these aren't exactly my scene either- not enough blood and *hardly* any gore. Anyway, where's your friend Jaime?"

"At the bar getting drinks. We kept trying to flag over one of the hostesses, but it was taking too long..."

I looked over towards the bar. She was talking to two guys, both attractive. I smiled, happy for her. Then I checked my phone- nothing. Just then, someone who looked like he knew Mike approached.

"Hey, Mike! What's up? I didn't know you were comin' tonight," the tall attractive blond shouted before quickly noticing me. "And...I didn't know you were dating someone," he added curiously.

I watched Mike's amused face, "well, not that I *wouldn't* date this beauty but... she's actually my cousin. Ryan, this is Lea. Lea, Ryan. We used to run the circuit together." *Circuit?* Honestly, I could never understand what the fuck these people (including my own cousin) were talking about.

"Hi," I said, "nice to meet you." *Damn is this guy hot.* I smiled uncomfortably.

"Hey, would you guys excuse me for a sec? There's an agent here tonight my buddy wanted me to meet. I'll be back in a few." And just like that he disappeared into the crowd leaving me standing there, alone, with a stranger. This wasn't the first time he'd done this. One time he'd left me alone with one of his creepy wannabe 'director' friends. Within minutes of listening to him ramble on about how he was 'buddy buddy' with Quentin Tarantino, I thought I was gonna kill him.

"Anyway...funny we've never met." I shrugged my shoulders. *I'll say.* I'd never even heard Mike mention him. Then again, Mike knew a lot of people. "You live here?"

Now how exactly should I answer that? "Not really, no," I sighed. "Actually, I'm leaving in a few days so..."

"Sounds complicated," he said. We moved towards an open high top. *You have no idea.* I remained silent. I hated awkward situations, especially with guys and *especially* with one who *wasn't* my boyfriend. "Unfortunately, I'm well familiar with 'complicated'- my girlfriend dumped me last week- we were supposed to be in Cabo this weekend."

"That sucks. Sorry. Popular place, I guess." *Is that the only place these people ever go?*

"What?"

"Oh, nothing," I said.

His smile was genuine, unlike so many guys I'd met out here, and I thought back to when I'd first seen Patrick's. "So, uh, where are you going back to?"

"Connecticut." Of all the times to meet a guy like this, I thought. Oh well. I smiled, checking around for Jaime. Fifteen minutes and she still hadn't returned with my drink. "Let me guess-musician, actor or model?" I laughed to myself.

"Fuck that-I'm a contractor," he chuckled at my supposition. "I just wanted a change of scenery, known Mike about six years. What about you? Modelling?" *What did you just say?* Embarrassed and flattered, my face blushed. "What's so funny?" he asked.

"Nothing. It's just...you said *model.* Yeah, uh, I don't think so. Plus, it's not exactly in my wheelhouse," I giggled, shying away, "I'm a veterinarian."

"Hmmm...could've fooled me. *Wow-* impressive." I felt my brain shut off nearly everything around me. "Uh...are you thirsty? Let's go to the bar and grab a drink." I looked for Jaime and still no sign of her, so I agreeably went along.

Meanwhile, on the other side of the rooftop...

"I can't believe I let you guys drag me to this," Patrick said to Walt. "I hate these things. On top of that it's been a long week and I'm not really in the mood for..."

"Which is *exactly* why you need a night out, *away* from your dog," Todd added, nearly shoving Patrick forward.

"Dude, are you blind? Look *around*- it's like a 360 degree, constantly rotating platter of hot ass," Walt laughed.

Noticing Patrick's lack of amusement, Todd cut in, "come on, man, you know he's not interested in that."

"Why? *Oh*," he said, "you mean you're *still* hung up on that chick who dumped you to go play with dogs and cats? She doesn't seem so smart to me now."

"She's a *doctor*- she doesn't *play*," Patrick said, obviously angered.

They looked at each other, "she dumped him."

"No one dumped *anyone*- it's called chasing your dreams- you should try it sometime. We were on a break- *are* on a break. Whatever, I don't wanna talk about it."

"Sure, a break. Whatever, man. All I know is the past few months you've been miserable as shit and *she's* the reason."

Just then Steve, the final part of their foursome, returned from the bar. "Here you go." He said, handing them their beers. "Why do you guys look so serious? This place is jammin'. Let's go mingle."

"Exactly," Todd complained, "we're at a killer party and Patrick's whining about some chick who deserted him, meanwhile we're surrounded by all this." Steve cocked his head as if clueless.

"She's not 'some' chick," Patrick stated, irritated, "her name's Eleana."

"Does it *matter*? She's not even fucking here. Just forget her, will ya?" Walt insisted.

Steve's face went sour. "Uh...*oh*, right, right."

They all looked over at him. "What's that look for?" Patrick asked.

"Nothing. Uh, Eleana? That's funny. I swore I heard that name when I was at the bar...but whatever- it was probably Ariana or some shit. Let's go..."

Patrick instinctively turned his attention towards the large bar across the dance floor and within seconds, his face dropped. It *was* her. She was standing at the bar having drinks with some dude, smiling and laughing. Here he was, upset at how they'd left things, miserable without her, ready to apologize for being so insensitive, while *she* was out having a good time with strange men at the kind of scene she *claimed* she hated. Had he been wrong for thinking those things, for waiting on her decision about the future? Or had he been a fool, just like he'd been before?

Immediately the guys caught on. "What?" Steve asked, "I thought you said she wasn't here."

"See? I told you man- East coast, West coast- they're all the fuckin' same, which is why you can't trust *any* of 'em. I don't know about you, but I'm staying single."

Patrick shook his head disheartened, his pride pummeled. "I thought this one was different."

"Why don't you go talk to her?" Steve asked.

"Dude, the guy's already paddling- you want him to fuckin' *drown*?" Walt asked.

"No, Walt's right. Let's just go. Didn't you say you got that VIP suite?" he asked.

"Yeah, it's waiting for us, along with those girls I met earlier. I see them now." They headed back inside.

"Hey, you okay?" Ryan asked.

No. I wasn't *okay.* They were far enough away not to notice me, but close enough to where I could see, and what I saw had been clear as day- I watched Patrick and three guys I didn't recognize make their way towards a group of girls by the sliding doors. They were laughing and seemed to be having a good time, exactly the opposite of what I was experiencing at that very moment. I couldn't believe it- Patrick had said he'd call me as soon as he got back into town, yet here he was, out at some party enjoying himself, in the company of women no less, and my phone hadn't gotten so much as a beep. It was becoming clear to me where his head-and heart- were at. I guess I *had* been stupid- he had already moved on.

"What?" I asked, trying to play it off as nothing, hiding the tears with one hand.

"You look like you just saw a ghost." *When I'm through with him he will be...*

"Oh, no. I just uh...thought I saw someone I knew." I turned back to him and smiled, sniffling. "Maybe we should go find Mike." Just then I saw Jaime coming from around the corner. It didn't take her long to notice something was wrong.

Chapter 59 ~ How to Lose a Guy in 10 Days

We hadn't stayed late at the party. Seeing Patrick had pretty much destroyed any chance enjoying the rest of the evening although up until that point it had been fun. I hadn't gone to search for him, not that I'd wanted to confront him anyway.

I waited until we were in the Uber to let Jaime in on what had transpired. She could hardly believe it and was fuming, demanding why I hadn't ripped him a new one. Patrick may have been well-liked by my friends, but those same friends would quickly turn as soon as they caught wind of dishonesty, Jaime included. She'd called him every name in the book, not that I'd blamed her. In my mind it was yet another thing pushing me to leave.

I was leaving in less than 36 hours, but I knew I couldn't get on that plane without at least *trying* to talk to Patrick. But what would I say? Should I even bring up last night or was there no point? Because what I'd seen had not only been obvious it'd been hurtful, and no matter how you spun it, facts were facts. Patrick had seemingly removed any evidence of us from his house. He'd found out I was in town but had blown me off for 'work'. He'd returned to L.A. *without* telling me and now, I was beginning to think he'd never intended to. Maybe he'd hoped I would just go away. If he *had*, his plan was working. I felt as though I was slowly being erased out of the picture entirely.

I slept in, hoping I'd wake up back on the east coast as if none of this had ever happened. As *if*. I got up, made myself a double espresso and sat outside, staring at the marina. I watched the joggers out on their morning routines. I still had yet to pack. Jaime had said I could leave a few things behind for when I returned to visit, although right now I couldn't imagine when or even *if* I'd be back. It was going to be a beautiful day. I'd gone for a long walk without my phone. I took a deep breath and listened to my messages when I got back. The first was from Jaime, checking in; the second was from my mom and the third was from Patrick. I felt a chill just hearing his voice.

I texted Jaime back that I was okay and I'd talk to her later. Then I left my mom a message. Before I could even dial Patrick's number, a text came through. Boy was the world changing fast. Never had I imagined that simple emoji symbols would ever turn into this shit. At first, I'd been opposed until I'd found myself texting as much as everyone else. But it hardly replaced normal conversation and when it came to matters of the heart, it was *anything* but personal and what I considered to be an easy way out when you wanted it to be. And now Patrick was texting to elaborate on his previous message, which made no sense- if you had two minutes to type a message, you had time to dial a fucking number.

Hey- can't chat now. Can you come over later this afternoon so we can talk?

"I mean, why not just make it easier on yourself and get it over with?" I grumbled, turning on the shower. I couldn't help it- I'd dialed Rachel's number the second I'd read Patrick's text. I needed to vent. I felt like grabbing my shit and heading to the airport right now. I just *knew* this afternoon wasn't gonna be good and the more I thought of Los Angeles, the more my stomach churned. "City of Angels, my *ass*," I said.
"Hey," she said, "maybe it's a59ood thing."
"*How*, Rach? Nothing about this is good."
"Look, you should be grateful."
"*Grateful*? For what, having been sucked into this *bullshit*? For being foolish enough to believe that I could actually be *happy* with someone like *him* in a place like *this*? I mean, how fucking stupid could I have been to think this would've worked? It doesn't even work out for these fucking people half the time."
"True," she said. "I meant that at least you saw for yourself, that you didn't have to hear about anything or see it somewhere."
"Oh, I'm sure I'll see something *somewhere*- it's just a matter of time."
"Just go over there and talk to him- you *need* to. You owe it to yourself *and* to him. Maybe there really *is* some explanation for his odd behavior."
"Yeah, I guess you're right. I just wish you were here."
"I'll see you tomorrow at the airport."
"Okay, wish me luck," I said before hanging up.

Patrick's house, Loz Feliz
I stood in the driveway after my Uber pulled away, staring out at the road. *If I could just leave a note then quickly run so I wouldn't have to face him...* But I knew that probably wasn't the right thing to do and so I was gonna do my best to keep it together, knowing it might be the last time I see him.

I inhaled deeply. "Well? Here it goes," I mumbled to myself. Immediately I heard barking. Before I knew it the door opened, forcing me to turn around. It was a strange feeling standing before him. I was so nervous, so wishing I was anywhere else, a complete 180 from how I'd come to feel about him after all this time together.

He stood there, his head cocked, a smirk on his face as Fenway jumped up on me, his tongue out for a big kiss. "Eleana, what are you doing out here? Why didn't you just come in?" he asked.

Finally, I found the courage to speak. It was already happening, the uncontrollable emotional rollercoaster that was about the ensue. "Oh, um, well I...didn't wanna just barge in..."

"Why? It's not like you haven't been here before," he said.

"Oh, right." He hugged me, kissing me on the cheek as he welcomed me inside. Not one 'I miss you' or 'It's so good to see you'. Was this how it was gonna be now? Just two people who act as if they never even shared one kiss? I followed him, Fenway hot on my tail, seeking affection.

"You want something to drink?" he asked. "I'd offer you an espresso, but someone swiped the espresso maker..."

"Oh, right, right," I chuckled slightly. "Sorry- I figured you weren't using it so..."

His smile lightened, comforting me momentarily and I felt that familiar magic between us. Maybe it *wasn't* gone after all. "You know I could never work that thing anyway. Plus," he paused, "you got me hooked on the French Press. I even travel with one now. Want some?"

I nodded. I just hoped I wouldn't gag. We sat outside on the patio. Fenway hopped up right beside me and lapped my face, as if unaware of any awkwardness in the air. But it was just the opposite. Animals were far from stupid. He sensed something was off. It was almost as if he was giving me extra attention because *he* himself knew he might not see *me* again.

"Calm down, buddy, calm down. Looks like he really missed you," Patrick said lightheartedly.

"Yeah, I guess." *That makes one of you.*

Our gazes hung on to one another, unable to waiver. I wondered what he was going to say. Maybe he'd apologize or ask me to stay. Maybe he wouldn't, but I still hung on to hope. I opened my mouth to speak but he beat me to the punch.

"Eleana, sorry things have been so hectic lately and I'm sorry for the short messages earlier, but...honestly I really hate texting- they end up sounding so impersonal." *Really, buddy? Your messages sucked even more.* "I figured it's best to talk in person and believe it or not, I *did* want to see you." *Maybe I was wrong about being wrong. Maybe he does still care about me.*

"I uh...I wanted to see you, too. Patrick I..."

"No, let me go first, okay? This is hard enough for me," I nodded willingly. *'I miss you'...*"You know all this time we've known each other, it's been... I've never had a connection like that with anyone, ever, and I want you to know that no matter what, that means a lot to me." *You mean a lot to me- I'm sorry, for everything.*

I stared at him, waiting for more.

"I never thought I'd find someone like you, but then I did and things were great until..." *Until I screwed up and didn't give you the chance you deserved...* "Until all of a sudden, they weren't. And maybe some of that was my fault. Maybe I didn't realize the kinds of things *you* wanted, that *you* needed and for that, I'm sorry." *Go on...* "Look," he continued, "You and I have both been through a lot these past several months and I know you've had a lot on your plate and I've tried to look past all that- I've tried to stay positive and give you the space you need, hoping that you'd make a decision about the future. But I don't know if this arrangement is gonna work anymore. I..." *What?*

I looked at him and gulped so loudly the dog even turned his head. "That's it? *That's* what you had to say? *That's* what you had me come all the way over here for, to be lectured to?" I was mortified. "And here I was expecting an apology. Maybe you *should've* just texted it to me," I huffed, "then maybe it wouldn't have been so *hard* for you."

"*Apologize?* Wait a minute- what about *you?*"

"*Me? You're* the one who was out with a bunch of hookers!" Shocked by my statement, he stood up. "That's right. I saw you last night with your friends and...and those *girls* or whatever. 'I'm gonna call you as soon as I get back?'; 'I'm so sorry I had to fly up to Vancouver for yet another one of my bullshit lies but go ahead and enjoy dinner without me...'. Having your brother do your dirty work for you these days- *nice.* You're a real class act, Patrick."

"That's not true."

"Oh yeah? Which part, the hookers, phony meetings or the scapegoat story?" I asked angrily.

"It wasn't phony," he argued, "it was important. And you should talk. I can't tell *what's* the truth with you anymore." *What?* Confused, I threw my hands up. "Not fun when you get caught in a lie, is it?"

"What did I lie about?" I asked.

"I *saw* you." *You what?* "That's right- I saw you last night, too, getting cozy with some guy at the bar."

"Excuse me?"

"So, how'd you make out? Did you score?"

"You *asshole.*" I stood up abruptly, tears beginning to stream down my face.

"Right- *I'm* the asshole. Then who was that guy?"

"Nobody," I continued to sob.

"Just like *Nate*, right?"

"No, not just like...I was with my cousin." I wiped my face haphazardly, unable to control the tears. "I can't believe this. I came here thinking we could talk, that maybe I *had* made a mistake, but I was wrong. Apparently, I've barged in on *your* new and improved life, one that *clearly* no longer has room for me. This whole thing, right here?" I asked, pointing to us, "was a mistake right from the start. When everyone said I was crazy for trusting someone like you, that all you'd do was hurt me, I ignored them, insisted you were different. But I *should've* listened; I should've *known* I could never be for you and this fake-ass, fucked-up bubble-of-a-world you live in out here? They were right about that, too- it could *never* be for someone like me. So, go ahead- make your big movies and your big money and sleep with all the dumb ass groupies you want to, because clearly that's what *you* want."

"What are you saying?"

"I'm saying that I'm gonna make this even easier for you. I'm getting on that plane tomorrow and I'll be out of your life forever and you won't have to worry anymore- I won't bother you again."

Sobbing, I turned around and headed for the front door. I didn't even give him a chance to come after me, not that he did.

An hour later…

"Yo!" Kevin asked as he made his way through the house. "Hello?"

"Out here."

"Oh, *there* you are. I stopped at the packy on my way ov…" Before he could get any closer, Patrick had swiped a bottle out of the six-pack. "Don't you want a bottle open…okay- never mind," he added as Patrick hit the bottle's top at the perfect angle against the side of the table. "Hmmm- I never saw *that* on your resume. Anyway…" He stopped himself, noting how unusual it was for his brother to chug a beer so fast. "Hey, slow down, I only got two of these…wait. What's up with you?"

Patrick sat there, shrugging his shoulders. It didn't take Kevin long to realize he was upset about something.

"Wait- Where's Eleana? I thought she was coming over." Patrick simply nodded and rolled his eyes, "she did."

"By the look on your face I'm guessing things didn't go too well."

"*Real* fuckin' observant," he answered rudely.

Kevin sat down next to him, glaring. "Care to elaborate?"

"Not really."

"Good," Kevin attempted to copy his brother's crafty beer-opening tactic, "I've got all night."

"Apparently, so do I. Here, give me that," he said, opening the bottle with ease.

"What?"

"She *left*. She's leaving-tomorrow." Patrick continued staring out at the pool, the reflection of the sun dimming gradually with each minute. "I heard her dialing Uber and then she was gone."

"What do you mean, she *left*? I thought you guys were gonna talk, that you were gonna explain things, *apologize*. She was looking forward to seeing you, you know."

"Hmmm-Could've fooled me."

"What's with the coded language?"

Patrick sighed deeply before continuing, "you're right. I *was*...until I saw her last night getting' some guy's fuckin' number."

The shocked look on Kevin's face was a rare one. He abruptly stood up.   "What? Where?"

"At that party Walt dragged me to, the one at The W. I didn't even wanna go but now I'm glad I did- or else I never would've seen her true colors."

"You mean the one with all the half-naked chicks and all the fireworks? Come *on*, that's not Lea's scene. You sure it was her?"

"Apparently things have changed way more than I thought..."

"Come on, you don't really believe that. Did you ask her about it?"

"Of *course* I did. She said he was nobody."

"And you didn't believe her. So, then what?"

"She told me she was leaving tomorrow and she took off."

"And you didn't even *try* to go after her?"

"She didn't exactly seem like she wanted me to. Kev, what am I supposed to think? She acts all weird for months, keeps the biggest job of her life a secret from me, then lies about a guy she *claims* there's nothing going on with and to top it all off, she's out getting guy's numbers while she's crying to you that she misses me."

"Give her a *little* credit- her dad fuckin' died. And she didn't exactly cry..."

"I don't know, man. Maybe people were right; maybe *she* was right. Maybe this was always a losing battle- with her there and me here; the different lives we live. You said it yourself, she doesn't fit into this world..."

"That was *before* I knew her. What is she a fucking *alien* now? You sound like an idiot."

"Maybe I *am*; maybe I *was* this whole time, for thinking that it could work."

"You always said she was different- in a good way. What's gotten into you? This isn't like you to give up so easily. Even *I* thought you guys were great together," Kevin said, "*everyone* did."

"So did I, Kev; so did I."

"You sure about this?"

"I'll have to be."

"If that's what you really want."

"She made it pretty clear- it's what *she* wants so... it's probably for the best."

"Well you're my brother- I'll stand by you even if I don't agree with you, which I *don't*, just so we're clear. The family's not gonna get over this," he added, sighing.

"They're gonna have to- *I'm* gonna have to."

"I just hope you're sure about letting the best thing that's ever happened to you walk out of your life, because you may never get another chance after this."

"I know."

"By the way, what the *hell* is Uber?"

The sun was still high in the sky when I left Patrick's, but I knew it wouldn't last long. As much as I didn't want to think about it, it was time- to leave the unhealthy things behind and go back to my life outside of Patrick's- the life I once had before. There was no looking back now.

"Ever wonder how something could be so beautiful and so depressing at the same time?" Jaime asked, sipping her wine, as we both watched the sun in its final act of the evening.

"Yeah," I sniffled. My eyes were still puffy from just a short time ago, yet I tried to remain positive. Just like Patrick this gorgeous evening sky, the one I'd fallen so hard for a few years back, now also brought me great sadness. What was once one of my favorite parts about being out here was now a constant reminder of him. I knew in my heart I'd done the best I could, but it was going to ache for a while. As Jaime and I sat watching the sky's colors quickly morph, my heart felt the same heaviness as the sun, its weight dragging it down closer and closer towards the horizon with each minute and there was no fighting it now- tomorrow would have to be the start of a new day.

Chapter 60~ Hot Tub Time Machine

One month later...

July had come and gone quickly. Summer was in full effect yet somehow, I wasn't in the beachy mood. It was completely unlike me to rush along this kind of weather, but I just couldn't shake my summer blues. The sooner it was apple pie season, the better. Work was busy, I'd been active with my nephews and Rachel and I had been able to hit the beach on weekends. Still, every time I was at the beach, I nearly broke down- even though the scenery was completely different; even though the sun set on the *other* side. It didn't seem to matter- I was miserable.

I hated the way Patrick and I had left things, but what could I do? It was officially over and I was right back at the starting line- to the life I'd had before I'd gone on that crazy west coast path to self-discovery. But at least I'd learned a few things- like taking chances, especially on seemingly unattainable men (not that I'd kept him); that I was actually capable of maintaining a relationship and above all else, that I could learn to trust again. But then of course the inevitable had happened- it'd gone to shit.

I kept telling myself that it'd been for the best- that in real life the jock and the nerd *don't* actually live happily ever after, that maybe the whole point of all this had been to end up back here a stronger person with a fresh, new outlook on life and love. Patrick had literally been a dream come true and those stories hardly ever involved yellow brick roads or fairy godmothers. Maybe someday I'd see the silver lining, but right now I could barely see over the mounting pile of crap on my desk.

"Hello?" Mrs. Potts said on the other end.

"Oh, yes, Mrs. Potts, sorry about that. I was just reading through your bloodwork I mean, Benny's bloodwork. Everything looks good." *Jesus, Eleana.*

"Are you sure? You don't sound so sure," she responded worriedly. *Not really,* I thought to myself.

"Absolutely. Nothing to worry about- *trust* me."

"Okay. Cuz he's my baby, *you* know that- I'll do *anything* for him."

"Yes, I know." *You gotta love some of these people...*I paused after hanging up, noticing the envelope sticking out of the pile. "Shit," I said aloud, hoping no one heard me. I'd totally forgotten to respond to that email I'd gotten about an upcoming meeting. I'd left the invitation on my desk as a reminder- *that* had obviously worked well.

I quickly opened my email, sighing. I regretted that I'd gotten involved but seeing as it was crunch time, I didn't have much choice. Several others had already backed out. It was Rachel who'd originally encouraged me, plus it had been a good distraction. She reminded me to stay positive and focused not just on work, but on social aspects, like the upcoming Guns n' Roses concert we had tickets for *and*...my 20-year high school reunion. `

Initially I'd declined to help- hell I wasn't even sure I wanted to go- but when our reunion page on Facebook began blowing up with desperate pleas for volunteers, I foolishly agreed to help. God knows why- I'd never been on any kind of board, except the high school paper- but even Andrea Zuckerman rose higher in the ranks than I had and although she hadn't actually *dated* Brandon Walsh, at least she'd gotten to kiss him. I wasn't an outcast, a nerd or a loser; I was just shy- the plain, quiet girl with a big smile. I'd had friends, just not popular ones. I hadn't gone to one party. I hadn't dated one guy and the one guy I *would've* dated had been way out of my league anyway.

It's not that I hated my classmates; it's just as far as most of them were concerned, the truth was I really didn't give a fuck. Especially when it involved punk-ass, filthy-rich, spoiled brats like our Class President, Christian Spencer, who had everything handed to them on a silver platter and never had to work a real day in his life. Not that Christian had ever actually *done* anything to me- he was just annoyingly preppy. Still, the thought of having to sit on any other board right now besides a veterinary one was putting me near capacity- *not* that I couldn't handle it.

Compared to my younger, naïve and shier self, I was a completely different person, one most of my classmates wouldn't even recognize. Initially I hadn't cared about this reunion but then I thought- why *not* go and show off a little? After all, I had the medical degree and my own newly budding business. The only thing missing was the 'someone' in Hollywood I *used* to date. Not that Patrick would have gone. I may have come from an upscale community but most kids I'd grown up with weren't that bad. Still, my town had its share of snobs: snobs who got BMWs for their birthdays, threw huge parties while their parents were in Europe and who got into the college of their choice because of a family name or shitloads of money.

Whitney Osgood's family didn't just have money, they had a vault. They were descendants of the Vanderbilts and she never let anyone forget it, either. She designated herself the head of every club she belonged to and of course, had elected herself second in charge of this reunion and now I was gonna have to deal with her, too. I hadn't seen her since high school, but I remembered her- the way she pretended to be better than everyone else; the way she dressed in Ralph Lauren from head to toe and stuck her nose up in the air as she walked down the hall stroking her blond hair like some fucking Standard Poodle in the Westminster and mostly, the way she treated people (even her own friends) like they were second class citizens. But I guess people could change. Maybe she'd turned out to be a decent human being. After all, it *had* been 20 years.

"So," Rachel asked, "where's the 'final' meeting?"

"Shit, you make it sound like The Last Supper," I said, placing my coffee mug on my desk.

"Man, I wish I could go with you as your lesbian date or something. Anyway, not to bring it up, but it's too bad you couldn't have shown up with some hot guy…"

"You mean, like Patrick?" Dead silence. "Come on, you were gonna say Patrick," I insisted, sifting through some papers.

"Okay, fine, yes."

"It's okay. I guess I need to get used to this being my new normal."

"Since when was anything with you two *normal*?"

"Anyway, I think The Goose. Hopefully it's not long- I really don't wanna be around them any longer than I have to."

"I thought you said they weren't too bad?"

"They're not, really."

"It'll be fine. I wouldn't worry about it- you get along with *anyone*. If only you were this version of you in high school, you might've actually had a chance of dating the captain of the football team. What was his name again?"

"Chase Bradford. Oh my *God, stop* will ya?" I could hardly control myself.

"Sorry- I couldn't help it. Do you know if he's going?" she asked curiously. "He's local, right?"

"I don't know. Why?"

"No reason…"

"It's a reunion, not a time machine. I highly doubt that if he *does* go, he'll even notice me. He hardly did in high school and he sat next to me for two years." I noticed a phone call coming in. "Hey, speaking of the reunion, I gotta take this- it's Dean." I ended the call and texted him. Within a minute he was calling. Apparently, I wasn't going to be able to get my work done.

"Hey," I answered, "I was gonna call you after I was done…"

"Hey, baby!" Dean exclaimed in his usual flirty voice.

"I'm gonna assume you didn't even hear what I just said about work," I said.

"I *heard* you- I just wanted to say that." Any opportunity Dean had to use one of his favorite *Austin Powers* lines, he did it.

"Right. Anyway, as I was saying, I got these calls to make so…"

"Don't you have email?"

"You know the veterinary world is far more personal than the human version. We actually *like* our patients. But we are going paperless soon, which means I won't have to all this writing. Of course, I'm a shitty typist so we'll see how that goes. So, what's so important it couldn't wait till next weekend?"

"Nothin'. I just wanted to hear your voice."

"That's *it*? Come *on*, I've known you since the 3rd grade, well enough to know when you're hiding something."

"Who says I'm hiding anything? I can't even call my oldest best friend and check on her?"

"Hmmm…why don't I believe you?" I asked, giggling to myself.

"Okay, fine. I wasn't sure if you'd heard and I kind of wanted to give you a heads up."

"Not that I don't want to hear your voice, but you could've just texted me."

"Yeah, I know, but I didn't think this would sound good in a text."

"*What* wouldn't sound good?" *Gulp. Now what?*

"You know how during reunion time rumors always start to surface about random shit?"

"Yeah..."

"Well, there's one well, two actually, that I got wind of that I think you'll wanna know about before next weekend."

"What makes you think I really care about any rumors involving these people?"

"Well, actually, they have to do with you."

What? "*What?* Why me? Dean, we've been out of high school for 20 years. What could *possibly* have to do with me? I never even dated anyone. What did I get voted off the island? Good, I could free up some time."

There was a moment of silence on the other end. "Surprisingly, no."

"Then what?"

"It more or less has to do with who you've been *recently* dating." *Oh, shit.*

"I *knew* it. I knew this was gonna happen. Maybe I shouldn't go. Do you think it's too late to back out now? I'm sure Whitney will enjoy sucking up more of the spotlight."

"True. But if you don't go, you won't have a chance to take advantage of the next rumor I had to tell you about."

"I can't *wait* to hear this one."

"I heard Chase Bradford's back in town." *What?* "*And* he's single." *Fuck me.*

Chapter 61 ~ The Breakfast Club

Reunion board member or not, I was still uneasy going in without my friends. Suddenly I was feeling even more uncomfortable than if I were at some Hollywood movie premiere. It was undoubtedly intimidating and unfamiliar being around the rich and famous-at first, they were like figures in a wax museum until you got up close. But real wealth was a completely different world; one that people like me don't fit into and one you weren't necessarily welcomed into with open arms just because you drove a Lamborghini.

People who came from family money were on a whole other level of privilege *and* crudeness. Even if you had the ways or means to get into one of their elite 'clubs', if you weren't born into it, you were still an unwelcomed guest in their Mickey Mouse Clubhouse. I just didn't get it-and neither did any of the friends I'd grown up with. We were the ones who lived in the paltry Cape Cods and farmhouses, whose blue-collar parents didn't have silver spoons to feed us with. And sitting in my car waiting for the guys to arrive, I wasn't sure I ever *would* get it.

They'd barely entered the lot and I knew it was them- speakers full bore, the echo of that distinctive voice tearing through the air. Just a few notes and instantly I was back there. I can remember hanging in the school parking lot or at the beach, crankin' up tunes and having a good time. The late 80s had been one of the most creative periods in music history and we had the privilege of experiencing it. It wasn't just the era of the rock band, with groups like Motley Crue and Guns n' Roses at the top of their game; Madonna and Janet Jackson had moved to the forefront of dance; Bobby Brown had left New Edition, while N.W.A. and DJ Jazzy Jeff and the Fresh Prince tried to mimic the success of L.L. Cool J. and Run DMC. And at the tail end was the birth of alternative and grunge.

By 1989 we'd made it through our freshman year and had our own little group of misfits. Dean had had a guitar pic in his back pocket since we'd met. In high school he'd walk the halls in his SKIDZ or torn jeans, bottoms rolled up over his Converse sneakers, plaid shirt tied around his waist, singing to Jimmy Hendrix, giving the finger to any preppy kid who tried to mess with him. The minute Skid Row's album had debuted, he'd played that cassette tape so many times I thought the ribbon would shred. The blaring words from Dean's car stung my ears sending a rush of memories through me. I pictured us doing our best impressions of Axl Rose and Sebastian Bach. Back then there were no cell phones or social media- just a bunch of kids enjoying each other's company.

Twenty years later I was proud of how close we'd all remained, which was more than I could say for most people we grew up with. Christian Spencer, Whitney Osgood and their popular crew had seemed close in high school, but you wouldn't have guessed it now. They were more like strangers and I could see right through the bullshit façade.

Not being popular had never seemed to bother Dean or the other guys- they beat to their own drum, which made them well-liked by everyone from Christian to the jocks. They'd even gone to parties and I was always jealous because I hadn't had the self-esteem to join them. As successful and confident as I now was, the past still hung over me and I couldn't shake the feeling of being back in high school, a meek girl surrounded by a majority I never really knew.

I watched Craig and Bryon step out of the car. They hadn't changed *one* bit- stuck in the 90s forever. They all had the same hair, the same smiles and of course, the same smart-ass personalities that I had sorely missed.

"Hey, *baby*," Dean said, going in for a hug.

"Reunion chair, huh? Popular now?" Craig said, following suit.

"They were desperate," I answered, laughing.

"*No*, they weren't- they needed someone who could take charge," Dean commented.

I eyed him, smirking, "Where've you guys been? I've been waiting here half an hour."

"What do you need us for?" Craig asked, "didn't you help plan this? You and Whitney Osgood must be besties by now."

"*Right,* my wildest dream come true," I paused. "Just because I helped doesn't mean I actually *like* them...wait. Did you guys stop at the bar first?"

They went silent for a moment before BRYON spoke, "no- of *course* not. We were at Dean's."

"That explains it." I shook my head and rolled my eyes. "You guys clean up pretty nice."

"What," Dean added, "no leg warmers or Madonna bangles?"

"Funny. I was just about to ask you where your Z-CAVARRICI's were. And that was middle school, Dean."

"*We* do- look at *you*, Lea. How come you didn't dress like that in high school?"

"She didn't have the *body* to dress like that in high school. Sorry," Bryon caught himself.

"You're right." I sulked, thinking back to senior year. It's not that I was fat, I was just frumpy, with a definitive lack of style. If I'd looked anything like I did now, maybe Chase Bradford *would've* noticed me... I stared at the grandiose front doors, not at all ready to venture inside.

"Lea, are you okay?" Craig asked.

"Yeah, I'm...fine."

"You don't look fine. What are you bitchin' about? Not only are you one of only *two* doctors in our class, you've got your own business and you're dating an actor, so I'm pretty sure you have more than enough to boast about when people ask what you've been 'up to'..."

I looked at him, sighing before answering, "not anymore- we sort of broke up."

He gasped as if in shock, "*what*? When?"

"Just over a month ago. I don't wanna talk about it- I just wanna get inside, do a little dancing and get out..."

"How the fuck do you expect to drop a bombshell like that then act like it's nothing?"

"Because it *is* nothing. Can we just go now?"

"Wait, wait." I caught a glimpse of Bryon out of the corner of my eye, coming at me with a bottle, and I turned back around.

"What's that?" I asked, raising my voice.

"What's it *look* like?" The small flask-shaped bottle with its signature black and white label stared at me. "You need a shot," Bryon said, handing me the small cup.

"You're not supposed to bring that here. You're gonna get us in trouble."

"Come on, Lea, this isn't fuckin' prom. Besides, what kind of high school gathering would this be if we didn't sneak in booze?"

"Shit," Bryonsaid, you're even straighter than I remember. Maybe you *have* turned into Whitney Osgood."

"Okay, fine, fine, I'll do one."

Five minutes later we were standing in the middle of a huge banquet room surrounded by bold blue and white decorations with name badges pinned to our chests. The infamous mascot in the form of a super-sized wave dangled from the ceiling. Admittedly, it had turned out well and from the looks of things people were pleased.

"So, *this* is what the inside of a country club looks like," Craig commented.

"Right," Dean added, "I guess I can say this officially checks off the last box on my fuckin' bucket list." We all cracked up- none of us had ever been high enough on the totem pole to have earned an invite to places like this growing up.

Quickly my smile faded. "Shit, there's Whitney. Catch up with you after." She was waving me down so overanxiously from across the room it irked me.

As I walked over, I looked around. It was the exact opposite of what I'd expected. There were no clicks or small groups hiding out in corners and everyone seemed to be having a good time. Maybe I'd been wrong. For the most part I'd always gotten along with people; we were just in different circles and the popular crowd rarely let outsiders in.

I got a closer look as I continued walking- some had clearly aged better than others, but most looked the same. Some had brought spouses or dates and for a moment I wished Patrick had been here, not that he'd have anything in common with these people. A-list star or not, people tended to flock to anyone famous. My luck I would've spent the whole night standing there while all the females in the room hit on him, so I guess it was fine.

"Eleana, *wow*- this place looks great! And so do *you*," she exclaimed, eyeing my dress. "Is that Kate Spade? I *love* it!" *Can we say ass-kisser?*

"Uh, you know, I honestly can't remember," I lied, "it was probably on sale. Besides, I don't think they sell Kate Spade at Kohl's." *Who am I kidding? The word 'sale' isn't even in her vocabulary.*

"Oh my God, you're *so* funny!" she said loudly. I noticed Christian strutting over with his trophy wife. *What an ass.* "Anyway, I absolutely *love* it. So," she continued pointing around the room, "people really seem to be liking this. I think we did good. Maybe we can work on the next reunion together."

Not likely- I barely survived this one. I smiled curtly at her, "ah, maybe, you never know…"

Before long, Christian was standing in front of us. "You both look nice. This is my wife Kristen. Kristen, Eleana, and you remember Whitney." I couldn't help but find everything about him irritating, from the way he dressed to his weaselly, untrusting smile to the demeaning tone in his voice. Maybe he wasn't such bad guy. Maybe it wasn't his fault he'd grown up so wealthy he never knew any better. Or maybe he was just an *asshole*. Either way my impressions of him now hadn't changed much from years ago.

I bit my tongue, smiling. "Hi, nice to meet you." *Keep smiling. It'll be over before you know it.*

She was exactly as I'd expected- beautiful, petite, somewhat quiet- the perfect Stepford wife. Those were a dime a dozen around here and not a single one of them actually served any real purpose than to reproduce and take orders from their rich husbands. I don't care *who* I thought was attractive in high school, you couldn't have paid me enough money to marry into their families. Well, except *one*, maybe.

"Yes, you, too. I love the decorations."

"Thanks," Whitney and I both answered.

"That's right- the girls did it all. That's not really my thing..." Christian smiled almost dismissively. I wanted to vomit; *and* punch him. *Girls? As if all women can do is fucking decorate. If only I had a scalpel on me right now...*

Instantly my grin flattened and my eyes narrowed. "Well, Whitney and I *did* come up with the idea, you know so..." she looked at me. Most people remembered me as shy; they weren't used to this 'grown-up' version, the one who wasn't afraid of opening her unfiltered mouth. If I was this outspoken and confident back then, I would've blown Christian Spencer out of the water in an election. Without much else to say, he took his wife by the arm and walked away.

"Thanks," Whitney said. "You know, I always thought he was kind of a dick."

I turned to her and smiled, "you don't say."

Two hours later, things were still running smoothly. Drinks and hors d'oeuvres were flowing, and people were being far more social than I'd anticipated. Surprisingly I'd made it to the dance floor at least twice. Well, I couldn't let a Third Eye Blind or Bel Biv Devoe song down...But the biggest surprise of the night hadn't been that I'd enjoyed talking with classmates I hadn't seen for years or that I'd impressed people with my career or even that I'd been told by just about every guy in the room how great I looked.

I peeked over my shoulder. Remarkably, most of the class had shown up, pushing our total upwards of 200 attendees. To have such a great turnout was almost unheard of. It hadn't been a bad night so far- the mock 'awards ceremony' was sure to be a hit- I giggled to myself at the then "most attractive couple" who obviously wouldn't regain their titles tonight.

It was getting dark. A few caddies remained on the still lit-up course's sand traps and putting green. The water of Long Island Sound shimmered under the moon. It was a pretty picture, yet it hardly compared to the one that I'd admired on the Pacific Ocean almost a year ago today. Never in my life would I have expected a fucking golf course to have any remote effect on me. No thanks to Patrick Thomas. I wondered what he was doing right now...

Great- I'm gonna start crying in the middle of my God Damn reunion. Before my internal emotional battle could continue, an unfamiliar, deep voice muttered something behind me.

"Hi, uh, Eleana, right?"

You have to be fucking kidding me. I shook my head, irritated as I turned around. "look, if you're that dude who was hitting on me earlier, don't even think about it. I may be in heels, but I will fuck you u..." *Oh shit. You're not creepy stalker guy.*

Shocked, the tall attractive blond took a step back and I gasped, embarrassed. "Not quite the answer I was expecting but...okay. You know, of all the chicks I've pissed off over the years and believe me there's been a few, I don't think any ever said anything like that to me before."

His smile hadn't changed one bit- and neither had his physique. Looking at him now, you'd think he was still playing college football. Yup- Easton Chase Bradford was a completely different image from the jackass waiter who'd tried to get my number earlier- and what a beautiful image he was.

"Uh, *oh*, I'm sorry- I thought you were someone else," I gulped. *Understatement.*

"I *hope* so," he answered, his grin a bit loftier. "Is this a bad time?"

Still in shock that he was standing there, I paused before answering. "Uh, no, I was just..."

"Planning your attack on any poor, unsuspecting guy who approaches?" For a moment I was back in 11th grade English only this time, I wasn't the same drab girl who's biggest accomplishment was serving volleyballs and editing the school paper- I was a successful doctor with a lot to show. *Then act like it, Eleana.*

"*No*," I laughed, "there was this guy...nevermind. I was just getting some fresh air. Uh, shouldn't you be inside hitting on some newly-divorced, Botox-ed prom queen wanna-be or...hanging with Mike Maloney and the rest of the..."

"What?" he asked. I shrugged my shoulders and smiled jokingly. "Come on, say it."

"I was gonna say football team but..."

"No, you weren't."

"Okay, fine, I was gonna say jock." *What is he doing out here? And why is he talking to me?*

"You look surprised."

"Well 'undetermined' *was* next to your name," I scoffed. "And...surprised that you'd be out here? Uh, *duh.* The last time I saw you was 1993 at the Thanksgiving football game."

"Yeah, well, Mike convinced me. To be honest, I don't really talk to many people from our class."

"I didn't expect that," I paused, "you all seemed close to me. The popular crowd. You guys hardly even noticed people outside your 'world'."

"'World'? We all went to the same school and being popular isn't everything. Eleana, we sat next to each other in English class for two years- of *course* I *noticed* you." *What did you just say?*

"You know what I mean. Sorry if I ever made you uncomfortable..." I shied my head down. Twenty years later and still I felt meek around him.

"You mean, that time you gave me that stuffed animal for Valentine's Day?" *Jesus. Does this guy remember that?*

"I was hoping you'd long since forgotten. I couldn't help it- I was young with a crush." *Did I just say that?*

"It's fine, don't worry about it. It was sweet." *What did you just say?*

"Sweet? You had a girlfriend, and I was such a..."

"It was cute. Besides, Phoebe was a bitch. I don't even know why I dated her." I looked around. We were the only ones out here and then it hit me. I was alone. Outside. In the dark. With Chase Bradford. I could barely keep myself together.

"So," he started up again, "*doctor*, huh? Impressive. And I thought I was cool because I worked for my uncle's law firm and drove a Porsche."

Chase may have come from money, been captain of the football team and one of the most popular guys in school, but he'd always been nice to everyone, including me. Even when I'd crushed on him in front of his friends. At 6' 2" and well-built, he was an intimidating guy- a *hot* one at that- and he was standing out here, now less than a foot away.

"Ah, yep. How did you know that?"

His smile grew widely, "it was next to your name on the board. So...you still live around here?"

"Yeah, I paused. What's your story?"

"Other than just coming off a horribly well-publicized divorce, losing my house and still trying to put my life back together? I'm good."

"Oh, I'm sorry." I felt bad for him. Maybe he *was* right- popular or not in high school, right now it really didn't matter. It *was* a good thing I wasn't with Patrick anymore. I was glad not to be anywhere near a spotlight these days.

"Thanks. It is what it is. What about you?"

"Me?" I asked, suddenly shy again.

"Uh, huh." He leaned in a little, resting his chin on one hand.

"Oh, uh, well...no kids, never married, hence I do not know what divorce is like but I *do* have an idea on seemingly great beginnings, bad endings, public humiliation and trying to put your life back together so..."

Intrigued, he leaned in further. "*Really.* Huh."

"You have no idea."

"I guess we both needed the fresh air then." For a moment he didn't move. Then suddenly he blurted out something completely unexpected. "I always thought your eyes were brown," he muttered in a sexy voice.

"Man, was *I* a dumbass in high school."

I looked into those gorgeous blue eyes and smiled, "well, I *did* help you on a paper once..."

"That's because I lost my notebook. Eleana, did you forget I had one of the highest GPAs in our class? I *meant*, why didn't I ever try this before?"

"Maybe because you had a girlfriend. Or maybe," I added, "it's because I was about 20 pounds heavier with really bad clothing choices."

"You weren't 20 pounds heavier..."

"Oh please. I can't even look at that stupid yearbook picture."

He laughed. "Well, right about now you look amazing, which is more than I can say for a lot of other people, including my soon-to-be ex." *Especially Phoebe O'Connor.*

"You're just being nice. You were always nice to me so you wouldn't hurt my feelings."

"Ok, maybe then, but not now. I don't remember you being this cool in high school."

"I wasn't. I came out of my shell later on." He stared at me, unwavering.

"Hey, would you maybe wanna grab a drink sometime? No pressure."

"A drink? With the captain of the football team? Sure, I mean, why not?"

He smiled again. This guy had sexy down to a tee, no pun intended. "Cool, what do you say we go back inside and enjoy the rest of this reunion?"

Whatever would happen with Chase Bradford didn't matter- he was a nice guy and judging by the brief encounter we'd just had, we'd more than enjoy ourselves on a date. If something more came out of it, great. But I hardly expected it to.

Chase and I parted ways. I may have grabbed his attention, but a part of me still felt like the same old Eleana Camioni-the one who *wasn't* ever going to be good enough to fit in with a popular crowd *or* into the life of Chase Bradford. Not-so unlike Patrick, Chase and I were of two different worlds and the chances that we'd make it any further from his bedroom were slim. Still, it felt nice to be doted on by the captain of the football team, even if it *was* twenty years later and as for his bedroom? Well, you couldn't sign me up fast enough.

I hadn't even made it within ten feet of Dean and Bryon before the comments started flying.

"*Hey* now," he smirked. I watched as the both of them laughed.

"What?" I stared them down like I was about to kill them.

"*Really*? Come on, spill it."

"Spill what?"

"What do you think, we didn't see you out there with Chase?"
What?

"We were just talki..."

"Bullshit," he laughed, "you were doing *more* than just talking. You only had a crush on the guy for like six years."

"So, what? It's not like anything's gonna come of it...he just got divorced. Shit. I didn't realize how long I was out there. I'll be right back." I only had five minutes before the ceremony. I was about to open my bathroom stall when I heard them come in. I got up on the toilet seat and pretended like I wasn't there.

"Oh, my *God*. I can't believe this," one of them said angrily. "Hey, can I borrow your lipstick?"

"Sure," another one answered. "What's up?" I didn't recognize their voices. I figured it would be awkward if I came out now. Plus, I was curious.

"Phoebes, what happened?" *Phoebes?*

I heard a loud sigh followed by a near scream. "Patty was out on the terrace and guess who she just saw Chase getting cozy with...*Eleana Camioni*. Can you believe that? First, I thought she was kidding and then two other people said it, too. What the *fuck*." *What the fuck is right. Someone saw us? Oh, great.*

"What? Eleana Camioni and Chase? No way. Not possible. She's not even in the same league as us. Just what the *hell* is she trying to prove anyway?" Carefully I took a breath so they wouldn't hear me. I felt like one of Jason Voorhees' victims, waiting to be killed.

"I don't know, but I'm gonna put an end to it." Phoebe said angrily.

"Calm down. The guy just came off a nasty divorce. Let him have a drama-free night, huh?" one of the other two girls said.

"How about *she* should lay her hands off? You know she was dating that guy, right, that actor? He dumped her. And now she thinks she can just come into *our* reunion all high and mighty. Well she better think again." I gasped, quickly covering my mouth.

"That's not what I heard. I heard she was sleeping with all these guys and she dumped *him*; left him stranded." *What? So not true. God, I hate tabloids.*

"Well," I heard Phoebe's obnoxious sigh, "She's messing with the wrong bitch. *I'm* the one who's supposed be there for him in his time of need, *not* her." *He just told me how he felt about you and you think you're gonna make a comeback? Dream on.*

"Okay, okay. Let's go to the bar." *Like that's what you assholes need right now.* "It'll be fine, don't worry. Let's just try to enjoy the rest of the night. It's not like Chase would ever be serious about her anyway."

I stepped out of the stall, still in shock. Just how many people had seen us? Still, I had the right to talk to Chase Bradford if I wanted to. I didn't get it. I may not have been best friends with any girls in my class, but I hadn't had any enemies and I may have hated Phoebe O'Connor because she dated Chase, but I was a kid. Whatever was behind her reasons for hating *me* so much I couldn't let it get to me, especially now when I had to go back out there.

Halfway through handing out the awards and still no sign of Phoebe or her cohorts. I was relieved. I spotted Chase off to the side and felt even more relieved. He was still here and still smiling at me, the same way he'd been earlier. I smiled back.

"And now, the moment you've all been waiting for," Christian announced. "The award for "Most attractive male, 2012 Edition", goes to...Chase Bradford." Everyone clapped and cheered. He strutted up to the podium modestly, his dimples taking a front role.

I listened, waiting for the next name to be called. "And, the award for "Most attractive female" goes to...oh. Turns out she's already up here." *Good for you, Whitney...* "Uh, Eleana Camioni." *What?*

Shocked, I looked over at Chase before looking back at Christian, forcing a smile. I couldn't believe it. *Me?* Christian handed me the trophy. I wasn't even holding it for two seconds before lightning struck.

"Just what do you think you're doing?" Phoebe had reappeared out of thin air.

I looked at her, unsure of how to answer her idiocy. "*Excuse* me?" I stood there, reveling in my moment. "Well, right now. I'm holding this trophy. What's your problem?" I asked.

"Phoebe," Chase chimed in, "what *is* your problem?"

"My *problem*? *I'll* tell you what my problem is- *her*." She pointed right to me.

"What did I do to you? And I thought you'd left or...were passed out somewhere."

"You think that just because you dated an actor and lost a few pounds you can just show up and be popular. Well, I got news for you, you'll *never* be one of us! Maybe everyone else is fooled by this *façade*," she pointed at me again, "but *I'm* not. I know the *real* story." The entire room went silent. *Gulp.* What did she know that I didn't? "I know what you did- you slept around and practically ruined his career and I'm *not* gonna sit here and watch you try to do it to Chase, too."

Just what the fuck do these people read in the tabloids? "Do what, exactly, *talk* to him? Maybe you didn't realize, but this is 2012, not 1992. You're not dating him anymore. He's a grown man- he can do what he wants."

"Listen to yourself. 'he can do whatever he wants'," she added cloyingly, "what are you still in *love* with him? Did you bring him a stuffed teddy bear or write him another love note? You're kidding yourself if you think he'd would *ever* wanna be with someone like you. You're not even good enough to be inside a place like this..." I felt my eyes water a little.

"That's enough, Phoebe." Chase stepped in between us as I stood there, now speechless.

"Or what, Chase? You *really* wanna drag your family's name through the mud some more by getting involved with this trash?" Chase went silent. I could tell he was angry but somehow kept his composure. I, however, would never have been as strong. In a flash Phoebe was on the ground, but not because of me- she'd tripped on the edge of the dancefloor.

I could feel all the eyes still on me. Had everyone actually believed her drunken rantings? Visibly upset, I walked around her fallen body and headed for the door. Of course I hadn't made it as far as I'd wanted to.

"Hey, hey," Dean had followed me. "Are you okay?" he asked, concerned.

"Yeah, I guess, but in a way I *did* leave Patrick behind. When things got weird, I bailed, but it wasn't anything on purpose. Not that you'll read *that* in any paper." I held my head down.

"Like anyone's gonna take what she said seriously- she's wasted. And, you *wish* you were some Hollywood whore." Dean had always been good at making me laugh. It was one of his strongest attributes. But right now, I wasn't sure it was enough to turn my mood around.

"Is that supposed to make me feel better?" I asked.

"Maybe not, but a nice stiff one probably will," he smiled offering up a hug. "We've *all* had bad relationships, some of us worse than others, but in the end it all turns out for the best and in your case? I'm sure the best is yet to come."

"Thanks," I smiled. "But maybe was she right about getting involved with Chase. I don't want to make his life more complicated."

"Would you stop worrying about what *other* people think? You're better than that. And you're not gonna scare Chase off. I saw him back there defending you, not that you needed any help. For a second, I thought you were gonna hit her."

"I *was*." We both laughed.

"So," he continued, "what do you say we wrap this shindig up and head over to The Goose?"

"Oh, I don't know. I think I might just head home, you know, snuggle up with my trophy and dream about the date I probably *won't* ever get to have with Chase Bradford."

"Bullshit. Let's go, Camioni."

Chapter 62 ~ The Secret of My Success

Thursday August 30th

"Come on, Camioni. I caught you staring down at least five times during that meeting. What's up? Waitin' on a booty call?" Nate laughed.

"*No,*" I answered snidely, "that's your territory, not mine."

"*Ouch.* Not anymore. I'm engaged, remember?"

"Well, I haven't seen her stop in for lunch lately so maybe I forgot," I teased. "Anything I should know?"

He let out a heavy sigh, "other than we've had to push back the date because she keeps changing her mind?"

"About what? I thought she *wanted* a pink theme," I laughed. "You mean, it's *not* November?"

He shook his head. "Actually, to be perfectly honest I'm kind of fuckin' relieved."

"Not having second *thoughts,* are we Peterson?" I wasn't trying to be coy, but deep down I really didn't think she was right for him. I just wished he would realize it before it was too late. Not that you couldn't just get a divorce and *not* that I had any say in the matter.

He leaned back, seemingly offended, "Uh, no, smart ass. It's just with the hospital shit, it's one less thing off my plate right now, that's all. You don't think I'll go *through* with it?" He raised one eyebrow at me as if in the middle of a tit for tat.

I shrugged my shoulders, "I don't know...it's just you didn't sound so sure and you wanna be *sure,* right?" I smirked back.

"Maybe you don't know me as well as you think," wink, wink.

"Guess not." *Yes, I do.* "Well when you *do* decide on a date, let us know." *Yak. Can you call out sick to a wedding?*

"Enough wedding shit, who were you waiting on? Don't tell me Mr. Wonderful has made a comeback in the sequel."

"Ha, funny. No and...*no,* not after what I did anyway," I was sulking a little.

"Lea, what you did was choose *yourself,* your career and your future. If a guy's not on board with that, then fuck him."

"Gee, tell me how you *really* feel," I looked at him.

"Honestly, I liked the guy but...he kind of rubbed me the wrong way."

I leaned in, curious for more. This was a surprise, to say the least. I wondered why he was saying this to me now. "How?" *Like Tina is some kind of fucking prize...* "You mean, because he's famous with lots of money?" I joked.

"No, *please*, dude. I'm not envious of that shit. I just think you deserve better, that's all."

"Wow. Where is this suddenly coming from? And why didn't you ever tell me before?" I really wanted to know. "And by 'better' you mean...who exactly? *Please* tell me it's not *you*."

He paused a moment before continuing, "I don't know. I guess I didn't want to ruin your big moment; you seemed so happy. I hadn't seen you like that in a long time..." he dazed off. Then it hit me- *had* Nate had genuine resurfaced feelings for me and could just never bring himself to tell me? Or was I crazy?

"Oh," I said.

"Lea, it's just my opinion. You don't have to agree. I guess it doesn't really matter anymore anyway so..." He was right about that one. Nathan Peterson was going to be a married man soon while I was now miserable, single, and alone. I'd screwed up twice, each time with a guy I'd really cared about and now it was too late. Patrick, and now Nate, would be out of my life forever.

"But," he went on, "you *still* have to tell me why you were looking at your phone so much. Come on, let's hear it." It was amazing how guys could turn emotions on an off so easily. In a matter of seconds Nate had turned back into his cocky, masculine self.

"Okay, fine. I ran into this guy at my high school reunion a couple of weeks ago and we sort of hit it off. He said he was gonna call but...after what happened he probably won't."

"Why not? Didn't he *look* at you?"

"Now's not the time for jokes, Nate. Basically his old girlfriend accused me of being a whore, ruining Patrick's life, and tried to attack me."

"Oh, please. No one's sober at those fuckin' things. They probably didn't even pay attention," he reassured me.

"She did it in front of the entire class, on *loud*speaker," I said, crossing my arms.

"No shit." He could hardly contain his laughter.

"Stop laughing."

"I'm sorry- I can't help it. Oh, come on. I'm sure you kicked her ass."

"I didn't have to- she fell all on her on own."

"Okay, so, how was that *not* funny?" I shrugged my shoulders. "What happened next, you had pig's blood dumped on you? I'm sure it wasn't that bad."

"You weren't there."

"I would've been if you'd asked me."

"That's because you'd never turn down an open bar," I answered smugly.

"Okay, true, but also not true. I could've been your date- made people even *more* jealous. Then they wouldn't have had *shit* to say," he smirked.

"Then my chances of going out with Chase *really* would've been zero- you would've cock blocked me."

"Hey, only guys can say that."

"No, they can't."

"Did you say *Chase*? What kind of fuckin' name is that?"

"What kind of name is *Nate*?" I joked.

"Seriously- that's his name?"

"No. His first name's Easton. Everyone calls him by his middle name."

"Must be a rich Connecticut thing."

"It is."

"Whatever. I'm sure he'll call- just give a little time. You know he'd be stupid not to," he winked. Just then, his phone started buzzing. Quickly he looked down. "Speaking of calls, it's Tina. I better take this or I'll never hear the end of it." *Since when do you not hear it from her?* "See you Tuesday?" I nodded. *Wait- Tuesday?*

He smiled as he hit the answer button. He got up and left the room, leaving me alone with my thoughts, which were now all scrambled after our conversation. Since when had Nate Peterson given out dating advice? And since when was he the one moving on with *his* life while I sat here lost, trying to figure out where my own was going? Nate appeared cool on the outside, but something was bugging me. Despite his lame attempts at disguising it, I felt something was off. I closed my folder and went to find Maureen. After looking in her office, I finally found her- in Justin's.

"I hope I'm not interrupting anything."

"No, no, come in," Justin said. "What's up?"

"We still on for tomorrow night. I've got to go shopping so..."

Maureen's face went sour, "uh, tomorrow? Oh crap. I screwed up. Justin and I decided to head out to Long Island right after work. I'd invite you to go but..."

"It's Labor Day Weekend. Oh my God." *That's what Nate had meant by Tuesday.*

"We just wanted to take advantage of the long weekend that we somehow both got off."

"It's not a big deal. I'm sure I can find something to do...you guys have fun. Oh, and pick me up some wine, will ya?"

For New Englanders, Labor Day meant more than just a symbol of the end of summer (and a plethora of *JAWS* marathons); it was the official end of beach season. But that's where global warming gave us *one* advantage. September had historically been the beginning of fall with changing leaves, blooming apple orchards and the first smells of burning fireplaces. But in recent years we'd seen warm weather until October which meant with kids back in school, some of the most quiet and relaxing beach time of the entire year.

It was after 8 pm by the time I'd gotten home. It'd been a productive work meeting and after nearly three months I was finally starting to get into somewhat of a groove. There was a newly hatched feeling of accomplishment, different than before. I felt more needed, more important and above all else, prouder of the person I was becoming. I was beginning to wonder if maybe all this Patrick stuff *had* been for a reason; if this *had* been the right choice for me, just like Nate had been trying to say.

Patrick and I had been apart before, but this time we were no longer together; It was really, truly over. Maybe this time away from him *had* been what I'd needed. I was starting to see my life in a new light. '*My* life', I thought. The way *I* chose it to be, with or *without* a guy. I had to get myself back on track and into my *own* life- not the life of someone else's- and I could be successful. But what was the true secret to anyone's success, not just in work or relationships, but in life? This whole time, had I just made it all more complicated than it really was? Was there something I'd been missing?

Success wasn't about trying to please everyone else. And it wasn't about checking off some stupid mental list or trying to force your life to be complete in a way that would or could maybe never even work. I thought back to what my dad had once told me- in one of his nonvulgar, inoffensive moments that *hadn't* involved long, drawn out (well, that depends on your definition of 'long') war stories or government conspiracy theories. My father wasn't the most poised or well-spoken but every now and then, he'd spout words of wisdom in some way, shape or form, just when you least expected.

Picture it, Connecticut, 1992: You may not think an ex-SEAL would have any for his teenage daughter about to go off to college, but he'd surprised me. I don't recall his exact words, but it was something along the lines of "the greatest measure of a man's success isn't how many wars he's made it out of, how many kills he's had or how many medals he's earned- it's how much of his heart he's willing to put on the line for what he believes in without compromise, without expecting reward or recognition. People who constantly seek success are going about it the wrong way."

He'd also pointed out the fact (as he had done many times before) that without heart and a strong belief in your purpose, you'd not only fail miserably, you'd also be remembered as a coward or even worse, a coward who let his fellow men down. But just when I'd thought he was done, he'd surprised me yet again:

"You're gonna be a great doctor, honey, but even if you don't, it doesn't matter as long as you put your heart-and everything you fuckjin' got- into it. Just be the best you can be."

"Dad, this isn't the Army," I'd said, mistakenly interrupting his speech.

"You're Goddamn right it's not; *fuck* those pussies. Stop talking and listen. Don't let yourself get caught up in whatever bullshit everyone else is doing- you might lose your focus, lose sight of the target and when that shit happens all hell can break loose. Trust me, I've been there. Stay on track, stay focused and for fuck's sake stay away from them college boys."

In a way it'd been some of the most sound and heartfelt (not to mention brow-raising) advice I'd ever been given, just a little rough around the edges. But that was my dad- rough on the outside, soft on the inside, one of the greatest men to ever have lived (in my book). I wished he was here to see how far I'd come and how much he still meant to me and after all this time, how clearly I still remembered those colorful words. Well, sort of.

Maybe if he were here, he'd have some new words of wisdom for me. I hoped that he was proud of what he saw down here. Despite all his idiosyncrasies, he'd had this way of making me feel like everything was going to be okay, even when he was sick; I'd had a sense of security. If he were here, he'd probably tell me that I hadn't fucked up too badly and that everything would be just fine; that I'd made it through some tough battles; that I'd done pretty well for myself and that all I really needed to do was to stay on point and get back into focus. And, more than likely, he'd tell me to just go to the shooting range and target practice because besides cleaning his weapons, shooting them always made him feel better. It also helped keep distractions out of sight, out of mind. Of course, *some* distractions would *always* find their way back in.

Chapter 63 ~ The Wedding Singer

The weekend came and went faster than I'd expected. I felt refreshed, recharged and ready to take on what I knew would be a very trying week or as it's known by its *real* name, a shit show. Going back to work after a long weekend could be challenging, for several reasons. You might want one (or two) more day(s) to relax, you were still feeling the effects of all the partying or you just didn't want to deal with people. In the veterinary world, it was almost *always* the third reason that won out.

I really loved my job but there were times when I hated it. People who worked in other professions didn't have to deal with what we did (on so many levels). After some time off, they just went back to the office and resumed their lives- logged onto a computer or changed someone's oil or deposited checks. Doctor's offices reopened, saw appointments and answered phone calls. If someone had an emergency after hours, they went to a hospital or a walk-in clinic. For us? Yeah, *right*.

An all-too common occurrence with sick animals? People waiting it out. Sure, there are plenty of caring and responsible pet owners out there, but there are just as many *irresponsible* ones. Countless people wait all week to see if their pet gets better and when they don't, they call our office, usually on a Friday, 10 minutes before closing. Then there's the second group who gives it another day (that'd be Saturday), just in case their pet makes a dramatic turnaround and when they don't, they call- at 10 minutes before closing. And then there's the *third* group of winners who in my book don't deserve to be pet owners, the ones I like to call assholes. These are the ones who were gonna call three days earlier but didn't, because they had better things to do like barbeque or go boating and rather than take their beloved pet (who's been vomiting for several days and now is critical) to the 24-hour emergency hospital they call your office (who's already slammed because of all the other people who did the same thing) and expect to get in whenever they want and not spend too much money. Fucking people- and you wonder why so many of us in this profession think about leaving it at least a dozen times in our career. Quite frankly it was scary to know what was out in the world.

I arrived at the office early so I could get a jump start before the chaos, although that statement could apply to almost *any* day at my office. We were a 24-hour care facility. I didn't work any late or emergency shifts, but I had patients to follow up on from before the weekend and sometimes that list got long. I aimed to leave on time, get home and leave work behind. Not that that was always possible, as *all* of us in the medical field know. So, if that meant coming earlier, I was all for it.

By 10:30am, it'd already felt like noon. I'd seen three emergencies, in addition to my regularly scheduled appointments. I received a text from Maureen to come help her with a case and so I went to find her in one of the treatment rooms.

"Hey, what's up?" I asked. "How was the Island?" I knew that smile. It meant she'd had lots of sex, while I'd spent my weekend polishing off two bottles of crappy champagne, not that I was celebrating anything.

"Oh, it was *great*."

"I bet it was," I smiled.

"I haven't been on the North Fork for so long, I forgot how beautiful it is- all the farms and wineries, ocean..."

"Sounds perfect."

"It was well, *almost* anyway." Her face went sour.

"Why?"

"It was fine until Justin got that disturbing text." I waited. "Wait- you *don't* know?" she asked, lowering her voice.

"Know what? Is everything okay?"

"You mean to tell me halfway through the day at this fucking place and you haven't *heard* anything? Wow, I thought word would be out already."

"Okay seriously, you're beginning to freak me out. Did somebody die?" I scooted closer to her along the counter.

"*No*." She let out a huff before leaning in. "The wedding's off," she whispered. I looked at her, clueless. "*Nate's* wedding." *What?* "They called it off. Actually, Tina called it off- right before she broke up with him." *Holy Shit.*

"Not to quote Joey Lawrence on this one but, *whoah*."

"I'll say. We were right int the middle of a romantic dinner, too. Sort-of put a damper on the whole evening but don't worry, we made up for it the next day," she hinted.

"Ew, gross. You're gonna spoil my lunch."

"Whatever- you'll probably eat a protein bar anyway. So," she continued, "I kind of thought Nate would've said something to you."

"I haven't seen him." I kept checking to see if anyone was listening in. You never knew what little sneak would be hiding around a corner in this place.

"Not even a text?" she asked in disbelief.

"Not even a text. You know I don't talk to him much outside of work. And I stopped asking him about his love life a while ago. It's not my business."

"Oh yeah, like when?"

"Like after he told me to. Satisfied?" Miffed at her line of questioning, I crossed my arms. "Just stop. I know what you're gonna say."

"What am I gonna say?" she asked.

"Oh, I don't know- some snarky comment about going to see if he's okay. He doesn't *need* me. He's got Justin, plus any one of these new techs, too, at his disposal. I'm sure he'll be *just* fine."

"Or maybe he won't," she argued. "He really cared about her, you know." *Whatever.*

I shook off her comments as best I could. "Speaking of need, I thought you 'needed' my help with a case..."

"I just made that up. But while you're here, may as well give me a second opinion on this CBC. I was thinking of adding a PCR flea and tick panel."

After speaking with Maureen, I went to radiology to check on a patient who'd been admitted for radiographs for a suspect cruciate tear. I was just about to leave when I heard two female voices in the hall. I couldn't help but listen in myself.

"Did you hear?" one of them asked in a suspicious tone.

"Yeah. Poor guy," the other said.

"I know, right? I was thinking maybe I should ask him out." *What are they talking about?* I peeked out the door to see who they were- no one I recognized. *Must be new.* They were in their 20s, full makeup and scrub tops so tight I thought they were gonna rip any second. Or maybe that was the point.

"Let me know how it is," the second one giggled.

I hated whiny giggling sounds about as much as I hated the braindead girls they always seemed to come out of. What the fuck did girls do- connive and scheme the second a guy is broken up? And was it a new thing to actually *share* the guy like he was some piece of meat? I felt bad for the guy, whoever he was however, a part of me wished I'd been like that at their age...

"Definitely. I'm sure I can get at *least* a few meals out of him, along with the *rest*, obviously. Guys like Nate are totally vulnerable when this happens."

That did it. My blood was about to boil over and when it hit these two idiots, they were gonna scream their pretty little heads off. I stormed out of the room, unable to control myself.

"Um, excuse me. What do you think you're doing?" It took them way too long to even notice I was talking to them. The shorter redhead crossed her arms at me.

"Uh, can I help you with something?" *Really, bitch?*

I tilted my head at her, pointing to the black block lettering on my lab coat. "Hmm...see this? I *doubt* it. You must be new here. Just so you know, it's against hospital policy to gossip while you're on the clock *and* in the hallway. It's a distraction to other employees."

"What are you the *owner*?" the other dumbass finally spoke up. *Oh this one's real smart.* "Maybe you shouldn't listen in on other peoples' private conversations."

"Um, first of all- *so* not private- you're in a hallway. Second, maybe *you* should mind your own business." *And stay away from people almost twice your age.* "*Jesus*, the guy just broke up with his fiancé. I highly doubt he's gonna go for the 'I wish I was a porn star in the 80s" look. If *I* were you, I'd stick to what you know best, like ridiculously caked on makeup and...body shots. And by the way, I *am* one of the owners so if you want to keep your jobs, I suggest you take my advice more seriously."

The look on their faces was priceless. *Good. I scared them.* But it hadn't been all me. They were staring at something –or someone- behind me. I turned to see Nate standing there, the smile on his face so big it could've charmed the pants off a snake.

"Yep, I believe she's right," he said as they scurried off like a couple of rats.

"Oh, uh, good morning, Dr. Peterson," I recovered.

"Technically it's afternoon. So, I guess you heard. Shit, bad news *does* travel fast," he said.

"Not to *them*- apparently they thought it was *good* news," I laughed.

"*Really*. So, you're sticking up for me now? Thanks, but I'm okay."

Why didn't I believe him? "You sure?" I asked.

"Nah, not really, but whatever. I was gonna call you but I'm guessing you already found out."

"Yeah, Maureen told me."

"You mean you didn't hear the version where I have a month to live? Although, I gotta say, the cut she left still hurts like a bitch."

"Nope." He was right. Not only did news travel fast, it had an overwhelming tendency to morph into a complete untruth. "So, wanna tell me what happened?"

"There's not much to say. She decided I wasn't what she wanted. Oh, and she was fucking someone else. So honestly, I'd rather just forget her and be done with it. But as we both know that's not so easy to do. What can I say? At least she didn't leave me at the fuckin' altar."

As much as he tried to make light of it, I could tell Nate was hurting and I felt horribly. Whatever had happened, whatever mine or anyone else's opinions of Tina had been, I had been happy for him or, at least, I'd *tried* to be. I still cared for him and I hated to see him like this. Sometimes people could go on a path of self-destruction in the face of a something so sudden and I didn't want to see that happen. Despite moving ahead with wedding plans, he'd become a better friend to me in recent months than he ever had been- through all the stuff with Patrick and my dad, the hospital, he'd helped me to see things more clearly, like my future- Shit I never thought I'd say that about Nate in a million years...

"You're right- it's not. Well, if you ever wanna talk, you know where to find me," I smiled. "Well, I guess I better go. I have an appointment."

"Yeah, me too. Thanks, Lea."

A few hours later I was in my office filling out records when I heard Nate come in. I stopped what I was doing and looked up. "Hey, looks like you made it through the day in one piece," I joked.

"Yea, mostly. Anyway, I was thinking about what you said earlier, about getting out. What are you doing next Friday?"

"Gee, let me check my busy schedule- nope, sorry. Got a hot date," I chuckled.

"Seriously?" he asked. "Does that mean 'what's his name' finally called?"

"No, *not* seriously." *So not seriously.* "I don't expect any of *those* in my foreseeable future." Sulking, I played with my pen.

"Whatever, his loss. Oh, good. I mean, *good* that you're free, not that he didn't call."

"Why?"

"I have two tickets to a tasting dinner or some shit Tina and I were supposed to go to but..."

"But you didn't wanna take just *any* office skank?" I joked. He stared at me, partly annoyed. "Kidding, kidding."

"Besides, everyone knows office skanks are only good for *one* thing," he laughed.

I rolled my eyes, "ew."

"Hey, you brought it up. Anyway, I didn't want them to go to waste. I offered them to Justin, but he can't go so..." he paused. "And you know you're *way* better looking than the office skanks; plus, you have a brain," he teased.

"Gee, thanks?"

"Anytime," he smiled.

"Wait a minute. You don't drink wine and no offense but somehow I don't picture you at a fancy dinner eating escargot sipping cordials."

"I'm Irish. I drink fuckin' *anything*. Hmm..."

"Hmmm...*what?*" I asked.

"I guess there are some things you *don't* know about me, Camioni. Anyway, you in?"

"Um, sure, why not?"

"Cool, see you later."

Chapter 64 ~ Star Wars Episode IV: A New Hope

The rest of the week I was on edge. I wasn't sure why Nate's broken-off engagement had thrown me so much, but it had. Being friends with someone you either had feelings for in the past or perhaps still did could be difficult, even if those feelings were ill-defined, which mine obviously were. To complicate things further, I hadn't just 'had' feelings for Nate- he'd had them, too, and we had acted on them, but that had been a long time ago. Part of me was relieved about Nate's break up; the other part felt guilty for even thinking having those thoughts. I'd left Rachel a message that night, but it wasn't until the next day I heard back from her.

"So, let me get this straight- the girl postpones the wedding- *twice*-, bitches about him spending too much time with his friends, even though he works with them, and *now* she decides she's done with him? Who the fuck does that?" she asked, clearly as pissed as I was.

"People who don't give a shit about other peoples' feelings. I don't really know much more."

"You mean, he didn't *tell* you? I thought you two were close."

"Not *that* close. Not that I ever really liked her but that's not my problem; he can take care of himself." *I hope so.* "Honestly between you and me, I am a *little* worried. Nate has this way of acting like everything's fine when it's not."

"Maybe you two should go out and talk or something."

"Ha, funny you say that because he asked me to go out next Friday."

"*Really.*"

"That's what I said."

"You should go. You could use the distraction, to take your mind off you know who," she said.

"I don't need *that* kind of distraction, not that it'd help anyway."

"Hmm, *really.*"

I rolled me eyes, not that she could see them. "The guy just got dumped weeks away from the altar."

"Whatever. You said it yourself- no one liked her anyway which means, he probably didn't either."

"I think he more than *liked* her, Rach, otherwise he wouldn't have been willing to marry her." *Why is that I want to throw up every time the words Nate and wedding are in the same sentence?* "Anyway, I'm not gonna swoop in for the kill just because he's single, that's not right."

"What's *not* right is you sitting around burying yourself in work when you should be out having fun, checking out the dating scene. I'd join you, but I've got my own ball and chain to deal with."

"Hey, I *heard* that!" It was Tom. He must've been close enough to hear her conversation.

"Oh *chill*," she yelled back, "I'm just kidding." She lowered her voice, "actually I'm not- I'd be interested in seeing what's out there these days."

"I can still hear you!" Tom called out.

"Damn him," she joked. "Anyway, think of it this way- you've known him for a decade; you're already friends; he makes you laugh. It'll be fun if nothing else."

"Yeah, I guess. It's just one night."

"Speaking of dates, don't forget we have that thing next weekend with the moms. But we should do something this Saturday if you're free."

"It's *not* a date and I can't. I promised my brothers we'd go shooting."

"Sounds thrilling. Whatever you say."

"You should try it sometime, you know, get in some target practice in case you get really pissed at Tom," I laughed. "It's surprisingly fun- once you get over the whole fear of holding a loaded weapon part. Plus, it's good for letting off steam."

"Right. Good old Camioni family bonding time; tempting, but no thanks. Say hi to Donnie and Anthony for me. And do yourself a favor- go out. Maybe you'll surprise yourself and actually have *fun*."

"Okay, okay. Well, I'm sure it'll be entertaining, to say the least. Nate has never disappointed in that department." *Or others...*

"Wish I could be a fly on *that* wall."

"Why? All you'd see is Nate on the prowl."

"On the *prowl*? I thought you said you were worried about him."

"I *am*. It's just...that's what guys do when they need to get over someone- they hunt for prey. *Trust* me- I've seen him in action plenty of times."

"Hmmm...I *bet*. Well that *does* sound entertaining."

Long Horn Hunt Club

The three of us met at Donnie's and were in Hartford by 11am. Central Connecticut was beautiful this time of year and further upstate the leaves were beginning to turn, which meant fall wasn't just around the corner, it was already here.

My dad and brothers always brought nothing short of an arsenal to the range and it was interesting to see the looks on peoples' faces when they saw what was inside their bags. They were fun times. This time however, one of us couldn't make it. It'd been six months since my dad had died and over a year since I'd held a gun, and this was definitely one of those times that would never be the same without him. Normally he'd be giving everyone pointers like he ran the place, the same way he used to tell dive instructors how to dive whenever we were on vacation...

'This is how you make an entrance without the enemy knowing you're coming...' or, 'no matter what you do, *always* check your O Valve...' or, my personal favorite and the one that used to scare the shit out of any poor, unsuspecting tourist who drew the short stick and ended up on the same dive charter as us, 'when you're sitting there floating in ice cold water, waiting what seems like a fuckin' eternity for your team to come get you and all you got left is a wet cigarette and an already lit match...'

Going shooting with my dad had been the same experience, but at least he knew what the hell he was talking about and if it's one thing he never fucked with, it was safety. Unfortunately, Anthony had inherited my dad's knack for talking longwindedly and acting like he knew everything, which I had to say could be really fucking annoying sometimes, like now.

"So, Lea," he said, "how's work?"

"Ah, good." Normally I didn't mind talking about my job with my brothers, but for some reason all I kept thinking about was Nate. My brothers may have been off the hook at times and just as unobservant as any other male on the planet, but they could still tell when something was bothering me. Unfortunately, the fact that Anthony had brought that up had struck a nerve, one they both noticed immediately. Me? I just wanted to start pulling triggers.

"*Good*?" Donnie asked, "like business-wise, or good as in you're fakin' that shit because of what went down with Patrick?" Donnie was always to-the-point. In fact, most times he went straight for the heart when you least expected it. Later on, you appreciated it; in that moment however, you fuckin' hated him. Without a word, I hit the target dead-on and smiled. Sometimes I *did* surprise myself. "Damn, Lea, you sure you haven't been shooting since last year?" he asked, impressed. Well he *had* been instrumental in my training.

"Jealous of my skills?" I asked, avoiding his question.

"Ha, ha, funny. As if you could compete with this..." He had a point. I'd hardly pass as G.I. Jane. "Seriously though, nice shooting."

"Must be all that penned-up energy from lack of sex," Anthony chimed in, laughing. It wasn't easy to insult me, mostly because of all the shit I'd taken from both he, Donnie and my dad over the years but still, these kinds of conversations were hard not to hear, not to mention embarrassing, especially at a gun range and especially if you were the only female around.

I smirked cloyingly at the two men next to us before answering, "oh, shut the fuck up, Anthony."

"Just kidding, Lea. Seriously though, you doin' okay?" I nodded.

"Okay, good, cuz I was gonna set you up with this buddy of mine..." And back to guys and their hooking up tactics.

"Uh, *no* thanks, Ant. I'll be okay, not right now."

"You sure?" Donnie asked. "So like, you haven't even *talked* to him? HOT RANGE!!" he shouted before shooting.

"No."

"I saw his new movie." Anthony added.

"Yeah, I'm sure it was *great*." I rolled my eyes.

"Sorry, didn't mean to upset you. But you wanna know what I think?" Donnie asked.

"Not really," I answered. "I mean, if you're gonna say I made a mistake or how I should've done things differently or how much you really liked him...do me a favor- *don't*."

"I wasn't. I was gonna say I know it was probably hard because we all could see how much you really liked the guy or whatever, but I'm glad you stood your ground. You didn't falter and you went after what you really wanted without letting the bright lights of Hollywood stand in your way- that's what good soldiers always do."

"You mean, there are soldiers running around Hollywood?" I joked. "Jesus, now you sound just like dad. I'm not a soldier."

"You're one of the toughest fuckin' people I know, even tougher than some of the guys I've worked with. I *meant*- you didn't give up on your dreams; pretty sure you'll have your own house soon and don't worry, you'll find your guy. I wish *I'd* accomplished all that shit. Eight years with the Teams and all I've got to show for it are battle scars, a few less friends and far too many fucked-up nightmares."

"That's not true. You make a killer Pakistani flatbread." The three of us laughed. "And you got all those Arabian rugs for us..."

"Funny," Donnie pouted.

"You've got *us*, dude."

"Thanks, dude." It wasn't often my brothers hugged. They were seven years apart and sometimes more different than alike. Still, when you were in the presence of Camionis, you felt the love- and everyone knew that as much as Camionis could fight, they had more love and more heart than almost anyone around.

"Patrick was pretty cool, though," Anthony added.

"Yeah," I said, "I guess he was." I smiled to myself as more shots rang out.

"Ok, enough bullshit. After this, who's up for some wings?"

What Donnie had said kept running through my mind. Could he have been right about there still being a silver lining? Or had Patrick been my last hope? One thing's for sure- I was no fucking soldier and as much as I wished for some magical powers, I sure as shit was no Jedi, either.

But then I thought about what The Force was and who the Jedi were and it hit me- Leia wasn't a Jedi, yet she still had the power of The Force within her, because it was in her blood. Luke was far from a Jedi when he was young yet because of his destiny, he was able to harness The Force and become one. Between the destruction of their home planet and the loss of everyone they knew including their parents, Luke and Leia had to endure so much and ended up being stronger because of it. And through it all with the help of their friends, one thing always remained- *hope*. And it was because of this hope they were able to overcome tremendous challenges and evil.

Hope- they never lost it no matter what was thrown at them. I knew I had to do the same. Maybe my future *wouldn't* include Patrick, but I had to believe that when the time was right, I would find my person. Or maybe, he'd find me. I had to remain strong and with my family and friends around me, I knew I'd be okay- If only I could just get through my night with Nate.

Chapter 65 ~ *Forgetting Sarah Marshall*

Friday, September 14th
Lyndhurst Mansion, Tarrytown, New York

"Wow, this place is amazing. What's it called?"
"I don't fuckin' know- I found it online." A typical Nathan Peterson lackadaisical response. Sometimes I wondered how his clients took him seriously. "I was trying to be..."
"*Romantic?*" I asked, chuckling.
"Shut up." We got out of his car and stared at the meticulously manicured, sprawling grounds, still part of the old Rockefeller Estate. And this was the *front* entrance. I couldn't wait to see the view from other side. On a clear day the New York skyline was visible down the Hudson River.

I'd worn capris and a sleeveless top. I had to admit Nate looked good, almost *too* good, in his khakis and shirt. We were escorted to an expansive back terrace made of stone. Lanterns and candles were scattered about long, skirted tables as if for a wedding reception and I smiled, realizing that for the first time in a long time I felt at ease. But as we sat down and I noticed the night's menu, that ease quickly left me.

"What?" Nate asked, noticing the dour look on my face.
"I guess there's always bread and butter..."
"This isn't the fuckin' Olive Garden," he sighed, shrugging me off. "If you're complaining about the menu, don't worry- I got it covered."
"You got it *covered?*"
"Oh, come *on*, Lea. Y5u didn't think I remembered that you hate seafood?" I sat there silent. "Now what's *that* look for?" he asked, raising a brow.
"Nothing. You just...surprised me- that's all."
About halfway through dinner I noticed something about Nate. He'd always had a calm demeanor but tonight he seemed different, in a way I couldn't quite put my finger on. The attention to detail, the charisma- It

was almost as if I was meeting him for the first time- in *another* dimension, of course. Sitting in front of me now, drinking a glass of red wine…this was *definitely* not the version I'd met way back when. That Nate would've probably had tickets to a Monster Truck Rally or a football game…

"Yo, Lea." I had unknowingly drifted off. "Hello?"

"Oh, sorry," I answered.

"You okay?" When I didn't answer immediately, he went on, "look- tonight's all about *us*- no exes, right? That was the deal."

"I wasn't thinking about exes…" *Well, in a way I was, I guess…*

"Good, because we're only here to have a good time. Man if this is how rich people eat, I don't know how they're all not fuckin' starving. Am I the only one who's still hungry?"

"Not really," we laughed.

"Thought so. Wanna get outta here? There's this bar near my place. If you don't want to…"

I contemplated my options: I could either end the night here or…let the fun continue. A part of me thought it might not be such a good idea to join him; the other thought why the hell not? Because the truth was, I didn't really *want* to go home. I was beginning to wonder if Rachel had been right about expecting the unexpected because so far, the night had far exceeded any of my expectations.

A half hour later we were at McFly's, drinks in hand, watching the drunken show around us. Karaoke was always a crap shoot of entertainment, from the crowd to the DJ to the completely random list of songs chosen by a majority who could barely even see straight, let alone read flashing words on a screen. Sometimes it was even more fun to watch than sing.

"Hey," he said, "you should go up there. I'd go with you, but I sing about as well as I fuckin' dance so…"

"Very true," I giggled. "Nah, my throat's too dry. I wouldn't sound good."

"What the fuck does that mean? Half these people are wasted- no one's gonna criticize you except *you*."

My mind drifted off to our second year in Grenada. Maureen had talked me into singing in the school's talent show. It was the first time I'd ever sang in front of a lot of people and I'd been scared shitless but after all the compliments I'd received, my stage fright had improved. That didn't mean, however, that I loved being in front of a crowd.

"Hey, remember last term when my family came to visit and I took them to the talent show? Man, Jenna wanted to cut out early and I wouldn't leave because you hadn't gone on yet. She was so fuckin' pissed she barely talked to me for the next three days."

How could I forget? They'd only been dating a couple of months, not long after *we'd* hooked up, *after* I'd ruined things and lost him to a sneaky little bitch who'd probably been eyeing him for months and won him over by giving good head. I'd sucked it up and pretended to like her, that I was happy for him. The truth was, I never *did* and I never *was*- just like with Tina. But you can't complain about not liking who someone is with when you've pretty much given up, can you?

I smiled, "yea, that was pretty funny. I could feel her eyes searing through me from the audience, fake smile and all. Must've been a fun weekend for you," I joked.

"Yea. But you killed it that night and you know what was even funnier? My parents kept asking me why I was with Jenna."

"Oh? Why?" I looked at him more serious.

"Because they liked you *way* better. In fact, they *loved* you. Guess they were right on that one." *What?*

"You never told me that," I said.

"Yea, well, we all make mistakes we have to live with," he smiled. "Anyway, seriously you should go up there- you know you sound *good.*"

"If these people are wasted, then how can they tell if I *sound* good?" I argued playfully.

"I don't give a shit about what they think- *I* wanna hear you."

"Oh," I blushed. "Um, I don't think so. Maybe next time."

"Why don't you at least *try* to enjoy yourself, Camioni? Jesus."

"I *am* enjoying myself."

He stared at me in disbelief. "*Bullshit.* You're feeling sorry for yourself, just like you've been doing ever since you got back."

"No, I *haven't.* What's that supposed to mean?"

"It means, you don't look like you've been happy for a while."

"Maybe I haven't. What do you expect after breaking up with my boyfriend of two years? I'm gonna be instantly, magically happy?"

"No, but you could at least *try*, you know, go on a date or…or find some random guy to have sex with. That always works for me I mean, with girls."

"Oh, yeah, sure. Let me just pick one out right now from this stellar selection," I answered sarcastically, scanning the bar. "I mean, there's *so* many to choose from. Should I go for the grossly overweight biker or the douchebag with the skinny jeans and the earring? And I tried that- he never called."

"So get back up and try again. Who says you're out with one strike?"

"Why is it so easy for guys to rebound, jump into the sac with I don't know, *anyone*, almost immediately? You sound like you're already over her."

"Of *course* I'm not. And…what makes you think it's easy? Maybe we're just better at compartmentalizing. We *all* have needs, Lea." *Gulp.*

"Compartmentalizing...right. Your fiancé just fucking *dumped* you- you mean to tell me you can just forget everything you're feeling and be with someone else?"

"Depends on who that someone else *is*," he smirked.

"Okay, fine. Then if you're *so* good at it, why haven't you slept with any of those annoying techs that are always eyeing you?" I crossed my arms, angry.

"You sound like a jealous ex-girlfriend," he said. "Shit, give me time- it's only been two weeks. You've been single for two *months*. And I'm not that cold-hearted. On the other hand," he said, cutting me off, "if you'll excuse me, I think I see a potential winner." *Of course, you do.*

"Ahhh...Okay, fine. Wouldn't wanna cock block you or anything," I sat there, arms still crossed.

"Exactly. Thanks. I won't be long." He winked before getting up and stroll confidently towards a cute blond at the bar. It was impressive actually, the way she seemed to be instantly drawn to him, falling under a Dracula-like trance.

"What the fuck? Do you see this shit?" I asked the guy sitting next to me. He ignored me and continued drinking his whiskey. A wave of irritation and disgust came over me. Maybe I *was* jealous. *Fuck it.* I walked towards the DJ booth. I hardly compared to Pat Benetar, but I could sing some of her songs decently. I knew every word and without missing a beat or reading a screen, I belted out the lyrics.

Meanwhile, across the bar...

"Anyway, I totally get what you're saying...hey, are you even listening?" the blond blabbed.

Barely paying attention to her moving lips, Nate turned around. "Uh, yeah, sure, whatever," he answered, waving her off.

"Wow, she's really good. Ooh I *love* Joan Jett."

"Yeah, she is and that's Pat Benetar," he answered, correcting her.

"Who?"

"Shit, never mind. Uh, excuse me, I gotta go."

The audience screamed loudly. As I handed the mic back to the DJ, I noticed Nate reappear out of nowhere, clapping, with a somewhat triumphant look on his face.

"Wow even *better* than I remember. I guess your looks aren't the only thing that improves with age," he smiled.

"Well, I figured you might have had a small point earlier, about having fun, I mean. Back so soon? What happened with *Coyote Ugly*? Too much air between her ears?" I laughed.

"Hmmm- nothing," he smirked "Just wasn't interested I guess."

"*Not* interested? In a hot, younger girl with fake tits who'd probably do you in the bathroom right now if you asked her to?" I replied, laughing at him.

"Tempting, but no. What's that look for?" he asked.

"Oh, nothing." We stood there, neither of us speaking.

"Speaking of fun, I think I've had my share of this place- let's go."

Maybe it was the change of scenery or the alcohol. Maybe it was the company I was in or the fact that I couldn't help but notice the way he'd looked at me all night. Being out with a past romantic interest could have consequences; there were a slew of memories involving Nate, memories I'd tried to forget- not that I ever could. Up until now, I'd thought *I'd* done a decent job of compartmentalizing- I saw him often; I owned a hospital with him. Not once had I faltered; not once had I given in to any feelings I feared might be resurfacing.

For all these years I'd tried to keep him where I thought he'd belonged, in the past, but looking at him now, I wondered- was that where he was supposed to *stay*? And whatever the reason for how I was feeling right now, one thing had just become abundantly clear- I'd been a *hell* of a lot lonelier that I'd thought. So much for compartmentalizing.

It was almost midnight. The two of us stood at Nate's front door, still laughing at the half-naked elderly woman who'd nearly attacked him as we left the bar.

"Thanks for tonight. You were right," I said softly. "I'm glad I came out. I had fun."

"Of *course* you did- you're with me." His smile beamed almost brighter than the streetlights. "You know I never disappoint," he added.

"I'm glad, too." I swayed slightly off balance. "You sure you're okay to drive home?"

"Um, yea well, no, probably not. I'll text Maureen…"

"That's stupid. You should just stay here. It's not like I don't have the room." I shrugged. "Come on, I don't bite. Well sometimes, I guess," he laughed, opening up the door. He *was* right about that.

I haphazardly set my bag on the kitchen counter as Nate opened his fridge. God he was attractive. There'd always been something different about him. He was more of the laid-back, country boy- about as far from my 'type' as I ever thought possible. He'd also been far from perfect, but so had I. Maybe there was some truth to the saying; Maybe *this* time, timing *was* everything.

"Night cap?" he asked, holding up two beers. Instantly I recognized the blue and gold label.

"Where'd you get those?" I asked, walking around the small kitchen peninsula. "I haven't had one of these since…"

"Grenada?" There was an air of flirtatiousness stirring. Our fingers brushed each other briefly.

"Um, yeah."

"Those were good times," he opened each bottle without even looking down.

The look in his eyes was utterly familiar. "Yeah, they were. Not that I'd want to do school all over again but... sometimes I wish we could go back..."

"Sometimes I think the same thing," he said.

"So," I cleared my throat, quickly trying to change the subject, "about Iowa- ever think you'll go back? I mean, all your family's there."

"I don't know, *maybe*...someday. I like it here. You?"

"Right now, I see myself staying. Seems there's more reasons keeping me here than not so..."

"Speaking of reasons," he said as he turned on some music, "didn't see anything *good* tonight, huh?" I investigated him sharply, knowing exactly what he'd meant.

"No."

"Did you at least even *look*?" he sat back down.

"*Yes*. Oh, right. I was supposed to pick some random prey to fuck. Is that how you guys do it?"

"Honestly, I'm not gonna say I haven't." I swear, Nate could really piss you off and with one smile you'd forget what you even were upset for.

"So then, *honestly*- why *didn't* you get that girl's number?"

"Why are you so fixated on what numbers I did or didn't get?" he moved closer to me on the couch.

"I'm *not*-it's just she seemed *so* your type." I smiled evilly.

"And what *is* my type exactly?" he asked, inching even closer.

"*Not* Tina," I uttered under my breath, not realizing he'd heard me.

"Ahh, so the truth finally comes out." *Oops- I guess he heard that.*

"What?"

"Come on, Lea. It's not like I didn't already know."

"Know what?"

"How much you didn't like her."

"What?" I faked. "I...*liked* he..."

"Just like you *liked* Jenna? No, you didn't. Admit it-you didn't think she was right for me."

"I never said..."

"You didn't have to. Just like you don't have to say what you've been thinking all night. 'Cause I've been thinking it, too." *Double gulp.*

"And what's that?" My throat suddenly dry, I had no defense, because we both knew he was right. All evening I kept thinking about how things used to be. I missed those warm, tropical days on an island few of us had ever heard of let alone stepped foot on: A bunch of strangers from all over who'd become- and remained- good friends, some of us *more*. I wished we could go back- that *I* could go back- and say what I'd wanted to say, what I'd needed to say. But I didn't have to.

His answer was simple and to the point. In fact, it was so on point, I didn't have time for any comeback. Without saying a word, he planted a kiss on me so enchanting, so powerful, it rendered me helpless, which was just what I'd needed. Barely able to control ourselves, we laughed hysterically all the way into the bedroom, half-dazed as clothes dropped to the floor, piece by piece.

The next morning...

I hadn't had a night like *that* in a long time. By early morning I could barely even move. I could've stayed in bed all day. Then I heard it. Nate's phone woke us both out of a sound sleep. He rolled over to answer it.

"Shit," he said.

Barely awake, I rubbed my eyes. "Let me guess, duty calls."

"Yeah. Hey, you look good in my college football shirt," he leaned in and kissed me. "Almost *too* good." He kissed me again. "This dog's gonna need a scope so..." I pulled him onto me and began kissing his neck.

"I know- you gotta go in. Think maybe we have time for one more round? Who knows? We may never get this chance again," I smiled.

"They don't need me for a couple of hours so, yeah, I think I can handle that."

"You sure?"

"Definitely," he said, pulling the Iowa State shirt over my head. "*Good.*"

An hour later, we were in the kitchen. I smiled to myself, watching Nate half-dressed, as he threw two bagels in the toaster.

"How's the coffee?" he asked.

"Good, thanks. I needed that. Last night wasn't too bad, either." I winked.

"It was *great*. Haven't had a night like *that* in...too long. Was the bed comfortable?" he leaned over the peninsula.

"Bed? If I remember correctly, we were on the floor half the time," I chuckled.

"Yeah, right. So, about last night..." He stopped himself as he looked at his phone, "Shit- that's Justin again."

"It's okay. We don't have to rehash anything. It was what it was. It's not a big deal," I sulked slightly.

"Yeah, it *was* but...we should talk. Dinner next week?"

"Sure."

"Look, I gotta run- now there's an acute abdomen that just came in and needs an ultrasound, probably will end up in surgery but anyway...Help yourself to anything you need- shower, clothes, whatever. Just lock the door on the way out."

Chapter 66~ Step Up

"You know I only agreed to this because you said you'd come. Otherwise, I would've stayed home. I mean not that I don't love The Fab Four, but who the hell combines wine tasting and The Beatles?"

"Who the fuck knows, but I *guess* we've gotta do the obligatory mother-daughter shit with them *once* in a while," I joked.

"True, true- the price we pay for being the spawn of Beatlemaniacs," Rachel added. "Anyway at least we get to drink and not have to worry about driving. Whoever came up with the idea for a wine bus was a fucking genius. *The wine trolley? Maybe not so much.* "I swear they act like it's still 1964. I mean, do Bunny and Lorraine think Sir Paul is going to randomly show up in upstate New York on his way to London?" She was right on- They *did* still think they were teenagers. Then again, so did we.

"I guess it could be worse," I said, "we could've ended up with mothers from *Valley of the Dolls*." We broke out into hysterics at the crazy thought of being raised by pill-popping lushes. Neither of our mothers were like that however, they never denied doing pot every once in a while.

Rachel and I were standing at a wine barrel gazing out at the beautiful scenery. Not that Baldwin Vineyards was much of a 'vineyard'- It looked more like the bunches of vines my grandparents used to grow in their backyard. Although upstate New York was home to several wineries like this one, most weren't true 'vineyards'; in fact, most didn't even grow grapes- especially reds- because they just couldn't thrive in the climate. The Shawangunk Wine Trail was 60 miles north of New York City in the Hudson Valley and right in the middle sat New Paltz, an adorable, hippie town not far from Woodstock.

"Definitely," Rachel agreed. "Speaking of Beatlemaniacs, where are those two?"

"Last I saw them they were in the middle of debating over Paul versus John. I just let them be, no pun intended. So, how many more after this one?"

"I think two."

"I've barely made it *this* far. I had enough last night to last me a while." I shook my head disappointedly. Although last night had certainly been anything *but* disappointing...

"Oh yeah, how have I *not* asked you yet? How *was* last night?" I looked off then back at her, silently shrugging. "Oooh..." She knew me well enough to know that my flushed cheeks hadn't been from wine. I cleared my throat, cautious as to who was nearby. The last thing I needed was input from the mom peanut gallery. "Come on, spill it. I'll keep an eye out for the Bobbsey twins."

"It was fun. And dinner was...*good.*" I smiled to myself.

"Let's hear it."

"Well," I said, now looking towards the large red and white barn, "like I said, dinner was good, and afterwards...we went to a bar near his place for karaoke."

"*And?*" she asked with anticipation.

"And...you were right. I haven't had that much fun in a long time."

"Of *course* I was." She watched my expression become more pensive. I looked down, guiltily, giving myself away. "Oh, wait a minute. Did you two do what I *think* you did?" I nodded and smiled, ready for the onslaught of questions. "So, how did that happen?"

"How do you *think*? Alcohol."

"And...how was it?" she asked.

"A helluva lot better than I remember. I don't know. For some reason, we ended up clicking."

"Since *when* have you guys ever *not* clicked? How did you leave things?" *In the bedroom.*

"That's a good question- I'm not entirely sure. We're supposed to meet up this week and...talk. But I don't know."

"Know what?"

"Last night was unexpected and unexpectedly great, but I'm just not sure how I feel."

"What do you mean?"

"I mean, something feels different."

"Maybe it's *supposed* to. I mean, look at how much each of you has been through, how far you've come...and now you're partners. I never would've predicted that shit. Maybe it *is* meant to be with you two," she added.

"Or maybe it *isn't.*"

"Why do you always have to be so negative?"

"I don't know- maybe because I always find a way to *fuck* things up. Somehow, even when they're going right, they go wrong."

"*You're* wrong."

"*How*, Rachel? Nate was nothing but great back then and I screwed it up. You'd think I'd have learned something from my past mistakes and been able to hold onto a relationship, onto Patrick. Instead I managed to fuck that up, too. I'm scared I'm just gonna do it again. It's beginning to feel like a curse."

"I think you've had one too many tarot readings."

"Then tell me- how do I change it? How do I get over this?"

"Maybe you can't get over it. Maybe the only way is to face it head on."

"I'm not sure I have it in me."

"Yes, you do. I'm your best friend- I *know* you. You're being stubborn."

"Maybe I *like* being stubborn."

"Then I guess you'll like being alone forever. Being in a relationship *is* scary, every day, for lots of reasons. And merging your life with someone else is even scarier- I know. But if you never take that leap of faith, you'll never know what it feels like to be with the one person you love and cherish more than anything; the one person you'd give your life for if it would make them happy. When you find *that* person, there's no running; there's no turning back. It's like you're two magnets stuck together and even if you tried, you couldn't separate. I can't even picture my life without Tom anymore. He may drive me fucking nuts, he may be a royal pain in my ass sometimes, but I *love* him; he's the one for me. There won't ever *be* anyone else- not in *this* lifetime anyway."

"When you say it that, it sounds so permanent."

"Love *is* permanent, Lea. When you love someone like that, it stays with you. It may change or grow over time, but it never really goes away. You think you feel that way about Nate?" she asked.

"That's the thing- I don't know. I think I've always felt something *like* that for him, but it's just not the same..."

"You mean...as with Patrick? Look at me, Lea. I *knew* it- you still have feelings for him, don't you?"

I kept my gaze, a sad look in my eyes. "So? I doubt he still feels the way he said he did..."

"How do you know that?" she asked as I shrugged my shoulders. "Did you forget how you met the guy in the first place? I mean, the odds of that were like one in a million and look what happened? Who says the odds can't be in your favor again? Look, let's just go over there and get our sampler, okay? We can rehash this later."

We snagged two stools at the bar. Within seconds a woman handed us menus. "Hello, ladies, ready for your tasting?" We nodded eagerly. "Great," she said, pointing to the menu. "You can choose from the white or red tracks and if there's anything else you wanna taste, just ask," she winked kindly. We both agreed to whites and in an instant our glasses were poured. "First, we have our unoaked Chardonnay, aged in stainless steel barrels for 5 months. It's still got that toasty note with a hint of pear, but without the harshness."

"Ooh, that's good," I said, sipping it slowly.

"Yeah, not bad," Rachel agreed. We were halfway through our tasting when I heard three girls come up next to us.

"Remind me the next time we come to one of these things to drink *beforehand.* I swear, if my mother blurts out one more tidbit fact about George Harrison, I'm gonna shoot myself. I had to listen to that shit the whole ride here," the tallest of three commented.

Normally I didn't listen in on other peoples' conversations, but it was kind of hard not to seeing as they were inches away. Rachel and I giggled to ourselves at the odd similarity.

"I mean, at *least* take us somewhere we actually have a chance of running into single guys. They wouldn't be caught dead at a place like this- look around."

They were right. Our moms acted like this was *the* place to be, just because it involved The Beatles when in reality Paul McCartney would probably balk at a 'Magical Mystery Wine Tour'. They were also right about there not being anyone in the vicinity of our age in sight. Most guys wouldn't go near a winery; breweries and distilleries were their obvious first choice.

"I don't think there's a guy here under *60*, let alone 40," they laughed.

"Hey, speaking of celebrities…you're never gonna *believe* who I saw downtown the other night." I kept an ear open, knowing that it was probably someone neither Rachel nor I would care about. "I was at the Towne Grille with Tracy and in walks this hot-as-hell brunette. I didn't recognize him at first but…"

"Who?" one girl asked.

"Anyway, it took me a minute to figure it out- It was Patrick Thomas." *What did she just fucking say?*

"*American Justice*, Patrick Thomas?" one asked.

"Tom Clancy's hottest new *star*, Patrick Thomas?" the other queried. "Holy shit." *My Patrick Thomas? Holy shit is right.*

Rachel snapped her head around so fast I thought it was gonna fall off. I thought I was gonna fall off my chair…

"Are you sure?"

"My friend works the bar and she said he's in town filming or something."

I watched Rachel's eyes widen as she mouthed to me 'what?'. I mouthed back to her, 'I don't know'. Just then my hands began shaking uncontrollably.

"Wow. I can't believe that. Here?"

Our jaws both nearly dropped to the floor. I *had* to know more because it just didn't seem right. He *couldn't* be here. I leaned in, interrupting. "I'm sorry but, did you say you saw Pa...uh Pat..."

"Patrick Thomas?" Rachel finished asking for me.

"Oh, yeah. And get this- apparently, he's looking for a house in the area, too," the girl said.

"Oh...*really*," Rachel paused momentarily. "Did your friend happen to hear how long he might in town for?" She smiled as I sneered at her.

"I think a few weeks, not sure. You guys must be fans, too. I've practically been in love with the guy for a decade," she said. *Join the club, honey.*

"Yeah, I mean, *who* isn't?" Rachel joked. I sat there quietly stirring in the background, as they continued their conversation.

"Totally. He's so hot. And recently single. Guess I'd be too after what the *last* girl did to him." *What?* That got my attention even more than before. I just *had* to hear this shit.

Playing along, Rachel spoke up, "*oh*? What happened? I just assumed it was the same as every other carbon copy Hollywood romance- boy dates girl, relationship can't survive the spotlight, they break up," she teased.

"Or..." the girl said, "she uses him to get *into* the spotlight and then dumps him. Apparently, she was a real bitch- left him high and dry in the middle of his cancer scare for another guy. I heard she's not even that pretty. Whatever he was doing with *her*, I have no idea," she blurted. *Cancer? Jesus Christ these tabloids. You wanna see bitch? I'll show you...*

"*Huh*. You don't say?" Rachel probed further, holding me back as she winked. "Must be *really* hard to get over a girl like that. That's too bad." She kicked me.

"Ouch!" I cried out.

"Not *that* hard. He didn't seem too upset the other night when he was talking to a bunch of girls. Are you okay?" she leaned around to ask me. I nodded, speechless.

"Who knows? Maybe one of us will be lucky enough to end up his rebound while he's here," she winked again before nudging me. They all laughed aloud before saying goodbye and scampering off.

"Would you stop fucking hitting me?" I said angrily.

"Are you getting all this?" she murmured.

"Of *course* I am. I'm right here," I scoffed.

"Well, were you *listening*?"

"Yeah, I was, actually- to all the *bullshit*. *Cancer*? Made me see things *so* clearly now."

"Like what? And you know firsthand none of that shit's true."

"But maybe they had a point- I have no idea what he was doing with that girl, either."

"Well *I* do."

"Enlighten me."

"He was in *love* with you. Just like you were with him; just like you still are."

"Okay, fine. Maybe I am...a little, but it doesn't matter anymore- it's too late; just like with Nate. The past is the past and I can't change it."

"Who says you need to change it?" I looked at her baffled. "Look, I love Nate; I always have. I think he's great; I always have but...I think the real reason, which you already know, that this time doesn't feel right is because you guys weren't *meant* to be."

"And you think I'm meant to be with Patrick," I smirked.

"Exactly," she affirmed.

"Let me guess- you think that just because he's here that I should go find him, pour my lonely heart out to him and when I do, he's gonna forgive and forget like nothing ever happened? What's next? We ride off into the sunset on his white horse and live happily ever after?"

"Hmmm...maybe, yeah. I think that could happen- if you *wanted* it to."

"That's stupid- What *girl* wouldn't *want* that to happen to her?" I asked, annoyed. "That's just not reality."

"A girl who's too afraid to let somebody love her and who essentially continues to deny herself the happy ending she so desperately wants *and* deserves. Reality is whatever you want it to be. Figure it out yet, *doctor*?"

"I'm sorry, Rach, but we don't always get what we want. You said it yourself. Besides, he has my number, or *had* at least, he knows where I live. If he wanted to call me, he would have; if he wanted to see me then he *would* have. He *doesn't* need me, Rachel- he never *did*."

"You've got it all wrong. *You're* the one who needs *him,* and he needs to know that. Patrick Thomas is right here, right now- *your* Patrick Thomas. You can't let him leave without telling him, and you can't let him get away again, Lea."

"Wh..."

"Shut up- I'm on a roll here," she insisted. "Anyway, as I was saying, you still have a chance to be truly happy- *if* you want it."

"It doesn't matter what I want. What am I supposed to do, make an ass out of myself again and hope that it has the same outcome? Show up on some movie set and profess my undying love? I don't think that's gonna work this time. No, I'm pretty sure he'll take one look at me and tell me to leave. I mean if I were him, I don't think I'd want me showing up embarrassing him, either."

"Yes, *yes*, you need to make an ass out of yourself."

"Gee, thanks."

"No, I mean, he *needs* to see you- that's the only way. You've gotta fight for him or at least, *try*. You're my best friend, Lea, and I love you more than anything, but I've never seen you really *try*. You need to tell him how you feel; that you love him and you can't live without him; that he's the only one for you, that you knew it from the moment you met..."

"Where'd you pull that bullshit from?"

"I read it in a fuckin' magazine once," she joked. "I don't know, you needed some kickass words of encouragement so...here they are."

"Is that how Tom won you over?" I laughed.

"*Fuck* no. Tom never said anything *like* that. It was more like, 'what are we beating around the bush for, let's get hitched, babe'. You know what I think? I think maybe you needed the time apart so that you could see your life *without* him like, *really* without him. And maybe in some weird way Nate was meant to help you find your way back to him.

What if Patrick's been trying to find his way back to you and he didn't know how?"

"I don't think so, Rach."

"What if *this* is the how?"

"Sounds like a pretty backwards twisted yellow brick road to me, one I'd probably get lost on."

"Well, you've been pretty fuckin' lost *without* him, so what have you got to lose? Just *do* it; *find* him, tell him everything. You'll never win him back unless you do. This may be your last chance at a happy ending, and you know it."

Chapter 67 ~ Never Say Never Again

I thought long and hard about what Rachel had said. My mind was going in a million different directions and I couldn't focus-at *all*. By Wednesday though, there was no avoiding it any longer. Nate and I were supposed to go out for drinks and as much as I had originally wanted to, I was now thrown by the onslaught of things that had happened over this past weekend.

My first inclination was to call Patrick, yell and scream at him for not having told me he was here but then I thought, that was so obviously wrong. I mean, why would he even care? And although Rachel had had some valid points, *I'd* had an even better one: that if he'd really wanted to see me, he would've called. He knew where I lived, he knew where I worked, and he knew the whereabouts of at least one family member or friend. Still, I couldn't help but wonder what he might say if we *were* face to face, and I'm not so sure I wanted to hear it.

Nate and I met at his place and walked over to the restaurant. I sat, admiring the views of the river while I waited for him to return. I watched him up at the bar. He was as handsome as the day we'd met and still smooth as ever with the ladies. Looking at him now, this all 'grown-up' version of the Nate Peterson I had met way back in anatomy and physiology, brought so many memories back. Good or bad, my time spent in Grenada was some of the best of my life and I wanted to hold onto to those memories forever. If only forever were possible.

In a matter of seconds, Nate was back with two martinis. "Pretty cool place, huh?"

"Thanks- this looks great."

"It *better* be- I told her to make it *extra* dirty," he winked.

"Well, cheers then," I smiled, talking a sip. "No thanks to you, I love these things. Which is never good, considering..."

"Considering what?"

"That one too many usually gets me into trouble," I joked.

"Oh, oh, you mean…"

"Yeah." And that's all I said. It was a well-known fact that I wasn't good at this kind of conversation.

"Right," he answered. "About the other night," he continued, "that was fun I mean, I had a really good time, almost *too* good."

"Me, too," I said. His face turned serious. "What?"

"Nothing, it's just that look you always give me."

"*What* look?"

He sighed, "that never-ending, sexy-as-hell Camioni look, *that's* what." I blushed uncontrollably. "Gets me every time, ya know, always has. That's always been my problem with you."

"Problem?" I took a larger sip this time. I had the feeling he was about to go deeper.

Silently he stared out at the river before looking back at me. "You remember when we first met?"

"Well..."

"Second week, first term. A bunch of us were out at The Boatyard. I was at the bar trying to drown my sorrows because my girlfriend had dumped me; I was pretty fucked up. You came up to me and you what you said?" I sat there, literally stunned by his recollection. "You said, 'everything okay?' And *I* said, 'yeah, I'm good, whatever.' You put one hand on my shoulder and you said, 'now why don't I fuckin' believe you?'."

I swallowed the huge gulp that had now formed in my throat as I thought back to that night. For some reason I hadn't remembered it in the detail that he apparently had.

"And you know what I said next? I said, 'Eleana, right?' And you nodded, still smiling, 'Where have you been all my life?' And of all the things you could've said, you said, 'I don't know, *Connecticut*- does it fuckin' matter? I'm buying the next round and you're gonna forget that bullshit.' You stung me with those golden-brown hazel eyes and that incredible smile and I just thought, *wow*. I knew right then and there we had something special, something I'd never had with anyone else before; something I've never had with anyone else *since*." *What?*

"Why are you bringing all this up now? Is this about the other night? 'Cause..."

"Sort-of. It made me realize that there's something I should've told you a long time ago. Eleana, I've loved you since the first time I saw you...and every day since. I think that's why it's always been so hard for me to move on. Every time I've tried to forget you, I can't. Look, I know that we both had a lot of bullshit that went down when we were in school and maybe things turned out the way they did because it was in part out of our control, but that doesn't mean I ever *wanted* them to be. I never thought anything bad about..."

"Nate, I never stopped caring about you, either I just..."

"I know."

"No, you *don't*. I...had feelings for you, too, more than I ever said. I should've told you."

"I know, Lea; believe me, I always knew." He smiled.

"You *did*?" I asked.

"Of course, I did. The other night was...amazing. I haven't had that in a *really* long time and then I realized why; it was because of *you*—*you're* the reason; you've always *been* my reason. I wish things could've been different and for that I'm sorry. And I wish I could be with someone like you and feel that all the time, the feeling I *didn't* have with Jenna or Tina. I knew someday I'd find it again. Being with you has brought up a lot of great memories and I don't want us to lose any of those."

"Me, neither..."

"But I also started thinking that as great as it *was*, as *we* were, that for some strange reason, this time it feels *different*, like we're more like..."

"*Friends?*" I cut him off, knowing.

"Yeah," he sunk his head. "Are you mad?"

"*No*," I said quietly. "I felt it, too."

"I mean, don't get me wrong, it was pretty fucking great, *you* were great, but something just felt off. At first I thought seeing you and getting to know you again, that maybe it was finally the right time for us, but then I saw how you looked at Patrick. You've never looked at me like that."

"Patrick?"

"Yeah. I mean anyone would be an idiot if they didn't see it. When I saw you two, I knew I didn't have anything close to that with Tina. She wasn't the one for me. Just like I don't think I'm the one for you."

"What? What are you saying?"

"I'm saying that, as your 'friend' and someone who knows you pretty intimately since we just had sex the other night,,,,"

"Shhhhh..."

"Oh, sorry, nobody's listening. Anyway, I'm saying that the right guy for you is still out there, and *I* think...he's closer than you think."

"If you're still talking about Patrick, that ship has sailed..."

"Why? Because you freaked out and bailed?"

"Excuse me, I did *not* bail and I did *not* freak out. I...wait a minute. Since when are you on *his* side? I thought you said he fucked up."

"I never said he 'fucked up'. I said you could do better. *You* fucked up."

"Oh *really. How?* So, you were lying when you said all that shit about him?"

"I was just fuckin' with you. I was trying to make you feel better. I figured you needed to hear from someone that you're great no matter what. Lea, neither of us needs someone to make us successful;

we can do that all on our own. Finding someone who has the potential to make us even greater, now that's something I don't think most people find. I know I haven't, but maybe I will someday and if I'm *really* lucky, with someone as amazing as you. Who knows? But *you*? You found your guy once; you need to get back out there and try again. Don't quote me on this but I think if you do, you got a good shot at getting him back."

"*Back*?"

"And in case he didn't tell you, in case you were wondering what the big mystery was, Patrick didn't just give up and he didn't just walk away- *you* did. He backed down because *you* gave up on *him*. You never gave him a fair chance." He paused for a moment before continuing. "You never told him how you really felt, did you?"

"How did you..."

"Because I know. I've been there, remember?"

"Nate, I never told you how sorry I was..."

"It's okay. It was a long time ago."

"No, it's *not* okay. All that stuff you were saying before. I just could never say it."

"Don't worry, Camioni- I still love you, too. Besides, you *did* sort-of make up for it the other night, so I guess that makes us even..."

"Ha, very funny, Peterson." We both cracked up, still watching each other.

"I'll go and get us another round."

"Sounds perfect," I winked. "And...Nate?"

"Yeah?" he asked.

"Thanks."

"For the other night? *Anytime*," he joked.

"No, well, yeah, but no. Just...thanks.

Chapter 68 ~ My Cousin Vinny

Friday, September 21

Regret wasn't the only thing that could eat at you- so could reflection. So far this year I'd lost my job, my boyfriend and my father, only one of which I'd fully recovered from. Since I'd traded in my once thrilling dual life for an old, mundane east-coast one, a lot of things had changed- some for the better, others not so much. Ever since Patrick and I had split something inside me was off. A part of me felt broken and despite my trying to deny it, I just wasn't the same without him, even with Nate back in my life and maybe it was going to take even longer to get over him than I thought.

Despite what I'd said to everyone including Rachel about letting things go, I actually *had* tried to contact Patrick, but someone else had answered and the emails I'd sent had been kicked back. It didn't take Sherlock Holmes to figure out the mystery. It was like he'd purposely dropped off the face of the planet and didn't want to be found or maybe, he just didn't want to be found by *me*. But could I really blame him? I guess I could've tried to contact someone else like his brother, but what was done was done and I didn't feel that anything I said or did would've changed Patrick's mind because the truth was, if you couldn't even establish contact with someone you were once so close with, they more than likely didn't want you to. I had gotten the hint, and the hint was loud and clear.

And then that night with Nate had happened...and happened...and happened...and although I was engulfed in yet another 'blast from the past' moment in time, one that would no doubt stick out in my mind as one of the best ever, the way I'd felt afterward had been just the opposite of what I'd expected. Days later Nate and I had gone out again, only this time it hadn't led us back to his place- it led me back to somewhere I'd forgotten, a place that after all was said and done, made me happier than any other place I'd ever been. The thing was, it wasn't a place at all- it was a person, and that person *wasn't* Nate after all.

Patrick Wade Thomas, the guy who'd played a superhero on TV but had turned out to be my real-life hero; the guy who every girl wanted but who I'd *had*, until I'd so foolishly let him go without a fight. And I *should* have fought for him, for *us*. I should have given us the chance we deserved but instead when things got rough for me, when I was faced with too many terrifying challenges, I did what most scorpions *wouldn't* be caught dead doing- I put my stinger between my legs and flew away, all the way back to the east coast where I would never have to worry about it again (or so I'd thought).

Having that heart-to-heart with Nate had not only been cathartic, it'd made me realize some things: 1- that I'd always love him and have room for him in my life; 2- that no matter how badly you screw up good friends always understand you and have your back and 3- it's never too late to open or *re-open* your heart for the right person. Despite the fact that I should've told him how I'd felt a long time ago it was okay, but not just because we'd forgiven each other, but because we both now knew exactly where -and *what*- we were meant to be.

It's not unheard of that reconnecting with an old flame can be 'enlightening' in certain ways and everyone knows old feelings can resurface or lead to places you least expect *when* you least expect them to. But to think that you could tell one person that you would forever love them, while realizing you were *in* love with someone else all at the same time? Now *that* just sounds fucking crazy; But that's exactly what happened. While not yet over my ex-boyfriend (that'd be Patrick), I'd hooked up with another past love who wasn't yet over *his* ex-girlfriend/ex-fiancée (ie- Nate), which made me realize how completely and utterly in love with the first guy I was (that'd be Patrick again)- a guy I'd never really fallen *out* of love with in the first place, the *same* guy who I just found out was in New York. If that wasn't a wrench being thrown into an already fucked-up socket...

Not only was Patrick here and *hadn't* told me, now he was looking at *houses*? Since when had he decided to buy a place here? Weren't his parents and sister back in Minnesota? He certainly hadn't said anything the last time I'd seen him, not that it'd been the most pleasant of circumstances. Still, I wished so much that I could go back and tell him how I'd felt, that I could've just put my feelings into words, words that might've landed us somewhere other than where we were right now- apart.

Nate had made me see how stupid I'd been and that maybe it *wasn't* too late. But honestly, I wasn't sure I had it in me. If only there existed an algorithm in one of my medicine books for winning back the famous ex-boyfriend you so foolishly left behind to pursue your not-so glamorous career of putting animals back together...

Yonkers Raceway, Yonkers, New York

"I told you, Ad, I don't know the first thing about this shit. You're lucky if I throw a dollar at a slot machine once in a while."

My cousin leaned over and read the screen in front of me, rolling her eyes with attitude. "Look, all you gotta do is pick a fuckin' horse. It's not that hard. *You're* the one with the medical degree. Don't think of it as gambling, think of it as a game where you can win money."

"Isn't that gambling?" I smiled.

"Oh, shut the fuck up, bitch. Now, who you pickin'- 'Razor's Edge' or 'Cannoli'?"

Since 1907 New Yorkers had been enjoying betting on first thoroughbred and now standardbred horse racing at Yonkers Raceway, renown for Sea Biscuit's 1936 win. Although I heard people rave about The Belmont Races and The Kentucky Derby, they just weren't my thing. To me horses belonged on pastures and dogs belonged in homes, not on tracks, in pens or in stalls. Still, every now and then I went for the social aspect of it and also out of respect for my family because that's just what Italians did. Of course, these kinds of places never lacked entertainment, and my cousins were definitely entertaining people.

Adriana must've asked me to go to the track with her about a dozen times this year and each time I'd turned her down. Finally, I caved and told her I'd go. As if shooting wasn't good enough quality family time on my *dad's* side of the family...*this* side loved the old Italian past times of Baci, dice, cards and OTB- anything and everything they could bet on. And leave it up to my cousin to consider the race track a good place for quality girl bonding.

"Shit, I don't know- both. Why not?" I asked. "Who you pickin'?" Why was it that every time I was around my New York family I started talkin' like *I* was the one who came out of the Bronx?

"I think I'm gonna go for 'Pizzaiola' *and* 'Stargazer'. Maybe we'll win. Enzo won almost two grand last time," she added. "Speaking of Enzo, where the hell is he? He said he'd be here."

"You tell *me*- he's your brother."

"Don't remind me."

"I *won't*," I smiled to myself. "You said he was coming from the pizzeria." Yes, it was true- nearly half my cousins owned pizzerias, delis or 'shops'. The other half were mechanics, contractors or by default, worked 'in construction'. Of course, everyone knows that only half of Italians who say they're 'in construction' actually do any...

"He was picking up Vinny on the way."

"Uh, oh. Now there's trouble."

"Tell me about it. The other week he called me stuck in Fordham and needed a ride."

"For what?" I asked.

"You don't wanna know." Of *course* I didn't. I tended not to ask questions where they weren't welcome. And this was one of those times.

"He still doin' that shit?"

"It's easy money, what can I say? Plus, he ain't that smart, you know that."

"So's picking up dog shit."

"Yeah, true, but he probably won't stop at this point- he's got it good. I'll tell you one thing- I ain't pickin' him up from there again- it's fuckin' shady."

"Most of the Bronx *is*, dumbass."

"Yeah, I know, but he's family."

"Well, not *really*," I laughed.

Technically Vinny wasn't our cousin at all; we weren't related (Thank God). His dad and my Uncle Jimmy (Adriana's dad) had been best friends since they were kids. Adriana and Enzo were like siblings to me growing up, so I'd pretty much known Vinny my whole life. A common thing with Italians, your closest friends and their kids became 'adopted' cousins. As a result, in addition to the dozens of cousins most of us had already been blessed with, we acquired even more. Generally, it was people your parents were *so* close to, they trusted them with business or family matters, a sort-of secret code.

My theory? These adjunct family tree branches were for more support or more likely, to intimidate other families. Because there was no doubt that the more family you had, the more intimidating you could be, and the more people might fear you. But everything comes with a price, not that everyone necessarily cared. Most old school Italians I knew, male or female, believed that it was far better to be feared than loved, even by your *own* family, because it all came down to respect, which led to power and control. And if you could have that kind of power, would you really give a shit if anyone loved you?

Not that my family was in the mob (that I knew of), but I'd always suspected some of my 'other cousins' like Vinny were. Some things in movies were true; others weren't, but of all things people ever heard or saw in mobster movies, one thing remained accurate- once you got involved with that shit, it was nearly *impossible* to get out unless of course, you chose the easy way...

I could understand the temptations and even the perks that came along with it but the older I got and the more I learned, the more that kind of life scared me. Because although men like Al Capone, Bugsy Siegel and Joe Gallo no longer existed, there were still plenty of their kind around- they just knew how to go undetected. And if Vinny remained careful, he'd stay under the radar *and* out of trouble while making money in the process, as long as he did what he was told. In addition to doing various 'errands' and 'odd jobs', he also worked in construction and helped out at my cousin's pizzeria. There was almost no one he didn't know in all of Westchester.

Just then, two young, dark-haired guys dressed in t-shirts and baggy jeans approached. One sported a Yankees hat and the other one with the Italian flag. I could see the gold crucifixes sticking out of their shirts. They could've been twins, if not for the difference in height. As they walked up, they were laughing.

"Yo, cuz, what's up? Sorry we're late. Been here long?" Vinny said.

"Nah, just a fuckin' hour," Adriana teased, "where the fuck were you two?"

Enzo spoke, "had to drop somethin' off quick- sorry. Hey, Lea," he leaned over for a kiss.

"Yeah, sorry. We still got plenty of time before the race starts. What do you guys want? I'll go get it." I opened my purse for a twenty. "I got it- *forgettabout* it," he insisted.

"Thanks, Vinny," I smiled. "We're kinda hungry, too."

"No problem. I'll have Tony fix us up a bunch a shit. They got great nachos. Be back in a few." They swaggered off around the corner.

"Jesus," I said, watching them. "Is there anybody he *doesn't* know?"

"I don't think so," Adriana said. "Last year he scored us front row passes to Jay-Z."

"No shit."

"Anyway, we got some time before they get back so I can ask you. What's this I hear about that guy you work with?"

I set my wine down and looked at her. How in the *hell* in another state and county where I didn't even live and barely knew anyone other than my family she could know about who I worked with was ridiculous- *and* next to impossible.

She noticed my shocked look and continued, "I guess you forgot how many people *I* know."

"Oh, so you *didn't* hear it from anyone in the family," I stated.

"Believe it or not, *no*. Not this time."

"Then who? And exactly 'what' are you referring to? Not that it's anyone's business," I argued.

"Danielle. She works at Lyndhurst Mansion and happened to recognize you last weekend while on shift. I guess she didn't want to interrupt you…"

"The *fuck*? Interrupt *what*? Two friends of the opposite sex aren't allowed to go out to dinner?" I asked, still annoyed she'd brought it up.

"You tell me. Danielle said you looked like more than *that*," she smirked. "So, were there any *benefits* that came along with it? She said he was pretty hot."

"Maybe, but it was a one-time thing." Damn, why was I such a bad liar? "I think I need a break from the mental shit that goes along with actual boyfriends for a while," I said.

"Isn't that what you've been doing for the past four months?" I nodded. "So, does this mean you're done with *all* men right now, even *Patrick*?" I crinkled my eyebrows at her suggestion. "I mean, isn't he here, like upstate, filming or something? Aren't you gonna go see him?"

"Now, how the *fuck* do you know *that*? And no, I'm *not*."

"I just *do*," she shrugged. "So, is that what you really want, Lea? To be completely miserable and alone while someone *else* steals him away from you *and* your chance for a...whatever you wanna fuckin' call it?" I sat there, silent. "I don't think you do."

"Nobody *stole* him away- he left," I insisted.

"I thought *you* were the one who left. Look, the way I see it you got two choices: you can give up and run away scared like you always do whenever someone gets too close or...you can conquer you fears and go after what you've always wanted, what you've always been too afraid of."

"I don't think I know what that is anymore," I sulked.

"You're *so* full of shit, Lea. I've looked up to you my whole life; hell, I wanted to *be* you- but not now. You've never been afraid to go after what you want. You went to college and medical school and now you own your own practice- but when it comes to guys, you really suck at it, you know that?"

"Yeah, well, none of us are perfect."

"It's not about being fuckin' perfect. If *I* was perfect, I'd be 5'9" and have guys like Vinny workin' for *me*...it's about being happy with your life, Lea. After all you've experienced these past few years, haven't you *learned* anything?"

"Yeah- you can't always get what you want. Oh, and the sand *isn't* always more sparkly on the other side."

"Shit, you have a *lot* more to learn than I thought."

"What does that mean?" I asked.

"Drink some more wine and I'll tell you."

Chapter 69 ~ The Goonies

Sunday, September 23rd

"Hey," I said, as I stood nervously on the doorstep.

Rachel was shocked to see me when she opened the door. "Hey, not that I'm not glad to see you, but what the hell are you doing here? It's 9:00 on a Sunday."

"Can I come in?"

"Of *course* you can come in. It's not like anyone's running around naked," she smiled.

"Sorry I didn't call first. I figured if I didn't jump in the car and come over here, I would've had time to talk myself out of it."

"Out of what?" she asked, as we went inside.

"Okay, so, about what you said. I was out with my cousin the other night and I started thinking. After my night with Nate..."

"*That* night?"

"No, *no,* not *that* night; the *other* night, as in...Wednesday."

"Oh," she said, relieved, pulling up a chair. "Come on, sit down. I'll make us some espresso."

"Ah, no thanks. I've already had three- any more caffeine, I won't be able to drive," I said.

"Okay, seriously. You're scaring me. What's up? You don't look so good."

"I don't feel so good, either."

"Why? What happened with Nate?" she asked, concerned.

"Is that a *trick* question?" She glared at me as she turned around for a mug. "I'm kidding. You mean, what *didn't* happen?"

"What the fuck are you talking about?" she asked.

"Nate and I went out for drinks, like we'd planned and...he kind-of, sort-of told me he loved me; he always has."

"What?!" I nodded. "I knew it. That's *great,* right? Or...*not?*" she changed her response when she saw my face. "What did you say?"

"I told him I loved him, too."

"So, what's the problem?"

"The problem is...I'm not *in* love with him. We both realized we've made mistakes and..."

"You're *killing* me over here." Tom had come around the corner causing both Rachel and I to momentarily pause our conversation. "Why do you women always have to make shit so long and drawn out? Just get to the point," he went over to grab some coffee.

"Give her a fuckin' break, will ya?" Rachel said, smacking him as he walked by. "She's been through enough this year, don't ya think?"

"Okay, fine, sorry, Lea. You know I love you."

"Anyway, go on," Rachel pressed, shooing off Tom.

"Well, we both agreed the past should stay in the past to make room for the future and the only way for that to happen is for us to remain friends, and *only* friends."

"Oh, I half-expected that..."

"That the martinis would've worked their magic again?" I snickered.

"Maybe," she winked. "So, what now? Why the impromptu visit?"

"How do you feel about a little ride up to the country?" I asked.

"What do you mean? We *are* in the fuckin' country." Her aggravation arose.

"You know, Rach, despite what you wanna believe, we *are* still in civilization," Tom argued, just to piss her off.

"Hmm, you could've fooled me," she huffed at him. "Anyway...*ride*...another winery?"

"No," I said, shaking my head. "Rhinebeck- Patrick's aunt lives there."

"*Patrick*?" Tom asked. "Wait, I'm confused- didn't you guys break up?"

"What else is new?" Rachel rolled her eyes at him again. "They did, but he's...back."

"What, here?"

"No, in Rhinebeck, we *think* anyway," she cut him off. "Lea's gonna win him back."

"Hurry up before I change my mind." Rachel grabbed her keys. Tom began to follow. "What do you think you're doing?" she asked him.

"What does it *look* like I'm doing? I'm coming with you."

"No, you're not- this is girl stuff."

"You sucked me into the story- now I *have* to see what happens. Plus, you might need backup."

"Good point, but I'm driving. Let's go."

An hour later we were in Rhinebeck. As we pulled in, I thought back to last year's Thanksgiving. It was the first time I'd seen him in weeks; he'd been home briefly from filming. It'd started out as a great weekend, until we'd run into Nate and his girlfriend in the city. I smiled to myself for a moment, thinking about the tidal wave of shit that had happened since. Who knew I'd end up here?

The past had really caught up to me hard and fast and I'd barely been able to handle it. But the past was the past, I thought-I couldn't worry about it anymore. All that mattered was the future, *my* future, a future I could suddenly no longer envision without Patrick. Nate and Rachel had *both* been right- he needed to know- everything- and if he shut me out, then at least I'd know and I could put that chapter behind me and finally move on.

My hands trembled as I opened the car door and walked up the front steps. The was far from the feelings of excitement and anticipation I'd had during my last visit. I knocked on the door and almost instantly Aunt Jennie answered. She was as surprised to see me as I was that I'd actually made it all the way here.

"Eleana...what...what are you *doing* here?" She looked just as beautiful and well put-together as I remembered, about the exact opposite of what I looked like right now. Still I didn't care, as long as I could see Patrick. Her smile quickly faded as soon as I told her why. "Oh," she said, "well, um, he...he's..."

"I understand if he doesn't want to see me..."

"No, I mean, he's...not here. He left a little while ago."

"Oh," I lowered my head, "do you know when he'll be back? I *really* need to talk to him."

Her face went dour. "I'm afraid he's not coming back." *What?* "I'm sorry, honey, he's headed back to the city. Said he had a bunch of work to do in preparation for the convention Monday. I think he's flying back to L.A. immediately afterward."

"*Convention*?" I asked, saddened by the news.

"Some comic thing. Honestly if I could help I would, but I don't even have his new number." *That makes two of us.* "He didn't say where he was staying, either."

"Oh, okay. Thanks anyway, I guess," I said, defeated. *I guess that's my sign.*

"Are you okay?"

A tear started in my eye as I tried to play it off as if I actually were. "Never mind, it's nothing. It's just...too late. I'm too late, that's all." *Story of my life...*

"Eleana, look at me." I glanced up. "It's never too late to tell someone you love them. Believe me, I know." She smiled once more and then I headed back to the car.

"So, is he here?" Rachel asked anxiously.

I shook my head, "no, he's gone."

"What?" Tom asked, "what do you *mean* he's gone? Is this the right house?"

"He *was* here, but I guess he left to go back to the city."

"Well, what are we waiting for? Let's go."

"She doesn't know where."

"So, then *call* him."

"I *can't.*"

"What do you mean you *can't*?"

"I mean, I don't have his number and neither does she. He...changed it and I think I know why."

"Maybe it's not because of you, Lea."

"It doesn't matter anyway. He's going back to the west coast Monday- This was just another dead end."

I felt defeated and lost. There was nothing I could do about it now; I should've told Patrick when I'd had the chance but instead, I'd freaked out and bailed, just like Nate had said, and now he'd never know how I really felt.

That evening, I didn't feel like seeing or talking to anyone. My phone was inundated with calls from my mom, my brother and yet another 'friend' of a friend who had some stupid ass question about one of their dogs on a Sunday night...I almost dialed Nate's number, but I stopped myself. I turned on the TV but of course the first thing on was the last scene from *Sleepless in Seattle*, where Meg Ryan and Tom Hanks finally meet at the top of The Empire State Building. "Perfect," I said aloud, "just fucking *perfect.*"

And so there I was, back where I'd started, alone and disappointed, in both fate and myself, stranded with no hope left for redemption or a relationship reboot. I had every intention of telling Patrick everything I hadn't been brave enough to say, from the very beginning all the way up to the part of the story where I was lost without him. In less than 24 hours Patrick would be gone, maybe for good. If only I had been more brave; if only there was more time. But there wasn't, and I didn't have one minute to waste of what was left.

As I sat on my couch watching the unique casting duo on my TV screen work their magic as they'd done so many times before, I thought...maybe all hope *wasn't* lost; I might still be able to win him back or at least, give it my best shot. But it would mean finding the courage to be bolder than I'd been my entire life. It wouldn't compare to a rendezvous at the top of The Empire State Building but still, it had the potential makings of a happy ending. After all, this wouldn't be the first time I'd beaten such odds- it was only four years ago that I'd accidentally 'walked' in on a hugely publicized panel discussion involving my then (and now still) celebrity crush *and* an entire TV show cast. *Wait. Wait a second...*

If I was truly intent on listening to my heart, I had to act fast. But just how was I going to find him? I'd have to know exactly when and where Patrick would be so I could get him alone...and if I did, would he *listen*? I weighed out my options but the only plan I could muster up was crazy. No, scratch that- it was fucking *ridiculous* and far from failproof. I mean, could it even work? Maybe, but the problem was I didn't exactly *have* a plan. My other problem? There was *no* way I could pull it off without some major help. I knew just who to ask, but it was no doubt gonna leave me owing lots of favors and be...

"...a *fucking* long shot. Are you sure about this, Lea? I mean, it sounds a little fuckin' crazy, even for *you*," my cousin said on the other end.

"Yeah, I'm sure and *yea*, I know," I answered.

"Okay, but only if you're sure. Once it's set in motion, there's no turning back. And...it's probably gonna cost you."

"That's what I'm counting on," I said.

"Let me make some calls." She hung up.

Fifteen minutes later Adriana was back on the line; because the truth was, there was really only *one* person she needed to get a hold of.

"Wow. That was fast."

"I'm good, what can I say? Anyway, here's the deal. I don't know how you got this lucky but...turns out Vinny knows a guy who knows a guy whose brother does security at you'll never guess? The Javits Center."

"You're *kidding*."

"Nope- wish I was, because now you just roped me into this shit," she complained.

"Come on, you *love* getting roped into shit with me. You act like we're doing something illegal."

"You mean like the time we made all those prank calls and the next day the cops showed up at my house asking questions? No, thanks," she laughed. "But funny you bring that up cuz it's gonna involve some uh 'stuff' you may not wanna do."

"I'm not gonna have to *kill* anyone, am I?" I joked.

"No, asshole, but you *are* gonna have to think outside the box a little and break some rules."

"Meaning?"

"Exactly how far are you willing to go for this guy?"

MONDAY, SEPTEMBER 24TH, 2012
NEW YORK COMIC-CON

"I can't believe I agreed to this," I uttered as we stepped off the train and onto the platform.

"*You*? It was *your* fuckin' idea. Are you kidding me? I called outta work for this shit."

"I think they can make pizzas without you for a day. If it makes you feel any better, it's for a good cause. And you don't look half bad, either, for an alien..." I joked.

"Bitch," she joked. "He better be worth all this. Right now, I'm not even sure *you're* worth all this. My ass barely fit into these leggings."

"Then stop eating all those calzones."

"Fuck you. Walk faster."

"Kidding, and what are you even talking about anyway? What are you, a size zero? What's this?" I asked, as she handed me something.

"I got you an extra Metro Card for the subway. Think of it as your doubloon. Let's go." Thirty minutes later we arrived at The Javits Center and were out front in the middle of the masses of fans.

"Who are we waiting for again?" I asked as I watched all the people in costumes go by.

I had a brief flashback to summer 2008 in San Diego. Comic-Con; an alternate universe even more whacky than Los Angeles itself. I'd run into an inconspicuous Patrick Thomas outside before meeting him again inside *out* of disguise, so to speak. For all I knew this time, Patrick would sick his people on me, throwing any last chance out the window, and *me* out onto the street.

"Vinny said his friend would have someone meet us out front with passes," Adriana said. "I think I see him now." Out of nowhere, a burly guy about 6 foot plowed through a crowd of screaming fans to reach us.

"Yo," he said gruffly, "you Adirana?"

"Yeah," she answered back just as rough. At under 5 feet, she may not have seemed intimidating...until she opened her mouth.

"Come wit me. Here, yous put these on." He hurried us inside and quickly ushered us towards an alcove off to one side. "Ok, wait here. Someone will be here to get you in a few minutes." He ran off, answering a call on his headset.

As we stood there waiting, I looked around. Oddly familiar scenery, I thought. I fixed my cape and adjusted my mask, letting out an uncontrollable giggle.

"What's so funny?" Adriana asked.

"I was just thinking- here I am on this wild rescue mission to win back Patrick and I look like a fucking idiot. Why couldn't I have been Wonderwoman? At least that costume's attractive."

"Hey, you asked me for a hookup, you got it- signed, sealed and delivered well, *almost*. Let's not be too fuckin' picky, huh? I mean at least it's form-fitting. Let's just hope this works."

"Why wouldn't it work? Between Tommy Ugatz and whoever else they got on the inside, I feel like this is more *Oceans Eleven* than *The Goonies*. I keep waiting for Matt Damon and Brad Pitt to walk around the corner..."

"Don't we both *wish*..."

Chapter 70 ~ Return to Me

They weren't kidding when they'd said a few minutes. As if we were in fact trying to pull off some big money-stealing scheme, another guy showed up almost exactly 90 seconds after the first guy had left us. We were led down a long hallway to a set of large double doors.

"This is it. They're scheduled to start in less than ten minutes. Everyone knows to expect you guys, uh, ladies, so no one will bother you," he smiled, "you know, in case either of you causes a, uh, scene."

"A *scene*?" I asked.

"Oh, there's probably gonna be a fuckin' scene," my cousin answered sarcastically. I shot her an angry look. "So, what do we do now?" she asked.

"Just wait here. One of the security guards will let you in." In a flash he was gone.

"So, what are you gonna say?" she asked.

"I have no idea," I said.

"Wait a minute. You just made me go through *all* this trouble and you don't even know what you're gonna *fuckin'* say?" she argued. "How the hell do you expect to 'win' him back then, brainiac?"

I shrugged my shoulders indecisively. "I figured I'd just say the first thing that comes to mind when I see him."

"Well? Anything coming to mind yet? I mean, it doesn't get more down to the fuckin' wire than this, Lea."

"Not really."

"Great."

Just then the door opened and a security guard rushed us in. Again, we were ushered through the crowd only this time, we kept going until we were close to the stage so close, I almost panicked. We both looked at him.

"*These* are our seats?" I said.

"You guys got front row section, backstage passes, the whole nine yards so...Good luck."

Immediately I turned to Adriana. "What does *he* know, too?"

"*What*? I *had* to tell them something," she smiled sneakily.

"Yeah, some story. I hope it works out for ya, doll," he said before leaving.

It didn't take long for the room to fill to maximum capacity. Although not quite as large a room as the last time I'd been in this 'situation', there had to easily be 300 people in here. Most were loyal fans, anxious to ask questions and get the down low on any upcoming projects; the rest was a mix of photographers, reporters and security scattered throughout in strategic locations. The lights flashed and after a brief announcement the members of the cast of *American Justice* walked up and across the stage from right to left, one by one. I knew them well, especially the last one, who'd gotten his own special introduction.

Ninety days may not seem like a long time in the grand scheme of things but to me, it had felt like an eternity, even with all that I'd had to keep me occupied. He looked different somehow; I couldn't quite put a finger on it. Was it relief that he was no longer with me? His recent rise to fame? Or was it some newfound love, one that he'd be asked about here today? I let out an uncontrollable gasp at the sight of him, catching a girl standing next to us off guard.

"Are you okay?" she asked.

"Yea, she just uh, swallowed her gum, that's all. She *loves* Patrick Thomas, almost more than life itself," Adriana said. "Ouch!" I whacked her.

"Don't we *all*," the girl said. "I can't *wait* to see him backstage after!"

"Yeah, *us*, too," she lied.

If we even got backstage...I thought. If I messed this up, we'd be headed straight back home empty handed. I sighed deeply and stared up at him. His hair was medium length and he'd grown what looked to be a decent scruff on his face. He was as handsome as ever, clearly too handsome to be with someone like me.

"I hope you're ready," Adriana commented. "It's now or never." I smiled curtly at her as the presentation began. *Me, too.*

After about 30 minutes of watching old clips and interviews, the audience grew anxious for more, while I suddenly grew more anxious to leave. I'd had no idea the cast of *American Justice* would be here, especially since the show had ended more than three years ago. But apparently, as we'd just seen on the big drop-down screen, a spin-off was in the works.

And now, the moment everyone had been waiting for except maybe, me- the cast would speak freely about their past experiences on the show, future plans and glimpses into their lives off screen. And after that, their attention would be turned to the audience for questions, where fans would finally get the answers they'd been searching for, making their trip here worth it. For me, it would be a chance to finally redeem myself and to see how this story would end. *Just don't run...*

Nearly every hand in the room raised and as I turned around to examine the crowd, I felt my nerves rise up further. This was the real thing now. I had to just do it. Several minutes went by and it wasn't long before they called on someone in our direction, but it wasn't me- it was Adriana.

"Yes the ah, alien over here in the second row," the panel discussion leader said.

"Hi," she answered. I stared at her- not an ounce of fear in her eyes. You'd have thought she'd done this before. "Yeah, I got a couple quick questions for Patrick." Just then he turned our way and panic began to set in as I watched his face.

"Hey there," he said kindly.

"*One*, is it true that you've been house hunting here? *Two*, I was just wondering if there was anyone in particular you really miss, uh, *working* with the most."

"Well, that's hard to say," he laughed, glancing over at his castmates, "they're all extremely talented…"

"Yeah, right, I'm *sure* they are," she uttered dismissively, "I mean someone who *isn't* here but if she, I mean, 'they' *were*, it'd sorta complete the whole reunion thing ya got goin' on."

Patrick's confused look said it all. Yep, he thought she was nuts. "I don't quite understand the question."

"Uh, ya know?" she asked, grabbing me by the cape, "my *friend* can probably phrase that better than I can so…" She pulled me closer to the mic, lowering her voice, "now's your chance."

"What?" I asked, now completely freaking out.

"Take off your mask," she almost whispered.

"No," I tried to say quietly without drawing too much attention.

"*Yes!*" she insisted, raising her voice.

"*No!*" I said, louder. Just then she ripped it off my head and I froze, unable to speak.

If there were ever a moment in time I'd wanted to suspend, jump out of and replace myself with someone else, this was it but unfortunately, I had no disappearing powers. My costume didn't even light up. It didn't matter because it was too late- Patrick had already seen my face and judging by the stupefied look on his, I could feel the odds were now definitively stacked against me.

"Uh…um…*hi*," I finally was able to say. He didn't speak.

This was my chance; my *last* chance. I had to go for it- and whatever was about to come out of my mouth I'd have to live with. I just hoped it wouldn't come out sounding like a bunch of mumbled nonsense.

"Um, I was just wondering if, *if*, there was anyone you *did* happen to miss, who in your opinion might have left the show prematurely, who maybe you wished would've stayed longer. And if that someone later on realized she'd made a *huge* mistake by going off on her own and how sorry-and stupid- she was for leaving in the first place, would you consider having her back?"

My heart dropped as I heard the audience, now silent, await his response. It became *so* silent I thought for sure Patrick could hear my gulp from where I was standing. Everyone including the cast members, who by now had also recognized me, listened intently. I watched Patrick, who remained visibly caught off-guard by my impromptu appearance. I wondered what was going through his mind, seeing me standing there, some ridiculous caped crusader. I had no doubt that he now thought *I* was completely out of my mind, and probably now wondering why he'd ever gotten involved with me in the first place…

Was he even going to answer me, or would he shoo me away for ruining yet another major press conference? I waited, unable to stop my legs from shaking yet unable to run at the same time. Then finally, he spoke.

"Well, that depends," he answered cautiously, still wearing a serious expression.

"On…*what*?" I asked nervously.

"Just how *sorry* is she?"

"Sorry enough that she'd do anything, including masquerading around Manhattan as some gaudy, second-rate superhero, for another chance just to…to tell him…"

"Tell him *what*?" he asked curiously.

"That she was wrong for leaving behind the best thing that's ever happened to her thinking she'd be fine when in fact, she's *completely* miserable and lost without him. That she's not afraid anymore. That if it's *not* too late and if he still feels the same way, she might still be able to ask him to be hers in front of all these people because if she doesn't, she'll regret it for the rest of her life?"

I had blocked out just about every noise around me. It was like all I could see was a clear path between me and Patrick. All I kept thinking was how the *hell* I had managed to say all of that and still be standing?

"Oh, well in *that* case…*yeah*, I guess I'd have to *seriously* consider it." There it was- the smile I'd been wishing and hoping for, the one I had missed so terribly.

There was a precipitous uproar amongst the crowd. Lights began flashing nonstop from all angles and the next thing I knew, we'd been ushered away yet again only it wasn't outside- it was to some dimly lit backstage-type area. Adriana and I looked around. There wasn't a soul in sight but for two big security guards.

"So, is this where we get bags thrown over our heads and taken out back?" I joked.

"Probably," she laughed.

Just then a door opened and a young woman motioned us inside. "Okay, wait here," she said, pointing us towards a couch and empty chairs in what looked like a waiting room. "He shouldn't be too long. Make yourselves comfortable. There's coffee and snacks over there."

"*He*?" I asked.

"Patrick," she answered, "when he's done signing autographs, he'll meet you in here."

Adriana walked over to the refreshment area and poked around. "Want anything?"

"Ah, no thanks. I think I'm gonna throw up," I said.

"Suit yourself- I'm starving." She grabbed herself a bagel and a Diet Coke and sat down. "Oh, look, there's even a TV. I wonder if they've got you on replay," she laughed.

"*So* not funny right now."

"So," she continued babbling, "what are you gonna say *now*? I mean, I don't know how the hell you're gonna follow *that* up..."

"Funny, thanks. Honestly it's all a blur. The words just kept pouring out. I don't even know if any of it made sense."

"No, not really, but don't worry," she assured me, "if it's on tape maybe they'll play it at the wedding." She shoved another piece of bagel into her mouth.""

"Oh just shut it. For all I know, he's just coming in here to personally escort us out of here."

"*What*? I just figured that's next."

An hour later we were still waiting and I was beginning to wonder if Patrick was gonna show. *Maybe he changed his mind.*

"He didn't change his mind. Did you see all the riled-up fans in there? They've probably been waiting half their Twittering-Instagraming-Facebooking lives to be this fucking close to him. You should know how crazy they can be- you used to *be* one of them. Actually, you still *are*." I shot her a nasty look before getting myself a drink. "What? You gonna argue with me? *Look* at you- you were so desperate you asked *me* for help," she said, laughing.

My back was still facing her when I heard the door open. Patrick had walked in, apparently right in the middle of our discussion.

"She's right," he said.

I spun around, my jaw nearly dropping to the floor. I stood there, in awe that he was standing there, even more so that we was agreeing with her. *Now you decide to be tongue-tied, Eleana? Come on, say something.* "Uh, hi," was about all that came out.

He looked over at Adriana, seated comfortably on the loveseat. "And you're..."

"Adriana, the cousin. We met last Thanksgiving, at my mom's." Her smile, even through her mask, was conniving as all hell.

"Oh, right, right. I remember. Nice outfit," he smiled.

"Anything for family and by that I don't just mean this uncomfortable-as-shit *leotard*," she sneered back.

"Oh you mean, *you're* the one responsible for this?" Patrick asked, pointing out the both of us.

"Responsible? Fuck no. I just laid the uh, groundwork, if you know what I mean..." Clearly he didn't, judging by his confused look.

"Ah," I interrupted, "what she *means* is that she helped me carry out the, uh, plan."

"Hmmm, however you did it, I've never seen anyone pull this kind of thing off."

"Yea, well, not everyone has *Vinny*," she said.

Immediately Patrick looked back at me for clarification. "Let me guess, another cousin?"

Adriana and I both shrugged our shoulders, grinning, "not...*really*," we said. Still confused, he stood there.

"Nevermind. It doesn't matter. I'm just glad you actually saw us, I mean, me."

"Did you think I was gonna have you kicked out because you snuck in here?" he asked.

"*Excuse* me, nobody snuck- we had *passes*," Adriana said abruptly, shutting him down, "and I hate to break it to ya, but you wouldn't have been able to so..."

"Anyway, it was impressive...and also this was kind of the last place I expected to see you. I figured if you were gonna crash anything, it'd be another wedding."

"Oh, right." I hung my head bashfully. "So, does this mean you're glad to see me?"

He walked over and without saying a word, leaned in and kissed me. "Does that answer your question?"

"Ugh, alright, alright, I'm convinced already," Adriana interrupted. "Excuse me while I go outside and fuckin' puke," she said and left.

I was in total disbelief that my plan had actually worked, that Patrick was still standing here and that I still had a chance to make things right. "So," I said, holding his hands, "about what I said in there.."

"Wait, you're not thinking of taking any of that back, are you? Because you *can't*- it's out there, and I'm pretty sure someone's got it recorded, *this* time."

"Ah, no, it's just...there's *more*," I answered.

"*More*? How could there be more?"

"There's something important I sort of...left out."

"I'm listening."

"Patrick, I'm in love with you. I have been for a long time, I just couldn't say it. I was afraid that once I did, you'd change your mind about being with me and find a reason to leave."

"Why?"

"Because of almost every other guy before you, because of *me*. I've always been afraid of things not working out, of being disappointed. I guess I just learned that if I was the one to leave first, I'd never be hurt or let down…"

"So that's why you left. Eleana, look at me," he said, holding my chin up, "I wouldn't have done that and I'm *not* every other guy- I'm *me*, the guy who's still in love with you, too, who never fell *out* of love with you. I never wanted you to go but you gave up without giving me, or *us*, a fair chance. The way you looked at me that night…it really hurt me. I just assumed I wasn't what *you* wanted anymore; that everything you wanted was back home and I couldn't compete with that…"

"Compete with what?"

"With your job and your friends and…"

"*Nate*?" He shrugged. "Patrick there's *nothing* there I mean, there *was* but that's…that's over. We're just partners and good friends. It was never a competition, but you're right- you deserved better than me- you still do. I've never thought twice about giving 200% of myself to everything I've ever wanted…and the one time in my life when I really needed to come through, I didn't. When I finally got everything I thought I'd always wanted…I realized I was wrong. I was still missing something- the one thing I let slip through my fingers because I was too afraid to fight for it. I'd give anything to have it back." The tears were streaming down full force as I pleaded to him.

"And what's that?" he asked.

"Us. You may not have needed me, but I *always* needed you- I was just too stupid to see it."

"And what about the hospital and your dreams? Your future?" he asked.

"I'm looking at it. Patrick, I don't care about any of that anymore well, I *do*, it's just…right here, right now- *this* is what's most important. The rest? We'll figure it out- together. I know it will all be okay now. I don't want to be afraid anymore- I want *you*." I pulled away from him for a moment and reaching into my pocket.

"Lea, wh…what are you doing?" Patrick asked.

"What does it *look* like I'm doing? I'm getting down on one leotard, which hopefully won't rip," I said as I kneeled down on the carpeted floor.

"What the hell is that?"

"It's a ring pop- we got 'em from one of the vendors," I smiled. "Just give me your hand, will ya?" I grabbed his left hand with both of mine and looked up at him, "Patrick Wade Thomas, will you marry me?"

"Just tell me, and be *honest*, if I say 'no' is that guy Vinny gonna barge in here and break my fingers?" he asked, half smiling.

"Nah," I laughed, "Vinny doesn't like to get his hands dirty. He'd probably send someone."

"Gee that makes me feel *so* much better."

"I'm kidding. So…is that a 'yes'?"

"Only if you wear this outfit for the rest of the night. I swear you look better in a superhero costume that *I* do."

"Deal."

Chapter 71 ~ Ever After

Spring 2013
Sonoma Coast, California

It was a beautiful spring day in Northern California. Yeah, I know, the east coast girl who swore her wedding would be in the midst of a New England fall had officially crossed over to the dark side. A part of me felt like a traitor for making my family and friends travel across the country, but the other part of me didn't care, because in my mind I had uncovered the best of both worlds- a sprawling vineyard that overlooked the ocean, a one-of-a-kind gem, tucked away on the Sonoma coast where few would expect to find it- kind of like Patrick.

I never dreamed in a million years (well, maybe just a *little*) this kind of thing could happen to me but here I was, thousands of feet up in a tower like a princess, about to be rescued by her prince. I gazed out the enormous arched windows, still in complete amazement that I was even here. Acres upon acres of lush, green forest and rolling hillside surrounding flourishing vineyards, all overlooking a gorgeous backdrop of deep blue sea. If I closed my eyes, I might have believed I'd been transported to the south of France, Tuscany or perhaps The Cliffs of Moher. It was so flawless and so exquisitely picturesque that it almost wasn't real. Kind of like my life had been for the past five years.

It had been a long and crazy ride filled with lots of ups and downs and I knew there'd be more ahead but that was okay because I was finally ready to take on whatever life wanted to throw at me. It wasn't going to be easy, but life wasn't meant to be easy, was it? I mean, how are you supposed to live and learn without ever being challenged? And there had been *plenty* of those, *that's* for damn sure.

We were all standing in a room atop a castle, built piece-by-piece from stone that had been flown in from Italy. It practically clung to the western edge of the continent, appearing to magically float above San Francisco Bay's coastal fog, affording it unrivaled views of the majestic Pacific Ocean. Napa may have been well-known for its scenery, but nothing compared to what we were now looking at in my book, not that that was doing me any good in the anxiety department.

"Okay, it's getting close to that time. How you doin'? You okay?" Rachel asked.

"Is that a *trick* question?" I responded shakily, half-dressed.

"Rach, she's about to merge herself to a fucking movie star...how the hell do you *think* she's doin'?" my cousin Adriana said.

"I'm gonna have to agree with her on this one," I heard Mac chime in.   "Here, Lea, have some of this," she said, handing me a champagne glass.

"Shouldn't we be saving that for *later*? I mean, it wouldn't look too good if the bride stumbled down the aisle," Adriana added.

"That's true, Mac," my mom said. "Honey, everything's gonna be fine. When I married your father, I was just as nervous." As much as my mom was trying to help, it wasn't doing a damn thing.

Adriana and I looked at each other before I finally spoke, "ma, when you married dad you were 19. You knew him for like three months."

She quickly hushed me as if that weren't true. But it was- my parents had met at one of those dances like in *An Officer and a Gentleman*. My dad had been stationed at a local Naval base in New York. At first I'd been appalled, because I could never imagine what the hell went through someone's mind to do something so ridiculously out of character. Right now however, I was feeling the same way, questioning myself again...

"That's beside the point," she said. "Just calm down and try to relax. Everything's going to be fine." Normally her smile would've at least partially reassured me but right now, it wasn't.

"Come, on, Lea," Kelly agreed, walking over. "You should have this anxiety stuff down by now. I mean, it's *not* like you haven't been in the spotlight before. What's a measly 150 people? Plus, I didn't come all this way *not* to be able to crash *your* wedding. Now, that just wouldn't be fair."

That made me giggle a little. She had a point. It hadn't been that weekend in San Diego or that day at the animal shelter that had turned my world upside-down. It'd been that crazy day of winery tasting when I'd unexpectedly befriended a girl named Kelly and her fiancé, Dylan, unaware of who her brother was. It hadn't taken long to learn it was Patrick Thomas and before I knew it, she'd introduced me to her whole family *and* invited me to her wedding. After that well, my life just wasn't the same.

Everything had come full circle and I was truly happy yet at the same time, I was sad. There was still an emptiness I couldn't shake. I had everything I needed but still, there was one thing missing. I wished more than anything my dad could've lived to see this day. He wasn't much of a 'scenery' guy, but he would've loved to have seen this place (and maybe even tried to stir up some family drama in the process, which would've no doubt made for a more entertaining day...).

"Where's your veil?" Kelly asked.

"Here," Mac said, handing it to my mom.

"Just beautiful," she commented, a tear down her face. "Patrick's one lucky guy."

"I'll second that," Kelly joked, making us all laugh. "Oh, I almost forgot. I have something for you, from Patrick."

Surprised, I glanced down at the light blue box as she handed it to me. I instantly noticed the note on top.

"Eleana,

When was it we first fell in love? That magical dance at Kelly's wedding? Our first date? I can't say because honestly, I can't picture a time when I haven't been in love with you. From the moment we met, you had this way of looking into my soul and seeing me like no one else could. I look at you and I see not just a fiercely independent, successful woman, but a force unlike any other and one I envy.

Though the world may sometimes see a fiery exterior, I have never known such grace or compassion. Your ever-growing heart amazes and inspires me to be a better person. As beautiful as you are on the outside, your inner beauty is incomparable- you are just as kind, loving and selfless as you are resilient and strong, and you always see the good in people. These are the reasons I love you; without evidence I just do.

You may think you don't fit into my world but Eleana, YOU are my world; The truth is, you have always been the one who was too good for me. I know you're afraid that we might fail or let each other down or that I might one day leave you, but that could never happen. You have always believed in me and you may not realize, but you have saved me and that makes you MY superhero. I believe in you and in us and I know there's nothing we can't do together because when you love someone, it's not just for now or for a little while, it's forever.

They were right when they said "Home is where the heart is", because although we have often been apart, you keep me grounded; when I've been lost you bring me back to a place that feels like home. You are my best friend, my perfect match and my forever home and I cannot imagine spending one more day of my life without you.

You might be wondering how I got this. A while back, your dad gave it to me. He said that if we ever made it this far (reluctantly, of course) that I was to give it to you. He told me that if I ever hurt you or if I lost it, I'd never live to see another movie set...He also made me promise that if for some reason he couldn't be here, I was the one who should walk you down the aisle because it would be my turn to take care of you, and also that that's what a real man would do. Well, he must've known something we didn't, because not only did he trust me with his only daughter, we made it.

This may not be a 'typical' family heirloom but since we both know your family and since it is technically blue, I think it more than qualifies. It'll reassure you that your dad is here for you, now and always, just like I will be. I can't wait to stand by your side today and begin our lives together. I'll see you there.

Love Always,
Patrick."

"What is that?" I heard someone ask.

I recognized it alright. All this time, I'd thought my brother had it. It was my dad's Navy Cross, one of his prized possessions. I couldn't believe he had just passed it over to Patrick. I had only seen it twice- he kept it locked away along with all his others- and he'd had a *lot*. Another tear began formed and I tried to keep it together. God knows I hadn't even left the bridal suite yet...

"Is that a...*medal*?" Mac asked.

"Yeah," I finally answered, trying not to cry, "it's my d...it *was* my dad's. His Navy Cross." I held it loosely in my left hand, cracking a smile.

"It's your something blue," Kelly reassured. "Don't you see?"

"Yeah," I whispered, suddenly feeling at ease, well a little anyway. *Yeah, I guess I finally do.*

"I think it's cool," Rachel added. "So, where should we pin it?"

"It looks like it weighs a fuckin' pound," Adrian joked.

"Almost," I laughed.

"How about in your bouquet?" My mom's suggestion seemed the most appropriate and in a matter of minutes, we were headed outside.

It had turned out to be a near-perfect day- the sun was shining, it was in the upper 60s and a rare occurrence this time of year, the fog had lifted, offering up crystal clear views for miles. There was only one thing left to do- walk. If I could just get myself to move. My heart fluttered uncontrollably when I saw him. For a moment I was back at Kelly's wedding all over again, uncomfortably numb surrounded by a bunch of strangers, wearing someone else's dress. But I wasn't- I was in a dress that *I* had picked out, surrounded by close family and friends, with a handsome-as-ever groom of my own, waiting for me.

The bridal party had taken their places up at the gazebo as had the groomsmen, all but one, leaving me to fend for myself. I looked down at the narrow path leading down to the ceremony site, about to take my first step and it hit me. This was *actually* happening. To think that six months ago this wasn't in the realm of possibility and now here I stood about to finally do what I had never had the courage to do: to love someone unconditionally, to let them love me back and take care of me the way I so needed. I knew when I had met Patrick I hadn't been ready to do that, not just because I hadn't found the perfect guy for me but because I hadn't been able to see myself fully through the eyes of someone else. I felt like I'd won the jackpot with Patrick. My dad once told me never to sign on the dotted line unless I was 100% sure of what I was signing up *for*; well, I couldn't have been surer about Patrick. From here on out, he was the only man I could ever see myself with.

"Okay, dad, here goes nothing," I said, gazing up at the blue sky as I touched the Navy medal, now a part of my bouquet.

Suddenly one shoe began to move and then the other, and I slowly and cautiously made my way down to Patrick. His back was still facing me. He stood at the beginning of the aisle, his hands neatly folded over each other as he patiently waited. I couldn't wait to see the look on his face when he saw me. As I got closer, I could hear the music playing and a nervous tingling sensation coursed through my body. I heard voices rise as everyone had taken notice of my appearance and just then, Patrick peered over his shoulder and smiled.

Our eyes met and there wasn't a doubt in my mind that I had made the right decision. Everything that had happened these past several months, good or bad, right or wrong, had culminated in this very moment. This was it; *he* was it. I was unafraid and I was ready.

"*Wow*. I'd say you look beautiful, but beautiful's not even a good enough *word*," he said.

"Gorgeous works," I smiled.

"Actually, I was thinking more along the lines of breathtaking." With one finger I gently caught a tear, but it wasn't mine. I had never seen Patrick cry. "Man, that's embarrassing. *I'm* supposed to be the one wiping away *your* tears," he laughed softly.

"Oh, don't worry," I said, "you'll have plenty more chances." I winked, wiping the tear away. "You sure you're okay?" I asked.

"I am now- *you're* here. So, you ready to do this thing?"

"Oh, *hell* yeah."

"Geesh- good thing we didn't book a church," he added, making us both chuckle.

He took his left hand and clasped our fingers together before raising my hand to his mouth and kissing it. I looked up at him longingly. He sure was a picture out of a storybook- those beaming green eyes, that innocent yet alluring smile, the body of a god; wisps of dark hair moving almost in sync with the breeze...and he was all mine- for *good* this time.

"Here," he gestured, holding his left arm out. "Now hold on tightly. The ground's a little uneven at the bottom of those steps. I'd hate to see the beautiful blushing bride go head-first before we even make it up there," he smirked.

"Funny," I answered, leaning up to kiss his cheek, "don't worry- I won't let go- I *promise*."

"*Good*, 'cause I wasn't planning on letting you get away this time," he whispered.

I observed the guests, heavy with anticipation as they waited for us. The large, wide-open gazebo was set amid an outdoor garden grove and decorated in trellised vines and baby blue flowers. Rows of chairs had been set up on either side of the aisle and surrounding it the beautifully landscaped gardens framed by acres of lush vineyards. Beyond the rolling hills in the distance you could see the various hues of blue ocean waves.

I took a deep breath as we began to walk, answering him back, "I was just going to say the same thing." And off we went, on our biggest adventure yet. Now this was better than any happy ending I could have possibly imagined.

You know I'm a dreamer
But my heart's of gold
I had to run away high
So I wouldn't come home low

Just when things went right
It doesn't mean they were always wrong
Just take this song and you'll never feel
Left all alone

Take me to your heart
Feel me in your bones
Just one more night
And I'm comin' off this

Long and winding road
I'm on my way
I'm on my way
Home sweet home

-Mötley Crüe

Made in the USA
Middletown, DE
21 December 2020

29631221R00225